A PERFECT
KNIGHT
FOR
LOVE

Books by Jackie Ivie

A PERFECT KNIGHT FOR LOVE

Jackie Ivie

ZEBRA BOOKS
KENSINGTON PUBLISHING CORP.
http://www.kensingtonbooks.com

ZEBRA BOOKS are published by

Kensington Publishing Corp.
119 West 40th Street
New York, NY 10018

All Kensington titles, imprints, and distributed lines are available at special quantity discounts for bulk purchases for sales
promotion, premiums, fund-raising, educational, or institu-
tional use.

Special book excerpts or customized printings can also be
created to fit specific needs. For details, write or phone the
office of the Kensington Special Sales Manager: Kensington
Publishing Corp., 119 West 40th Street, New York, NY 10018.
Attn. Special Sales Department. Phone: 1-800-221-2647.

Zebra and the Z logo Reg. U.S. Pat. & TM Off.

ISBN-13: 978-1-4201-2400-2
ISBN-10: 1-4201-2400-5

First Printing: September 2012

10 9 8 7 6 5 4 3 2 1

Printed in the United States of America

Chapter 1

AD 1689

Limitless . . . that's what it was. And stretching as far as the eye could see.

Amalie inhaled with pure joy, focusing a moment on breaking clouds tinted with a setting sun. Everyone else had dismounted the coach, stretching and yawning as they cleared the door. Amalie ignored them. She knew what they'd be looking at: a hastily erected posting house whose wood was so new it contained slivers, or one hewn from rock looking old and worn before it got finished. They'd also see a collection of horseflesh that might taint any decent stable, before being accosted by more robust and uncouth humanity. It would be exactly like the last stop, and the one before. The only good thing about this one was it was the second-to-the-last one she must visit.

Amalie exhaled and watched the mist from her breath for a moment before it dissipated. It was all so beneath her. She had more immense things to ponder than jostling through a crowd to a sparse attic room, eating a lukewarm and probably unappetizing sup, and bedding down on coarse sheets atop a hard bed. She had freedom. The moment they'd crossed the border she'd felt it. She was free. Absolutely, totally—

She tripped, spinning into a tangled mass of skirts and traveling cape before landing in a bruising cradle without much give to it.

"What the saints?"

Amalie slapped her hand against a massive chest having a total lack of softness. Nothing about him felt remotely soft. Or anything other than hard. Heated. Male. Amalie squinted up at him.

"Good catch, Thayne."

"Now lasses just come raining from the heavens for him, too? 'Tis vastly unfair of fate."

"Hush. All of you."

The man moved his chest with the words and that moved her. His head came around the brim of her hat next, showing the unfairness of the entire exchange. Handsomeness such as his existed only in some night-fantasy capacity. And those, she'd never admit to.

"'Tis fain easier to use the steps, lass."

He had a thick Scot accent that teased her ear. It also required a moment or two to decipher what he said.

"Th-thank you."

He tied her tongue with the view, and then tangled her words with the size and strength of him. She didn't know where her wits had gone. It was just so completely unexpected. Her palm flesh itched and tingled where it touched solid male through a too-thin muslin shirt, there wasn't but a bunched band of plaid cloth intersecting him near her knees, and she was having trouble breathing.

"Nae thanks necessary, miss. It is . . . miss?"

He lifted his brows, showing off light-shaded eyes. They combined with perfect features and thick reddish-brown hair. He was extremely tall. Either that or he stood on the loading stool. Amalie could see beneath the coach she'd just fallen from.

"Y-yes." She sounded weak. And she stammered. It was better than remaining stunned and silent, but not by much. It wasn't possible to converse properly with him, though. Her mouth didn't work.

He let out a pent breath and turned his head. "All's well, lads. She's unwed."

"That's MacGowan luck for you."

The reply caused chuckling about her. The man holding her didn't join in. He turned back to her. Amalie licked her lips and ordered her heart to cease the gallop of beats. It didn't work.

"'Luck?" Amalie asked.

A grin split his face, sending his handsomeness right into beautiful. Amalie's eyes went wide.

"'Tis luck I'll na' be accosted for my actions."

"Actions?"

"I caught you."

"True," Amalie agreed. "But I . . . don't understand."

"A husband might find my action objectionable."

"He would?"

He cleared his throat. It rumbled through the chest she was pressed to. "'Tis na' exactly the catch. More the delay that has ensued afterward."

"Delay?"

"I've yet to release you."

"Oh. Then, do so."

"'Tis muddy through here."

"Now, I truly must object—"

He stopped her words by gathering her close enough their chests touched. Then he took large paces through the muck of the stable yard, moving muscled flesh everywhere she touched.

He was accurate about one thing. It must be muddy. He

slipped more than once and that got her gripped even more tightly.

"Iain? See to the door. And you, Sean! Fetch a mug of something."

"Specifics?"

"Mead! Fetch mead. You ken mead?" Her captor asked the last, dipping his head to her and giving another quick smile.

"Ken?" she asked.

He blew a breath through his lower lip, lifting stray locks at his forehead with the motion. "A bit of mead works well at untwisting knots from a coach ride."

"Put me down," Amalie replied.

"What if I say . . . nae?"

"Surely that's ungentlemanly."

He tipped his head to one side as if weighing it. Then he bent sideways and slid her to the wooden floor, keeping a hold on her elbow as if she needed it. She hadn't been mistaken. He was worse than tall. He was gigantic. Amalie looked over at the fourth button down on his too-thin shirt. She'd probably fit beneath his arm. She cleared her throat. It sounded weak.

"I really must leave you, sir. But I do thank you."

"I'd best see you to a prime spot first."

"Prime . . . spot?"

She may be at his side rather than plastered to him but her reaction hadn't improved. She glanced up into clear, green-blue eyes and darted her look away.

"For your rest. And meal."

"I've a room reserved. I do *not* sit in the common room." Amalie knew she sounded autocratic, but it was too late. She could only hope he didn't notice.

"You the governess expected by Clan MacKennah? The one from London-town?"

He'd noticed.

"Y-yes." Her voice wavered again. Still.

"Sincerest apologies. Your rooms have been . . . borrowed."

"What do you mean . . . borrowed?"

"They're na' available to you at present."

"Release me at once. I'll take this up with the innkeeper." Her lips set. If he knew her better, he'd know what it meant.

"Nae need. The man's well satisfied."

"Satisfied? How? And with what?" Her voice was growing tart and acidic. Both signs of her temper. Amalie worked at controlling it.

"With copious amounts of silver. What else?"

"That's impossible. My room is booked and paid for."

"It's still been taken."

"You can't take a room."

"It's done, lass. Come. I'll see you a sup fetched and mead."

"You stole my room?"

He gave her that innocent looking smile again. "You canna' steal a room, lass. I've but borrowed it. I'll return it. You've my word."

The thick brogue attached to the words was no longer interesting. It was irritating and annoying. Everything about him was. Her voice rose.

"Unborrow it, then. This instant. Rooms have been reserved for me all along this route. And unhand me, as well." She tried pulling her elbow from him, but all that happened was he tightened his thumb and two fingers.

"I ken as much."

There wasn't much of his previous joviality to the words and no leeway in his grip as he twirled her forward. Then he forewent any appearance of a gentlemanly escort to march her across the room, using long loping strides that slid her feet, sending orders above her head the entire way.

"Grant? Clear a spot nearest the fire. You, Sean! A chair. Iain, my cloak. And get me a plaide. A dry one."

He dragged her across the common room as if it wasn't crowded, went through a portal, and entered another room.

Amalie's heartbeat was so pronounced it pained her throat, while her mind flashed through every warning and dire consequence she'd been forced to listen to during the last few days.

She'd been told a Scotsman was barbaric. How ancient villages had been raided by Vikings, and those in turn became governed by Highlanders. Supposedly the culture hadn't progressed much since. She'd been warned how any veneer of civility got wiped away by the Covenanters of the '60s. It had all seemed so far-fetched and ridiculous. And she hadn't paid enough attention. That much was patently obvious.

"I'll scream. I swear." And if her voice would work beyond a whisper, she'd have already done it.

"Hush!"

He moved with the word, folding her into an embrace of sorts. She'd known he was large, muscled, heated, and solid. Being clamped against him with her head tilted upward was unnecessary proof. Amalie opened her mouth but he'd forestalled her with a barrage of brogue-filled words, colored with what sounded like genuine fear.

"'Tis nae whim, lass! You ken? You need to quiet and assist. 'Tis life or death!"

Light whooshed from the fireplace, flaring with the influx of air from an opening door. Amalie didn't see it. She was suffering too many impressions at once. All of them strange. Odd. Foreign. Hard, heavy heartbeats at her nose. The odor of rain-wet wool. Huffs of breath touching her cheeks. The sensations combined to bombard her, making her tremble slightly within his embrace. All of it was unwarranted. Unladylike. Unbelievable. His arms tightened, pulling at her pinned hair, crushing her bonnet out of his way as he lifted her. She heard a whisper and then everything went to absolute shock as his lips came down on hers.

Amalie fancied her first kiss a chaste one, delivered upon promise of a betrothal. A quick meeting of her lips with those of a shadowy suitor, with her hands upon his shoulders while her breasts heaved toward him. She'd relived it often in her mind. She knew the pose by rote. Yet the moment this Thayne's lips touched hers, it obliterated absolutely everything.

Her hands were trapped between them, branding her palms with heat. A thunder of heartbeats tapped at her palms. He was rock hard, and his chest wasn't the only portion exhibiting that. Everything felt hard. Unyielding. Even his lips. They weren't soft, romantic, or remotely shadowy. They were rigid, bruising, and hot enough to scorch. Pings of sensation hit at her nose. Breathing was especially difficult as it mingled with the force of his.

Then she felt something so horrid, she was grateful her eyes were tightly shut as something completely illicit and totally alien happened, exacerbating the blur of hummed sound in her ears. An odd flurry of thrills ran over her head, down her spine, and all the way to her toes, before racing back. From there the shiver went right to center at each breast tip, making them tight and sensitive. There wasn't any way to stop it or control it. Amalie didn't know what the reaction was. She'd never felt such a thing before. And worse! The man holding her somehow knew. The instant flinch in his frame and his quick intake of breath told her.

Amalie heard the thudding of boots, then angry words, all of it coming in disjointed snippets of sound. It was akin to eavesdropping on a party from the nursery—back when that's all she'd known. The words carried threat and then she heard a clank of sound that could very well be a sword leaving its scabbard. And she didn't even know what that sounded like.

"MacGowan!"

More sounds of metal filled the space between heartbeats in her ears, more footsteps, and then more words, angrier and more threatening in tone.

"I'll have your head!"

There was a bit of quick grunts, sounds that could mean blows, and Amalie stiffened. The man holding her did the same. Cold invaded, stealing her breath, and muting the warmth. Even his lips felt cold. Then someone behind him spoke loudly and with a bit of amusement coloring the words.

"'Tis clearly a mistake, lads. We've got the wrong MacGowan."

Sounds of a scuffle died. With it, the ability to stand. Amalie sagged into Thayne.

"Someone should put a leash to your laird."

The man holding her gave the slightest reaction to the conversation behind him, grasping her even tighter somehow.

"Well . . . you ken how our Jamie is."

"Keep him from my daughters. Or I'll send him to hell. You hear?"

"Aye."

More words got exchanged in the room behind her, blending with the noise in her ears, before she heard footsteps leaving and a door close. That's when Thayne finally pulled his lips from her, lifted his head, and lowered her to her feet. He didn't release her. His continued touch was horrid and yet heaven-sent. Her entire frame was trembling and her knees didn't feel like they'd hold.

Her captor went in a twist to look out at the room, granting her a perfect view of thick muscled neck with a grosgrain ribbon attached to a bit of stubble on his chin. Amalie blinked. Her bonnet had come untied? It was one of her plainest, without any lace, bows, or feathers, but she couldn't afford to lose it. She narrowed her eyes and concentrated on the mundane misplacement of her hat. As if it mattered.

She hadn't lost anything. She could feel the bonnet trailing from her shoulders.

"That was close." Somebody said it from behind MacGowan's bulk.

"'Twas Dunn-Fyne?"

The words rumbled through the chest she was still pressed to, making her gasp, which made him harden even further. And all of it even worse as she could swear she felt thighs against hers. Even through her skirts.

"Nae. Ammon."

Thayne swore. Amalie held that gasp, yet still he hardened somewhere as if she'd reacted, sending prickles of annoyance through each palm where they still pressed against his chest. The man was worse than she'd been warned.

"And Glen-Gorrick."

"They doona' suspect anything?"

Thayne answered again, with another resultant tightening of something in his frame. Amalie's fingers got cursed with every nuance of him. And his shirt wasn't helpful in the slightest.

"You heard. They think you Jamie. Out for a bit of rape and pillage. As usual."

"'Tis a foul night, lads. Full of accursed deeds."

This time his arms moved, pulling her closer, and that just wasn't fair. Or reasonable. And it was making everything spin.

There was a chorus of 'ayes.'

"Nae sign of Dunn-Fyne?"

If he said one more thing, she was going to open her mouth and scream. It would be better than swooning.

"He'll na' be far. Ammon's his mon."

"Christ. And his Mother Mary."

He spit the curses out, moving her with them. He followed with more words, said in a language she couldn't possibly comprehend. And then he took a deep breath, held it for long heart-thumping moments before releasing it.

"That was close. And my actions are totally unforgivable. I doona' even ken why I'd ask, but I should still try. Lass?"

Amalie turned her head and shut her eyes the moment he'd moved back to her. He probably gave her a bit of smile to

match the cajoling tone in his brogue. As if handsome looks
and charm would grant him forgiveness. It had probably
worked before, though. Not today. And not with her. She
wasn't listening, and for certain she wasn't looking.

"You believe me, doona' you, lass? 'Tis a matter of life or
death. I swear."

He whispered it to the area above her ear. The spot instantly tingled. She lifted her shoulder against it, opened her
eyes, and felt her jaw drop at the sight of drawn swords and
what looked to be mallets his men held at the ready.

"Thayne! Quick! There's nae time! She's *dying*!"

Everyone pivoted to face the speaker who'd opened a door
on the opposite side of the room. His hissed words got an immediate response. Amalie wasn't given a choice. Thayne
simply lifted her and followed, running up the two flights of
steps that should've echoed with the volume of boots.

If he'd just give her a moment, she'd tell him. She believed
him. She did. This much intensity and action had to have life
and death at its core. She no longer cared about the stolen
room or the outrage of her first kiss. She was overcome.
Shocked. Scared. She needed to be alone to work through it.
Amalie's known world was structured, soft spoken, rarely
disturbing, closely organized, and scripted. There wasn't
anything dramatic about it.

The room they'd purloined was in the attic, small and
sparsely furnished, as a second-class paying passenger deserved, and it was crowded. It reeked of poorly washed linens
and sweat, while grassy-smelling smoke came from a fireplace that hadn't had the flue opened enough. Or they were
using wet wood. Or something. Amalie's eyes smarted the
moment they'd arrived. Then, she was blinking against the
sting. Through a candlelit haze she heard the sound of whispered voices and the soft sound of weeping. And the muted
sounds of what had to be an infant getting suckled.

An infant?

"How . . . is she?"

Thayne's voice was soft but it was the only soft thing about him. The words echoed through where he'd pressed Amalie; close . . . like a shield. Both his arms were about her torso, just beneath her breasts, pressing immodestly where they shouldn't. Which was another stupid mundane thought. None of this was modest.

"She's dying! Dinna' Pellin say?"

"Save her, damn you! 'Tis why I brought you!"

"You canna' change fate, Thayne MacGowan. Regardless of how oft you try."

"Shut up."

The words were ground out. Thayne moved forward, toward a small sagging mattress on an equally sagging bed frame. He went to a knee, folding Amalie into a kneeled stance with it, and reached with his free hand toward the woman propped against ecru-shaded linens that matched the color of her skin.

"Mary?"

He touched her cheek, moving Amalie forward with the pressure of his chest against her head. The move connected too much male to where her bonnet should have been protecting, which was just another stupid worry in a world of new ones.

The woman rolled her head toward them. She didn't look to qualify as a woman yet. She was little more than a girl. And she'd been severely beaten; often and recently. Her blackened swollen eyes and the myriad scabbing and bruising couldn't hide it.

"You . . . see . . . the bairn?" The wraith whispered it.

"In time," Thayne replied.

"She's . . . perfect."

"You were na' to have it until we reached the castle."

The girl smiled in such a slight gesture, it hurt to watch. "Pro . . . tect her, Thayne."

He nodded.

The girl pulled in a shallow breath. Two words came out with the exhalation of it. "From . . . him."

"Aye."

He cleared his throat, showing what this meant to him. Amalie's eyes pricked with unbidden emotion and she blinked rapidly against it.

"You . . . promise?"

The words were a hint of whisper, followed by another shallow, barely discernible breath.

"Aye."

This time his voice did crack.

"And you?"

The girl moved her gaze to Amalie.

Me?

Thayne's arm tightened, squeezing. The man was worse than a barbarian. He was a brute.

"Promise it!"

Thayne's hissed warning was barely audible. Amalie nodded. The girl on the bed sighed softly, rolled her head back to look toward the ceiling and closed her eyes. They watched her take another breath and let it out. Then there was nothing but silence. Cursed, complete silence. Then sobbing started again from somewhere in the room behind them.

"Somebody handle the wet-nurse! Jesu'! Easy, though. We need her. And fetch Grant. Gannett. Michael. Alex. And Rory." Thayne stood and turned away, barking orders with a gruff voice.

"Present."

"Done."

"Ready."

Thayne held Amalie as voices punctuated the space, forcing her to continue the unforeseen and unwarranted insertion into private matters. Dreadful matters that she didn't want to comprehend or address. Amalie was certain whatever she'd interrupted was sordid and scandalous, even before they'd gotten an innocent Englishwoman involved . . . through no fault of her own other than a careless step on the feeling of complete freedom. Or what was freedom if she could just escape. That was the most important. She had to get loose and then she'd run. Far and fast. She didn't know what else this Thayne might be capable of.

His arms tightened as if he second-guessed her thoughts. He spoke again, filling the room with low-voiced orders. Only now there wasn't a hint of weakness or emotion to his tone.

"Get Mary's body to Castle Gowan. Afore another minute passes. We've nightfall for the assist and na' much else. Dunn-Fyne's on our heels. Already."

"So many? 'Tis too risky."

"Nae option. They've eleven leagues, four burns, and Caryndale to cross. I'll na' trust her to anything less. Wrap her and go! Quickly!"

"That'll leave you with just four men, Thayne!"

"Aye. But I've got this for a ploy."

Thayne stood, lifting her to show what he meant. That's when she knew exactly what he was capable of.

Chapter 2

He must've forgotten what chivalry felt like but couldn't imagine why. Or how. Or when.

It seemed like his entire life Thayne took responsibility and punishment for Jamie's escapades. That was the lone way to keep their sire from guessing the truth about his favored son. That, in turn, kept the laird of MacGowan from brutality and drink. And that bit of chivalry kept their mother from her bouts of melancholy. At least until the old laird passed on and the dowager duchess followed him into the crypt less than a season later. It hadn't even been a year since Thayne had suffered every curse of chivalry when he'd watched Mary leave him . . . without a word of the cost. Or the heart-burnings. Or the betrayal.

All of which were old issues and even older secrets. Thayne had ever kept secrets, practiced chivalry without a murmur, and taken blame without one word of defense. He'd also reaped the punishment . . . and then the pain. He should be used to it.

Thayne shifted atop his horse, lifted his head, and blinked on dry eyes that hadn't time for grief. Chivalry was cold. Lonely. Friendless. It always had been. And now it was guilt-ridden as well.

He bowed his back, rested his chin atop the wench's head and looked unseeingly at the gloom-cast path. The air was heavy, filling each breath with cold and wet and the promise of more. Inhalation brought moistness that tugged at his chest before he released it. Such ague-spiked mist was the cause of Sean's coughs as they came ever closer together and louder. Thayne could also blame the inclement weather for Mary's early labor and subsequent death. He didn't. It was his fault, and his burden to bear. That was the curse of chivalry.

The lass in his arms whimpered slightly at the beginning of every breath, reminding him of barbarity and guilt. She wasn't doing it consciously. She'd been asleep since they'd entered this forest and well before rain hampered their progress. Or she was an expert at relaxing her frame in a parody of sleep. Thayne smirked. He truly wasn't caring one way or the other and it was a large improvement to the thrashing and closed-mouth screaming she'd done when he'd first subdued, gagged, and then trussed her up in bonds like a holiday game hen. He hadn't meant to but she didn't give him the choice. She either didn't understand the dire reality of their situation, or life meant little to her.

She hadn't made it easy. That helped with the guilt. She'd been wearing so many petticoats it was nearly impossible to find and secure her legs. The lass dressed for a fit of winter blizzom and it was but late spring. Foolish. What would she do if the weather turned harsh? At the time, he'd thought mayhap she wore so much to cut down on baggage. That wasn't abnormal. She wouldn't be the first one to wear her wardrobe on her.

One look at the trunk swaying behind Sean atop the lead horse manifested that falsehood. It wasn't her lone one. They'd had to fetch all three trunks in order to make her sudden disappearance look like a usual event. Such a foolish, naïve, untaught wench. Traveling alone with three leather tooled trunks cast with silver-smelted fastenings was an open invitation to perfidy.

Thayne shook his head slightly, rolling his chin atop her head. That earned a slight sting from where she'd hit him. He supposed he'd earned it, but that was more of her foolishness. It's what got her hands bound. Then he'd slashed most of her undergarments away with his dirk, just to find her legs and stop the kicking. Thayne huffed another breath and watched it fog before his face. His chin bruise wasn't the lone one she'd landed. He had more than one blow to his legs from those pointed boots of hers. For that, she'd lost them as well.

All of which was odd. For such a tiny thing, this particular wench fought like a griffin. Which was strange. She didn't look strong. Or fight-filled. She was small. And she was all woman. She felt it, for certain. Smelled it, too.

Thayne eased out another breath at the thought. He wasn't immune to this forced proximity. That was more oddity he'd have to face. But, not yet. He had enough to manage at the moment with keeping them alive. It would take four days to reach Castle Gowan. If they avoided Dunn-Fyne. The path was also beset with thieves and clanless scoundrels, threatening trouble and dealing death. Aside from all that, Thayne's group reeked of weakness. Five fully armed and mounted MacGowan clansmen would normally be given a far swath, but five Clydesdales that looked spent invited trouble. The continual sound of Sean's coughing only added to it.

None of it could be helped. Thayne had spent every bit of horseflesh just to reach Mary in this abused notion of chivalry; without one thought to the consequences, and even less time to doubt or change the plan. In consequence, all five mounts were road-weary and carrying a clansman or a burden of a trunk having the same heft. They moved at a walk pace. With bowed heads and slow strides. He'd put the bairn and her nursemaid in the center, right behind him. He'd hoped any sounds they made might get muted that way.

Thayne straightened, lifting his head from the sweet-smelling mass of hair. The MacKennah governess had locks as dark as a shadow-filled section of Castle Gowan's tower and as slick and shiny as a moonbeam. He'd been wrapped within it before he'd finally gotten her subdued. He hadn't known hairpins could hold such volume when she'd been finally quieted, spread on her back beneath him, glaring with spark-filled amber-shaded eyes. Eyes that color should've been warm and welcoming . . . but not from this lass. The golden hue of her eyes was nothing but cold-cast and hard; akin to metal. Slick. Inanimate. They'd looked as welcoming as a witch's teat in winter. And just as cold.

Thayne stretched, using that to wrench his mind from further thought of the woman in his arms. He had enough to worry over, without adding the English lass he'd been forced to steal.

Sean coughed again, putting frail sound into the air. Thayne moved his glance. He really should've sent Iain to the front. Perhaps then they could hide weakness. The infant cries were hushed when they came, but to Thayne's ear, just as frail-sounding. Even the light was against him as it glimmered on a stark treeless hill, rain-washed and covered with opaque fog, making the ground look off-kilter and indistinct.

He'd breathe easier if they could reach the forest at the end of this particular drum. He might even allow a bit of rest and a fire. Among trees and deadfall they could shelter and cover over what an easy mark they were. It would also provide the perfect ambush spot . . . if one were so inclined. Thayne considered it and tossed it aside. He knew they'd have to take the chance. Staying out in the open was foolhardy.

He'd been right about the ambush.

The form of Mary's husband loomed out from the fog the moment they reached the tree line. Without a bit of warning, men on horseback swarmed from right in front of Sean's horse, Laird Dunn-Fyne at the fore, sword at ready. He was accompanied by countless men that all looked the same.

Sean's mount stopped, too tired to even give a lurch at the surprise. He was followed by the others. Thayne's stallion, Placer, needed subduing. Thayne had to pull the reins to halt the Clydesdale. Around him, he felt Iain, Pellin, and Gavin working to get all five horses flanked, facing outward. For defense. It wouldn't have mattered. Death was being dealt. And he'd earned it.

That's when Thayne knew exactly what chivalry reaped: absolutely nothing.

The horde closed in silently, threat and menace on each face. Thayne reached for his claymore and that's when he got the first clue the lass wasn't sleeping. Her fingers gripped about his thigh. That was accompanied by the lurch of her entire form up and against him, sealing her head beneath his chin and forcing his head back.

"Halt, MacGowan!"

Thayne didn't answer at first. Nobody did, although those about them started closing in, adding restless horse noise to the night. Then even more men came from behind Dunn-Fyne, bearing torches.

"You've nae answer?" Dunn-Fyne was yelling it despite the absolute stillness.

"Nae need," Thayne answered easily.

"What?" The man was still shouting. It didn't do much except make the lass in front of Thayne tremble.

"You requested a halt. 'Tis needless. We've halted."

There was a bit of stillness following his words before Dunn-Fyne lifted his sword higher. He raised his volume as well. "Now unhand my wife or face your maker!"

Thayne sighed heavily. "I've na' got your wife," he answered.

"Unhand the wife or I'll take her from your dead frame!

And that'll save me the trouble of drawing and quartering your sorry arse!"

Thayne reached up and pulled the plaid from the top of the lass's hair. Even in the torchlight it was obvious she had dark brown hair, not the light reddish locks Mary had been noted for. And pursued over. And had poems written about. Some of them from Thayne.

"That is na' my wife!" Dunn-Fyne yelled.

Thayne smirked. "I just said as much."

"Who is she, then?"

Thayne shrugged, large enough to move the lass with it. And then swallowed, although it resembled a gulp. Chivalry was a decided blasted curse.

"Well?"

"A wench of little renown and less frame. Now allow us to pass. We've naught you want."

He felt the woman stiffen and moved his sword hand from the hilt of his claymore to wrap it about her waist. He passed it along his kilt as he went, drying the moistness from his palm. She wasn't just trembling anymore. It was a full-out shake. Thayne tried for a reassuring grip, pulling her against his chest to lift her slightly above the saddle with the hold.

And just then, the hours-old bairn decided to wail and everything in the world halted to listen. Any gap between horses was eliminated as Dunn-Fyne moved, pushing into the defensive huddle Thayne's band made. The infant's wailing increased, punctuating the night with sharp heart-stirring cries.

"Where is my wife, MacGowan? I'm in complete earnest now. I'll cleave your head from your shoulders and split you in so many pieces, they won't find enough of you to bury!"

Thayne cleared his throat. "I have na' seen your wife. Lately."

"Then whose bairn is that?"

It was useless to disclaim it. The babe had been seen to, but there were still the sounds of suckling.

"Hers." Thayne moved his chin, sliding it against perfumed strands of hair with the gesture and ignoring the sting from his bruise.

"Lad or lass?" Dunn-Fyne asked.

"'Tis clear she's a lass, mon." Someone else answered it.

"I meant the bairn! Is the bairn a lad or lass?"

Thayne narrowed his eyes. Every Highlander knew Dunn-Fyne wished a male heir since he'd produced but three daughters from his first two wives. *Make that four daughters and three wives now*, Thayne amended. Perhaps if the man ceased to beat and starve his women they'd gift him with more than girl bairns.

"Lass," he answered finally.

Dunn-Fyne wasn't fooled. He knew the babe was his. It felt as if he knew the entire story of how it happened. It was in his eyes and on his face. As was the complete disgust and bitterness. And then the cunning. That put Thayne's entire frame into one hard and ready state even before the man spoke again.

"Unveil the woman."

"You've held us enough for one meet, Dunn-Fyne."

"Unveil the woman . . . now."

"We've a camp to set up. And rest to be had."

"I'll na' ask it again, MacGowan. I'll be forcing the issue."

Dunn-Fyne moved his horse alongside Thayne's, pushing the steed's shoulder into Thayne's right leg and pinning his claymore in place. There was nothing for it. His left hand pulled the plaid to the girl's shoulders, showing the piece of cloth he'd gagged her with. As well as how bonny she was. *Curse women and their beauty!* Thayne watched the man absorb all of it.

"Unbind her."

Thayne shook his head.

"I've tired of your play, MacGowan, and I've a wench to rescue. From the looks of her, she may even appreciate the rescue. She might even appreciate a real man when she has one a-tween her legs. Unlike your sorry hide."

"Dunn-Fyne—"

As a threat, it didn't work although the lass had gone stiff. Thayne didn't know if it was the shock or the idea of a rescue from him. The laird of Dunn-Fyne leaned forward in his saddle, slipped his blade beneath the gag-cloth and without much movement slit it open. Then he leaned back, folded his arms across a lapful of table-girth and waited, his brows lifted and a smirk on his lips.

It felt like they all waited. Even the babe had quieted to a whiff of sound as it hiccoughed slightly. Thayne felt the lass's efforts to free her mouth, using her tongue since he still had her arms bound. There wasn't a quiver to be felt anywhere on her.

"For shame, MacGowan." Dunn-Fyne was clicking his tongue as he spoke. Then he grinned enough to show rotted teeth. "You resort to stealing wenches now?"

"She was na' stolen. Exactly."

"I wonder whose clan will be seeking justice this time?"

Dunn-Fyne's men chuckled at the last. It was added as a reminder that it was usually Jamie with this problem.

Everything was going wrong. Worse wrong than when he'd lowered Mary from her tower into the skiff and rowed from Fyne Castle's black sides. Bad luck had been his companion as they'd ridden away, begging the saints to allow them to reach MacGowan land before Mary's birth-labor made it an impossibility. Even worse luck and just as vivid was this particular girl falling into his arms. The absolute worst had to be what this lass was about to say. And there was nothing Thayne could do to stop any of it.

The lass had her mouth freed. She pushed the spit-soaked cloth out with a tongue that was probably gaining strength for the mix of hatred she was going to spew about him and everyone attached to this mission. Struggling was futile. Fighting the same. The lass had his fate in her hands and Thayne had little doubt what she'd say and what would ensue. It was strange how fully free he felt as he realized it.

"Well, lass? You need a sip of whiskey for speech?"

She shook her head at Dunn-Fyne's booming words. She also turned imperceptibly closer to Thayne. He tipped his head slightly and raised a brow.

"You failed to speak . . . sufficiently."

It took a moment to realize she was addressing him. The only indication was how angered Dunn-Fyne looked of a sudden.

"I did?" Thayne asked. The words growled. It felt like his throat was closed off with cotton wool.

She nodded.

"I'll be doing the speaking, MacGowan!"

Laird Dunn-Fyne's threat came with the blade of his claymore at Thayne's chin, forcing his head upright again. The move used her head as a fulcrum to make the slant more vicious. Thayne swallowed and felt the blade scrape his throat.

"Then speak," she said.

The woman he'd stolen had a sweet voice, calm and collected and holding just a hint of reproof. As if she faced a bevy of admirers that had gotten out of control and not a bunch of Highlanders dealing death. All of which was gut-clenching strange given the circumstances. It served to get the sword moved from atop her head, as Dunn-Fyne pulled it back, placed it across his knees and considered her.

"Well?" she continued, adding a lilt of humor that bounced off Dunn-Fyne's dumfounded look.

"Your name?"

"Amalie . . . uh . . . MacGowan. Of course."

"MacGowan?"

Dunn-Fyne's look was probably the match to Thayne's, if not the entire grouping of men about them.

"A woman usually takes the name of her husband upon wedding with him," she replied with a slight condescending inflection to the words.

Dunn-Fyne pulled back. Thayne attempted the same although a nerve pinched his middle-back, wrenching him into a stiffer stance. He already knew what she was going to say and was powerless to stop it.

"You're wed to MacGowan?"

"If you're referring to the man holding me, then yes. I am. And he knows it."

The lass put every bit of affronted dignity in her speech. It was an amazement to listen. Thayne's jaw dropped slightly. He had to turn aside to cover it.

Dunn-Fyne shifted atop his saddle, or the horse moved restlessly with a pinch from his knees. Whichever, it jostled the claymore against Thayne's thigh, reminding of the consequences of chivalry. He set his jaw and turned back to Dunn-Fyne.

"Is this truth, Thayne MacGowan?"

Thayne sucked in a huge breath, eased it out, and then made the reply. "Aye." He was actually surprised it came out as full and calm as it did.

"Without banns posted? And without clan approval?"

Thayne nodded.

"And without one word of the happenings to Clan MacKennah and your betrothed?"

The lass in front of him jerked slightly at that information, bumping her head into Thayne's jaw. The way he'd clenched his teeth prevented the clack of them giving away any of it, although he reaped a painful jar against his bruise.

Thayne nodded again.

"I believe I'll need your words. Loudly. As if proclaiming to all."

"Why?" Thayne asked.

"For the fate that's being dealt. And to make certain of our hearing."

Thayne pulled in another long breath. Let it out. Did it again. Words came with it. "I'm wed to this woman. And she is wed to me." His voice had a croak running it, but it was the best he could do.

"And you, lass?" The chieftain of the Dunn-Fyne clan boomed the question out, unnecessarily loud and abrasive. The humor in his voice was easy to spot.

"I don't understand all the nonsense. You heard me already."

Dunn-Fyne's face shifted to a frown as he leaned closer. "I wish to hear it again. Or he faces the consequences."

That was stupid. Thayne was already facing them. They were pounding one after another through his head until an ache formed right at the top of his nose behind his eyes.

"Very well. I'm wed to Thayne MacGowan. There! You heard it. Again."

"And just when did this wedding take place?" Dunn-Fyne inquired.

"About nine months ago. Or I wouldn't have a child, now would I?" The lass had regained her superior-sounding voice, almost as if she lectured a servant. But that was ridiculous. Thayne knew her status. He'd checked when he filched her room. He had to admit she possessed bravery and a tongue skilled at lying. He almost believed her.

"Ah . . . that's right . . . the wee bairn. You claiming it, are you?"

"Of course," she replied with that superiority-stained tone.

"And you, MacGowan? You claiming the bairn as well?"

Thayne nodded and the pounding behind his eyes accompanied it.

"I see."

He did indeed. Dunn-Fyne saw all of it and enjoyed it

immensely, if the grin splitting his beard was any indication. Thayne felt like a salmon: hooked, netted, and then lifted nakedly to be appraised for delectation. He concentrated on the thud of ache in his head, coming with each rapidly increased heartbeat.

"I doona' ken the kidnap, though."

"Ken? What is this word *ken*?" the lass asked.

"You were gagged. Bound. I've decided the why of the gag. With your sharp tongue, I'd have silenced you, too. After beating you senseless."

Her gasp was impossible to hide. As was her jerk backward. Thayne tipped his head sideways to avoid another bruising, while tightening his grip on her waist to keep her seated.

"Your wife needs a heavy hand, MacGowan," Dunn-Fyne informed him.

"Why do you think she's bound?" Thayne replied.

"Foolish wench." Dunn-Fyne was amused again. "Now that I find difficult to believe."

"How so?" he inquired.

"You? Wedded? Fair enough . . . although 'tis powerful odd to do it like this. Unlike your brother, you're levelheaded. Honorable. Trustworthy. Leastways you've that reputation . . . until now."

Thayne didn't answer. No one said anything. So the man started filling the space with more words as if they were needed. "I've been surmising some things as we've talked, though. And after a bit of viewing of your bride, I believe I do accept it. Even if she is one of *them*."

They all knew what he meant, except maybe the lass. Thayne would have to start thinking of her with her given name. He didn't recollect it, though. He'd have to ask her for it again. The bairn started another bit of wailing, high-pitched and weak-sounding through the mist. Dunn-Fyne turned to listen. Everyone watched.

"Your offspring does na' sound to have much strength." Dunn-Fyne had a sneer to his mouth when he turned back.

Thayne lowered his eyelids to regard the man, ignoring the ache behind his eyes that came with each heartbeat. "So?" he finally asked.

"This must come from mingling Highland blood with Sassenach." The man spit after the last word, making it sound even more insulting.

"Lowlander," Thayne replied. It sounded like he was speaking through clenched teeth because he was. There wasn't any way to hide it.

"Lowlander? Borderlands, then?"

"Aye."

"My condolences."

Dunn-Fyne burst into a large guffaw of laughter that echoed weirdly in the fog once he finished. Nobody joined him. They might as well all be stone.

"Accepted," Thayne replied.

Chapter 3

What a wretched turn of fate. As well as being completely and totally outside her control or realm of experience . . . or even her imagination, vast as that was. She'd never believe any of this if she wasn't living it.

Amalie had often engaged in wordplays and playacts with her brother Edmund. They'd spent hours together pretending to be explorers, or warriors, or anything other than what they were. Not only did the hours pass quicker, but it was the lone way to escape the sickbed into which Edmund had been born. He'd probably find this entire debacle amusing, if he'd lived. But if he'd lived, none of this would have happened. She'd never have been ordered to accept the Duke of Rochester's heir's hand in wedlock and put on bread and water until Father thought she'd acquiesced. Foolish man. He should know his only surviving offspring wasn't the fainthearted sort. Nor was she one to sit back and let fate deal her a losing hand. Oh no. She was in charge of her destiny. All she had to do was pretend at being cowed and beaten, do the best acting of her life, and then follow her escape when it appeared.

Such self-reliance, imagination, and courage were her saviors more than once. And she'd have done anything to

escape Rochester. Amalie shivered again at the thought. Anything. Being safely ensconced in a Scot schoolroom, teaching
two young ladies had seemed the perfect hiding spot, too.
She'd have time to think of her next move and wait for Father
to reconsider his edict. It hadn't sounded as mad then as it
undoubtedly was now. She hadn't had time to evaluate and
ponder, however. Why . . . being on that particular corner
when the real governess-to-be had been mowed over by a
carriage right in front of Amalie—and then seeing the poor
woman into a lane where she poured out her story—had been
pure luck; heaven-sent and fated.

If only Amalie had the sense to keep her footing at that
carriage step, none of this would be happening. She wouldn't
be sitting with her back against a tree, wrapped in not one, but
two of their plaid blanket-things, smelling like wet scratchy
wool. She wouldn't be wearing her hair in a huge twist between her chemise and gown where it too itched. She'd never
be outside in a copse of trees while a stretched animal skin of
some kind kept rain from her, although it did nothing for the
damp wet ground-mist that permeated everything else. It even
crept up through the thick weave of blanket she lay atop. And
she'd never be regarding the man she'd actually declared her
husband as he whittled away at a piece of wood when he
wasn't looking across their fire at her for no known reason
she could decipher.

It was enough to make the only daughter of the Earl of
Ellincourt grit her teeth to stay the screams. Or the faint. Or
seizure. Or whatever response gently-bred young ladies were
expected to suffer when being held captive by a small group
of barbarians named Clan MacGowan who'd gotten themselves a dangerous escort of more barbarians named Clan
Dunn-Fyne. And all of it under threat of death.

Of course, any reaction would only work if the lady in
question allowed herself that sort of idiocy. And if it would
actually do any good.

Amalie looked down at the bundle of sleeping babe the wet-nurse had placed in her arms and sighed slightly. Such a tiny thing! In need of loving and nurturing. It was a mistake to cuddle it close and feel any stirring of emotion. Any fool would know that. Not only was the babe nearly too weak to survive but there wasn't any way Amalie Ellin was staying about to see to the mothering of her. She suspected that loving this baby girl and then giving her up might be worse even than losing Edmund. She wasn't staying to find out; deathbed promise or not. And if that barbarian Thayne thought differently, he could just join the list of other men without a thought to their skulls.

As if he called, Amalie looked across at him again and got another of his dark, enigmatic looks containing what looked like anger. If he wanted to hide emotion, he should probably grow a beard like the others, or he shouldn't clench his teeth. Such a stance did little except define and shape a sharp jaw. Or the flickers of fire were lying. He had nothing to be angered over. *Nothing!* Besides . . . he'd started it. He'd practically authored it. She couldn't claim a child and no husband! Not when facing this Dunn-Fyne horde.

All of which was probably hidden in the look she gave Thayne, trying her best to remain unblinking and just as expressionless. She sighed heavily, moving the child with it and then worked at ignoring the little sucking motion the babe made as it snuggled closer to her. It didn't do any good to trade looks with him. He looked immune to it, and her eyes started to smart. She had to resort to looking aside to keep from betraying anything.

Amalie blinked against the sudden sting. She wasn't used to going without sleep for so many hours. They'd put a large piece of stretched skin atop their bonfire, but it was so low it sent smoke into the clearing before it could get obliterated by rainfall. That could be the reason for tears. It wasn't emotion. Oh no. Never. She didn't cry and wasn't about to start.

Besides which, she'd chosen this . . . or something like it. She'd already decided that no matter what awaited her, any fate away from Rochester was better than wedding him.

The space glimmering in front of her eyes got shadowed and then filled with the huge frame of Thayne MacGowan, crawling onto the ground beside her. He then compounded that surprise by spinning onto his back, showing one tanned and naked upper leg that didn't get covered as his plaid cloth settled into place. It was vaguely threatening with a view of muscle and strength. She had no need of the reminder. She'd already been held against more male than she knew existed and a lot more than she could handle. He should wear more. And he should wear it properly. Not just tossed on like an afterthought. They all should, although every other man in the makeshift camp paled if compared to this one.

Thayne acted like he knew the bent of her thinking as he just reclined there, breathing slowly and with deep breaths that raised and lowered the broad span of his chest. He hadn't shed his shirt but since it was fashioned of thin muslin and was now soaked with rain, it wouldn't have made any difference. The fabric was useless as a cover. It filmed every shadow and bump and rope of a muscled physique few claimed. Edmund certainly hadn't. Nor Rochester. Nor had her father. Or any other male she'd ever seen. Thayne MacGowan looked primal and uncouth and menacing even as he portrayed complete lassitude. He kept his head atop bent arms, looking at the tanned skin above him as if he lay atop feathers and not the blanket-covered decaying deadfall of shed leaves.

Amalie held her breath through countless heartbeats, waiting for the moisture atop her eyes to dry. She cursed silently as more tears joined in, making it inevitable what would happen if she blinked. She thanked the tears at the same time for making him indistinct and blurred.

"I've come to ask you something," he finally said. He was

using a soft low tone with a hint of brogue. "Actually . . . I've come to ask you several things."

Amalie would've answered if her voice worked and if she wasn't fighting what couldn't possibly be full-out sobs. She refused the emotion. The rivulet of shivers up and down her back and climbing her shoulders were hard to endure. They'd be worse if she had a witness to it. She knew it instinctively.

She nodded and looked away into the dark mass of plaid-covered lumps of men. Although the view was firelit, rain-washed, and then tear-blurred, it was still easy to spot the large quantity of Dunn-Fyne men sleeping just on the other side of a fallen log. She tipped her head to send one tear trail into her temple while the other one went down her nose and then she righted her chin again, giving him her profile.

"I'll na' have it bandied about that I'd nae interest in my family. Either my new bairn . . . or the wife."

He was worried about gossip?

"You ken?"

She'd decided the word ken took the place of 'understand' most of the time. It seemed to stand in for 'know' as well. And for what should be 'easily apparent.' Or whatever else they wanted to use it for. She nodded.

"I also need you to cease the invite you've proffered me all eve. I'm na' immune. You ken that as well?"

"In . . . vite?" Her voice was missing. It didn't seem to matter.

"Aye. Invite. To enjoy you. All eve. Just as I said."

"I never—!" Her exclamation had a hint of sound attached to it this time. It carried every bit of her shock, too.

"I've nae wish to consummate our marriage. Well . . . actually I do, but 'twould go better if I weren't surrounded by Dunn-Fyne men at the time."

Amalie sucked in a gasp, pulled in tears with it, and choked. That started a coughing spasm that filled her eyes worse than before, dislodged the infant into a berth at Amalie's

far side, engendered several grunts and snorts from all the humanity about them, and got a fit of whispered swearing from
the man beside her. It also got her hauled down onto her back
beside him, while a leg went over her thighs and his hand covered her mouth. The move scraped her legs. She could feel the
minute sting of it as well as the caress of air atop her knees and
if she thought of it, higher still. All of which formed a lump in
her throat where it thumped with every heartbeat while the
babe kicked and squirmed against the grip she'd put on it. She
was surprised it wasn't screaming.

"Life or death, lass! Doona' you ken anything?"

He hissed it in her ear, sending heat that created shivers.
And threat of more. The clamp of his fingers indicated how
much more. As did how he'd shifted to an elbow, putting himself above her and in a position to make certain she understood. That was before she factored in where he'd put his leg,
holding her in place with a limb so heavy the pulse thumping
through her had moved to her upper thighs.

Amalie nodded quickly and viciously.

"I'm moving my hand. Nae sound. Agreed?" He whispered it, making it infinitely worse as more shiver accompanied his breath.

She nodded.

"I'm trusting you. God help me."

He lifted his hand. Amalie watched his eyes. She'd specif-
ically noted their blue-green color since he was forever putting
her into a close range when she felt the most awkward, but she
hadn't factored in how thickly lashed they were. Nor how well-
formed. Capable of holding her gaze with a look that created
a riot of more shivers that flew all over her, centering with
horrid accuracy at each breast tip. Again. She watched him
flick a gaze to her lips and then her bosom as if he knew!
Exactly where and what!

Amalie had to look away. And quickly. She fixed her sight
on the flap of stretched skin above them where the animal's

head had once been. She was still watching it when Thayne looked back at her face. She didn't have to check. She knew. It was in the heightened rate of his heartbeat next to her arm, the stronger huffs of breath, and the stir of something at her hip where his groin pressed against her. All of which was more barbaric and crude than before. And then her entire frame made it worse as she spasmed oddly right up against him.

The immediate reaction was a responding lunge against her and then a huffed breath across the bridge of her nose. He lowered his head again to her ear. "You doona' ken the least in orders, wife, but you're fain bonny. And gifted. I'll say that for you."

Amalie went stiff as what had to be his tongue finished the whispered words. She jerked away and then endured a chuckle that caused worse tremors atop the wetness he'd tongued into place. All of it because she had no choice. He was practically astride her as if it were normal and acceptable—and with an infant beside them! Amalie felt the babe settle back into slumber as if that was also accepted and normal and comfortable, too.

Well . . . how was she to know? She hadn't anyone to ask. She'd always shied away from imagining close physical contact with a man. She knew instinctively it wouldn't have helped. She couldn't have known what to imagine. Right here in this copse, in the open and surrounded by more men than she dared count, this Thayne fellow obliterated everything. Not only was he more male than any woman should have to deal with, but he knew it. He also knew how to use it. On unsuspecting females. And to a punishing level.

"I almost doona' miss my freedom."

Her intake of air didn't have much impact although it moved the babe slightly. She felt Thayne's lips moving along her cheek . . . toward her mouth. To kiss her again? Without one bit of asking? The most horrid quiver started deep in the private regions of her body as if in accompaniment, making everything spin and whirl.

"Leastways, to the degree I should."

Lying in his arms wasn't gaining Amalie a thing. And soon, it was going to reap worse. She could tell as fingers spread about what was left of her skirts, gathering petticoat-depleted cloth about one side and lifting her, matching her fully against his loins. Her eyes flew wide and her trembling worsened. That just made the limbs holding her harder and tighter as a tremor scored him. It was impossible not to see goose bumps as they lifted the opaque white fabric from his skin. Amalie had never felt so odd; her breath was coming in sharp short bursts, while her entire body felt like liquid weight. It was held in place by him and being fitted around him, and there wasn't much on her that felt capable of stopping any of it. He went to a push-up position, above the babe, parting her legs and then settling something, hard, foreign, and heated right between her thighs, splitting them. Just above the knee. She had to do something! Anything! And it just wasn't fair that not one soul had warned her about this sort of experience.

"St-stop! Please . . . stop!" The squeak was barely audible at first.

"Say something to match your frame." His voice was accompanied by a slide of motion as he bowed above her and maneuvered further between the sensitive skin between her thighs.

"You . . . must stop—!"

"Nae," he responded.

"I'll scream! I will!" The huffed words had fright and shock at their core. And somehow that stopped him.

"What? Why?"

"I swear . . . I will!"

"You prefer death?" Thayne's whisper was harsh as he

lowered back onto his side on the blanket bed, somehow keeping their loins connected. And worse. It felt like it pulsed against her with a movement of its own!

Amalie's eyes went so wide it pained. She didn't dare blink as he looked down at her. There wasn't a hue of any kind to be seen as he gazed at her for long moments while his heartbeat continued to pound against her belly. Swift. Strong. Relentless.

"You doona' wish this?"

"N-no." The whisper was hers but it was choked-sounding. It didn't sound like a refusal at all. It sounded eager . . . and breathless.

"Truly?"

"Tru . . . ly."

"Why did you tell them we wed, then?" he asked.

"I . . . had to."

"Why?"

He'd guessed something of her distress for he was easing from her, sliding away as he moved. He left one leg atop her, pinning her. As if he needed it to prevent escape. That was needless. If she tried to stand, she suspected she'd fall.

"Be-because you . . . told them the babe was mine."

"True."

"I cannot have a baby."

"Well, I sure as the devil could na'," Thayne replied.

"It isn't amusing."

"Agreed." He'd sobered at her tone.

"I mean . . . I can't have a-a-a newly birthed baby."

"Why na'?"

"I don't know the . . . particulars, but I think there are doctors involved . . . and s-s-sometimes surgeons . . . and I-I-I think it's very hard. I probably couldn't be moved."

"I've carried you everywhere. That's nae issue. Only my men ken why."

Space and time away from the intimacy he'd forced on her was strengthening her voice and giving her back her wits. As well as making everything cold-feeling. She'd worry over that later.

"Very well. What about the rest of it?"

"What 'rest of it'?" He mimicked her exactly, although his barely audible voice was two octaves lower in tone.

Amalie stuck out her lower lip and blew a sigh. "When you tell a lie you have to be able to back it up. And continue the farce. You didn't."

"How so?"

"You gave me little choice. Without any time to think, I might add."

"Why doona' you make sense?"

"Claiming you is the lesser evil under the circumstances. Can't you see that?"

"Lesser evil? Me?"

He pulled his head back as if insulted. Amalie barely avoided giving in to the twitch of smile.

"Life or death, remember?"

"What are you speaking of now?"

"Exactly what you did."

"I must be stewed, lass. You make nae sense. None."

"You told them I'm the babe's mother."

"True. You already argued it."

"You didn't think it through!"

"You're a shrew. With a nagging bent. That's it. Is na' it?"

Amalie's response came through set teeth. It was soft and cursed but it was still loud enough to waken. Thayne stiffened completely. She matched his held-breath state as they waited for the movements about them to quiet. She didn't move the entire time and he didn't, either. All that happened was her heart rate increased until it owned her hearing.

Thayne finally blinked, tipped his head to her ear again,

releasing his breath as well as her gaze. "Perhaps we should save this . . . for another time."

Amalie managed a nod and that got her what felt like a lip touch on her neck. And that just got her another round of shivers to fight.

Chapter 4

She'd rarely spent such a night. Amalie stayed still for several moments, willing sensation back into her limbs. Her mattress had never felt so hard. She felt weak, too, just like during the weeks of slow starvation Father ordered. And she was filled with ache. Massive ache. Everything was heavy: her legs, arms, neck . . . all leaden.

Her sleep had been filled with an endless span of dreams, peopled with savage demons, steep cliffs with bottomless drop-offs, and cold deep water that pulled her under, making it nearly impossible to surface for a gasp at air. But throughout there'd been the form of a man. Tormenting her. Teasing her. Protecting her. And not just any man, but one conjured into being just for her. Formed with jaw-dropping features, shoulder-length chestnut-colored hair he wore pulled back, and clear aqua-shaded eyes. There was more. He'd been a huge muscled man, capable of wielding any weapon to her defense and easily assisting her when she needed it. It was a shame he was just a dream.

Amalie stretched and connected her head with something solid and bulky. Alive. And grumbling. Then it was angered.

"Watch the chin! I'm bruised and swelled already."

Amalie yanked her eyelids open, tried to sit at the same time, but was pitched back by an arm of unbreakable strength. She didn't guess the unbreakable part. She found out. She tried. All that happened was the hold tightened to a punishing level, a leg went atop her hips, and a face came into view. Amalie spent several moments of huffed effort pushing against him before admitting defeat. Her fight hadn't done much. The man who held her was just as massive and unbending as he'd been in her dream. He was as handsome, too. Even with a mass of lengthy, ungroomed hair falling across his forehead. She added to that. He also looked amused. He didn't even look winded.

"You're an odd spit. Thinking to best me? And at wrestling?"

Amalie bucked with her entire body. Nothing much happened, other than his limbs flexed to hold her in place.

"You . . . are not real," she informed him haughtily.

One of his eyebrows lifted, showing a flash of blue-green. The man had stunning eyes. No wonder she'd dreamt him.

"I dreamt you. That makes this unreal and therefore it's not happening," she continued.

He was definitely entertained now as a smile split his face, revealing a full set of white teeth.

"What . . . is so amusing?" Amalie asked.

"You called me a dream. Me."

"My mistake. I meant nightmare," she replied.

"Lass, you more than dreamt me. You up and claimed me. Afore all."

He said each word distinctly and solidly. That gave them more weight and that just seemed to add to the entirety of his bulk.

"I did not. Nor would I. Ever."

"Oh, aye. You did. Proclaimed aloud and with perfect words. Binding words."

"Let. Me. Up." Each word was punctuated with another

heave of her entire frame, or what she hoped was her entire frame.

"Na' yet."

She had to cease fighting him. Her strength wasn't up to it and her face was probably red with the effort. It humored him, too. Amalie narrowed her eyes and glared at him and received a full grin for her trouble.

"Why not?" She was about to use her cross voice. The one reserved for the stupidest servant. She hoped he was prepared.

"'Tis unsafe. Too many men about."

That stopped her words and then it evaporated every bit of the just-awakened confusion. Her heart moved to mass in her throat, nearly closing it off. "Where . . . is the babe?" There wasn't any sound to her whisper but he knew what it was.

"With her wet-nurse. Filling her belly. Eating. Exactly as I'll be doing. Once I've taken a moment to . . . uh . . ."

His voice trailed off and Amalie watched as it looked like his neck darkened and then his chin. *Men blush?* She wondered it before wondering why she cared. And further, if he wanted to keep the emotion hidden, he should wear a collar with his shirt. Or at least fasten his clothing fully, rather than leave it gapped to mid-chest, revealing skin-covered sinew she'd snuggled against all night. That's when Amalie stopped every thought before she got her own blush. He hadn't been mistaken about bruising, either. There was a dark shadow along the edge of his jaw. His chin didn't look swollen, however, or he was more sculpted than seemed possible.

"Seek the privy?" she added to assist him.

He glanced toward her and then looked away again. Nodded. And went an even rosier shade.

"That bothers you?" she asked.

"I've na' been around lasses much," he replied. "And never one I'd wed."

Amalie stiffened, realized that mistake as every portion of

her collided with him, and then pulled in on her cheeks. She hoped he'd know disdain when he saw it and tried to make certain he heard it. "You're mistaken, sir," she replied. "We are not wed. Further, I wouldn't wed with you if you were the last man, I repeat—*last*—man I ever run across."

He pulled in air, pushing his chest and belly into hers, flicked his glance to her, and then he shoved the breath out, cursing her with heated warmth all over.

"We're already wed, lass. 'Twas your mouth saying the words."

"No."

"Aye."

"N. O." She spelled it this time and added a head shake for emphasis.

"By declaration. Among witnesses."

"I . . . refuse."

"I dinna' wish it, either, but trust me. 'Tis Scot's law. We're wed. Legal and binding."

"If you didn't wish it, why didn't you stop it?"

"Because I value life. I want to finish with mine. You heard Dunn-Fyne's words. Drawing and quartering is nae fit way to die."

"This isn't happening. It isn't true, and it certainly isn't right."

"Trust me, lass. 'Tis true. And serious. You're wed to me. Just as you spoke."

"That was playacting!"

"Keep your voice down!" He rumbled the threat and made certain of it with a hand atop her mouth. "Doona' you ken a word I say? I value life. I just wish you placed the same value on yours so I would na' have to do it!"

Amalie didn't doubt him anymore. Everything on him looked earnest and truthful. And ready to make certain of it.

"Trouble with the wife, MacGowan?"

"Nothing I need an assist with. But I thank you all the same, Dunn-Fyne."

Thayne turned his head to answer the snide voice of their captor. Amalie didn't need to look and verify it. The unpleasant ripple of shiver going all over her was enough proof of who stood there. As well as the volume of men he had with him.

"You certain?"

"Aye."

"Any wench gave me that much issue, I'd see her whipped."

Amalie's eyes were huge and unblinking, probably reflecting absolute horror at the man's words.

"My thanks for the advice," Thayne replied.

"Some wenches react best to a whip."

Amalie tried to shut off her hearing. She wasn't listening to such things. Not in this lifetime. And not about her.

"She worries over the bairn."

"Sounds and looks more like she worries over your lusts. And perhaps . . . their nearness to the bairn's birth."

Thayne swallowed. Amalie felt the motion. "That, too," he finally replied.

"Well! Doona' let me stop you."

"All in good time, Dunn-Fyne. The wife's barely left the birth-bed. As you just brought out."

Dunn-Fyne chuckled. He was still laughing as he moved away, taking his snide words with him as well as the shuffling noises of his men. Amalie shut her eyes.

"You believe me now?" Thayne whispered.

She nodded.

"You'll keep quiet?"

She nodded again.

He sent a breath across her nose and released her mouth. Then he moved his head to continue his whispering, this time at her ear. More than his head moved. It felt like shoulders, chest, belly, groin, and legs all undulated along and atop her.

"He kens the truth about us. You hear me? And what he does na' ken, he suspects!"

She waited, listening to every single heartbeat as they raced through her ears, revealing her fright. Waited some more.

"The man is na' stup't. He kens the wee bairn is his, as well."

"Why doesn't he do anything about it, then?"

"Why should he? Think, lass. He's got me hooked, netted, and fileted. He's fain satisfied with the turn of events. Can you na' see it?"

"You're heavy," Amalie told him.

Thayne pulled in a huge breath, if the amount of weight pushing against her was any indication. And then he let it out. Loudly and with a large sigh sound. He lifted his upper body onto his elbows to regard her with unblinking earnest aqua-shaded eyes. Amalie felt her heart flutter slightly before she could prevent it. She could only hope he didn't note it.

"We move, we do it together. As one. In reach of one another. You ken?"

Amalie waited a moment before nodding.

"You cleave exactly to me. Always. 'Tis the lone safe place. And the lone place to keep everything else safe as well! Including Mary's bairn. You ken that, too?"

Amalie puzzled that before shaking her head.

"I've noted how he looks at you. If he gets close enough, he'll grab you. And then he'll ravish you, and then—! Are you still a maid?"

She put every bit of anger that question deserved in the look she gave him. It worked. He understood the answer.

"I'll remedy it as soon as I dare."

"What?" The word squealed.

"Softly, lass! Soft! Jesu'!"

He continued with more whispered curse words, shifting his body with the intensity of it and putting weight atop her that had a crushing value to it. About the only thing he wasn't doing was holding her mouth.

"Can you na' listen through anything afore reacting?"

"You're . . . too . . . heavy," she managed to reply. He lifted onto his elbows again, and this time, he even shifted his hips to one side of her.

"We'll try again. Pray, listen fully this time. Dunn-Fyne's a wife-beating, heartless son-of-a-banshee. He's na' above taking another man's wife. 'Twould be a fitting revenge against me. If he so chooses."

"Revenge?"

"For the stealing of his wife. He'd consider taking you a just and fair act. And righteous. He'd probably rape you in full sight of all. Brutally. You saw how he treated Mary?"

Amalie choked, held the scorch of reaction until she had it under control and breathed with the slightest cough accompanying it. It still burned every bit of her chest. He took it for an answer.

"This is the Highlands, lass. Up here, if a man canna' hold what's his, he's nae right to claim it in the first place."

"You-you'd allow it?"

"How am I to stop him?"

"But—"

"Doona' fret. There'd be nae allowance. I'd die fighting. 'Tis better."

"Better?"

"Dunn-Fyne finds your maiden wall, he'll put light on our lie . . . and then I'm a dead man. As are the others about us. Except . . . perhaps you. But you'd most like be wishing for death."

"You just told me . . . he already knows." Shock altered her voice.

"I did. And he does."

"I don't understand this at all."

"You doona' need to! Trust me. And another thing—I need to ken your name. Uh . . . your given one."

"Amalie," she replied automatically.

"You're na' the governess?"

"Y-yes," Amalie stammered on it. She knew what was coming next, too.

"That does na' sound right. I canna' recollect the name, but . . . you're certain-sure it's Amalie?"

"Of course." She'd forgotten one of the rules of lying. Always keep the story straight. Amalie nearly groaned.

"Fair enough. Amalie. I'll work at remembering it. You're to stay at my side. Leastways 'til we reach MacGowan land. Or Dunn-Fyne ceases this humiliation of me."

"Humiliation?"

"Our declaration is all that's standing between us and death. And I include the wee bairn in that."

"You expect me to believe he'd hurt his own babe?"

"She's his fourth daughter. Unwanted. Another mouth to feed and drain his coffers for dowry. I doona' ken if he'd harm her for certain, but whether she lives or dies means little to him."

"Now I really hate him," Amalie replied. Thayne's lips curved slightly.

"Enough to obey? As a proper wife to me?"

"Very well. I agree. I'll act the part. For now."

"I doona' ken if you listen proper but I'm beginning to doubt it. You *are* my wife. 'Tis of an unbreakable nature, and . . . brace yourself. There's more."

"More?"

"I'm betrothed to the MacKennah lass. This marriage will restart the feud."

"Feud? Did you say . . . feud?" It just kept getting worse and there didn't seem any way to stop it.

"MacGowan Clan's rich. Settled. We hold a castle, three lochs, and a seaport. Na' so MacKennah Clan. They march right alongside the sea, but on rock-strewn cliff attached to naught save bog. They've leagues of worthless land and bloodthirsty clan. Little in wealth. A betrothal was arranged in exchange for ransom over a score ago."

"Ran . . . som?" Sweet heavens! Were her ears deceiving her? *Ransom?*

"You ken now why he's allowing me to live? Dunn-Fyne has full vengeance for any slight. We *gave* it to him."

Her voice was missing. Her mouth just kept opening, then closing, and nothing came out.

"You also ken how things could change should you get . . . seized? And a maiden wall discovered?"

She gulped. Blinked against moisture that accompanied what felt like absolute frost invading her limbs. Gulped again.

"You'll stay at my side? Without argue?"

She nodded. The next moment he was on his knees and backing out from their shelter. He took her with him.

Things looked little improved as dawn lengthened into mid-morn, the day awash with rainfall that shaded everything to gray. Thayne lifted his face to the drops and then shoved fingers through his hair, pushing it back onto his shoulders before resuming a hold about the woman before him. It might be worse. They could be facing a cloudburst of huge strength and duration, turning every bit of land to hoof-sucking bog and stopping travel. He wondered if the lass guessed that particular spate of luck.

Or even if she cared.

The woman was amenable to whatever he asked; without argue, comment, or delay. She'd have a difficult time running from him without boots, but she gingerly tiptoed about, staying at his side. She was with him to fetch a tin of water, watched him drink it before refilling it for her. He could see once she returned—following the length of rope he'd looped about her waist—that she'd used the water to wash her face and attempt to braid all that hair of hers. She hadn't seen his frown. She should've left her hair as it was, pulled back and hidden. He'd probably been a little rough when making certain a MacGowan plaid covered her, but she hadn't balked. *Women!* She already knew Dunn-Fyne lusted for her. Showing womanly attributes was adding unneeded complication. Especially with the extent of attributes this lass claimed.

If Thayne believed in luck, he'd have to count himself in it with the woman he'd claimed. Fully. As the morn lengthened he felt even luckier.

She'd stayed at his side while he set Iain to saddling horses and Pellin to cooking. Pellin was a great cook. Could usually create sup with little in supplies and less in equipment. Dunn-Fyne couldn't fault the aroma of fried gruel cakes, even as it blended with fresh rain smell. The lass had been at Thayne's left side the entire time as he shoved three cakes into his mouth, one after the other, quickly chewing and swallowing, while never moving his hand from the hilt of his claymore. They all did the same. Such a manner of eating was usual when accompanying enemy clan. They all ate in silence without cutlery or even plates.

His wife wasn't used to such. It was obvious as she tore her cake into pieces to fit into the cup, barely touching and then blowing at her fingers from the heat. Then she nibbled on one little piece at a time. Thayne glanced at her as she did it and waited but she hadn't made one act of argument over any of it.

She'd kept her head bowed and rarely raised her eyes. Twice, in fact. Thayne sucked in on his cheeks and considered it. No . . . it had been three times. This Amalie had glanced up at him thrice, showing spirit and fire and how well hidden it all was. That was fine with him. As long as they kept the charade long enough to reach MacGowan land, he'd be well satisfied.

Thayne shifted and resettled on the hard leather of his saddle, brushing his groin against the woman's thigh with the motion. She'd settled into the spot in front of him with one glance, telling him wordlessly how much she disliked their closeness. Thayne hadn't cared. Much. The lass was formed too well, with bonny features, slender waist, lush thighs and woman-area, while her breasts tempted him with every upward move of his arm. She seemed fashioned for pleasure. Those reminders added to the satisfied part. If Dunn-Fyne saw fit to see them bedded down in a reasonably private way, regardless of whether they'd reached MacGowan land, Thayne wouldn't fight off consummating this marriage of his.

His mind wandered where his body couldn't and he let it, clenching deep in his lower back, feeling the heavy pronounced thump of heartbeat as it started and then heightened, elongating and thickening him. Thayne tilted forward slightly, so he could fit where he wanted, tightening his thighs against the horse at the same time he drew back, bringing her into place. He barely kept the groan from sounding. This woman was perfectly formed. Lush. Even sideways atop him and covered with skirts and plaid, he could sense her haven. Beckoning. Enwrapping. Undulating.

She didn't help him, but she wasn't fighting either. At first. Thayne stifled the chivalrous instinct the moment it surfaced. This woman was made for pleasure. And they were wed. It was his right to be and do exactly as he was. She stiffened and made a strange gurgling sound before tightening her buttocks to move. Thayne hardened the arm looped about her until she ceased. He should've known not to trust her. There wasn't a woman birthed that did anything without argue. Nor one that didn't know how to tease and tempt. And annoy. But he couldn't stay annoyed long. She was too womanly and had such a luscious smell about her that he bent his head and inhaled, filling his lungs with her smell before sending the gust of it with enough force it ruffled what material the rain hadn't weighed down.

"Thayne . . . I—"

He shushed her with a warning at her ear, at the exact moment he fitted her atop him again, twisting her forward-facing to slide against her. He held her in position, his left hand atop her belly, enjoying pulsing motions he didn't bother controlling. Despite her gasp and how her hands hooked about his arm like claws.

He chuckled at her antics, and then the voice of Dunn-Fyne interrupted, waking Thayne to reality and danger. And making him acknowledge it.

"More trouble with the wife, MacGowan?"

Thayne pulled in a lungful of air, lifted his head, and turned toward the man. His wife had ceased breathing, if the form in his arms was any indication. She was in a full tremble, though.

"Nothing I canna' handle," he replied, on the released breath.

"She acts more like a maid than a wife."

"Because she prefers privacy?"

"Because she fights you so. I've been watching. And pondering."

"She likes a good argue, Dunn-Fyne. As do I. I doona' like my women cowed. Or beaten."

"Hmm. Pity."

Thayne looked at Laird Dunn-Fyne, astride a like-size Clydesdale, but due to the man's smaller stature there was little choice but to look down. He watched as the man acknowledged it and then hated him for it. And started evaluating and deciding his options again, without one word being exchanged.

Dunn-Fyne had full lust for this Sassenach governess. Thayne couldn't alter it, even swaddled as she was in a thick bundling of green, red, and black plaid. Dunn-Fyne also lusted for revenge. He spent some time looking at Amalie, debating which one suited him best. All of it was easy to spot. Thayne's mind whirled but nothing else moved except the horse beneath him. To portray marital discord of the wife might work in their favor. But Dunn-Fyne may find it more enjoyable to take the lass's maidenhood and break her spirit, exactly as he'd done with Mary. Thayne gulped and felt the resultant pop in his ears as he waited and watched.

"I've been thinking, MacGowan. I may have need of another wife. Should Mary na' be located. Or found to have died. A man canna' be without a wife and son. I'm thinking on the lines of a feisty one this time. Bonny. Young. I also like them . . . maidenly."

The man drew out each word to get a reaction. The lass went deadly still in Thayne's arms, making a deadweight. He would've suspected a faint except for each catch of breath she made, pushing her breasts against where he held her upright. He cleared his throat.

"This here's nae maid, Dunn-Fyne. She's my wife. For nigh a year."

"So you both . . . say."

"True. We both spoke on it. You heard. We're wed. And nae woman has two husbands. You ken the law."

"She only has a husband while you live. True?"

He finished with a kick against his horse, sending it into a canter and leaving them. Thayne watched him without expression, although the strength and rapidity of his heart beating was impossible to control. The lass was gagging, if her reflexes were accurate. Or perhaps she sobbed. Either reaction was hidden by how she'd turned her head and settled it exactly atop Thayne's heart, stopping the ragged beat before restarting it in an even faster and harder pace.

Chapter 5

"Well, lass?" His voice came out higher pitched than he wanted it to, and with a hint of tremor. Thayne cleared his throat before trying again. "You've na' much time. Perhaps one eve."

"This isn't happening."

Her whisper sent warm breath over his upper belly.

"You say that oft. I doona' think you ken what it means."

"It's . . . a denial."

She said it in a hint of voice that heated up the area about Thayne's heart before turning to a squeeze. Then it moved to a twinge through his arms before it coiled and spread warmth right through his belly. Thayne lifted his head, looked over the woman's head at the mass of horses before him and gulped. He'd never felt such a thing. It was akin to the weak-kneed reaction he'd had when he'd won his first battle, but much worse. This feeling suffused his features with warmth while everything else about him grew strange-feeling . . . almost soft, pliant, and weak. Thayne narrowed his eyes, clenched his jaw, and looked unseeingly at the rain-washed view until whatever the emotion was abated and left. He couldn't afford weakness. Not now. Not ever.

"Denial does na' change anything, lass."

"I'm not listening."

She said it to his chest, sending more heated waves with her voice. Thayne needed to move her. It was too dangerous to keep her close to his heart and he didn't even know why. He shifted her back sideways to him, using his free hand. Then he made certain of her position by placing his hand on her forehead and holding her against his shoulder. He kept the reaction from showing as she snuggled into the spot as if she belonged. His arms trembled slightly before he could stop them.

His arms trembled? Not a good sign. He hoped she didn't spot it and assign meaning. Getting his voice firm and steady was his next issue. He waited three heartbeats before trying. Then a fourth.

"Verra well . . . lass. Deny it. It does na' alter it."

"Verra?"

For a woman who'd just been near faint with weakness she was remarkably cool-voiced and argumentative-sounding. Thayne studied the bleak sight of rain peppering the surface water of the loch before bending his head to whisper in the vicinity of her plaid-covered ear.

"You heard him?"

She nodded.

"He'll take you. Rough. With little care."

She shifted as if his words bothered her.

"He'll hurt you. Purposefully. With pleasure."

"And . . . you won't?" she asked.

"Nae." Thayne stopped, licked his lips, and then continued. "Well, mayhap I will, but I will na' want to."

"You'd hurt me?"

She asked it in a little voice that hadn't much sound to it. Thayne knew he was flushing. He couldn't help it. He'd never been in such a position, pleading of private matters while surrounded by enemy clan. He wouldn't believe it if he wasn't actually doing it.

"I'd try and be gentle, lass, but . . . when there's a maiden wall to breach . . . well. Uh. 'Tis na' wholly easy. Sometimes . . . there's pain. Na' purposeful pain, but it canna' be helped."

"Is that your offer? Pain?"

Thayne was exasperated. It sounded in his next whisper. "Sometimes! With the first. Uh . . . regardless of a man's size or intent! But it can be . . . altered a bit. Made less painful. If you ken my meaning?"

She shook her head. Thayne went a full-bodied flush. Red. He didn't need to see it, he felt it.

"I'd . . . be gentle. I mean I'd prepare the way . . . but well . . . uh"—he stopped, gulped, and continued with a harsher tone—"dinna' you receive instruction on things a-tween a man and wife?"

"My . . . husband is supposed to explain . . . things . . . of that nature."

What voice she had was nonexistent toward the end. Thayne had to bend his head to hear it and that just made the warmth about his heart swell again. He hardened it against her and his voice sounded it.

"Will you just answer?"

"Very well. The answer is no," she replied.

No?

Thayne's head lifted and his eyes widened, gaining him raindrops for punishment, and then he narrowed them. She'd promised to obey him and already she disavowed her own word. He didn't know why he bothered asking. "Lass, he'll take you!"

"So will you," she informed him.

"But he'll force you."

"And you won't?"

He took several deep breaths and forced a calm state. The lass had no idea how close to a shaking she was. "Of course I'll force you! To do otherwise means death."

"See? You offer force with pain. Just like him."

"I'm your husband," he informed her.

"No. You are not," she replied, stretching out each whispered word as if intoning them in that fashion made it more official.

"You canna' disavow it still. It's the law."

"It's not my law."

"Jesu'!"

"I'm not used to hearing such words spoken in my presence, either."

Thayne's mouth dropped open. He felt like a lad being upbraided by his sire. She sounded exactly like a governess. In the whispered cool tone it felt even more effective.

"You—you—" He was unable to finish. He didn't know what the rest of it was.

"This continual use of profanity around me. It's ungentlemanly . . . and unseemly. It's not furthering your proposition . . . such as it is."

"I-I. I—"

Anything he attempted would be another curse. They filled his mind. Thayne settled with closing his mouth and watching the hovering mist that obscured where the loch met the mountain they'd soon be climbing. *Women!* He was beset with women trouble! That's what chivalry reaped—a whole lot of women trouble. He counted more than two hundred heartbeats, until they slowed and took some of his ire with them. He bent his head to hers again.

"You see that drum ahead?" he asked her.

"Drum?"

"The top of the hill. Just ahead. You see?"

She nodded.

"That's the time you have."

"T-t-time?"

Her stammer had a shudder that matched it. That could be a good thing, Thayne decided. If it got her seeing sense.

"Dunn-Fyne will call a halt soon. For rest. And food. Ale.

And then we climb. A path follows the drum of that hill. And on the other side is a meadow. Surrounded on three sides by trees and rock. Protected. For camp. Anything farther and he's tempting ambush."

"Am . . . bush?"

"We're that near MacGowan land, lass. That near! I can near smell it! Dunn-Fyne kens it as do the others."

"Why stop, then?"

"You doona' listen to anything, do you? He continues on and it's risking ambush. There's na' much in cover for a span. MacGowan clan is immense. We hold many leagues of land. And what we claim, we keep."

"I don't understand."

Thayne ground his teeth together. He could feel and hear it. "You've got until we reach that meadow to decide. You already ken what'll happen if you choose wrong."

"You'll . . . all die."

Thayne flicked a glance to her. "Nae," he replied finally. "I'll use force. 'Tis exactly as he'd do, only I'll use a lot more violence to it and hope it works."

"What? Why?"

"To make certain there's blood! Jes—!" Thayne bit the rest of the curse off.

"B-blood?"

She looked shocked. She had her eyes wide with it and her lips open for air.

"Make the choice. 'Tis easy! I'm nae braggart, but I've been known as considerate. You may even find pleasure. Most women do."

She stiffened.

"Come along. Decide. You wish me angered, too?"

"I don't know why you're angry. I'm the one being forced. My lone choice is which man."

"Nae, Amalie. Your lone choice is whether I'll use force!"

She gasped, either at his words or how he said it. Thayne

didn't particularly care. Dunn-Fyne had stopped his horse some distance ahead to let his men pass by in single-file. Thayne watched as each man reached water's edge and dismounted, letting reins dangle as mounts got watered and men relieved themselves. Not one of them sought privacy. He could tell it bothered her as she sucked for air then swiveled to plant her face into his chest.

Oh, dearest God!

Amalie kept her eyes tightly shut against further assault as her heart beat so stridently it hurt. She'd been warned. She'd been rewarned. She'd been naïve. Even marriage to the Duke of Rochester was better! She might have to put up with his fat moist hands touching her and listen to vacant conversation since he had the mental capacity of a child, but at least she'd be protected! Cosseted! Secure in her position. Safe! She'd never have to watch a pack of bearded, uncouth men acting little better than the horses they rode!

Amalie shuddered in place with distaste and fright. And defeat. She was ice-cold. She'd been warned about how uncivilized the Highlands were. How castles and lands were held by chieftains acting like kings . . . making laws and dispensing justice. Here a man's worth was based not just on which clan he hailed from and how rich they were, but on how strong he was, how many men he commanded, and how many obeyed. Amalie had been told Highlanders thrived on proving a man's worth. They took land and belongings as a sign of it. Women were nothing more than chattel, to be used and discarded once they'd served their purpose.

Amalie had listened to the woman from the posting coach with skepticism. She'd suspected envy, since the other lady was old and plain, and going to a position in a much lower ranking household. She'd dismissed the warnings as little more than bedtime tales to frighten and entertain. Now she realized the other woman had spared the sensitivities with her descriptions.

How stupid and naïve could she have been?

Amalie missed Dunn-Fyne's first words once they reached him. She guessed at their content from Thayne's reply as it rumbled through where her nose was pressed.

"Well . . . I did have her gagged," he said.

"You need help . . . you ask."

Amalie shoved closer to Thayne's bulk as the sound of a whip slashed the air. But neither horse moved, so it had to be her imagination, or her fear, combined with how open and insecure and out-of-place everything felt.

"You're blocking us from our rest, and the bairn is crying for her mother."

Thayne's solid tone of voice matched the solid strength of each heartbeat. Hers were flying through her ears, each one making her more and more light-headed, while his sounded as steady as the lap of waves upon the shore.

"You still claiming the wee one?" Dunn-Fyne queried.

"I sired it. Why would na' I claim it?"

"And the wench?"

"Wife, Dunn-Fyne. Wife. This here's my wife. I'll be thanking you to speak correct about it."

The man grunted something. Thayne moved the hand with the reins to hold her back, cushioning and protecting. Or hiding her shaking.

"Until this eve," the man replied.

Thayne's hand started moving, running up and down her spine, where her plaid should be muting the feeling. Amalie sagged into it, trembling in place, while hearing the same words and seeing the same things over and over in her mind.

"I take it you've decided in my favor?" he finally asked.

"Don't let him touch me! Please? I'll do it! I will! But . . . don't let *him* touch me!"

A breath carrying what sounded like amusement brushed

her cheeks, warming the skin. Amalie cracked open an eye, then the other, and blinked. He was looking down at her with eyebrows lifted and his lips pursed in amusement. He had his hair pulled back, looking dark and shiny with the wet, and then a drop of rain dripped off his nose onto hers.

"You're the oddest thing. You argue endlessly with me, yet one word from Dunn-Fyne—"

"Please?"

"Lass." He lifted her, speaking the words against her chin and then along her jawline. Amalie sucked on a gasp filled with moisture. "You doona' listen to the smallest thing. I already told you. What a MacGowan claims . . . he keeps."

Amalie opened her mouth to answer, but he didn't give her the time. She was already smashed against him and that was made more intimate and more grasping and more everything with his kiss. Hard lips melded to hers, completely halting everything and then there was nothing but her and him and a surge of something warm and thrilling and breath-stealing.

She was in its thrall as he lifted his head, sending hard breaths all along her that matched the increased thump of his heartbeat. He was also holding her atop that strange hard lump of him again, and pushing against her hips to make certain of the connection, and groaning slightly.

"We must . . . slow this. Jesu', woman, but you're blessed. Fully. We need to cease this! And rapid-like. Right now. Or Dunn-Fyne has his vengeance full score."

Amalie had been swaying atop him, enjoying the tremor that scored the skin in front of her eyes. She stopped the moment she heard their tormenter's name.

"We canna' have witness to our tupping. You ken?"

"Tupping?"

"Aye. Tupping. You and me. 'Tis what happens with a man and woman. Can you na' listen to a word I speak?"

"I am listening. I've just never heard . . . it called . . . uh." Her voice trailed off. She'd never heard it referenced at all.

"'Twould be pure shame within hearing of the pipers, too."

"Pipers?"

"Aye. MacGowan pipes. Now, turn about like a good lass. We need a bit of rest and the bairn sounds as if she needs a cuddle or two, as well."

He didn't meet her eyes, looking instead out over her head. He had a rosy shade along his jaw as well. Then he put both hands on her waist and turned her forward-facing, or as close to it as her side-slung legs allowed. She felt him fuss behind her with the flat round bag-thing he carried at his groin, putting it flat between them. All of it mystifying and interesting. Especially as the flush moved up his cheeks. He didn't explain and she didn't ask. It was hard enough recollecting what she'd promised and what he'd do.

Tonight.

Amalie looked away before he'd spot her blush. Then she felt his thighs move beneath her, tightening on the horse as he motioned it back to a walk. That sent her leaning into the rock-like substance of his lower belly and the bag-thing, which got her a groan from him. He didn't speak. And she didn't question. She was afraid of the answer.

He'd been right about the infant. Mary's baby was at a full wail despite the wet-nurse's efforts to quiet her. The sound carried over the surface of the lake, making it difficult to spot where it spawned. Amalie could feel the tenseness in Thayne the closer they got. He also walked their mount faster. She didn't know it was to fling the reins at her and jump from its back until he did it, leaving her stranded and alone and bereft and easy prey.

And that got her Dunn-Fyne's unwavering gaze.

Amalie kept her head averted to slide off the horse in Thayne's wake, keeping the animal between her and Dunn-Fyne. The ground was wetter than it looked and soaked through her socks the moment she reached it. Amalie stood indecisively, one hand on the horse's mane and the other on her plaid to make certain it covered her. She hunched slightly to step atop her hem where it had to be warmer.

"'Tis such a weak bairn."

Amalie's breath caught. She held it until it burned before easing it out. She didn't have to look. She already knew who spoke. And where he was. And what he wanted. Shaking was overtaking her form despite effort to fight it, bringing faintness in its wake. Amalie fought the swell of black rising from where her blanket covering touched ground, blinked hard and fast while breathing quickly and shallowly until the darkness faded back into dull grayish-brown mud. Everything on her was cold now. Everything.

"Verra weak for a MacGowan," he continued. "Must be the mother at fault."

She tipped a glance to where he stood, exactly as she'd known. He was watching her from over the top of Thayne's saddle. Amalie looked away the moment her eyes verified it. Thayne ordered her to stay near to avoid this very thing, and then what happened? When she needed him, he wasn't here. And worse. In the hunched state she'd assumed, she looked and felt even more vulnerable. It was unbelievable. Amalie Ellin. Only daughter of the Earl of Ellincourt. Standing in a bowed position, terrified as she'd never been and weak-kneed enough to drop where she stood.

"'Twas an early birth?" he asked.

Amalie lifted her shoulders in a shrug, forced her fingers not to tighten on the wad of material she held to her throat.

"You ken why I ask?"

She shrugged again.

"You doona' feed your own bairn. 'Tis powerful odd. Na' many husbands hire a wet-nurse."

If she'd doubted Thayne's words, she was getting paid back. Fully. Amalie tried to shrug again but failed. Nothing worked at stopping how she shook in full-body tremors. She knew he saw it.

"You ken my meaning?"

Amalie had prided herself on a self-confident and fearless nature. She'd always exhibited it in her charades with Edmund, her dealings with others at court, her father's decrees. It's that strength of purpose she'd tapped when stealing the real governess's identity and luggage and undertaking a journey of this magnitude. She was known for bold fearlessness. Courage. Daring.

It was mortifying to find it all a sham when faced with true danger. She was also starting to cry. No matter how much she blinked and how quickly she breathed, or how tight she held her entire body. Nothing worked. And if Thayne didn't come soon, she didn't know what else might happen. All she knew was she feared it, to a near incomprehensible level.

"We'll speak more on this. You've my word."

Amalie blinked on moisture that kept flooding her eyes, making the view of lake and mist-draped mountain glimmer and blur and then glimmer again. How long she stood there, she didn't know. The edge of her plaid worked well as a handkerchief. She sopped at her face and then cupped her hands about it. All she wanted was to be back home. In her stateroom at Ellincourt Manor. Warm. Dry. Safe.

"What's happened?"

Thayne's voice accompanied arms that pulled her into an embrace of bulk, warmth, and protection. Amalie put her face firmly in the center of his chest and shook with the sobs.

"Well?" He lifted her enough her toes cleared the muck and wet and cold.

"You . . . left," she whispered.

"A moment. I was gone a trice. Mayhap less."

"He . . . he—"

"Dunn-Fyne?" He spit the name into existence.

Amalie nodded. "He—uh . . . he . . ."

"He . . . what? Come along, lass. Answer or no. Doona' leave me guessing."

"You left me."

"I saw your reaction to the others . . . so, to spare you, I—Oh, Jesu'! I canna' be with you every moment!"

"B-but that's . . . what you said. At your side. Always."

"You canna' have it both ways, lass!"

"Both ways?"

"I—uh—*women!*" The way he said it was another cursed word.

"I want to go home," she replied.

"Soon, lass. Soon. We'll be on MacGowan land by tomorrow eve. At Castle Gowan a day past that. With any luck."

Castle Gowan. Her mind conjured a building as dark and cold as the day about them. She shivered involuntarily. "I'm cold, Thayne. And wet."

"As is everyone. Look about. We're all cold and wet. Can you spare my ear the complaints?"

"But I haven't even . . . got shoes." She lifted a foot and touched it to his lower leg. He jumped slightly.

"Why dinna' you say something sooner?"

"I—"

"Christ! And His mother, Mary! You'll catch your death!"

He swung her into a berth in his arms, cradling her against him and placing her nose right against his neck. His steps were just as sure and swift as when he'd first held her in the stable yard. There was a pulse pounding from his throat against her, too. Sturdy. Strong. Powerful.

He probably didn't know it was the perfect restorative. Amalie wasn't going to tell him, either.

Chapter 6

She could feel him watching them. It continued throughout the rest period and wouldn't abate. Dunn-Fyne watched them. Every glance showed him watching. It got worse once they'd reached the meadow Thayne told her of. Despite supervising placement of the fire cover, ordering the score of men grouped about Thayne's small band, even when shoveling the stew they'd cooked into his mouth, ignoring where he dripped broth onto his beard. He was always watching her and Thayne. With a dark expression that matched his plaid.

Amalie tried ignoring Laird Dunn-Fyne but that just caused nervous suspense that made her limbs quake as if she was a fearful mouse and not a bold adventuress. The thought brought more self-loathing and self-recrimination. It was better to mimic Thayne and return every look without expression, while pretending a mothering nature she didn't know she possessed. She watched Dunn-Fyne as Thayne strapped the babe to her with a length of plaid material. It made an uncomfortable knot at the back of her neck, but Amalie didn't care. She cupped an arm about the babe who snuggled into it and slept.

The infant seemed to be the lone one.

Thayne assumed a position against a huge tree, beneath

wide branches that held another animal skin. He was propped against his saddle, his legs spread toward the fire and his right hand on the hilt of the long weapon that paralleled his leg, glinting occasionally with flickers of firelight. Amalie didn't quantify it as a sword. It didn't look like any she'd ever seen. The Earl of Ellincourt owned a massive armory. It contained all sorts of swords, handed down since the Crusades. They'd been long, slender weapons, never used. They hadn't been in her lifetime, anyway. Probably longer. The most attention they received was a polish cloth.

Thayne's weapon was long, thick, with a sharp edge that curved strangely before ending with a wicked point. It looked massive and unwieldy, and entirely capable of taking a man's head off. And it looked well-used.

Amalie was settled into the space along his other side, her head balanced on his upper belly where the steadiness of his heartbeat soothed and calmed the fear she still harbored despite every attempt at stifling it. From that position she could view Dunn-Fyne as he watched them. She didn't need any warnings. She was plastered to Thayne. She wasn't leaving his side for anything or anyone.

The air grew thick with moisture, imbuing the scene with dreamlike quality and making sparks from the fire sparkle before getting extinguished. Amalie blinked on the wavering image of horns sprouting from Dunn-Fyne's forehead until they disappeared. And then she shuddered. She had too much imagination . . . as always.

"Rain's slowing." Thayne lowered his head to her ear, pulling muscles she lay atop and breaking into her doze.

Amalie nodded slightly and continued watching Dunn-Fyne.

"'Tis a good thing. Provides cover."

"Cover." She repeated the word without comprehension, and watched the smoke between Dunn-Fyne and them undulate into dancing writhing forms. And then it drifted into the gathering mist, mutating into different shapes.

"Ground fog. 'Tis of great use."

"Fog . . ."

Her voice hadn't much substance to it, matching the scene in front of her. The flames were difficult to see through what had to be smoke. Odd smoke since it was held to the ground rather than floating skyward. At that low level, the smoke joined with the mist snaking about the tree trunks. Dunn-Fyne still sat across the fire facing them, but it was difficult to tell how watchful he was. His face was indistinct and vague and his eyes were shadowed recesses of black. Thayne's heart rate changed, nearly imperceptibly, and Amalie lifted her head. At that moment, there was a sense of movement about her other side, the one Thayne didn't protect. Amalie moved to check, but his hand stopped her, as if he knew. And then he dipped his head and explained in a soft whisper that echoed through his chest.

"'Tis but Sean. And Iain."

Amalie returned to studying Dunn-Fyne's indistinct features through haze that seemed thicker and full of dancing imps. Amid flickers of firelight.

"They've come to replace us."

Amalie murmured as if that made sense and squelched the yawn. It was entirely too comfortable and too safe-feeling, and added to that was the endless beat of Thayne's heart. She closed her eyes, settled her cheek, and the next moment she was spinning, pulled to her feet and jerked into place against Thayne as he slammed into the back of the tree, a hissed warning filling her ear.

"Hush!"

Amalie's heart filled her throat, trembling owned her limbs and there wasn't anything left to react to how he dangled her. She was entirely surprised the infant was still cradled against her breast and that her arm cupped it.

"Nae sound, lass! You ken?"

She nodded and craned her head with him to look back around the tree. At the site they'd just left. Dunn-Fyne hadn't moved. He was still endlessly watching them. Nothing looked changed. Or alert. Amalie glanced to where two forms had rolled into the spot Thayne and she had claimed. Yet another one filled where Sean and Iain had just been.

She was still assimilating all that as Thayne sucked in air and then he moved, quickly and quietly. No rustle of sound betrayed his steps, taken sure and swift through shrubbery that showered with spent rain and limbs that swayed and slapped without end. Then they were out of trees and onto open moor that was shadowed with rocks and other obstructions. That's when Thayne lifted her fully into his arms and broke into a run, as if there was a path and it was easily negotiated. Amalie held to the babe and kept gulping at a lump in her throat she couldn't speak around. Her voice was missing. And if she found it, she'd likely be screaming.

It was better to hide her face fully against him, scrunch her eyes, and pray. The thump of his pulse grew faster and harder, his breaths more strident and harsh, yet still he ran on, impressing her fully with his endurance and strength, taking countless steps over an unknown distance. And then without warning he slowed, spun, and knocked his back on what sounded like wood.

"Quickly . . . lass! Here!" His words were shoved through heavy breaths as he set her on her feet facing utter blackness. He was untying the knot at her neck as he spoke.

"But—" Amalie began.

"We've . . . little time!" The words were harsh and rapid, matching the exhalation of breath he used to say them.

"Time?" Amalie repeated.

"For tupping! There!"

The bundle of infant opened and was lifted from her. In the complete blackness, Amalie couldn't see what he did with it.

"But—your men?" Amalie asked.

"Took our . . . spots. I doona' . . . see what that has to do—make haste!"

"With what?" Amalie asked in a little voice she hated the moment it came out.

"Your clothing! At least . . . shed your plaid!"

She heard the sound of rustling that could be him removing clothing, but could be a sign of rats as well. All she knew was it was black and cold and carried a lone feeling that started a tremor deep within her.

"Where . . . are we?" she asked.

"Shepherd croft. Well built. Well-placed. Well hid. Private. Where are you? I canna' find you, lass! Amalie?"

He had his breathing back under control somewhat. The words were no longer sharp and huffed and spaced. She could sense his movements but despite how alert she was, couldn't hear them. Further, it was odd he asked. She hadn't moved from where he'd set her.

"Your men . . . know about this?" she asked.

"Jesu', lass! Of course they *know*! They're my Honor Guard!"

Amalie went hot with the all-over blush, filled with instant embarrassment and dismay. "They know what . . . we're doing right now?"

He gave a heavy sigh. Swore beneath his breath, and then answered. "They ken I was na' wed two days hence. And that I'm now consummating it. Keep speaking, I'll find you."

"B-but, Thayne, I—"

"You said you'd na' give me a fight!"

"It's just—"

Hard arms grabbed her, pulled her to a like hardness of chest and held her there. Everywhere she touched was bare skin, slick with a sheen of moisture and heated with the extent and duration of his run.

"Ah . . . there you are . . . mmm. Nice."

His voice turned low, to a croon of sound, as he ran his hands along her shoulders and then her arms, pushing the blanket thing with it. Amalie felt instant chill once the blanket fell but it got replaced by immense heat as his hands clenched about her and lifted, pressing her to the mass of him in order to just hold her there. For countless moments of time. And then his mouth found hers, prying her lips apart to lap at her tongue with his, and giving a full-body groan as accompaniment. Amalie's entire being flexed in readiness, startled and alert and entirely excited. She'd barely caught at the sensation before he moved his lips, trailing fire-spiked ice along her chin and to an ear. And once he reached there, he whispered words at her that started a riot of shivers. Amalie's shoulder lifted in defense.

"Sweet—! Ah . . . lass! You've been over-blessed with woman skills. Makes it nice—and sweet! Powerful sweet!"

He shifted, going to his knees and taking her with him, in a slant of provocation and something else. The sense of nakedness. Him. All of him. Wherever she touched, and wherever she tried not to touch. Her hands kept contacting, sparking before she lifted them, while Thayne's fingers climbed rapidly up her spine, sliding each button from its hole, opening the material to flesh that quivered at the touch. And everywhere she experienced shivers. Rivulets of them went over her shoulders to center in each breast tip, making darts of painful intensity and throbbing. Amalie felt the scratch of wool at her back, the rush of air at her bosom, and then the absolute shock as lips found her pointed nipple flesh. And started suckling.

Hammers hit at her, filling her frame with a pounding akin to drums. Those were chased by a torrent of shaking and a flood of feeling outside every realm of her experience and imagination. Her mouth went wide to allow a cry of pure reaction and that wasn't enough. She couldn't have dreamt passion and intensity such as those filling her veins. And then more of both until it all became a throb of thrill and anticipation and absolute want. Then that got chased by growing excitement and agitation that had her arching and bucking against him while her fingers clenched his hair.

"Ah . . . lass. I can barely keep from taking—! Na' yet! I've na' prepared . . ."

Whispered words unfastened him from her breast, touching on the trail of wet he tongued into existence as he slid back up, licking at her lips before taking the kiss. Amalie's hands found his, slid up his arms . . . reaching his shoulders before sliding the same way back, kneading and pushing against sinew and strength. She felt his arms harden as he lifted his upper body from her, his lips never leaving hers, sucking and playing and absorbing, and causing such a myriad of stimulation she was close to sobbing with the combination. She grazed her palms along his arms . . . reached his shoulders again, and dug her nails into him with the grip, seeking to bring him back. Closer. Again. More.

She barely felt him balancing, moving a hand to hers and sliding it to a hold against his chest. Until she understood. Amalie moved her hands then, spreading her fingers wide, pressing to his chest, where a heavy thump of heart tickled her palm, sending heat, moisture, and intensity. And then she slid her hand farther down him, exploring a roping of bumps and valleys all along him, learning the musculature of his lower chest, his belly . . . around to his back.

Amalie arched up from the wool-covered support, seeking to reach and match against skin he was denying her, her mouth open and keening a cry of frustration that hurt her throat.

"Easy, lass . . ."

She didn't want to go easy! She didn't know what it was she wanted, but slow and easy wasn't it. But then fingers reached the bare skin of her leg, making her lurch against him in a harsh and heavy fashion. He shoved a handful of skirt up, gaining chilled air on exposed skin, and then fingers replaced that, sending sparks. Amalie gulped for air as he slid his hand higher . . . grazing flesh. And when she exhaled, it carried a moan of anticipation and stimulation and pure need. She was afire with it. His fingers slid higher, wrapping about her to cup one side of her buttocks. Then Thayne tightened to lift her, yanking her against something so hard and foreign and large that she stiffened. Everywhere.

"Doona' fear. I'll be gentle. It's just—!"

He'd moved his kiss to her ear, whispering words that sent shivers racing to curse the rest of her. They sprang from his breath in a flood before pooling at her center, where he was sliding his hard shaft along her belly flesh and then back to the juncture of her thighs, moving closer to her core with each move. And trembling the entire time.

"Thayne! I—!"

Amalie's voice choked off as he angled his head into the space beside her shoulder, planting it on the wool in order to release his other arm. Fingers slid down her side, reaching her buttocks, and using full handfuls to lift her, holding her in position, creating an opening for him. And she was going wild. Her own lunges were trying to match against the heat and bulk filling the space he'd created. Then he stopped and a shudder ran him, strong enough to shift her along the fabric beneath them.

"Thayne?" Her whisper carried her tension. Desire. Inflamed craving.

But he stayed unmoving for the longest moment, save for where he pulsed in place, touching her innermost flesh and driving her into an arch of reaction that reached where he hovered.

"Ah . . . *lass*!"

The words were grunted as he moved finally, sliding along where everything was quivering and grasping and needy. Amalie was near bursting with the combination. He pushed his upper body against her, forcing her prone with the weight of him. Amalie was in a torture of inhaled breath, her hands gripped to his upper arms while her entire being felt poised in time, held alert, expectant, frustrated . . . and completely and totally ready.

"You're wet. But so . . . tight! I've but—*Christ*!"

He'd been huffing heated air all over her with the words, and then with the curse he'd stopped. Everything on him stilled. He wasn't even breathing while Amalie had her eyes scrunched so tightly, it hurt. Her throat felt raw with a denied scream. Her entire body was in a torment of expectancy, fueled by excitement and whirling with passion and fervor . . . and he stopped?

Light speared the darkness as the door flew wide, sending cold everywhere. It was accompanied by a slap of wood against an obstruction of wall. Within a blink, Thayne was on his feet and backed to a wall with her shoved between bare skin and peat insulation that crumbled onto her back. The boom of the door startled the babe into a cry from where she was suspended from a jut of log to the side of them. Amalie glanced at the make-shift cradle before looking at the mass of shadows in the aperture, highlighted by the torches they carried.

"Thayne?" The largest of the intruders bellowed the name.

"Jamie?" Thayne replied, the name rumbling through the back she leaned against.

The speaker stepped in, bringing a torch with him and lighting just about everything; Thayne's nakedness; the discarded plaid on the floor dented with the shape of her body; the squalor of the hut. Amalie glimpsed a large bloodied bandage on the other man's shoulder and bluish bruising about his eyes before closing hers and hiding as if that muted or changed any of it.

She didn't have to even ask. She knew the MacGowan chieftain instantly. He'd looked the same size and coloring as Thayne. And close to the same handsome features. But something was different. She'd have looked again if she could vanquish the weakness of a full-body flush and a space filled with embarrassment. Her ears got bombarded with the sound of clanking weaponry amid rumbling sounds of speech. That started the babe to kicking and fussing. Amalie wasn't capable of moving. Her knees wavered. She'd have fallen if the pressure of Thayne's body wasn't preventing it.

"Well. Well. Well. 'Tis my bairn brother, Thayne. Tupping a woman." The man had a huge voice with a deep brogue and a slurred way of speaking. He also laughed through the words, making him harder to understand.

"Jamie." Thayne's voice carried what sounded like threat. It vibrated through his back into where she'd pressed her cheek. It didn't affect his brother in the slightest.

"And doing it poorly, I see."

Embarrassment was an understatement. It was absolute horror. Unpleasant goose bumps ran her, feeling immeasurably worse where the back of her dress still gapped.

"You brought clan?" Thayne asked.

His brother was still amused, if his voice was an indicator. "More than enough for rescue from one small lass. Do you have whiskey?"

"Sporran," Thayne replied.

Amalie heard shuffling noises, the sounds of gulping, and the smack of lips. She peeked on the view of shadowed earth floor behind Thayne's boot heels and her feet. Nobody said anything until Thayne broke the silence.

"You could turn about, Jamie. Give us a moment."

His brother snorted. "A moment? You're selfish-fast, mon. Nae wonder the lasses prefer me."

Amalie went crimson-colored and then pale. She could feel it as heat followed by immense chill. It was easier to hide behind Thayne and put a hand over each ear. It didn't work. She could still hear.

"A moment to dress. See to the bairn. And the wife."

Thayne was talking through clenched teeth, if the sound was any indication. One of the men must have tossed a hank of plaid material at him. She saw the flick of cloth at his shin while his back undulated to catch it.

"Wife? Did I hear that right? *Wife?*"

"You heard," Thayne replied without inflection.

"You went and wed? Without word or approval?"

"Aye," Thayne replied.

There was a hushed reaction during which the baby hiccoughed. Amalie blinked rapidly and worked at controlling the shaking in her legs as Thayne pulled away to toss his plaid over his shoulder, brushing her head with it. She moved her hands to the front of her dress, checked for coverage, and then clasped them between her breasts. She'd rarely felt as open and unprotected and vulnerable.

"Did . . . you also say . . . bairn?" Jamie's shadow took a step toward the baby and she knew he peered into the plaid.

"You heard me," Thayne replied.

"So we did. True, lads?"

No one answered him. Amalie began to wonder how much whiskey he'd drunk to sound so unsteady and slurred. She watched the shadow turn fully toward them, making him look gigantic and misshapen.

"That the wife, then? The lass behind you?"

"Aye," Thayne replied.

"Stand aside. Let me get a look at her."

Amalie's heart moved. Or something. It felt lodged at the base of her throat, bumping against her clenched hands with the force of each beat, squeezing at her air passage. She could sense the room swaying and hoped it wasn't a swoon.

"Nae," Thayne answered finally; clearly, and with the same lack of emotion. She'd have gasped if she had breath.

"You should na' tell your laird nae," Jamie replied.

"Cease this and assist me."

"Gladly. Although I doona' usually share women."

Amalie really was going to faint. Little black dots hampered her vision and her legs refused to hold her. Thayne must've felt it, for he backed into her, pushing her against the wall and forcing her to stay upright.

"Cease frightening my wife."

"She's already seen your ugly arse. How can I frighten more than that?" Jamie asked.

"Enough."

Thayne said it in a low throb of sound. She'd never heard such a tone. Amalie knew a threat when she heard it. His brother must be immune, for all he did was sigh. Loudly.

"Come along, then. You're done rescued."

"'Tis na' just me. Dunn-Fyne has three MacGowan men and the bairn's wet-nurse. And my horse. I'll na' leave without them."

Jamie gave another sigh. "I can. And will."

"Assist me!" Thayne got larger somehow. Amalie could feel it.

"With what? Nine men? And me with a broke shoulder?"

"Loan me your honor guard, then. Nine MacGowan clan are enough."

"Eight. I'll need one."

"For what?"

"Setting up a pallet. Look at me. I'm useless. But I can guard your wife and bairn well enough."

"Jamie, I swear—!"

"Oh cease that and go," Jamie interrupted Thayne's outburst. "And try na' to start another feud. But if you must, fetch some whiskey. Yours will na' keep me long."

"The wife stays untouched, Jamie."

"'Tis but a few hours. Fraught with little save boredom."

"I'll ken if you touch her," Thayne continued.

Jamie waved his good hand. "Go. This tires me worse than a clan meet. I'll do little save sleep. You've my word."

"Lass?"

It took a moment to realize Thayne was addressing her. He'd swiveled his head over his shoulder to look back and down at her. It took a bit before she raised her eyes to his, and the moment their gazes touched, her heart did another un-bidden move, swooping to a large strong beat in her lower belly, warming and yet frost-filled at the same time. The sensation spread, making everything tingle. It was huge. Endless. Irrevocable. Untenable. And beautiful enough to cause tears.

Oh no. No. This couldn't possibly be . . . love? No. *Please, no*.

Amalie dropped her eyes and blinked, focusing on the dirty floor below her. It wasn't possible. If this was a feeling, she was ending it—immediately and totally. She couldn't feel anything for this rude, ill-mannered, uncivilized High-lander. She refused. She couldn't. She wouldn't. She didn't. Not him. No.

"I'll return. You ken?"

Amalie nodded. She didn't trust her voice.

"At dawn. And naught has changed a-tween us."

She nodded again, trembled for a moment, and ignored the impulse to sniff.

"Amalie?"

He was forcing her and he didn't even use touch. Amalie looked up slowly and had the exact same heart-dive feeling happen, despite moisture that made his image swim. The next moment she was pulled forward, felt a blanket wrapped about her shoulders where the instant itch of wool against her bare skin accompanied what felt like a kiss at her ear. Amalie stiff-ened as Thayne swiveled them as one, placing her before him. And then she scrunched a shoulder as he yelled a name.

"Gregor! Gregor MacPherson!"

"Aye?"

The man who shoved through the others looked Thayne's equal in size and bulk, but hadn't much that could be described as handsome. When he stepped around Jamie, Amalie could

tell he hadn't anything devoted to eye-pleasing. And she was
wrong. He was larger than either brother.

"You'll stay. Guard the wife. And bairn."

"Now . . . wait a bit there," Jamie protested. "I never
said—"

"MacPherson stays."

The big fellow nodded. He not only looked akin to bear
size but about as bright.

"You're to fetch for the laird, and then sit. With the wife.
You dinna' move. You let none touch her."

"You sound as if this were a love match. You? Ha." Jamie
snorted after he'd finished.

Hearing it spoken aloud, and in a snide tone, gave the
newly awakened emotion value. And truth. And complete
thrill combined with such a level of fear, Amalie was dizzy
with the combination. Then Thayne moved from behind her,
taking warmth and security away. She swayed for a moment
before catching against the wall. Nobody said anything as
Thayne departed, taking most of the light and all the humanity with him.

She didn't love him. She refused. Ever. No. Please . . . no.

Chapter 7

It took less time to return to Dunn-Fyne's camp than it took to leave it. Thayne suspected it was due to freedom from Amalie and the babe in his arms. Or perhaps it was the steady pump of excitement that built with each step he pounded into the sod at the threat he'd soon face, the leadership he was about to demonstrate, or perhaps it was the nearness of the fight. He told himself it had nothing to do with the fear he felt at leaving Amalie, or the effect of his brother's words. He didn't love her. *By all the Saints!* He didn't love anyone. Love emotion made one weak. He'd had it beaten into him that a MacGowan didn't have a weak bone in his body. Besides . . . even if he'd had the capacity for love emotion, it had died with Mary.

And that was that.

Harsh cries filtered through the mist-strewn copse of trees, adding impetus to Thayne's feet. The sounds heightened his senses to near-perfect pitch, making it easy to separate the wet-nurse's cries from Sean's low-pitched moan. Thayne slowed a step and then another until Jamie's archer passed him. Thayne tapped the man's shoulder before filching his extra bow. Another man's brush garnered a handful of arrows and then Thayne was pointing five men in one direction while the others stayed with him. Circuiting the camp had risk involved. A turned ankle could send a man down one side of the hill, while a false step could send him rolling right into camp.

Wet sod slid beneath boots with each step along the ridge soaked and loose with rainfall. Thayne went with each slide, bouncing from tree to tree to keep his footing, accompanying each movement with a hissed breath that almost drowned out sounds of torment. And then came Dunn-Fyne's voice as if he stood beside them.

"Tell the direction or I'll take flesh next!"

A whip cracked as the mist parted, giving a glimpse of firelight. It was a far span, but not impossible. Thayne went to a knee, flexing and pulling the bowstring into its fullest position with an arrow aimed at the sky. He couldn't stop the grunt of effort as he brought it down into firing position. The others hadn't seen or stopped, making his shot riskier. From between two of Jamie's Honor Guard, Thayne aimed and released. He was on his feet and running before Dunn-Fyne's man dropped, his fingers around the arrow in his chest, while another clansman fell at the other side of him.

That's when the loud cry came from the opposite side, staining the scene with confusion and a loud crash of something heavy as it lumbered through the trees. Thayne was on a knee again, targeting the man holding the wet-nurse, ignoring the thrash of bodies that charged a large log MacGowan men were using for a ram. Bodies were felled by the log, a claymore, or hand-axe from an attack on either side. Thayne ignored it; focused on the woman and her attacker; and then shot. Bow string glanced off his cheek as the arrow left it, finding its path directly to the man's eye.

Thayne marked the man's fall, which took the woman down, too. Then Thayne was moving again, leaping bodies and debris, barely avoiding a thrown dirk as he landed, aiming as he slid. That missile speared a Dunn-Fyne man's face right alongside his nose. The next arrow speared a belly. Thayne's last arrow found the space between one man's shoulder blades, turning him into a crashing projectile right to where Dunn-Fyne had gathered the last of his clansmen into a prickly, armed circle.

"I've returned, Dunn-Fyne!"

Thayne was at a full yell as he reached the clearing, diving into a roll that sent an enemy dirk landing on empty space. It earned the attacker a knife through his neck, sent the moment Thayne finished the roll and had room to toss. The man garbled liquid-filled words as he sagged in place and then fell forward, ramming the blade in fully. His death was followed by four more of them dropping to their knees as MacGowan Honor Guard knives filled the scene, sent from the same amount of hands.

Seven. That left seven to fight.

A quick glance showed the wet-nurse lived, putting woman-sobs into the scene from her rolled-up position. Thayne shoved the instant relief aside and rose from his crouch. Then he had to shoulder through three of Jamie's Honor Guard who'd filled in the space before him, protecting him with their bodies. He was shouting more words as he went.

"Drop the weapons or reap death, Dunn-Fyne. Your choice."

They heard steel hitting ground about the Dunn-Fyne men, and then cursing, but it was instantly muffled. Thayne waited, and got joined by the rest of Jamie's Honor Guard, with little more than scrapes and muck covering them. And then Sean limped into place beside him.

"Pellin?" Thayne mouthed.

Sean jerked with his head. A MacGowan man immediately took off in that direction.

"Iain?"

Sean shook his head. Thayne sobered completely.

"Dunn-Fyne! Show yourself!"

The grouping of men opened, allowing Mary's husband to limp forward. He'd taken a deathblow to his side, if the amount of blood dripping through his fingers was an indicator. They all knew it. Thayne's eyes flicked there before moving back to the man's face.

"I returned," Thayne told him.

"So . . . I see."

"You ken why?"

"You want . . . what's mine," the man replied. He took a breath mid-sentence and sagged slightly.

"Nae." Thayne pulled to his full height, sheathed his claymore, and stared down at the smaller man.

"You always wanted . . . my Mary. So . . . you took her."

"Nae," Thayne replied again.

"She dinna' want you. You ken?"

"Is that why you beat her?"

A shadow of a smile graced Dunn-Fyne's face, before it turned to a wince, and a stumble of movement. Judging by the blackish liquid oozing through his fingers and to the ground, he was on borrowed time. Thayne waited.

"She chose . . . me. You were . . . there. You . . . heard her."

"Aye." Thayne licked his lips. "That I did."

"She was . . . ever fine, MacGowan. Lush. Ripe. Woman . . . ly."

Thayne's back clenched and his hand tightened on the hilt of his sword. Beyond that, nothing moved.

"Tell it to your maker," he replied finally, and turned around.

"You just recollect that . . . each time you look at . . . the bairn's face. You ken? I had her. And you dinna'!"

A burst of fervor touched the words, alerting Thayne. He dodged sideways, and that sent the knife into his upper left buttock, rather than mid-back. It was a coward's throw. Thayne clenched his jaw to ignore it, but agony went clear through his leg from where the knife speared him, sticking his kilt with it. And when he tried to walk, the injury took him to the ground, much to his own disgust. Dunn-Fyne had worse. Thayne heard the man's death warble through a slashed throat even before he saw it. They all looked at the Dunn-Fyne man who'd killed his laird. And then Thayne nodded.

"Any man wishing to disavow Dunn-Fyne and join MacGowan, he's welcome!" Thayne struggled up from the ground to say it, but one of Jamie's men yelled it again for him anyway.

"I've a wife. Family!"

One of the Dunn-Fyne men answered it. It appeared he was speaking for others, as well.

"Those claiming such are free to go! Leave your weapons and go. Nae MacGowan will stay you."

Even leaning onto his uninjured leg, the knife wound burned. Thayne was forced back to the ground, ordering them to fetch Pellin. He had to hope the man was healthy enough to see him. He was still prone, on his front, when four of them hefted him to the fire, snickering and teasing about injuries to asses. Thayne was forced to lay still and listen. Every time he tried to move, the blade sent him back to the ground.

Pellin wasn't injured badly, although he had a slash on his cheek and more hidden beneath his shirt and kilt band somewhere. He winced occasionally, but otherwise lived. He looked to have taken the worst of the whipping . . . and Dunn-Fyne had been an expert marksman. Thayne didn't ask and Pellin didn't offer. The man simply took one look at Thayne's injury, moved to the fire to stir it, and then placed two wide-blade knives into the coals.

Thayne concentrated on watching the knives go to a bluish-red shade atop the bonfire tended by Pellin, whose shirt darkened in blood-glazed stripes. It helped mute the pain when whiskey was sloshed onto Thayne's backside, but did nothing against the removal of Dunn-Fyne's dirk. The flood of blood stayed the men's teasing. And then Thayne was arching in a silent scream of agony as Pellin burned him, although it took three of them to hold him for the chore.

Tears blurred the ground at his nose, despite every effort to stay them. Blinking sent them down his face. And nothing stayed the absolute agony. Thayne leaned his forehead into the ground . . . yanking in and shoving out breath after breath, and then he got angry. Curt. Foul-tempered and nasty toned. That made the shove to his feet possible, where he slashed an arm across his eyes and then limped to his horse. And if he could have mounted it without an assist, he would have. Thayne spent countless moments standing at his Clydesdale's side, willing strength into his arms, before he had to ask for help. That just started the teasing again, especially his sideways lean to elevate his injury from any contact. Thayne sneered more than once at Jamie's men and called his own taunts, before they were finally heading toward the hut, the wet-nurse somewhere in the line behind him. Thayne didn't look to verify it. He didn't think he could. It took every bit of concentration to absorb the throb centering at the bottom of his spine and radiating through every portion of him. There wasn't room for any other sensation.

Dawn infused the clouds with rose-shaded light before they cleared the forest fringe. It sent a fairy-tale look over the treeless landscape and probably did the same to the macabre scene that had been Dunn-Fyne's camp. Every step of the horse brought pain, every flex of any kind in his leg brought worse, and he knew they needed speed. They needed to reach the woodcutter hut and Jamie. Thayne would've commanded it, but he'd locked his jaw and set his teeth. It was the only way to stop the woman-cries from sounding.

The shepherd hut was a hovel of impossible description. It got worse the more she studied it as the torch slowly faded and then dawn started slipping in through the cracks. Amalie looked down at the babe in her arms and begged her to stay quiet. Just a little longer . . . until Thayne returned.

The babe hadn't spent an easy night. She'd been screaming with hunger and anger when MacPherson fetched her down. She'd continued her cries as Amalie juggled her, crooning and rocking and even dipping her smallest finger in the whiskey flagon-thing MacPherson held out for her before trying to give that to the baby. It hadn't worked. Nothing worked until the infant used up her strength and slept exhausted, her face red and covered with tears. Amalie hugged the babe close, defensively, especially when Jamie threatened to use a fist to stop the noise. She was terrified of what would happen if the wet-nurse wasn't there when the babe woke again. And what Jamie would do.

That's when she got a complete dose of reality and how unprepared and useless she was about any of it. Whatever happened, Amalie was powerless to prevent it. It preyed on her mind and filled her imagination until she panted with emotion. She hadn't known freedom came with fear . . . or that independence came with risk and peril. She didn't feel free. She felt small and insignificant and helpless and powerless. She fought tears more than once with the realization.

Everything Jamie MacGowan said to her made it all worse. Once the babe quieted, he wouldn't cease the words; cajoling, bragging, and occasionally getting angry from his side of the hut.

He'd been drinking. He'd gone through all of Thayne's supply and then MacPherson's. It made the MacGowan laird bold, crude, vulgar. Completely uncivilized. And then he got talkative. Jamie spoke on all kinds of things. Most of it meant to put his little brother in a bad light. He seemed to enjoy demeaning, mocking, and embarrassing Thayne. Jamie spoke of times when he'd done something especially odious and set it up so Thayne took the blame. Thayne was soft;

weak; foolish. Jamie had even gone past those words to tell
her of times he and Thayne had been keen on the same lass,
and then both had her by fooling her with how alike they
were. He claimed to be interchangeable with his "bairn
brother" once the lights were dimmed enough. One man was
as good as another, he told her more than once. Sometimes
one man was better, if she knew what he spoke of.

Amalie's upper lip lifted slightly in a sneer. She didn't have
any trouble following his words . . . and his intent. He'd gone
into depth on times when he'd taken uncountable women to his
bed. Some at the same time. Jamie claimed women flocked
about him, begging for his favors. They were his for the taking.
Always had been. Always were. Due to his name. And position.
His manhood. Prowess. Or mayhap it was his handsome face.
Or his record of braw' wins on the list. According to Jamie,
women were forever pestering him. Wanting him. Needing
him. Begging him for what he claimed Amalie also wanted
and needed.

He was ready to grant her all, now that he'd gotten a good
look at her. She was much too bonny for his "puny-ass"
brother, Thayne. Jamie was rich. Titled. Thayne had little unless
it was granted to him. By his brother. The MacGowan clan
chieftain. He informed Amalie she'd be wasting her time with
him. She should be dressed in silks from the East, satins and
velvets from Venice, and covered in Scot pearls of all shades.
The MacGowan laird would assure it. She just needed to order
MacPherson to step outside for a bit and Jamie MacGowan
would be hers. She'd have no regrets. He was twice the man
most men were. Even his brother possessed less "tupping
meat." At least, the women they'd shared always said so.

More than once his bragging got him a gasp of shock. That
was one of the times. He'd just grinned and asked if she
wanted to see for herself. That was when she'd first shifted
closer to the wall, hunching her shoulders against further assault. It wasn't the last. Nothing worked. He seemed to enjoy

her reaction since he regaled her more tales of male prowess and experience. All of it completely distasteful.

And totally frightening.

Amalie wasn't allowing that emotion. She thanked God silently that MacPherson was in the middle of the little croft, taking up most of the space in a cross-legged sit; Amalie at his back and the MacGowan laird in full sight at his front.

Amalie had never been around grown men. She'd always had servants and a governess at her side. Her father would never allow such familiarity. Thayne had seemed a creature from another world. Yet he had a sense of honor about him that his brother lacked. The more she was around Jamie MacGowan, the less he resembled Thayne. She doubted she'd ever have trouble distinguishing them.

As the torch sputtered and dimmed, he'd gotten lower-voiced. As if speaking secrets. Just to her. He'd moved to speaking of love. If she was looking for that, she had the wrong man. Thayne MacGowan would never love her. She might as well ken the truth. He'd been ruined by Mary even afore she'd wed with Dunn-Fyne. That must be why he claimed the bairn . . . and probably why he claimed Amalie as well. He needed a mother for the bairn. Thayne didn't want her. He didn't love her. He needed her. From all Jamie could tell, Amalie's lone value was as the bairn's substitute mother. That was the full truth; simple and straightforward.

He'd gotten slower-witted and softer and drowsier, yet still filled the croft with words. Jamie didn't know why she wouldn't let him demonstrate what love between a man and woman could be. How a wench could take a man within her and grasp the key to heaven at the same time. He'd show her. All she had to do was get MacPherson to move to one side. Jamie wasn't even caring if MacPherson watched.

He grew bored with his own voice and slept, his legs sprawled before him, his kilt-thing askew, showing off legs equally as long and thick as Thayne's, and his mouth wide and slack with the force of his snoring. And that's how the rest of the night passed.

Amalie lifted her eyes toward the myriad holes in the roof, letting in light. She sent an unspoken prayer through them. She didn't have anything else. It was dawn, her time was up, and Thayne hadn't returned.

"MacPherson."

She must've dozed. Amalie lifted her head from the infant's silent form, blinked on rose-shaded cheeks, and then looked over and up. The man who'd guarded her was moving, first to his knees and then to a stand that grazed his head against the beams. He was facing the laird, easily seen through daylight percolating through the roof and sides of the hut.

"Take the bairn and leave us."

MacPherson turned his head and looked down at her. "Thayne—"

"Look for yourself. Thayne dinna' return. Nor did my Honor Guard. 'Tis well past dawn. I'll repeat it just once. Take the bairn and leave. Now."

MacPherson reached for the babe. Amalie didn't seem to have any feeling in her fingers as they simply let the bundle go. She had her eyes on Jamie. He flicked a glance at her, imprinting absolute chill. Then he looked back up at MacPherson.

"You are to fetch my horse. Stand by it. You're na' to return, nae matter what you hear. Doona' fash it, much. I'll na' be that long."

"Aye, Your grace."

Your grace? Sweet heaven! Jamie MacGowan was a duke, too? No wonder he'd regaled her with tales of position and title and how many women it impressed! Amalie was panting. And she was trembling. There was no fighting a duke's command. Her father wouldn't even have the power. She was surprised Thayne tried.

She didn't dare stay on the ground. She willed enough substance into her legs to stand, wrapped her blanket securely about the ill-used gown, and ignored the scratch of wool against her bare back where the dress hadn't been refastened. It didn't help. Jamie MacGowan was a towering man, and once the wood bolt thing banged into place behind MacPherson, Jamie was an immensely threatening one. His first step took him to the center of the structure and the next put him right in front of her. Not touching, just standing, and huffing whiskey-tainted morn breath all over her.

"You thinking to fight me?" He lowered his head toward her. She didn't look up to check. She could feel it.

Amalie pulled the blanket tighter and kept her focus on lengthening each breath. She'd never been so frightened. She had to cease reacting and think! She wasn't an easy wench. She was Miss Amalie Ellin. His was a stupid question. She wasn't submitting without a fight. For some reason she knew if she told him of it though, it would please him. He might even want it.

"Is that what you want?" She tipped her head back to say it, met his gaze and kept it without blinking.

One side of his lip lifted. "Na' especially."

"Then yes. I'm fighting."

He pulled in a breath and let it out, sending sour breath over her again. Amalie held hers until the odor dissipated.

"You should see sense. We've a long ride ahead of us, a horde at our heels, and verra little time."

"Yet you waste it ravishing your own brother's wife?"

"You're na' his wife."

He stepped closer, forcing her back against the wall to avoid any touch. It didn't help. All that happened was a rash of shivers from the chill of the structure at her shoulders.

"Your law says I am," Amalie retorted.

Jamie lifted his lip again in a half-smile. It didn't make him look any less aggressive or menacing. "The same law makes you a widow, then."

Her heart thudded hurtfully and then kept radiating it with every following beat. It also made her voice shake. "You're wrong. Thayne was delayed. He'll be here. He will."

"Matters little, even if he does arrive. I'm the laird. I can have any woman I wish. This includes my brother's wife."

"But . . . last night." Amalie looked away. The words had come out breathless. Like a plea from a frightened young girl.

"Last eve? That was drink talking. Started when I got this." He gestured to his shoulder. "What you see and hear now is *me*. Jamie MacGowan. The duke. Male. Aroused . . . and needy. Did you ken you're way bonny? Does na' surprise me, though. Thayne has a verra good eye. Always did. Now, come here."

She didn't move. He didn't act like he'd expected her to either, since the moment he said it his good hand reached out, grabbed her upper arm and pulled her roughly against him. She'd been wrong earlier. He may not be the same hardness and strength as Thayne, but the difference couldn't be much. She twisted and kicked but without boots it was ineffective and hurt her toes more than him. She shoved her head at his bandage and all that happened was an oath, and then more of them before he had her against the wall, pinioned in place by hard thighs and the same sensation of belly and chest. He was breathing hard, too, cursing her with more odorous fumes.

"I can have . . . MacPherson bind you. You . . . ken?"

"Why? You not man enough?"

She shouldn't have taunted him. She knew it before he slammed her head into the wall with the pressure of his. Then she had to contend with his lips against hers, his tongue seeking entry between her clenched teeth. There was the hard, thick, and male portion of him shoving against her lower belly, too. That galvanized her into a jerk of movement, lifting her knee, and then she connected with a crunching hard blow.

The response was immediate and gratifying as Jamie dropped, freeing her. Amalie stared down at the mass of him, groaning and cursing as he cradled his groin in his good hand and rocked in place. She didn't hesitate another moment. She lifted her skirts, jumped over him, shoved open the door, and then she was running. She couldn't see where and she didn't care. The sunlight was too vivid and stupid tears were hampering her vision. She tripped, falling to her knees before regaining her feet, the harsh sound of her own breathing accompanying every step. Or covering over the sounds of Jamie's pursuit.

Amalie grabbed her skirts high and kept running.

Chapter 8

Mid-morn sun burned away any remaining fog and carved shadows all about the shrubs and rocks as they neared the hut. Thayne swayed with each step of his horse, a jolt of pain accompanying every one of them. Breath was sucked through his teeth with a slight hiss of sound, while anyone looking might have seen how white his knuckles were on the reins. The worst had to be that this injury was his fault. He didn't castigate Dunn-Fyne for the man's cowardice. It had been well-known. It was Thayne who'd turned his back on him.

They could all tell the scene about the hut was quiet, releasing a bit of the tension along his spine. Thayne should've given Jamie a bit of credit. And then the unmistakable form of MacPherson appeared from across the meadow. He had one hand holding what looked to be the bundle of babe while his other held Jamie's horse. He dropped the reins as he saw them and then he started lumbering across the space for the hut.

Fool!

Thayne was a fool to leave her. To rely on MacPherson. To trust Jamie. Guilt was a worse bane than even chivalry. And if Jamie had touched one hair on her head, Thayne was gutting him. As a unit, the horses all broke into a run, sending complete agony down Thayne's leg as he accommodated the pace. He barely gave it thought. The stone-weight feeling in his gut was far worse. He kept up with the others, but was unable to rein in his horse with a backward lean or pinch of his legs. His lock on the reins was the lone thing keeping him in position. Nobody noticed him overshoot where they were already dismounting, filling the space about the small croft. That's when he saw Amalie, running and skipping and looking altogether strange as she moved away. And that's why he was the first giving chase.

He'd passed her and had the horse broadside before she saw him. By then he'd slid to the ground and borne the shockwave of ache through his left buttock and down his leg. Thayne bent forward for a heartbeat and then two, forcing the sensation into a bearable throb, and barely heard his name cried. He looked up in time to catch Amalie's full-body lunge into his arms, forcing a limped step back, and another, and with the third one he went down.

Thayne slammed into the ground, losing every bit of breath as she kept saying his name over and over, clinging to his neck. And if that weren't strange enough, she was moving his arms about, trying to make them hold her. Thayne couldn't catch breath and scrunched his face on the new torment.

"Now . . . that looked painful."

It was Sean coming into Thayne's field of vision, looking down at him from his stallion before he dismounted. He was joined by three or four more of them, blocking the sun with their forms. None of it did a thing to gain Thayne a breath or mute any of the agony. He kept opening his mouth but nothing came out or went in.

"I hope he dinna' open the wound."

"Wound?"

Amalie shifted to ask it, gaining Thayne a bit of room to gasp for air. He used it for that, taking his belly concave on gaining a breath. It set his heart pounding, made his head throb, and filled the moment with the sound of bells ringing.

Lift her. He mouthed it. Someone shuffled but nobody understood or did his bidding. Their movements unblocked the sun so it could spear his face, too, blinding him.

He felt rather than saw Amalie slide from him and could sense, when he rolled his head toward her, that she'd gone to her knees in the grass beside him. Sun filled the air, looking like it radiated from her. She'd wrapped the plaid about her head and shoulders, shadowing her features, and with her long unbound hair, she resembled an angel from one of the mosaics at Castle Gowan chapel. Even with the black orbs swirling about her head. Thayne blinked. She had that perfect skin; womanly features, with a rose-red mouth and smallish nose; large eyes with long lashes; a perfect form, just made for tupping. Thayne narrowed his eyes to gain focus. He'd known the woman was beautiful, he must not have realized the extent of it.

"What's wrong with him?"

She craned her neck up to ask it. Thayne watched the faces above him start circling. Rotating. Swooping. Dimming. Like the densest fog before gaining volume and size. Disappearing. Returning. It made the throb in his head worse.

"Naught a good gulp of whiskey will na' cure."

Someone lifted his head and sloshed pure liquid fire into his mouth, then held it shut until he swallowed and jerked with the passage of it. And then he was coughing and sputtering and on his hands and knees to keep his innards in place while his eyes wouldn't cease watering. While everyone about him chuckled except Amalie.

The lass was crouched at his side, bent down to peer up at him. Thayne averted his eyes and blinked through moisture that made the grass swim and blur. He put his attention on that, since breathing was difficult, and then gradually, it changed. He had his wind back. And that just made the remembered pain start up in his buttock again. It was accompanied by a sense of damp. He didn't need to check. He knew he'd broken the wound open. But he was the only one who knew.

Thayne pushed with both arms to gain a crouched position, stiffening the moment his raw open flesh came in contact with kilt.

"Whiskey."

He ground the word out and lifted a hand, got a sporran delivered, and took a mouth-filling gulp. Then he took another, and swished it about before swallowing. He didn't look toward Amalie. He didn't want to see the expression that was probably on her face.

"Where's . . . the bairn?" he asked once he'd swallowed the third gulp. The whiskey hadn't helped his voice much. It was choked and rough-sounding.

"With the nurse. Getting suckled. Comforted."

Thayne nodded. Took another deep swallow, welcoming how it took the edge from everything. "My brother?"

"Having the same issue," one of them replied. The men about him chuckled again.

"He's with the nurse?" Thayne took another long swallow, more to prepare for the agony of standing than anything else. It wasn't working, but he didn't truly think it would.

"Nae. Just wishing so."

"His shoulder pain that much?"

"Nae. 'Tis more the injury the wife gave him."

"Amalie?" Thayne looked over at her. She returned his look, giving him nothing.

"He's groaning and moaning and saying she's gone and reived his manhood. With a hearty blow. The man canna' stand. Only crawl."

Thayne felt the amusement bubbling through his veins. His lips twitched but he held the smile.

"He's asking for time. Afore he has to sit his horse."

Thayne shook his head. "If I can ride . . . he rides. Give the order."

He pushed back with his arms, filling his lungs and then sucking in more air in order to prepare; controlling the shake and readying his legs. It took every muscle in his right side to get to his feet, where he wobbled with the effort. Amalie did the same move and stood beside him; silently questioning. With clear amber-shaded eyes that could easily belong to another of Castle Gowan's angels. Thayne shook his head to clear it. This little spit of a woman had protected herself from Jamie, and done fine work of it. There wasn't anything angelic about that.

He swiveled on his good leg to face where his stallion stood, placidly pulling on early spring grass while it waited. All Thayne had to do was get there. On his own power. He didn't let one oath or moan pass his lips as he took a step and then another, dragging his left leg along. He blanked everything until he reached the horse and just stood there, a full fist about horse mane, willing strength where there wasn't much. This was worse than a full day of challenge on the list. Draining. Humiliating. He didn't know how he was going to get into the saddle. And get his wife in front of him.

"You're . . . bleeding," Amalie whispered from somewhere on his right. Thayne hadn't known she'd moved with him, but he'd been so focused he wouldn't have heard had she stomped. He turned his head and caught her glance back from where the kilt was sticking to his backside.

"Aye," he replied.

"Bad?"

Thayne licked his lips and looked over the horse at the meadow edge. He shrugged. He didn't truly know and didn't want to know. Not yet. It wasn't a flesh wound. This was affecting movement and muscle. And Thayne wasn't giving it time to heal.

"We should rest."

"We're na' safe, lass."

"Dunn-Fyne?"

Thayne shook his head. "Nae. The mon's dead. But we're near MacKennah land at present."

"Mac . . . Kennah?" She split the name strangely. "Of the broken betrothal MacKennah?"

Thayne nodded. "Come."

He turned, put his hands along her waist and lifted her, giving a silent prayer his arms handled the effort and she weighed little.

"What will happen if . . . we meet them?"

"Castle Gowan is two days' ride. If we doona' waste time."

He was harsh, but she'd just have to allow it. He had to mount, using his arms more than his legs and getting his injured leg to swing into position behind her. And somehow he managed it. There wasn't but a shadow of shake attached to the entire move. That, and a groan he bit off.

She didn't understand these men.

The pace wasn't much above a walk, but each step had to be punishment and agony for the man holding her. Yet he never said a word. He needed rest. They all did. She knew his exhaustion due to the burden of his head atop hers once another man took the lead. And the steady rhythmic breaths that accompanied it. She'd have suspected he slept, but she knew different. Every time she shifted, he caught his breath, tightened his arm, and waited before settling again.

Other men sported bruises and cuts, while one looked to have gotten a severe whipping. They were all stoic. Not so their laird. Amalie heard Jamie's groans and curses sporadically throughout a day that lengthened into eve. Those were the other times she knew Thayne wasn't sleeping. Every time Jamie made a sound, Thayne would make a grunt-like response deep in his throat, vibrating against her cheek where she snuggled. It was as if the brothers had some unspoken contest of strength and stamina, and a woman wasn't granted knowledge of the rules. Only men.

It was stupid. More than once one of them had ridden beside them for a bit and looked down at the horse's side. She knew they were checking a blood trail. She'd seen it as well, the one time they'd stopped. Past mid-day, everything on her was aching, including her empty belly. Thayne had given her into MacPherson's keeping since he didn't get off the horse. He didn't look to have moved once she returned and was lifted back to him, given two of their dry griddle cakes and re-settled. Thayne had a white line about his mouth that forbade conversation even if she'd wanted it.

And a line of blood staining the stallion's side.

Nobody mentioned it. They simply remounted their horses and continued. She'd watched three of them ride faster, outdistancing the line. Amalie didn't know it was to get a camp set, fire going, and an animal roasting until they neared it. The sun was setting as they topped a rise and started down into a little valley. Amalie lifted her head and sniffed at the delicious smoke and food smell of the air. And then she tensed at the sound of running water.

It wasn't until they'd reached bottom that she saw why. A river split the valley floor, looking wide and quick-moving if the ripples splicing the surface were an indicator. It separated them from where she could see and smell fire, and that meant dinner. Her belly reacted as well as her mouth, salivating at the sound. She just couldn't see a bridge. She didn't realize they intended swimming the horses across until the lead one walked in. He was a MacGowan man, followed by a man in Dunn-Fyne plaid, and then MacPherson was at Thayne's side, grabbing their horse's bit and taking them in with him without one word of warning.

Amalie hugged into Thayne, burying her nose between the twin humps of his chest and desperately tried to keep from crying aloud with the fear.

"'Tis na' that deep, lass," Thayne whispered in her ear.

"I don't know how to . . . swim!" she told his chest.

"Hold to me, then."

She had just enough time to gasp before something shifted in the horse beneath them, everything on Thayne went taut and hard, and then they were both plunged over the side. Amalie's heart was thundering and her lungs ached and she'd already faced enough. She wasn't going to die! Not like this! Dark tendrils of death came for her and she fought them, kicking viciously where they held her. Heavy volumes of cold weight wrapped all about her and she pummeled at them, thrashing and twisting and fighting.

And then she was free, scrambling for footing, and standing in chest-high water, gasping for air that was filled with Thayne's cursing, while all about them was laughter. But before she could give him a good screeching, she slipped, going beneath dark coldness again. This time she didn't fight as Thayne found her and pulled her back to her feet. She didn't struggle as he held her in place when she kept slipping on slickness her toes couldn't grasp, either.

"Jesu'!"

Amalie put both hands to her face to shove her wet hair and just-as-wet plaid covering off to look across and up at him. Everything reacted the moment she did. It didn't help that he was glimmering in the reflection of water and that every bit of his clothing was plastered to him, delineating everything. Nor did it help that she was cold, and getting colder the longer he held her in place.

"You're na' much . . . for water . . . are you?" he asked, with a catch to each section.

"You did that on purpose!"

He tipped his head to one side, brought it back. "Na' true . . . although it does solve one issue."

"What?"

"I needed a dunk. For cleansing. As did the horse."

"You've never heard of a bath?"

"Aye. Just took one," he replied.

"We could've drowned."

Horses were passing on both sides of them, with men following: sodden men, walking through water that dissolved her argument. It wasn't easy, as more than once, a man slipped or went under; but it didn't look deep. They all looked to be grinning if she checked. She didn't. She did her best to ignore them.

Thayne looked like he was struggling with his own smile. "You finished?"

"With what?"

"Your fight."

"This isn't a fight, Thayne MacGowan. I haven't even shown you a fight yet."

It was a full grin he gave her now, and if he weren't so handsome and she wasn't standing in bone-chilling water she'd have an easier time staying angry.

"You two planning on staying there all eve, Thayne?" Someone yelled it from behind her.

"You just get those skeans hot!" Thayne shouted back at them.

"Skeans?" she repeated.

She slid. He caught her with tight hands on her shoulders. Then he huffed a breath all over her that chilled and annoyed. He spun her to face the same direction he was, pulled her sharply against his chest, and then took her with him for a step. He limped the next one.

"You could ask first," Amalie told him.

"What?"

"If I needed help. I didn't say, and you didn't ask."

He opened his hands, her foot slipped, and she'd have gone under again if he hadn't gripped her and hauled her back. This time he hooked an arm fully beneath her bosom. From that position, he couldn't miss the reaction as her heart hammered into him.

"You need help?" he asked, but he was laughing at her through it.

"Just get me out of this water." Her command would've had more substance if her teeth weren't chattering and her nose wasn't blocked.

He grunted a reply. She sneezed.

"You need to get those clothes off. Change."

"I am not taking my clothing off. I refuse!"

"Up here wet and cold . . . means death. You'll change . . . if I have to force it."

"I am not—"

Thayne took a step, stopping her words with how it dropped them into more water as well as the groan-touched breath he sent over her shoulder. She could tell he felt for footing before taking the next step. And then the following one, each one accompanied by the slightest hint of sound in his breath. She'd forgotten his injury, and what their accidental dunking may have cost. Amalie sent a glance up at him, over her shoulder. He had his face set in grim lines and nothing looked amused.

They reached shore and Amalie quickly turned her face, averting her eyes from how much bare skin was getting displayed as men donned fresh plaid things pulled from bags. Her action probably amused Thayne, but she was past caring.

"MacPherson?"

Thayne's voice hadn't much substance, but MacPherson must have been waiting for it. Amalie knew the man appeared before them from how he blocked the firelight with his bulk.

"Take the . . . wife. Get her . . . into dry clothing."

"Aye," the man replied.

"Thayne, I—"

"Go . . . with him."

"But—"

"Doona' make . . . me force it. Please?"

The whisper was touched with something indefinable, almost like a sob. With it, he diffused all her anger and argument. That was just cheating. Amalie stepped away from him, got lifted by MacPherson and then carried into the dark beyond the fire, and then he set her into a tight patch of stunted trees.

"Doona' move." He ordered it before he turned and walked away.

He didn't see her nod. As if there was need of it. Thayne was right. She was chilled, and the wet clothing sapped the fight right out of her. But her jailor was gone for what felt hours. Amalie wrapped her arms about herself and when that didn't work, went to a crouch. She was in a solid shake before MacPherson returned, carrying one of the governess's trunks, and carrying a lit branch for light.

She craned her neck to watch as he shoved the improvised torch into a crook of limbs, and unfurled a large, fringed plaid. Then he stepped out of the enclosure, lifted the blanket up, giving her walls that helped block the elements and any prying eyes.

She dropped the wet blanket cloaking her with frozen fingers that had trouble. It was easier to peel her clothing from her in rolls of fabric due to the sodden nature. It was probably more luck that the buttons hadn't been refastened since Thayne had opened them last night when they'd . . .

. . . *last night?* Oh, heavens. She'd almost given herself to a Highlander last night! And in a filthy hovel that no respectable lady would ever—!

She stopped the thoughts. They weren't helpful, although the blush muted some of the chill. Amalie sat atop the discarded garments to roll stockings off, clucking her tongue at the huge holes in the soles and brushing at the grit. She didn't take off the chemise. Not yet. Despite its dampness, it gave her one layer of protection from the encroaching night air. It did nothing to warm her, though.

MacPherson had brought the wrong trunk.

Amalie sifted through layers of gowns, all in muted shades, exactly as a governess would own and wear. She already knew they were meticulously sewn and some re-sewn, showing their age and usefulness. The other trunks contained the same. She sighed as she checked through everything, feeling for warm velvet, or at the least heavy cotton, and finding little save muslin and cambric, and then she got her next surprise. Undergarments crafted of what felt like sheer lawn were wrapped about gossamer stockings, and inside that was a shawl tied to a pair of satin slippers with leather soles. Exactly as any female would appreciate and love to wear dancing. And nothing like the modest, dependable attire the governess had in the other trunks. Amalie would've smiled at the governess's secret except she had her teeth locked to stay their chattering and opening her lips might make it worse. And in the very bottom of the trunk, she struck treasure as her fingers curled about a brush and comb. A real hairbrush. And comb.

She was just about to send MacPherson for a different trunk, when a low growl of absolute agony filled the night air, widening her eyes with fright and taking everything to an indefinable stop.

"That's . . . Thayne," she said, rising to her feet with the treasures in her hands.

"Aye."

"What . . . are they doing to him?"

Her voice rose in agitation. The same emotion quickened her movements to peel the chemise over her head, and shove on the lawn garment in its place. The governess had been thinner than Amalie, and this garment was sewn to exact measurement. It was tight on Amalie's hips and again at her bosom. And the straps were too loose once she had them in place. She was just finished hooking it when MacPherson finally answered.

"Branding him."

"What?"

Amalie stepped onto bristly forest floor in an effort to reach Thayne. She didn't feel it. She didn't feel anything until MacPherson caught her in the curtain he held and lifted her. The material about her was unbending and unmovable despite every lunge, kick, and squirm she made, and then it got worse. Yards of fabric wound about her until she had to stop, huffing and hissing at the man.

"Let . . . me go!" The words didn't have much sound, but it wouldn't have mattered. He didn't relax his hold, and Amalie could see how far the ground was beneath her since she was dangling upside down over his shoulder.

"You're na' dressed."

"But . . . they're *burning* him!"

He pulled her back over his shoulder and set her on her feet. It didn't make much difference. She was wound so tightly, she might as well be bound.

"They're torturing him . . . and you don't care?" His image glistened and blurred with tears and it was going to be full-out weeping if he didn't do something and quickly.

"He ordered it. Just as he did this morn."

"He *what*?" Her voice was back. If she had enough room for air, it would have been louder and even more shocked.

"To seal his wound."

"Oh." The word carried faintness. She was afraid she'd be right behind it.

"It stays the bleeding."

"My . . . God."

He pulled one end of the blanket, unfurling her to freedom.

Amalie crumpled the moment it released her and watched the tree trunks rotate from a prone position on her side. She felt limp. Weak. Wrung-out. Naked. Her legs felt like inanimate wood and her arms the same.

"Cease wasting time. Here."

A garment fell atop her. She looked up into MacPherson's unpleasant features and stuck her tongue out at him. It didn't do much. He simply pulled back and crossed his arms.

"Finish dressing. Get some sup. I've orders. And I canna' get me own sup until you're finished."

"Oh."

He worried over sup. Amalie pushed into a sit. Looked him over as he was her. From the size of him, it was probably a valid reason.

"And your bairn is crying."

The babe was definitely crying. Amalie could hear it over the sounds of men eating, moving, and a fire crackling with dry wood. There wasn't anything that sounded like Thayne.

"It isn't my *bairn*," she replied, using their word with the snidest tone she could manage. It didn't alter him at all.

"You claimed it."

Amalie sighed heavily. Nothing worked with the man. She was still in his control and he wasn't moving. She didn't know why she argued it. Aside from which, the lawn chemise was worthless protection from the night air, and her belly rumbled with hunger, too. She rose on unsteady legs with the dress in front of her and waited, giving him the exact same blank expression he was giving her.

A moment later he lifted the blanket back into position, proving he wasn't totally dim; just big and unpleasant-looking, and following orders without exception. She stuck her tongue out at his back again before finishing. It wasn't difficult to fasten the buttons once the dress was backwards on her. She'd discovered this method of dressing herself the first eve during this journey. It just took time, and her fingers were chilled, and the babe was still crying. And she still had to brush and re-braid her hair.

MacPherson had chosen one of the lightest muslins, making it easy to spot how cold she was and how embarrassing she found it. If he chanced a glance at the crossed arms in front of her breasts. He didn't. He simply turned at the mention of his name, nodded, lowered the blanket, and gestured with his head for her to precede him. She didn't have the choice, and the fire looked not only warm, but bright, while the meat they were slicing from their roast smelled divine. She knew it would taste as good. Perhaps better. He didn't have to tell her twice.

Chapter 9

Thayne was reclining atop another tartan that vied with his kilt on variation of pattern. He regarded the fire without any expression that might match the groan of agony she'd heard earlier. He held the babe in an arm, but she wasn't quiet. Her cries had increased along with kicking and flailing, if the bundle movement was an indication. Amalie lifted her skirt with one hand and started across to them. As if that was her place. The others looked too engrossed in eating and drinking to pay her much attention, and the wet-nurse was alongside one of them.

Thayne looked up at her approach and then frowned. Amalie bent to lift the babe to her, and oddly the infant ceased fussing the moment she reached there. Thayne wasn't the only one that noticed as movements about the fire ceased and everyone looked.

"You weren't holding her properly," Amalie finally told him.

"Well . . . I'm nae woman. Sit."

Amalie went onto her knees on the blanket beside him, sideways, with him in front of her and barely out of touch of her right knee.

"Cease staring! All of you! Sean, fetch sup."

He spoke with a loud deep tone, making the babe start.

Amalie put her attention to the little tufts of down-soft hair atop the babe's forehead and crooned to her, until she settled back into a snuggle of warmth against Amalie's bosom.

"She kens you," Thayne told her.

Amalie glanced over the babe's head at him and then darted her vision to his chest. It seemed safer but only slightly, since he'd failed to put on a shirt. She realized her mistake while looking over more male flesh than a woman should see. He was displayed as if for viewing, too, with a bit of wadded plaid material splicing across skin that rippled with every move, showing the muscle and strength beneath. She gulped in order to make sense; took a breath; gulped again. It almost worked. Her voice sounded indistinct in her own ears. As if she spoke from a great distance and through water.

"She just . . . recognizes soft. In a world of hard."

"She recognizes her mother," he replied.

Amalie turned her head and closed her eyes on the instant film of moisture hampering her sight. A band of potential hurt wrapped about her heart and started squeezing, accompanying every beat of it. She didn't dare answer until she had the sensation muted and then dissipated. She didn't have any feelings for this babe. She didn't. She couldn't. *No.* She added it to her plea against loving this Highlander and opened her eyes on one of Thayne's men, placing a huge platter of meat slices swimming in juice, onto the ground near her left knee.

"Here."

Thayne's belly flexed as he moved, drawing her eye despite everything she exerted, and stopping her breathing. He held out several slices of flattened black bread, smelling fresh and fragrant. Amalie lifted her eyes from the offering to his gaze and then quickly shied away. Maybe if she concentrated on something else, he wouldn't affect her so. Maybe.

"Use it. Like a spoon."

She moved the baby to one arm in order to pull one slice of bread from his hand without touching skin. Then she was scooping up a slice of meat, cupping it in the bread to hold it. At the first bite, she knew it was every bit as delicious as it smelled. Beside her, she sensed Thayne doing the same, although he devoured his in large bites, making three more of them, until there was very little sup left. And she was failing. The entire time. Nothing worked. She was aware of everything he did and every move he made.

"You finished?" he asked.

Amalie raised her eyes to his and everything stilled. Time halted, ceasing to function. The fire stopped crackling and snapping and sending flickers of light over them. She forgot how to breathe. Blink. Think. Then a log dropped, moving his eyes and releasing her. Amalie dipped her head to the babe's sweet features, hiding warmth that suffused her cheeks and then spread from there.

"Nearby crofter wife has vast cooking skills. Is na' amiss to a coin or two in payment."

Amalie swallowed. "I didn't ask."

"Dinna' have to. Here. 'Tis mead. Fresh drawn."

He was holding out a cup of dark liquid. Amalie reached for it. Chilled air felt like it rippled through her, making her tremble and doing horrid things to her breast peaks as they tightened into hard knots.

"You're cold," he observed.

She turned toward the fire and lifted her nose. "I usually have my baths in warm water in a warm room, followed by warmed towels." She looked unseeingly at the group of men eating and drinking and looking like a fest was happening.

"Scot inns must have changed."

His voice wasn't sarcastic, but it might as well have been as he pointed out the obvious. Amalie licked her bottom lip but it was the lone outwardly sign she gave. Inside, her heart pace had picked up and she knew her palms went clammy.

"I've held positions with luxuries such as hot baths before," she replied. As if a governess who looked and acted barely eighteen had prior experience.

"You'll na' be disappointed when we reach Castle Gowan then."

"Do you truly have to take me there?"

He'd moved . . . or something. His leg came into the scope of her vision, and she could feel the heat of him at her neck where a shawl should be protecting.

"I live there."

"Thayne, I—"

"And so will you. As my wife."

"Mere words. I refuse to believe them binding." She tried to sound authoritative. Even to her ears, it was breathless and young and frail-sounding. Amalie frowned at the muslin covering her knees.

"You canna' fight our marriage. 'Tis Scot law."

"It's not my law!" That wasn't her voice, either. Nothing about it sounded argumentative or defiant or anything other than feminine.

"Do we need this said again? Who we are does na' matter. You're on Scot soil. As such, you're under Scot law."

"There has to be a way."

"Mayhap. You'd need a powerful amount of gold, though."

"What if I . . . could find it?" she began.

"And only if the union has na' been consummated."

"If-if . . ." She was vibrating in place at the instant recollection of last night. And what he'd done . . . or almost done. His lowered voice brought the enticing, illicit emotions right back into being. Without any effort! Worse happened as she nearly giggled. Fear of exposing any of it made her voice cease working as he just kept talking, in smooth low-voiced tones that sent shivers atop those already racing her frame.

"Doona' fret. We'll consummate our union. I'm willing. I'm just na' my best with a wound, and an audience." He gestured toward the men about the fire as if she needed explanation.

"But Dunn-Fyne's gone. You said as much."

"He's na' the lone reason I'll keep to the law."

"He wasn't?"

"I give my word, I keep it. Unlike my brother."

At the mention of Jamie, her eyes went wide and met Thayne's, which was a huge mistake the moment she did it. Infinite moments passed while she was locked in place. Statue-still. The babe's coo of sound disrupted it, and then Amalie had to deal with another bout of blushing and nervousness and embarrassment. It was wrong, ill-advised, and absurd, but that didn't stop any of it. Nothing did.

"You forgetting Jamie?" he asked.

Amalie shook her head.

"Good thing. He's definitely na' forgotten you. And the un-manning you gave to him this morn."

Amalie scooted closer to Thayne, touching him. Then she went further. She rocked into a sit beside him with her thigh matched against his and the babe cradled in her lap. She hadn't thought through the move, she'd just reacted. It was subconscious, but it was still done. She didn't know how she'd be able to look at him again.

"You've made your decision, have you?"

She nodded.

"Good thing. Again. Since you already gave your word."

Amalie wasn't looking up at him. She didn't care what he said or how he said it. She wasn't looking.

"I need to ask something of you," he said.

"What?"

"I have need of another night. Mayhap two."

Amalie's heart pulsed into a complete throb of stoppage in her throat, paining her with the move. "For what?" she asked.

"Afore our consummation. Do you listen to naught?"

He was asking for a reprieve? Amalie felt an instant stab that didn't feel giddy with relief. It felt hollow and lost, and alone. And then she had to hide that.

"Try na' to show it."

Show what? There wasn't any way to hide the humiliation and embarrassment. All she could do was lower her face to the infant and breathe in the sweet babe smell of her. And tremble.

"You women. Your emotions are easily seen. And read. Your relief's an affront. I doona' wish any to ken I have na' done my duty yet."

"D-d-duty?" He thought her reaction was relief. Amalie couldn't believe the cool wash that filled her and then she had to try and hide that, too.

"I still might, lass. But 'twill be most painful. I might cry woman-tears. That would give my brother thoughts . . . and that I will na' allow."

"What?"

"He does na' ken my injury. Nor the extent of it. And I doona' wish him to."

"This injury . . . ?"

"I took a skean. Thrown by a coward's hand. Bone deep. Hurts like the devil. Hampers movement. Gives an appearance of weakness that has some truth to it. You ken any of that?"

"I can't stay with you, Thayne. I just . . . can't." And she didn't dare. Not for one more glorious, heart-pinging moment.

"You've nae choice."

"But . . . I just *can't.*"

He didn't understand. She didn't even fully comprehend it. If she allowed any further contact with him, she was afraid she'd never leave. This wasn't her future. Getting her father to release her from a betrothal was the goal. Once she got back to Ellincourt, she might even rethink that. Wedding with Rochester didn't sound as bad anymore. Her life would be one of privilege and luxury. He'd be easy to manage. He probably wouldn't even desire a consummation. She doubted he even thought of it, if he had any thought at all.

But wed to a Highlander? From a place so far North civilization hadn't even reached it? No. That couldn't be her future. Ever.

"I doona' have the choice, either, lass. Look to me."

Look at him? She couldn't.

"You don't . . . want me," she whispered.

"Na' true," he replied. "How many times must I tell you of it? If I was na' in pain, I'd be proving it. Right here and right now, and be-damned to any witness."

"You . . . don't even know me." And after what he'd just said, she didn't know her own whisper could squeak.

"True," he remarked.

"And I don't know you."

"True again. These things we can correct. Ask me something. We'll work on it."

"You're very stubborn."

"I've been so named afore. 'Tis nae dishonor. Find other words to flay me."

"Why?"

He sighed. All that naked flesh moved with it. It was difficult to decide where it was safe to look.

"We may na' be able to consummate our union, but we can work on correcting this lack of knowledge of each other. Ask something else. Something . . . personal."

"Why did they burn you?"

He cleared his throat. "I ordered it."

"Why?"

"Stays bleeding."

"I heard all that. But why? I-I . . . thought a wound needed to bleed for cleansing."

"A man can only lose so much blood."

She nodded slowly, brushing her nose against the babe. "You were afraid."

He tensed. "I'm never afraid."

"Of fainting."

"I doona' faint."

Amalie didn't say anything. Thayne sighed heavily. "Verra well, Amalie. I confess. A man canna' sit his horse if he bleeds overmuch."

"See, you were afraid."

"Who's to protect you, should I fall?"

"I don't need protection."

"You needed protecting the moment you were birthed. Or reached womanhood. I'm just wondering at the vagaries of fate that handed up the chore to me."

"I can protect myself. Look at this morn."

"That trick? Jesu'! 'Twill na' work on him again. Only the densest man falls for it twice. Jamie is na' dense. And who'll stop him the next time? And the score of men following him? And there'll be more! You're too bonny! And I tire of saying it. For a beauteous lass you should na' need the words. Have you nae mirror?"

She shook her head, more to stop his words than an answer.

"'Tis a huge mistake to own up to it, for a large-headed woman is worse than a shrew. But you're the type of woman . . . turns a man around. Gives him one thought and one only. Gets him to reacting. And wanting. And pining. Lusting. You're that bonny, lass. That lush. Christ. I should stay my own tongue afore I dig a bigger hole for myself."

It was too late. Every word sent shivers over her and Amalie had long since moved her eyes to his. The man was too handsome to be real and his words not only stole her breath but heightened the heat of the air about him. Every flick of fire glow that touched him highlighted and defined and caressed.

"Odd thing is . . . you claimed me. Me. At times I canna' believe my eyes. Or luck."

"You can't be saying these things to me," she whispered. Everything he'd said affected her. Her whisper was evidence. She watched as he flicked a glance to her lips before looking over her head at the fire, at all the men bedding down about them.

"I ken as much." He puffed his cheeks to blow air out. "Must be the blood loss loosening my tongue. Saying anything about it gives you power."

"Power? What power?"

He shifted against her, sliding slowly into a prone position, facing her. Then he reached behind him and lifted a hank of tartan over him, holding it aloft, like a tent.

"We've leagues to travel on the morrow, wife. 'Twill na' be easy. That's another mistake to admit, but there 'tis."

"Your wound?"

"And you on the horse in front of me . . . tempting."

"I do not tempt—"

He smiled. "Everything's an argue with you. You ken that?"

"I do not argue."

"You must keep doing so. It helps a bit. Oddly enough."

"With what?"

"Staying temptation. Want. Lust. I just spoke on them. Were you na' listening again?"

Amalie gasped.

"Come along. Settle. I doona' wish you out of arm's reach. Na' with my brother watching."

She scooted close to him and went onto her back, feeling every bit of the hard ground covered with one layer of blanket. The babe shifted atop her, making the uncomfortable position more so with the infant's weight. She heard Thayne's amusement as a whiff of air against her neck, before an arm wrapped about her ribs and pulled her sideways into an embrace that rolled the baby into a crooked arm at her front. Amalie stayed there for several moments, experiencing every bit of being fully against him; her shoulders to his chest, her backside to his belly, her legs against his. She didn't have enough barrier of clothing to prevent feeling every bit of it.

"Nice," he told the space above her head.

"Don't get too fond of it," she replied.

"Why na'?"

"I accept your embrace because the alternative is worse. I want you to know that."

She amused him, if the amount of movement at her back was an indication. "My thanks, wife. Truly."

"What for?"

"Claiming me."

"I didn't *claim* anything. This is forced."

"Sleep. We can bandy words later."

"Nothing's settled, Thayne."

"Hmm . . . ?"

"This. Us."

"'Tis been a long . . . day," he replied, yawning before the end word.

"For some."

"For all. You're safe. Settle now. Sleep."

He seemed to be accomplishing the action as he said the words. Amalie considered that with her own yawn. A clansman passed through her vision, walking silently and stealthily and taking her gaze with him. Through his legs she saw Thayne's brother, Jamie. He wasn't settled or sleeping. He was scowling.

At them.

Amalie slid closer to Thayne, felt an answering tension in his arm as he accommodated the move, and a snore went over the top of her head. She'd rather be exactly where she was more than anywhere else. It was the only place that felt safe.

It was really going to hurt when she left him. And that was her last conscious thought.

Chapter 10

"Three ways to cross Penkyll Glen and my bairn brother picks *this* one."

Jamie's complaint was loud and sour and carried on the rising wind. Thayne ignored it, as he'd done every other outburst. Despite how often they came or how bitter. The words had gotten worse once they ran out of whiskey to placate his brother.

Jamie was also wrong. There were four ways to cross Penkyll Glen.

This glen had been glacier cut and carried a quick running trout stream down its center. The soil was lush and fertile at the bottom, useful for spreading on a grain field. One path ran through the center. It was thick with tree cover, water-saturated, and night-dark. The sun rarely reached its depths and then only for a bit of midday. That kind of ground sucked at a horse hoof and then kept it. They'd have made little time and been bogged down incessantly. If the snows had thawed enough for the attempt.

Another way followed the ridge on the west. It was a narrow path in places, wide enough for one horse, while at times it widened for ten or more. It went above the tree line and was open to the elements on all sides. With a drop of rock shale on one side and a slant of grass-strewn hill on the other that sloped sharply to end at Gowandy Loch shores. It was the quickest route but also the most unsheltered. With the pipers and wind portending a spring storm, it wasn't the best choice. There was also a burn to be crossed at the glen's base. Thayne already knew it was swollen and dangerous. It had been when they'd taken that route less than a fortnight earlier. Now, there would be more runoff. That way was bound to be worse. To ford it took a man's skill and strength, and the same of his horse. Thayne wasn't risking it. Not with Mary's bairn . . . and not with his wife.

There was another route, used mainly by sheep and deer, running in a zigzag pattern up the east side. That one needed skill and dexterity and a fair portion of luck. If a man was desperate enough, the weather was perfect, and if he led his horse instead of riding it. Thayne wasn't willing to risk it, either.

That left the only other option. Thayne and Sean led the way onto a path strewn with boulders that seemed placed there strictly to keep the hill from sliding further. The juts of rock also gave travelers needed foundation for a trail that meandered along the hill, sometimes rising, sometimes not. It was at the tree line, giving them a bit of shelter from the cold-spiked wind. It was wide enough for two horses abreast, which is how Thayne proceeded. That way, they'd provide some break against the wind for each other. They'd been listening to pipes throughout the morn, carried on rising wind that smelled of moisture. He didn't need the warning. He already felt the spring snow. He'd order another tartan once they reached the summit.

"We'll never reach the castle! And drink!"

Thayne didn't bother tightening his lips at Jamie's tirade. Reacting was useless, arguing the same. They'd reach Castle Gowan . . . just not today.

The lass in his arms reacted though, stiffening slightly at the words. Or maybe it was the bitterness of their saying.

She'd no way of knowing Jamie was always like this once his drunk wore off. Either way, she'd do well to keep her concentration on keeping warm. And she should wear more. The light fabrics she wore weren't much protection against the elements. The moment he'd pulled her from the frosted dew-covered blanket this morn, he'd known it. She didn't say anything, but her lips had a blue-cast and she was trembling in place when they'd reached the horse. That sent his abused notions of chivalry to the fore again, gaining him the trouble of her body right against him, as he put her on the horse, mounted behind her, and then pulled the ends of his *feileadh-breacan* over his shoulder to wrap her to him. Sealing her against him and sharing warmth. And beginning a day of torment Jamie's words didn't pierce.

"We'll hit the storm this way! With naught in the way of shelter!"

Thayne sighed heavily. They couldn't avoid the storm regardless of which way they took.

"You hear me, bairn brother!"

It was better to keep Jamie drunk and somewhat pleasant. Parceling out whiskey would have been Iain's chore, had he lived. Instead, it fell to the lone member of Jamie's Honor Guard that Thayne still trusted, MacPherson. Thayne had relied too heavily on the big man, and he'd fallen asleep, allowing Jamie full access to their small keg. If Thayne hadn't taken this dirk and been so weak, he'd have seen to the task himself. Or at least, been capable of punishing MacPherson's lapse.

"Nae shelter! Nae fire! And nae whiskey!"

The best they could hope for now was to reach the summit of Penkyll Glen, get across it and through the moors, to reach their cousin, Grant MacGowan's farm. They'd have shelter then. And fire. And Jamie could have his cursed whiskey.

"You're nae leader, Thayne MacGowan! You ken?"

Amalie reacted at Jamie's words again or maybe it was just

pure perverse feminine nature to slide back and forth before Thayne, skimming lush buttocks about the area and making him wish he'd brought a different saddle. One with a leather rise to make it impossible to feel woman-flesh touching him. Starting a tingle he didn't staunch fast enough. That was followed by thickening . . . and that had his buttocks tensing for the assist. Thayne went to a hunch of agony, hissing air against her head.

"You shouldn't let him bother you so." She tipped her face toward him to say it, cursing his jaw and throat with warm breath.

"Doona' . . . move."

He managed the command through clenched teeth, got an upward glance at him through lush eyelashes before she looked back to his chest.

"I haven't," she finally replied.

And then she relaxed somewhere, pushing more curve onto him. Thayne tightened one arm about her, and trembled with stopping the near instant surge his groin made against her; and failed. Miserably. It almost kept the pain at bay as he filled the space beneath her, groaning with each outward breath.

"Well!"

At his motion, the lass finally got comprehension of his problem, and went into a purely stiff position, shoving his jaw upward with the move. Thayne looked out at the gathering storm, grasses that swayed with the wind, and easily seen path.

"You are, without a doubt, the most barbaric, uncouth, uncivilized . . . creature of my existence!"

She was speaking to the space in front of her, although he ceased listening after the barbaric portion. He could tell that Sean hadn't. The lad had a full grin as he looked over at them.

"Lass!" Thayne licked his lips and tried again.

"What?" She turned her head and gave him a half-lidded look, probably trying for contempt.

"Doona' move! *Christ*."

She gasped. He held her with a restriction she could barely breathe against, if the pressure at his forearm was an indicator. The pain of his wound was bad. The throb of need was worse. And he'd never had this issue. It wasn't right, sane, or warranted. It just was.

"You doona' ken the slightest in obedience, do you?"

"Obey? You?"

He gave a twinge in response, putting heat and bulk where she had no reason to doubt him. And got another gasp.

"I'm begging here, lass."

"I won't move. I swear."

She whispered it, but something in her lower parts disobeyed, and shimmied against him, earning a groan as full ache went all the way down his leg and back. And that pain didn't even work at staying craving and full-out need. He had a lust for his wife he couldn't control? Where was the justice in that?

Thayne sent his next curse out over her head and followed it with a full locking of every bit of him. The parts he controlled. There was something wrong that he couldn't stop his loins from pulsing again and again into woman curves that should have been wearing more. And not sitting almost atop him in order to toy with him.

"Cease that," she said. "Or put me on another horse."

"Nae."

"Brute. Beast. Cretin."

Even her whispered words of disgust failed to stop his arousal. There was more wrongness in that. He'd never faced such unadulterated lust. Always before, if he needed a woman, it wasn't hard to find one. They were ever about, pestering him. Or he'd work on the list until any urge save survival, passed. He avoided Jamie's wenches. All did, unless they wished to risk the pox. Thayne turned his head to the side, scrunched his eyes shut, kept a tight grip on everything, and prayed something would work. Anything.

"You calling a rest? Finally?"

Jamie's voice filtered through the lust surrounding Thayne. He opened his eyes on reins he'd pulled taut, bringing his horse to a stop. Looked over at Sean. Nodded. And waited as everyone shuffled from their horses. His wife had turned her face into his chest to avoid watching and that just made the torment last longer.

"Lass?"

"What?"

The whisper filtered over his chest and warmed his upper belly. And made him twinge against her again, which made her gasp again. Thayne licked his lips.

"You needing a rest?"

"If it will get me from this horse and you . . . yes."

"It will. Sean?"

"And keep me from it?"

Thayne unwrapped his tartan from about her preparatory to hand her down to Sean. She asked it as she slid into Sean's arms. There was an instant chill from losing her warmth, and it had to be worse for her.

"Nae." Thayne looked down at her.

"Why not?"

"I'll na' share. Na' with the way you ride," he replied.

Her eyes went wide, she pulled herself up, and she opened her mouth as though to upbraid him. Sean found it entirely amusing, as did the others starting to notice. Thayne flicked a glance, located Jamie, and returned to looking down at her.

"Bring her back to me. Doona' leave her side."

"Why can't I sit my own horse? You have enough of them."

She gestured to the riderless horses interspersed throughout their band. She was right. Thayne had more than enough horses. He'd taken Dunn-Fyne's mounts as spoils. Several were still saddled and carrying packs.

"True." Thayne moved his eyes to Sean's grin.

"Why can't I ride one, then?"

She had her hands on her hips and her head tipped back to argue with him. She really should be wearing more clothing, since every bit of her was easily defined. The laird was standing right behind her, watching, his face set and angry, and cunning. Malicious. All easily read and understood even without the drunk he'd recently come off.

"Fetch another plaid when you return with her," he told Sean.

"I asked you a question, Thayne MacGowan."

Thayne pulled in his cheeks and moved his eyes to her. "You'd have nae man at your back."

"I don't need a man at my back. Or anywhere else for that matter."

"That could set another man to thinking. And wondering."

"Wondering what?"

"How easy it would be to take you."

He'd mistaken her wide eyes earlier as they went huge and her mouth with them. Thayne inserted words before she managed it.

"You've reason for being here, Jamie?" Thayne moved his gaze to his brother.

"Nae."

"Then allow my wife passage. And Pellin? See the bairn secured."

He watched her walk through the men with her head held high and a sway to her hips none of them missed. She was a fine specimen of woman. With a quick wit and full use of her tongue. Yet she knew so little and argued so much. It was a decided chore to keep his wits sharp about her. Thayne was starting to like being with her. He nearly groaned.

* * *

A man at her back!

What were they? A pack of wolves? Amalie smiled her gratitude at MacPherson and then Sean for their assistance in holding blankets up, shielding her from the others, and at the same time she was annoyed with herself for doing it. She didn't want anything to do with them. She didn't want to thank any of them. She didn't want to like any of them. She'd been insane to think there was anything she felt for the man leading them. Regardless of what their laird said and did, it was obvious Thayne was leading. And Jamie wasn't. It just wasn't obvious why.

She stared up at Jamie MacGowan when he blocked her from returning to Thayne's horse. There was an unpleasant shiver running her back as she craned her neck to meet his eyes, but she ignored it and gave him her coldest look of disdain and disgust. He didn't move until MacPherson came from behind her and then Sean. That wasn't comforting. Nothing about this was.

She was standing at Thayne's right leg when Sean handed her another red, green, and black plaid from one of their packs. It smelled slightly musty, but was dry and thickly woven. Amalie wrapped it about her before she got handed back to Thayne. Once there, she settled sideways in the space in front of his saddle, completely ignoring him. He had an additional layer of blanket about him as well. Other than that, he didn't look to have moved from the horse. She didn't know if it was due to his male lust condition or his wound. Or maybe lack of need. And she didn't care, either.

"This is much better," she told him.

"Agreed. Did you check the bairn?"

"Secured to her wet-nurse. With straps. As ordered." Pellin answered it as he swung into his saddle. Amalie noted he had one of the thickly-woven plaids about him as well.

"You had the baby tied? To a horse?" Amalie asked Thayne.

"Have to. Storm coming."

"So?"

"You ever see a Highland storm?"

He was looking out over the path as he asked it. Amalie did the same and noted how it appeared blurred and vague and dark. A lot darker than midday. She shook her head in answer.

"You should give her a name," he remarked.

"Who?"

"Our bairn."

"Mary," she replied and watched his face go completely expressionless, although his arms seemed to tighten before releasing.

"Nae."

"You claimed it. You name it, then."

He nudged the horse into a walk. And then the wall of storm hit them.

Amalie had never been out in such conditions. Wind whipped water onto her, saturating the plaid about her into a sodden, heavy mass, and if Thayne hadn't lifted some of the back of it to make a hood about her head for breathing space, it would've been worse. The smell of wet wool surrounded her, warming and protecting against an onslaught that pelted exposed skin like sharp, cold darts. She folded her hands inward the moment the sleet hit at her fingers, and leaned against the solid comfort and security that was Thayne MacGowan. The horse plodded on. It seemed impervious to the storm, as was Thayne, the two times she checked.

The first was when they reached the summit of the mountain, getting a full brunt of the wind on all sides, hitting her with enough force to send her tumbling. Except Thayne's arm prevented it, holding her firmly in place against him. Amalie tipped the material and glimpsed his bowed head and slit eyes as he kept them on course, taking the pelting as if it were little. She knew now why he hadn't taken the path along the top of the valley, as wind swirled about them from every direction, bringing the pace to a crawl of movement.

Then they started across wind-whipped grass, lying flattened and covered with white specks that looked to be ice. Or snow. Amalie ducked back into the enclosure created by her hood, tucking her chin into where his heart continued to beat rhythmically and steady and securely. She hated to admit to any of it, but it was secure. Protected. She didn't like admitting to fright as well, as hours seemed to pass without any let-up in the wind. And no change in the pace.

The second time she peeked out at Thayne was when the wind altered, changing from a howling creature that attacked from all sides, to gusts that puffed around his body. Amalie slit open the blanket and looked out at rock wall, shiny with the pelting of snow it was receiving. She tipped her glance up at him then, and met his eyes, although he still had them in slits. Her heart skipped as he held her gaze. His eyelashes were spiked and interlaced, making him look beautiful . . . and dangerous. Then he smiled slightly at her before looking back up, and into renewed wind as they passed the rock wall.

Chapter 11

Thayne walked his horse into the stable and knew the others followed without looking. He didn't dare. He felt frozen into position. Any move might topple not just him, but his wife. That was reason enough to keep plodding through sleet as if the night contained a fully lit path and he had access to it.

That wasn't far wrong. Clansmen had been directing him for at least an hour, watching for, and gesturing him from well-protected peat-fed bonfires spaced almost within sight of each other. Without their help, he'd still be on the moor, getting pelted with death. And he knew it. Thayne hadn't even nodded to the MacGowan clansman who'd loomed from the sleet storm to take the bridle and lead. He'd rarely been as depleted. He just hoped he'd manage to hide it.

His brother didn't seem to suffer any ill effects. Jamie was off his horse and shouting orders before the last man had even entered the stable.

"Whiskey! First, I'll take a large whiskey and then ale. Then I'm desiring women, too. And after that sup! Nae! Mayhap, I'll sup afore taking a woman, but na' by far! And you! Bring me a change of sett! And be quick about it!"

Thayne forced his arms to unwrap from about Amalie,

placing his hands about her hips and used her to push right off the back of his horse, where he stood on swaying legs that hadn't much feeling to them. He slapped a hand to the horse rump for stability as the men about him praised, seemingly without end.

"He got us through the pass!"

"Can you believe it?"

"I'd have disbelieved it 'twere I na' part of it."

"Thayne's half eagle, dinna' you ken?"

"Oh, leave him be! Leave him to tend his wife and that weak-ass girl bairn! We've better things awaiting us! Or dinna' you hear me? I'm needing whiskey! And I mean to have it!"

Jamie shoved the stable door open enough to get his body through, sending cold air about Thayne's lower limbs. One by one Jamie's men followed, making the same shove and sending the same amount of frosty air.

"You'd best follow him. They'll be needing you to stay him. Especially from their women."

Thayne turned his head and looked at Sean. He didn't answer, but that seemed enough.

"Afore he gets well into a drunk and canna' be swayed." Sean spoke again.

"Surely the menfolk can handle it," Thayne finally replied.

"None here."

The clansman who'd led his horse apprised him of it. Thayne looked toward where he was standing. The plaid about Thayne was uncomfortably saturated, heavy but warm. It was also starting to put steam into the air as it warmed.

"Brian." Thayne greeted the MacGowan clansman by name. The man looked pleased.

"All the men were sent out afore the storm. They built fires—for signals as well as warmth. They're searching for lambs. 'Tis a vicious storm. A lamb born in this has to stand or die."

Thayne nodded, pulled in a breath, and straightened his back. Men were looking at him for guidance. His wife looked, too, from over her shoulder. Then he puffed his lips and sent the air out with a rush. If his hair hadn't been plastered to him with melting sleet, it would've ruffled.

"How many women here has the laird already . . . taken?"

"Four. Maybe more."

"Four? So many?"

"'Tis within riding distance of the castle, my lord."

"Give me names."

"I'm na' all that certain. I can only say Rachel, Marget . . . Ellyn. Mayhap even Marget's sister, Eve. As soon as the mistress finds out, she disdains them. You'll most like find them working the slops most days."

"Does no one see the danger in this? He's got the pox!"

Amalie gave a gasp. Thayne ignored it.

"He's our laird."

"Every MacGowan man has the right to a future with healthy bairns. Why dinna' Grant hide them?"

"None can fight the chieftain."

"How many are still untouched?" Thayne asked.

"I've na' seen all of them. But of what I've seen . . . they're verra young. Innocent. Grant's got three nieces come to live with him, recent-like. Orphans. One is the wife's relation. Two more just came up from Inverness. To gain employ, much as Marget and her sister did."

There was no help for it. The MacGowan clansman at Thayne's elbow was right. Jamie was their chieftain by birthright. His will was the law, and once he gained the title, the lone person who could stop him was Thayne, and that required a physical fight. More than once. To a punishing degree. He couldn't believe Jamie ignored the threat over the last time he'd been caught ravishing unwilling women. As if it was his right. The blame this time probably fell to Thayne, with his abortive attempt at chivalry, and his focus on Mary for over a year now. He hoped his legs worked for more than holding him up.

"Sean? Fetch the bairn and her wet-nurse."

The man grunted his reply. Thayne forced his right leg a step and then pulled the left to match it as he moved along the horse's side. His wife was looking at him with wide eyes and a look that probably reflected disgust and shock. Thayne controlled the flush with an act of will. He shouldn't care that she'd overheard. She couldn't stay innocent forever. She'd wed into the MacGowan clan. She might as well know the blackest of its secrets. Aside from which, it was her fault. If she'd kept her mouth quiet about being his wife, none of this would be happening. Thayne would've taken the time to escort her to the position of governess at the MacKennah castle, wiped his hands of her, and ridden away. Maybe.

"Come."

He lifted his arms with the command. She surprised him by sliding into them without a word of argument. But then she added to it. She moved to his left side and pushed her shoulder beneath his arm. The move supported his limp. He didn't comment on it and she didn't say anything. Someone shoved the door open against the storm to get them out, and then stepped out. Thayne followed, every step an effort to ignore pain and loosen legs that hadn't moved all day. It got easier the longer he walked, across the yard and through a gate that wasn't keeping much out as it crashed back and forth with the wind.

The main croft was thick with smoke from the fire, steam from drying tartans hanging along the walls, and the odor of stew. From the smell, he guessed at mutton stew, mixed with wheat and barley; hearty and filling. Overriding all the other smells was whiskey. Thayne stopped just inside the threshold and hoped the dismay wasn't evident.

Jamie was atop a stool, a lass balanced on his knee with another at his side. The one at his knee had her face averted.

The other had her hands tightly folded together and her head bowed. Jamie's Honor Guard were spaced about the main table, shoveling stew into their mouths. They were all drinking. Someone had opened a keg and spilled enough to make a dark spot in the earth near the fire. It only took a moment to gauge both girls' ages, another to ascertain their fear. Thayne sent his glance about the room to find the women most impressed by Jamie's presence. He didn't need names. It was obvious. There were women about who were older, well-rounded, voluptuous, and used to a man, if the way they caressed the men's shoulders and arms were any indication. Thayne had six spotted before taking his first step down from the stoop.

"This? Nae. 'Twas nae battle! I took a spill from my horse. Dense beast!"

Jamie's loud voice showed the amount of drink he'd already consumed as he patted the bandaging about his shoulder. It was also obvious the effect the whiskey was having on his temperament.

"Oh look! There's my bairn brother . . . his wife. And his bairn! At last!"

He waved an arm toward the floor as Thayne reached it.

"Come! Sit! Fetch stew. And more whiskey! He's earned it! He brought us safely to you!"

He shoved the lass off his knee and pushed her toward the fire. She barely caught the fall. Thayne's lips hardened. He took his own stumble, caught it with a hiss of pain and then righted, drawing on every muscle in his right side to handle the move. Jamie didn't note anything as he laughed harshly and loudly, before slamming his tankard to the table, making the girl at his elbow jump. Amalie seemed to make the same start, but it was halted by the weight of Thayne's arm atop her shoulders.

"You needing an invite, brother?"

Jamie was already belligerent. Hostile. And he slurred

the words. He didn't wait for the answer, either, as he yelled for another tankard of whiskey. That's when Thayne decided the best ploy. They needed time, an assist from Jamie's near unquenchable thirst, and Thayne's new wife. Thayne took a step forward but his wife didn't follow it. She was going to argue now? He pulled her forward with the force of an arm, sending more weight atop her.

"Don't make me sit near him, Thayne. Please?"

There were tears glittering at her eyes, or something close to them. And then there was nothing but glazed-over amber shade, looking the texture of a stone.

"Trust me." Thayne sent the whisper into an ear before turning back to his brother.

Amalie was going to sink beneath the weight of Thayne's arm. That was before she factored in what he asked her to do. She wasn't joining that monster seated at the end of length of smoothed wood they used for a table. She didn't even know what she was joining. Servant women laughed and slapped aside grasping hands as if it were normal. And the men! Amalie's senses hadn't taken it in fully. She didn't know men behaved this way. Or a society that allowed it. This wasn't a sup. It wasn't a fest. It was an unleashing of male power on anyone in the way. Amalie had never seen men behaving as these men were; loudly speaking with mouths full, gesturing with tankards that tipped ale, pounding on the table more than once with enough force to upset, grabbing at servant women . . . and all with the approval of their chieftain? She couldn't have imagined it. She was hard-put to keep her mouth closed against the complete shock. And Thayne asked her to trust him?

They walked around the table, gaining a position with a wall at their back. Thayne stopped. He didn't sit down. He worked at the knot of his soaked outer covering and once he had it unfastened, he handed it to one of his men. Or one of Jamie's men. Or even the man named Brian who'd led them in here. She didn't know names and faces aside from Sean and MacPherson and renewed her vow that she didn't want to know.

"Unfasten your sett and give it to Sean. For drying."

Amalie hugged it closer, feeling warm trickles of water between her fingers. She didn't know why she fought it. The wool was saturated, heavy, and not as warm as it had been earlier.

"Can't we just get some sup and return to the stables? We can bed down in there. I won't complain. I promise."

"You'd be alone with me. Alone . . . and I've still a consummation to achieve."

Amalie suffered every bit of the shiver that went all over her, and then tried to staunch it. "I accept," she managed to answer.

"Take off your sett, lass, or I'll force it."

"Please?"

"Chill breeds illness. Wet chill is worse. Unfasten it, or I will."

"I've little . . . beneath. You already know that."

He looked down at her, stopping her heart with the tenderness of his expression, and then he said damning words that stunned and frightened and appalled.

"'Tis exactly what I'm counting on."

"What?" Her voice trembled. It had something to do with his fingers working the knot at her throat. She didn't help him. She didn't fight him, either.

"My brother." He cocked his head in Jamie's direction as if she needed explanation.

"He's a lecherous beast!"

A hint of a smile touched his lips before disappearing. "Worse than Dunn-Fyne?" he asked.

She shook her head. Then nodded.

"Good. You're na' blinded to his true character. Now sit. Drink. Eat. Warm yourself with the fire."

"That all?"

"A smile would na' go amiss."

Amalie glared at him. "A smile?"

"Verra well. Nae smile. Will na' matter. There."

He had the plaid blanket unfastened and unfurled, releasing her to air that cooled the moment it touched. Her hair had mostly stayed in the braid, although stray tendrils were trailing about her face and she could feel them stuck to her neck. The crush of her cloak hadn't done her attire any good. The dress was wrinkled and clung to every bit of her. If she'd used sense last eve, she'd have donned more than the fine lawn undergarments for foundation. Then she'd have layered on as many dresses as she could. Regretting it now was a useless waste of time. Amalie avoided looking anywhere but at her hands as she pulled material from where it clung. Her efforts were useless as well since the material went right back as though plastered there.

"Doona' fuss so. 'Tis perfect."

"Perfect?"

"Here. Sit. Eat your sup. They fetched us a trencher and flagon of drink. My thanks, Brian."

Amalie looked down at a hollowed-out half-loaf of bread, filled with a mixture that sent more steam into air, coating her with more moisture. It wasn't needed. She already felt near naked. She could sense the reaction in the room about her. She didn't need to see it. She sat and watched as Thayne followed, although his came with a wince and a stifled groan.

"Why are you doing this?" she asked, in a quick whisper.

"Trust me."

"Trust you? You're mad."

"I can protect you, wife. Doona' fear so."

"I'm not fearful."

He snorted. Since he'd been drinking, it ended in a coughing spasm that took long moments to end. A quick look showed more men than Jamie paying attention.

"Eat. 'Tis verra good. And warm. Mutton stew. A Highland favorite."

"I can't eat unless I know what you expect."

"I expect you'll eat. Look bonny. Argue a bit with me. But still look bonny. Perhaps even slap at me."

Amalie studied him for long moments while her heart hammered in her breast, sending a high-pitched note through her ears. Thayne didn't look aside. He'd raised one brow while he waited.

"You want me to sit and look . . . bonny? What is that? Exactly? Feminine? Beautiful? Well-pleasing? Womanly?"

"Aye," he answered, giving her a nonanswer.

"Which one?"

"All," he answered.

Amalie tightened her lips. "It's not hard to act angered with you, Thayne MacGowan. Is that what you want?"

He nodded again.

"Why?"

"My brother needs his interest perked in something other than the young lasses he's grabbed. You've already gained it. I'm just reminding him."

Her heart fell. Her eyes went wide. Her breath got quick and fast. He was in perfect danger of getting slapped.

"You're using me . . . to gain . . . his attention?"

Her voice wasn't there for the full question, but he knew what it was as he nodded, slowly and without breaking the gaze. Amalie opened her mouth twice and closed it the same amount of times.

"You angered?" he asked.

She narrowed her eyes.

"Enough to slap at me?"

"Why?"

"Trouble in a marriage means comfort from outside . . . might be accepted."

"I've never been so slighted in my life. Never."

"Untrue. Everything Dunn-Fyne said and thought was a slight. Jamie, as well."

She opened her mouth to refute it and closed it again. This Thayne had a depth she hadn't guessed.

"You readied?"

"For what?"

He looked heavenward for a moment before looking back at her. "Slapping at me."

"I haven't eaten yet," she replied stiffly.

Thayne smiled slightly before attempting to look angry, but the twinkle of his eye gave it away.

"We've time. He's na' drunk enough. Na' just yet. So eat up, wife. Smile."

"There's no spoon," she told him.

"We doona' always have spoons."

"What do you use, then?"

In answer, he pulled a thin-bladed knife from his belt, wiped it along the kilt at his thigh and handed it to her. She regarded it in silence before moving her gaze back to him. The complete blankness of expression didn't reveal anything. Amalie tried to mirror him. She knew she'd failed. She didn't need his chuckle for proof. None of her past acquaintances would believe this. She could write it in a diary, but it wouldn't be believed there, either.

"Thank you," she said finally, and reached for the knife.

"You ready to slap at me yet?" he asked.

It was better to concentrate on the sup. Amalie turned to the stew and fished out a piece of meat, using the knife to spear it.

"One must be ill-bred in order to react with such a coarse, uncouth action," she told him.

"Even if one is a woman getting insulted?" he asked.

Her fingers tightened on the knife handle as she chewed, putting her full attention on the bite. The mutton was delicious, well cooked over a long period of time. The meat strands fell apart on her tongue where she toyed with them before swallowing. She turned and stuck the knife into the stew again, completely ignoring the man at her side. Or trying to.

"You like the stew?" He asked it as she stabbed at a piece.

"In different company perhaps," she replied.

He leaned forward, putting his weight on his right side in order to scoop a huge bite of stew out, brandishing a spoon he'd just disclaimed owning. Amalie went still, focused on the rough-hewn surface of the table where scrape marks from carving tools gave it an uneven surface. It was polished to a gloss that compared to the dining table at Ellincourt Manor. That was stupid. And odd. Why would they take such care of a wood slab when it wasn't hewn correctly in the first place? She studied the slice marks along the table's edge, guessing diners sharpened their knives on it . . . or something equally unsavory. She didn't move her eyes to the stew again until she had the complete anger covered over. She was trembling as she successfully speared a piece of meat and then leaned forward to pop it into her mouth, losing only a drop of liquid. She kept her mind on little things and not the large thing sitting beside her, toying with her; trying to get a reaction out of her.

"You . . . are no gentleman," she told him once she'd swallowed.

"Never claimed to be."

Amalie had to admit that truth as she reached for one of the hunks of bread they'd brought. It was hard-baked into a fist-sized roll, but once she stabbed a thumb through the side she found the interior soft, moist, and tender.

"Perhaps this treatment is more effective," he informed her.

"What treatment?"

"Ignoring me. Turning away. Making a man . . . wonder."

"Wonder no more, dearest Thayne. I am turning away. If there was another place to sit, I'd take it." Amalie put a bite of bread into her mouth with a delicate motion.

"There's one on Jamie's lap now. 'Tis probably due to you."

Amalie gasped and looked beyond Thayne toward the end of the table. She immediately wished it undone. The laird was definitely watching her, his complete regard taking the moisture from her mouth and making it difficult to swallow. He didn't have either of the young girls with him anymore.

"He likes his wenches young . . . true. But he also likes bonny. I'm thinking he's full in agreement to me that nae lass here fares well in comparison to the beauty of my wife."

"Thayne—"

The name came out as choked as it sounded. He held out the ale flagon to her.

"I already told you. You're safe. I guarantee it."

Amalie took a sip of the liquid and then a full swallow. It was nearly all water. She looked over the rim of the tankard at Thayne. He was drinking watered-down ale. Not whiskey. "This isn't ale."

He smirked. "Untrue. 'Tis na' aged enough. I believe they opened the wrong keg for me."

Amalie studied him for a moment. "Very smart, Thayne MacGowan. I still don't agree with your manipulations, but it is smart."

The smirk disappeared. "You should look more angered at me," he said.

"Why?"

"My brother."

Amalie resisted the temptation to look past him toward Jamie again, although that's probably what Thayne wanted.

"What do you hope to gain, Thayne? I'll not bed him. Ever."

"I'd na' allow it. I've already said as much."

The words sent the biggest sensation of warmth she'd ever experienced. It pumped through her, accompanying every beat of her heart. She was afraid it showed. With his next words, she knew it. And even if she guessed he spoke only to wipe the emotion from her face, it still hurt. Painfully.

"I've an aversion to his leavings. Or dinna' you hear earlier? He has the pox."

"I . . . heard."

The warmth was being suffused with cold. Coming from the calculation behind Thayne's answer and the lack of emotion he had when saying it. Her expression must be what he wanted for he nodded slightly.

"I want to go home." She did; with every fiber of her being.

"You said that afore. Answer's the same. You belong with me now. You *are* home."

Her eyes were filling with tears. Despite every control she put on it. It didn't work and nothing seemed to change. She was still sitting beside a Highland brute, being ogled by their chieftain, and ready to sob over homesickness. Thayne took the tankard from her hands and set it back on the table. It was probably because it had tipped. Amalie couldn't help that, either. She'd lost sensation in her fingers.

"Now you decide to cry?" he asked in a soft voice. He had his head turned toward her, as well.

"I never cry!"

"'Tis verra bright of you. Perhaps even better than a slap."

"What?"

"Keeping my brother's interest."

He shoved a half-roll into his mouth and started chewing as if he'd said nothing of importance. Amalie blinked until the table focused and the blur faded. She narrowed her lashes a bit.

"Why would you want that?" she asked him before he shoved another bite in.

"He's the laird. His word is law. Literal law."

"You don't always obey."

"You note that, did you?"

"I don't understand."

"I'm his brother. We've fought."

"You've . . . fought?"

Thayne nodded.

"And won?"

Thayne nodded again.

"That's why everyone obeys you more than him?"

"You note that, too?"

Amalie nodded and went pensive for a bit. "Do you fight often?"

"Only when challenged."

"Challenged?"

"Aye. Jamie oft issues challenges, especially when he's in his cups and I'm in possession of something he wants. Right now it's my newly acquired wife."

"I don't want to hear another word, Thayne MacGowan. Truly."

"I believe our ploy is working. My thanks."

"What ploy?"

"It appears I may give you over without a fight. And you'd na' mind it overmuch."

Amalie waited another moment. And then she slapped him.

Chapter 12

Amalie hated admitting it, but this Highlander had more than manly beauty and immense brawn. He was intelligent and cunning, too. That fact was in his brother's yell for more whiskey, using a voice full of merriment. Amalie didn't look toward the head of the table. She didn't need to. She could guess Jamie's expression. And his regard. And felt it for what seemed hours before he literally dropped off his stool. If he'd been sober, he'd have felt the pain of landing on an injured shoulder. As it was, he lay in a heap until three of his men hauled him around a blanket wall and into the other side of the croft. There he got dumped atop a pallet, where snores ensued from his complete stupor . . . without causing harm to either of the innocent girls. And without any fight.

Amalie looked over at the odorous lump that was Jamie MacGowan, dimly lit by firelight slipping beneath and around the blanket wall. He didn't look frightening or menacing, or anything resembling a man in command of his entire world. And nothing like a man who could take another's possession just because he wanted it.

Jamie MacGowan hadn't moved from how they'd placed him; on his back, limbs spread. His arms and legs weren't on the pallet, but once Amalie had gone to her assigned spot, she realized why. They had small pallets. Neither MacGowan brother would fit, unless he slept sideways, curled around his wife and babe, in a protective fashion. The moment Amalie thought about her current position, she banished it. She didn't want Thayne MacGowan curled about her for any reason; although . . . it did make for comfort and warmth and a bit of tingle deep within her whenever she sensed a breath touching her neck.

Fool.

That's exactly what she was. She should be fast asleep. The ride alone would've decimated her strength. The sup and drink should've made certain of it. She should be fast asleep. That way she wouldn't care how each of Jamie's snores reverberated through the structure, vying with the wind for strength and sound. Amalie told herself that's what kept her awake. It was impossible to rest with such noise. And then she tried to believe it.

She pulled the bundle in her arms upward toward her nose. The infant's nurse had seen to the babe and fresh linens wrapped her. There'd been a lot of sighs and soft voices about wee bairns and sweetness when an entire grouping of women brought the babe to Amalie. That was a signal of some kind, for once Amalie took the child they'd scampered away, climbing to the loft above. If that was their sleeping area, it was well designed. The rounded roof created little if any standing area, but it was probably warm and secure. It appeared to have a sturdy floor made from rough-hewn planks, like their table. Amalie slid her head slightly, tipping her chin as she looked at the shadow of assembled wood above her head.

Apparently, the Scots built well. This building looked sturdy, with log splits in the walls and dried peat filling any gaps between. It held the warmth from their fireplace and seemed impervious against the spring storm raging outside. She surmised this curtained-off area was reserved for guests and those clansmen too inebriated to walk across the grounds to their own crofts. Whatever the function, the room was close to the fire. Amalie had to admit it was warm. But she suspected being snuggled against Thayne gained that.

She stifled a yawn and thought sleepily about his Castle Gowan. According to Thayne's last whisper, they'd arrive mid-day. If the weather cleared enough for the ride and the new snow allowed passage. Amalie wondered if the castle had the same stoutness of construction or even enough volume and status to quantify it as a castle. Or if they had any of the amenities most homes were being fit with now-adays. She hoped she wouldn't look overdressed and over-elegant as Miss Carsten. Amalie settled further against Thayne. He tightened his arm as if he felt it, but nothing in his breathing changed.

Nobody told her how angry Jamie would be once he woke. Nor how vicious his words and the volume he said them. Nor how dark the looks he'd send her way once he'd stumbled to his feet and started bellowing in rage, startling even the soundest sleeper and making the babe wail. Amalie did her best to stay out of his way, standing on shaky feet to wrap the blanket fully about her, before leaving to find the babe's wet-nurse outside their curtain, and then sitting on a long bench against the wall. She stayed hunched into a ball in a tartan, wondering where Thayne had gone to while watching the women prepare breakfast.

Jamie noticed his brother's absence. He filled the air with taunts and threats from behind the curtained partition, even as women hurried there, burdened with large tankards of whiskey and fresh fried gruel cakes. Amalie didn't know how they managed to salve the laird's bad humor and didn't want to know. It was enough that sounds of slurping and giggling accompanied the silence.

She had her own grilled cake half eaten when Thayne

finally made an appearance, stepping into the building long enough to gain her attention. Then he gestured for her without one word of explanation. And it got worse. Amalie instantly obeyed.

"Hie to the stables. Get atop my horse. Sean waits to assist."

"Where are you going?" Amalie whispered.

"After my own meal. Be quiet and hurry!"

"Why?"

"Grant and the menfolk are returned. We've nae need of Jamie's company. And he has less for ours."

"Then . . . why are we sneaking about?"

"My brother's na' dense. He suspicions the trick played on him. He sounds angered enough to fight over it."

"Fight?"

"Save the words for when we've gone. Quick now. Afore he spots me."

"I don't understand this fear."

Thayne stood to his tallest, gaining every eye and then puffed out his chest to make certain of it. "I am na' afraid," he replied.

"Then what?"

He could pretend to be stubborn, but Amalie Ellin was well-known for it. She went to her tallest, making her head level with his chin, tipped her head back and glared back at him with the same expression he was using.

"Can you save this argue?"

"Admit you're afraid first."

He made fists of his hands and blew air over her, deflating his chest slightly. Amalie wasn't the only one to sigh in appreciation. She actually heard some of it happening in the room behind her.

"I've got the bairn to consider."

"Not . . . me?" Amalie cursed the little voice but that didn't stop it.

"Can you just obey? Please? This once?"

This once? He wanted her to obey always; without explanation, and usually with the threat of force. She didn't answer, but hoped it was conveyed in the look she gave him, before she stepped around him and obeyed.

He'd be glad to reach Castle Gowan, more so than ever.

Thayne decided it as the horse plodded through another bit of crusted snow. They'd started as a mounted band of four, leading more than a score of riderless horses that Sean and Little Mac controlled. There was no need of an escort on MacGowan land, yet the further they traveled the more clansmen appeared about them. It was due to the pipers atop every hill, their tunes interspersed with the fog that came from newly fallen snow battling spring sun.

It was slow going, but that was Thayne's fault. He could've stayed longer. Grant and all the men had returned. His cousin had a surfeit of hospitality, food, drink, and shelter. Staying at the croft would give the sun time to thaw and then dry the ground. As well as giving everyone time to rest. It had been tempting, but dangerous. Any time spent in Jamie's company was.

It would be different at the castle. Once there, Jamie would have to contend with his wife, a woman ten years senior to her husband, and a dominant force to be reckoned with. That's what came of wedding a Douglas clanswoman claiming a mass of bloodthirsty clansmen at her beck and call. But that was Jamie's fault when he'd been but twenty. Wedding her was the penalty for being caught abed with her in the first place.

Thayne shook his head. Jamie had a decade of wedded life with his harridan of a wife. It still amazed everyone who met her. The Duchess of MacGowan was a thin, lined, sharp-nosed, sharp-tongued shrew. Always had been. Thayne wasn't the lone one to wonder what force of nature she'd used to get

Jamie MacGowan into her bed in the first place. No doubt she'd used whiskey.

There were other reasons to be gratified at reaching the castle: Support. Sanity. Reason. Thayne wasn't afraid of fighting Jamie, despite Amalie's taunt. He was afraid of killing him. The four times they'd fought, Thayne won. The last time, he'd been nigh impossible to stop, pummeling his brother into a lump of raw flesh and muck. That was over Mary. Thayne had issued a warning as they'd pulled him off. Jamie wouldn't survive a fifth contest. Should he force it, it would be on the list within Castle Gowan's walls, with complete fairness and irreproachable witnesses.

Thayne would also appreciate a real bed beneath him. The canopied structure he slept within held an oversized mattress, stuffed with goose-down and straw. He'd seen it constructed four years back when his status became apparent with every one of Jamie's still-birthed offspring. Thayne MacGowan was the heir. Nothing Jamie or his duchess could do altered that.

Thayne just wished it had been enough to make Mary wed with him instead of that wretch, Dunn-Fyne.

Thayne shifted again on the saddle, silently groaning at the pain from his wound. His new wife settled right back into the space against him as though it was special made for her. She was sleeping, curved into a lean that put her head atop his arm and her buttocks fully against him, tempting him . . . if he wasn't constantly on guard for it. Thayne tensed against the urge, and when that didn't work, tried ignoring it by pondering things such as chivalry.

This rescue wasn't to take long. Or any lives. Mary had sent her missive for aid and he'd gone to her. It shouldn't have denigrated into primitive barbarity. He wasn't to gain a babe . . . and definitely not a wife.

Thayne had more to face. He had to see the bairn baptized, her birth recorded in the family bible, as well as this marriage. He had to oversee Mary's interment in the family crypt. He braced automatically for the heavy stone-feel about his heart that always came from thoughts of Mary, and then had to work at feeling it over everything else.

Odd . . .

Thayne looked out at the loch-filled vista, sparkling with sun on frost-fog, pulled his wife more securely against him, and blinked against a defensive wash of moisture from the bright view. He'd also be glad to reach the castle for a purely primal reason as well. He wanted time alone with this woman. In his huge canopied bed. It was probably a good thing she decided to sleep the afternoon away. If he had any say in it, she was going to be up most of the night.

It took longer than usual to round Loch Lingow. The ground about the lake was loose and shifted wherever his horse stepped, making it treacherous. That took his entire attention, which stopped the ponderings of his actions, but did nothing for the advancing power of lust. Nothing. Thayne had to admit it. He'd been cursed and its name was Amalie. Thayne pulled back into the saddle, pushed his filled sporran between them, and awakened his wife with the move.

And that cursed him even more.

This Amalie had beautiful light-brown eyes; the color of well-aged ale, fringed with lashes a shade or two darker than her hair. Thayne avoided looking into them, held his jaw tight as she looked him over, and then lost out. At the eye contact, he couldn't prevent his body's full pulse of movement, sending more blood to his groin, and that just got him more lust and more want and more need. Along with her consideration on all of it. Within scant moments, he could tell she'd assigned meaning to his motion and was preparing to use it. He moved his gaze to the view. It was better to look ahead.

"Sleep well?"

He cleared his throat to ask it, then fought a flush from happening throughout his chest, rising to his cheeks, and probably making his ears as red as the MacGowan plaid color. It didn't stay the twinge of his loins against his sporran, nor the fact she could feel it against her hip. And all because she didn't do anything other than look at him, as if studying him.

"Oddly enough . . . yes."

He could curse the instant glance he made down to her eyes, but that didn't stop it. Or change it. Or mute it. Or grant him relief from their locked gaze. Or anything other than give him more problems from his own body.

"I-I've never . . . slept . . . atop a horse."

"Nae?" The word came out rough, like he chewed on pebbles.

"I don't know why I slept so soundly. . . ."

Her voice trailed off. Her gaze didn't. Then she added to the torture with the tip of her tongue darting out to wet her upper lip. Thayne sent his gaze away, but not before another surge of want centered at his groin, pushing his sporran farther into her hip, although he pulled back and went to a forward angle to prevent it. And then bit back the cry at the movement on his wound.

He couldn't answer and she didn't act like she expected one. She didn't say anything. She just kept looking at him with those beautiful, bottomless, deep eyes.

He could tell her why she'd slept so well. Exhaustion was known to cause it. He only wished it worked with him. And on this lust emotion. He'd been awake a good portion of last night, encased in places his mind wandered and his body couldn't. Yet. He should've taken care of their tupping when he had the chance. Then maybe he wouldn't be suffering now. Nothing worked much as a dampener, either. Not even his wound. Thayne cleared his throat again. It didn't do much. He still sounded like he'd swallowed rocks.

"You need a rest?" she asked. There was a mischievous lilt to her words, making his flush worse.

"Nae. We've lost time."

"Time?"

"We'll na' make Castle Gowan afore sup."

"Sup?"

"Aye. Sup. As much as I despise it."

"Please don't tell me we have to playact with Jamie . . . again? Not every night. No. Please? And if so, I'm retreating to my rooms and staying there."

"Nae need. Jamie has his duchess to control him. 'Tis the formalness of the affair I detest."

"Formal? Did I hear right? Formal? The MacGowan clan?"

Amusement colored the words. Or sarcasm. He decided amusement was the better choice.

"The duchess is a Douglas. Schooled at court. French court. She's set the castle on the French style. I doona' find it to my liking. Na' many do."

"Right."

It wasn't amusement after all. It sounded more like skepticism and disbelief. Thayne glanced at her before looking back at the loch surface, squinting at the reflection of sun on water; calm and clear, without a hint of wind-ruff.

"'Tis usual to rest at this end of Loch Lingow. To . . . dress presentable." His voice sounded defensive to his own ears. But, at least it sounded like him.

"What . . . constitutes presentable? To a Highland castle run by a duchess schooled in the French court?"

Sarcasm and mirth carried clearly through those words. Thayne glanced at her before looking away. That's when he decided she could just find out for herself. She obviously had the Sassenach's viewpoint of a Highlander, and he had to admit, her experience so far would seem to justify it. She was in for a surprise. They were already in glimpsing distance of the castle now around every bend, if the warmth of midday hadn't created a layer of mist to hover about the loch's surface. He was going to find it very pleasant to watch her reaction when she did see it.

There were two main approaches to the castle. The landward side came over Mount Greaven from Inverness. There was a well-planned and built road, maintained as weather allowed. Arriving from that direction, a visitor looking down at the castle could appreciate the symmetry, if not the design. They could also see the six towers, two barbican walls—each one about a bailey—as well as appreciate the size, if not the full scope. The majesty of Castle Gowan was only apparent up close, where one could see three-story-high crenellated walls, and experience a thickness of twenty-seven feet of rock at the ground level. The mountain approach also highlighted the jewel-like setting of his home.

That was the direction Thayne's Honor Guard should've taken when spiriting Mary's body here. Thayne had taken the other way, around the loch. This way could be treacherous, as run-off from uncountable burns made all but the rockiest ground unstable, except in high summer. It couldn't be helped. He'd made the decision upon Mary's death and the fates could simply abide it.

This path took more time, however, since the path wove in and out of inlets and through forests bordering the loch. It also meant the castle would first be seen from well below it, where the eye could look up at a wall of rock rising approximately six stories above the lake surface. Thayne's forebears had built for strategic reasons, and more than once slain bodies of their enemies had dangled from those same ramparts.

Castle Gowan was situated at the confluence of two lochs, the spit of land going to an island when the tides were in. Such positioning made a well conceived defensive barrier. Constructed of rock quarried from Mount Greaven, the castle had an undeniable presence. And it was still intact; a rarity after Cromwell turned the cannons of the Covenanters onto most other strongholds. Castle Gowan held a unique position, for it was inaccessible by seagoing vessel. The Norsemen who'd conceived and begun it hadn't built it for staving off further raids by rogue Vikings. They'd built to hold gained lands against Thayne's ancestors, the Picts.

All of which made a historically significant, immense, and formidable fortress-like castle, silhouetted against the backdrop of darkening sky. The castle sat atop like-shaded rock, surrounded by a waterscape of deep blue and deeper aquagreen. Being at the base of Mount Greaven shadowed the castle each morn, but if the sun participated, the walls would be lit like old gold with every sunset, while the polished glass in every window refracted light like multifaceted gems.

To be from the clan claiming such a stronghold never failed to send a trill of shiver down Thayne's spine. This was no exception. Castle Gowan was in his blood, just as the land and clans were. He'd inherit it, God willing. Or his sons would.

His sons?

For the first time he got full measure of what had happened. His sons were to have been Mary's. Or . . . when Mary wouldn't have him, Thayne hadn't cared who the mother of his progeny was, as long as they were Scot. He hadn't fought the MacKennah betrothal. The MacKennah lass would do as well as any other once she reached the age of maturity. Her clan may be poor, but their antecedents went back as far in time as his did. Maybe further. And with them, a shared hatred of anything English.

No man destined to be a Highland clan chieftain would wed a Sassenach, especially without clan approval. And here, Thayne had done both. And worse: He couldn't find much regret over it. He bowed his head and got a nose full of Amalie's scent. God help him, but she was such a bonny one! Anyone getting a look at her might excuse his weakness. They'd never forgive it, even given her attributes, but they might understand it. The lass possessed massive feminine charms and the ability to wield them.

Blast and damn—!

The instant he thought it his loins harkened, pounding lust through his belly yet again. Thayne tightened his buttocks to stay it and that sent an unwilling groan as the flesh of his injury jolted. All of it made him slant forward, pushing the lass's head from his shoulder. And that just got him her unrelenting amber gaze again. Which just got him another round of flush.

Lord, but he'd be glad to reach the castle.

Chapter 13

They'd traveled what seemed hours, silent and steady, while Thayne trembled occasionally, groaned, and more than once resettled into his saddle, adjusting the part of him she was studiously ignoring, while at the same time wondering if a man couldn't control it any better than this. Not that she had knowledge, of course. All she had were the aborted moments in the shepherd croft—and that in the dark—with absolutely nothing between her nakedness and his except pure, unadulterated sensation.

That reminder jolted her slightly and had her scrunching her nether region against an itch she refused to acknowledge. Admitting to it meant she'd have to deal with it, and avoiding reality was one of her most insufferable traits according to her father. Amalie added to that. The Earl of Ellincourt had been backed in his opinion by her governesses—all three of them. As well as the elderly great-aunt who'd agreed to chaperone her entry into society. And probably everyone else who knew her well enough to have an opinion. Amalie Ellin avoided anything to do with truth and reality. Always had.

It was better than the alternative.

She blew the resigned sigh through her nose. She had to admit being atop a horse, held in a Scotsman's arms without opportunity to escape, and thrilling at the thought of what he'd told her would happen tonight, fully substantiated everyone's opinion of her. Running away to Scotland had been without substance and devoid of reality. All of which was definitely an insufferable trait.

Thayne's bag-thing touched her again and started a tremor through him at the contact. Amalie pulled away as far as she could. It didn't seem to be far enough. That was just confusing. As if he had no control over . . . *it*. That couldn't be normal. Could it? How was she to know? Nothing about any of the men she'd met, danced with, or accompanied to supper could be described as unable to control their man part. Or even indicated they possessed one.

That got her to wondering. About Thayne MacGowan, and the amount of maleness he wielded so easily and thoughtlessly. The act between man and woman couldn't possibly be as horrid as her great-aunt alluded, covering her mouth with a handkerchief as she whispered on it the one time. It couldn't be . . . or why would Amalie still have tingling deep in her belly? A rush of warmth? Shivers? The instant rise of her pulse beat? And there was worse. Her symptoms seemed to increase the closer they got to his castle.

Tonight.

Not only were the two days he'd given her over but they'd probably have privacy, as well. Whatever these barbarians considered a castle, it was bound to be private; secure and stout . . . and inescapable. It would probably contain food of some kind or another, too. That was a grand thought and Amalie's belly growled with hunger.

"We'll be arriving . . . in time for sup? Isn't that what you said?"

She pulled from the comfortable berth she'd assumed against him and looked up, and that created a gap in her words. Since the storm had seemed to precipitate the clear warmth of a sun-filled day, she shouldn't be surprised to find a golden haze of sunset on his features. It wasn't possible to keep her wits when facing a man straight from her own fantasies. Sculptured with a master's hand and hewn from flesh-covered rock. He had his hair tied back but strands had escaped, trailing to his shoulders, while aqua-shaded eyes held hers for long moments and the horse simply kept a slow walk, swaying them against each other. It was incredible. Impossible. She couldn't move. Think. Blink.

This reaction couldn't be all her fault. That was too unfair to contemplate. Thayne had to be the most beautiful male birthed or the pagan gods had released one of their own to earth. Amalie finally moved her vision to his chest where a shirt should be, then to his shoulders. Arms. Hands . . .

Nowhere was safe! She looked to the forest beyond him, sucked in on her bottom lip and hoped he wouldn't note her reaction and especially the why of it. She already knew she had too much imagination and she knew he was handsome enough to tie her tongue and drop her jaw, but she'd hoped further time in his presence would cure, or at least mute, the affliction. It was a complete blow to find that false.

"Here."

He fished about in the pack behind him, bumping against her head more than once with a shoulder before holding out another of their dry cakes.

"I'd rather await the sup prepared at your castle." She replied haughtily before making a lie of it by accepting the offering.

"You'll na' attend," he replied.

"I won't?" The surprise sent her gaze to him. She'd curse that move later, once she corrected the instant dryness that made swallowing the biscuit near impossible. She settled with moving the bite about in her mouth with her tongue, hoping for moisture.

"Nae."

She managed to choke down her food and sent another

dry gulp after it to find her voice. Then she flicked a glance to his tightened jaw as he looked out over her head, narrowing his eyes on the low slant of sunlight. Incredible. Masculine. Perfect. Reacting to the view of him just made her voice feminine and breathless-sounding. Much to her complete and total disgust. It was better to watch the trees beyond him. It didn't work. Her voice was still feminine and breathless-sounding.

"You'd have me . . . starve?"

His lips tipped into a smirk. "I dinna' say you would na' eat. I said you'd na' attend the sup."

"Why not?"

"The duchess would na' allow it."

Amalie straightened slightly. "Your mother wouldn't allow me to attend sup?"

"There is nae dowager. I speak of the duchess. Jamie's wife."

"I look . . . forward to meeting her," Amalie said. *And telling her a thing or two about her spouse.*

He shook his head. "Na' tonight. You're . . . na' proper."

He glanced down at her at the exact moment her face slackened. She didn't have time to alter it.

"I have never been so insulted," she told him.

"You've said that afore. You must get insulted oft."

Amalie set her lips. "I am totally proper, Thayne MacGowan. Totally."

"Proper . . . but na' acceptable dress. Nor is the way you're wearing it."

"Now, I'm thoroughly insulted, Thayne MacGowan. Thoroughly."

He smiled but didn't say anything, so she had to.

"I'm totally acceptable."

"Na' for the duchess."

"Are you truly telling me she'd find me unacceptable? Me?"

Her voice was rising. And it was stronger. The only sign

he gave was a wider smile, showing white teeth against his swarthy skin.

"Oh, you're total acceptable, wife. Total. You just appear to be . . . tired." When he answered, he used the arm about her to lift her, hauling her against him.

"Tired?" It was an argument. He should be listening closer.

"And . . . mussed."

"Mussed?"

"From . . . sleeping in your clothing. And other things."

"Other things?"

His lips were right at her ear. Amalie lifted a shoulder against it. It didn't work. Not much did. She still had a complete lurch through her frame, and it was matched almost instantly by his.

"All sorts of other things," he whispered.

"That is not . . . my fault." Nor was the soft reply as she swiveled to face him, putting her lips very close to his.

"True."

The word was accompanied by another push of his groin against her, and a tightening of the arm about her until every breath was a struggle. He also had his eyes scrunched. Amalie watched his face from a finger-length away and waited. She didn't have another choice.

"Jesu'! But you're a bonny one."

He opened his eyes, looked deep into hers, and then loosened his arm enough to lower her to the horse again.

"That is not an answer," she informed him.

"Bonny . . . and bristly. With an argumentative tongue that covers over honeyed kisses."

"Thayne." She was trying for a threatening note, but failed miserably.

"And sweet wet. Warmed. Just for me."

Her eyes were huge. She couldn't stop it as he put words into what he made her feel and what was happening.

"'Tis grateful I am to be near home."

"Near?" She was hoping for a tart tone but sounding feminine, breathless, and now ripe with wanton needs and urges, as well.

"Aye."

"How near?"

"Right behind you."

"Right—"

Amalie looked over her shoulder and immediately put her hand out on the horse's neck for support as she accepted every bit of shock at the structure looming from the mist, looking as if it sat atop a cloud, aglow with the gold-red of sunset. She'd never seen anything so massive, regal, awe-inspiring. Overwhelming. Immense. She lost every bit of her voice. It was impossible not to. Thayne had probably been generous when he called her unacceptable. There wasn't any of Miss Carsten's attire that would be. Only the wardrobe of the only daughter of the Earl of Ellincourt would suffice. And it had been left in London.

"Thayne . . . I . . . it's . . . uh . . ."

Her voice was missing as he twisted to put her back fully against his chest. Her heart hammered against the arm wrapped about her. She didn't know what her words would've been had she voiced them. The castle stole her words. It took her wits. And it severely dampened her self-confidence.

The fog about the castle base was thick, overhanging the shoreline they paralleled. From there it looked to reach out into the forest, like grasping fingers. Castle Gowan was the most amazing structure she'd ever seen, including Warwick and Alnsley. It dwarfed Ellincourt Manor. It probably did the same to anything save a royal estate.

"Doona' fash, lass. There's nae words needed."

He sent a breath of amusement at the end of his words. She knew why. It was payment for her earlier disdain.

"See that tower? The middle one?" Thayne took the arm from about her to point up at the tallest of them. Amalie craned her head back into him to look.

"Yes," she replied.

He put his arm back around her and she put her hand atop it. She nearly squeezed at the reassuring presence, but held back at the last moment. They were riding into the shadow thrown by the castle now and the setting sun put a massive formation of black silhouette over the landscape.

"Within that tower is a wheel-stair comparable to Fyvie. 'Twas added last century."

"What's a wheel-stair?"

"A staircase built of stone in a spiral. Counterclockwise. For defense."

"Defense?"

"To have a sword-arm free while defending, while the attacking force has nae such thing. That stair is wide enough to ride three horses abreast, too, more than the two built by Laird Seton."

"Who would want to do that?"

"A man attacking or defending his home."

"By riding a horse up a stair?"

"I dinna' say 'twas a normal thing. I only said 'twas possible. See the far tower? That one has two curved staircases. Wide ones. Gets men to the battlements quicker. 'Twas also of use in attaching the keep."

"Attaching the keep . . . to what?"

"The curtain wall. A free-standing keep is na' defensible against cannon fire."

"Cannon . . . fire?" She was losing her voice.

"You doona' ken what Cromwell's Protectorship was about?"

Amalie shook her head.

"The man was fond of cannon and used it. 'Twas the prime reason we attached the keep to the walls. The keep is verra auld.

Norman-built. Freestanding. Four stories high. Thick walls. Stout . . . but na' stout enough for Mons Meg and her ilk."

"Mons Meg?"

"You've na' heard of Mons Meg, either?"

Amalie shook her head again.

"What do they teach you in England? And what, by the Saints, did you intend the MacKennah lasses to learn?"

She opened her mouth and then closed it. Drat the man for finding such a weak spot.

"Well?"

"Tell me about this Meg," she answered finally.

He was amused enough to move her with his chuckle. "Mons Meg is a siege cannon, settled in Edinburgh since our second King James' time, although it's seen little use since the ascension war ceased. In 1603."

"Surely you jest. There wasn't a war then. I'm beginning to wonder at your education, MacGowan. Fully."

"Hate and mistrust of Sassenach goes deep. 'Twas paused for a bit when Mary's son ascended the English throne in 1603. That peace is now moot. Or are you na' up on the current state, either?"

"Current state?" Amalie racked her brain. There was the abdication last year of the deposed king, James Stewart, who'd fled to France with his pretender son. They were calling this new monarchy of Anne and her husband William the Glorious Revolution. Of course, she'd heard talk, but all of it had seemed immensely boring and of little import.

"They expect us to accept another removal of a rightful Stewart from the throne? The true king? 'Tis war they want, lass, and war they'll get. Again. And with that comes hatred. 'Tis all the Sassenach offer. And we can do naught save honor their threat."

Amalie gulped and it moved her head. She knew he felt it.

"Doona' fash it much. As my wife, you're now Scot. Or verra soon will be." He pulled her up against him to breathe

the words against her neck. "I'll order up a bath for you first thing. Heated. I'll have the same thing done to your towels."

"Thayne, I . . ."

Her voice trailed off. She didn't need a reminder of how condescending and scornful she'd been. The experience of being in the castle's presence was enough. There was a swell of sound in the air now, too. It emanated from figures all atop the battlements. She could see the pipers if she squinted. It added to the effect. They'd fully entered Castle Gowan's shadow, riding between two huge stone pillars and onto the first span of bridge. The structure was wood, echoing with first his horse's hooves, and then the sounds of so many behind them, Amalie tipped sideways to look for the reason. She was pulled back into Thayne's embrace the exact moment she gasped, securing her. In that glimpse she'd seen a sea of green, red, and black plaid-clad men following them. Some mounted, but most were on foot. Each of Dunn-Fyne's horses had a rider. Amalie looked over the looming barbican wall, rising from the rock foundation to create a massive gate front at the end of the bridge. They reached two more stone pillars midway across, holding a drawbridge. There were chains leading to the tops of each pillar. Her eyes followed one to a crenellated tower with arrow slits carved into it.

"'Tis a grand structure. Aye?" Thayne asked and all she could do was nod.

They'd reached the end of the last drawbridge and a portcullis of iron spikes long and pointed enough to spear a horse and its rider. Amalie glanced at it before facing the darkness of archway that opened into a stone walled alleyway, long and narrow. The moment the webbed gate cleared Thayne's head, he urged his horse forward, walking through another thick stone archway and into an inner bailey that was churned and uneven with slush-covered grass and mud. One of the near buildings loomed from the right, turning into an ancient-looking keep that was attached to the wall with a tower. It had the inflexibility of a Norman design, featuring large gray stone blocks, nothing save cross-shaped slits, and a two-story doorframe. At the far end of the inner bailey there was a building resembling a Renaissance Palace. The columns and carved statuary all about it faced them from across the length of the grounds. Amalie had a good look before moving her attention to the structures on the left side. These turned out to be thatched-roof crofts and fenced-off gardenplots, situated between two larger stone edifices that created another courtyard. And past that she could see more buildings.

Thayne continued through a corridor between the Norman Keep and another centuries-old building before turning to his left. She knew the stables before seeing them. The long, two-story structure ran along the wall, containing so many horses, she didn't know how he'd fit in the ones he'd brought.

"Each MacGowan chieftain put a mark on the castle. They add a wing, a tower, a structure. Such as that one. The one attempting to be fashionable."

"Which one is that?" Amalie asked.

"Just look." He gestured to the Renaissance building at the far end. "'Tis called The Palazzo. Our grandfather had that monstrosity constructed. Designed it himself after studying buildings throughout the Continent. Spent my grandmother's entire dowry on it. Such a waste."

"It's . . . beautiful," she remarked.

"Useless in battle. Na' one of those turrets could hold cannon, and but one archer. And look at the weakness of the design. An attacker would breach those windows in moments."

"Surely that isn't necessary in the inner bailey?"

"Betrayal comes from within, lass. Always. And the lone thing standing a-tween a man and death is strength and defense. In every aspect and every building. 'Tis what makes a clan rich. Proud. Strong."

"Barbaric," she added.

He huffed a breath. It sounded like a cross between annoyance and amusement.

"Jamie's duchess lives there. That woman gained vast ideas for décor and uses large sums to pay for it. She fancied The Palazzo for her backdrop and naught else would do."

His tone said more than his words.

"And that's . . . wrong?"

"Doona' you listen? She follows French fashion. All frills and nonsense . . . with regard to her entire household. Even the servants are attired in long, curled, powdered wigs atop their heads. Dressed in fancy short trews with satins, and laces and ribbons and gold-smelted embossed buttons. Most of her household hails from France. Nae self-respecting Highlander would wear such. They'd rather fall on their own claymore."

Amalie had seen some examples of proper court fashion. At Dilling's ball in Yorkshire, when she'd first been introduced to the dowager duchess of Rochester, starting this chain of events. Amalie hadn't met the reigning duke until much later . . . when the family already had the promise of her hand in wedlock and her fortune slated for the Rochester coffers. There'd been no witnesses to the meeting of duke and wife-to-be except four burly handlers hovering over the scene. No one ever saw the current title holder of Rochester . . . for a reason. And her father wanted Ellincourt progeny sired by that freak of nature? Amalie had to move her thoughts or gag. She'd forgotten how frightened she'd been and why she'd grabbed at this escape when fate put it before her. It was easier to recall the courtiers that had been at the ball, looking elegant and refined. Well-groomed. Clean. But extremely effeminate when compared with Thayne and his band.

"Does . . . your brother have to follow her fashion?"

"Why do you think he drinks so much?"

Amalie caught the slight smile on his face, and then matched it. She met his eyes, had the sound of her pulse crescendo in each ear cancelling out the drone of pipes and drums and humanity all about them, and that sent streams of heat rippling all through her. Everywhere. The feeling surging through her was immense; larger than the castle; bigger than breath. It stunned. Electrified. Awed. There was just this moment. This one time. This wonderment that began with shared humor before moving to fusion with him. And then it was gone. Thayne flicked his glance to her lips before scrunching his eyes, shutting her out. Amalie felt it and sobered instantly.

There was nothing in his eyes when he opened them again and she did her best to match that expression.

"Come. Enough dallying and history. I've a sup to be ordering. And then a bath. I may even join you."

He had to feel her gasp, even as she kept it from sounding.

Chapter 14

She was actually grateful Thayne didn't let her walk. She'd been dreading going on display with sodden material as her lone covering, while the amount of people made it difficult to make any kind of headway. Perched in Thayne's arms, she could feel him push through, crossing the span of courtyard to the Norman Keep. The crowd noise seemed to get worse once they walked up at least twenty steps. Amalie lost count as Thayne climbed, using his good leg first and pulling the injured one along. And then he walked beneath a thick arch supporting the doorframe, across a room with wood floor that pounded with the amount of boots striding on it, and down four wide stone steps into a voluminous space lit by torches high against rock walls and fires glowing from cavernous fireplaces spaced about the walls. If her mouth wasn't slack, it would have been at the sight.

"The original great hall."

Thayne informed her, although she hadn't asked. He proceeded to walk into the chamber, limping noticeably the farther they progressed. He stopped when it appeared they'd reached midpoint. The room seemed poorly furnished with long tables and benches widely spaced between them, but

there wasn't any amount of furniture that wouldn't seem
sparse and dwarfed; exactly as every man there looked.
Diminutive. Insignificant. Thayne stepped atop a bench and
then moved higher onto what looked to be the surface of a
long table. Then he turned about and without warning started
sending orders about the throng. Amalie's gasp got absorbed
by acoustics belonging to a cathedral. The room had to be
three stories or more in height. Otherwise, his voice wouldn't
resound from every corner. Nor would the answers he got, all
said in clipped male voices that echoed atop each other into a
blend of noise.

"Is my Honor Guard present?" Thayne asked.

"Aye."

Several male voices chorused it, making a crescendo of
baritone.

"The Lady Mary?" The query contained the slightest
warble in it. Amalie felt her heart ping a missed beat.

"Lying in state in the chapel. Per your instructions."

"Trouble?"

"Only . . . with Her Grace."

Thayne took a moment to digest that information. So did
Amalie.

"Services?"

"This Sabbath."

Thayne grunted, sending a rumbling through her with it.
"Nursery?"

"In order. Nanny's auld but willing. 'Anything for my
Thayne,' she said." The last was parodied in a querulous, old
woman voice.

Thayne smirked. "That you, Rory?"

"Aye."

"See to settling the bairn. Her wet-nurse, as well. My
chambers?"

"Readied. Have been since yester-eve when you dinna' appear."

"We hit a bit of storm, Michael. And afore that a scuffle with Dunn-Fyne."

"That where you get the extra horseflesh?"

"Aye."

"And your wound?"

"Dunn-Fyne tosses a mean blade."

Thayne didn't answer it. A glance showed the remark had come from Sean, standing on the bench just below them.

"'Twas luck we got to be safe and dry and warm here at the castle. With naught save saddle sores for our trouble."

"That you, Edgar?"

"Aye."

"For that you can ride to Ian MacGruder's croft. Fetch his sire to my side. Take Alex with you."

"Me? Why do I have to go?"

"You're his brother," Thayne replied.

There was a bit of grunting and groaning, and odd-sounding noises like slapping, before that batch of noise dissipated.

"Come along then, Michael. We'll take you . . . six with us. Now!"

"Pellin!"

Thayne didn't have to use the volume he did, but Amalie suspected he was speaking loudly to supplant the grumbling as men left the room.

"Present."

"See sup fetched to my chamber. Warmed. Fresh. Make certain of it."

"I'll cook up one myself."

Thayne grunted a reply, tightened his arms about Amalie almost imperceptibly, and then barked another name. "Gannett?"

"Aye!"

"See to fetching a bath. Make sure to heat it. In my chambers."

"You're taking . . . a bath?" There was a collective bit of laughter.

"Nae. 'Tis for the wife. And warm the towels, as well."

Amalie turned her head away, putting her cheek against Thayne's neck so the blush wouldn't be so noticeable. And then the blare of a horn came so quick and sharp even Thayne jumped, making the structure they were atop tremble as it took the brunt of it.

"'Tis Her Grace!"

Someone probably whispered it but the room echoed it into a declaration. Amalie turned her head and peeked.

Thayne hadn't been descriptive enough, but she was already learning that of him. He said what he meant and didn't waste words. Amalie watched as two rows of manservants formed, all of them sporting white powdered wigs atop their heads. They were adorned in green, formfitting velvet frock-coats and black satin breeches, with stockings so white they glowed light blue. Each man held aloft a long-handled torch. The man who'd blown the horn stood at the front of the cavalcade. He put his head back and yelled into the silence.

"All prepare to attend Her Grace, the Duchess of MacGowan!"

A woman stepped between the servants, proceeding with small slow steps into the room. Her progress was based on how quickly the farthest man could move to the front, making loops about each side to re-form the front of the lines, highlighting every step of the way with their torches.

"Sean? Take the wife and see her to my chamber. Now!"

Amalie didn't get another look at the duchess's approach. She wasn't given the option. She wasn't even given advance warning as Thayne tossed her to his man. She barely kept the scream as Sean caught her. Then he dropped down amidst the other clansmen and moved away, shouldering his way to the far end of the room and obscurity.

Thayne stepped down to the floor slowly, ignoring the wrench of his buttock wound. Once he reached floor, he waved the clansmen about him to part for the procession. He had to. MacGowan men were pressing together the closer Jamie's wife got, forming a human shield. They'd done it before, and that had gained him a command appearance to her chambers, which was far worse.

The duchess was dressed in what was probably the height of French court fashion, her dress of light yellow satin looked studded with jewels and draped with ribbon. She had a wide neckline running the tops of her arms and skimming a bosom. Or what would be a bosom if the woman actually possessed one. She wore the MacGowan emeralds. Large, perfectly faceted stones linked with diamonds flashed from where they perched atop the twin bony projections of her collarbone. The same stones glittered from the tiara atop her curled powdered wig. Her hairdresser had left two ringlets loose in a provocative manner, to caress each revealed shoulder. Her attire and entourage reeked of wealth and privilege and power.

It was completely wasted.

Thayne smirked slightly and caught more than a few chuckles and jostling from about him. She shouldn't take such time progressing across a floor. It gave the observers time to study her and come to the same conclusions. The woman was ugly-plain. Stick-thin. Aged . . . and wholly vain.

He knew of her wig despite how closely she guarded the secret. He'd been told about her thinning reddish-gray hair. He wasn't one for gossip, but some of the duchess's servants were fine-looking women and his Honor Guard weren't immune to listening to tales of the duchess, as long as it came with a kiss or two. No one needed to bandy tales, however.

The Duchess of MacGowan was unattractive, with pale eyes of a watered blue shade, light blond eyebrows and lashes, and a thin narrow nose that ended with a distinctive hook. That, combined with a recessed chin, couldn't be disguised. Nor could her dressmaker conceal her lack of womanly curves. The woman was plain, awkward-boned, and sharp-tongued. It was just as evident now as it was ten years ago when Jamie had first brought her.

"Thayne MacGowan has returned. At last."

They'd reached him, the amount of scuffling stopped, and she stepped to the front of her enclosure, tipping an open fan onto her revealed chest as she curtseyed. She said his name in a throaty tone that grated worse than a screech would. At least to his ears.

"Your grace." He tipped his head slightly.

"I was to be informed of your return."

She stepped closer to him, slanting her head to peer at him through artificially darkened lashes.

"Verra well . . . I've returned. You're informed."

"Wait!"

He'd turned to forestall any further conversation with her, but a skeletal hand grabbed at his upper arm. Thayne forced the instant knot of muscle to relax as her fingers groped him. His jaw locked and he narrowed his eyes to look above where she hovered at chin level. It helped, but not by much.

"I was to be informed the *moment* you returned."

She turned her voice into a sultry tone to match the skim of her fingers as she moved them about his arm. Thayne ignored it. She flicked her fan about her face and shoulders with little rapid-speed motions.

"I've things that need seen to. And nae doubt, you have guests at your fest."

He toyed with pulling from her grasp but kept it at bay. There were too many watching. Thayne hoped the rising flush was hidden, although according to Sean, her interest was no secret to his Honor Guard. Thayne hoped that's the furthest the news extended.

"I did as you bade . . . Thayne."

She took a skimmed step closer, flooding his nostrils with perfume that mixed with the powder atop her head. He turned away and held his breath to delay the reaction. It failed. The sneeze echoed through the chamber, causing more than a few chuckles. It also involuntarily tensed his frame and both arms. That just gained him a further clutch of her fingers about him.

"Oh my . . ." Her voice matched the complete cling of her hand, now kneading the flesh she held.

"What do you want?"

"You already ken."

She'd moved closer still, and went taller somehow, puffing out her meager chest for display as if it were something to be desired. The area above her neckline was moving rapidly as if she panted for air as well. Her fan was increasing the issue as it stirred the air, drying his eyes. Thayne's lips thinned.

"Thayne."

He moved his free hand to hers and squeezed. Hard. He'd had enough of this display at his expense. He watched her eyes widen a fraction before she looked down. He was afraid he'd be cracking bone before she released him. He was already turning when her next words stopped him.

"I thought you desired Lady Mary interred here."

"Those were my instructions," he answered.

"Well then, you owe me for allowing them."

Thayne swiveled back to face her, pulled to his full height, and crossed his arms. It didn't do what he wished. She didn't look intimidated. She looked even more interested. He watched her eyes drop to his chest before moving back to his face. She licked her lips and the fan moved faster, ruffling wisps of hair that sent more powder into the air. With all the torchlight she'd brought, the flecks were easy to see as they floated, some rising, and some settling back onto her. Thayne watched it all without expression.

"She should be interred in her husband's crypt. I can still have a message sent to him. In fact . . . I might have already sent one."

The words were clipped and short. Her voice had turned ugly and spiteful. This was familiar territory. As such it merited little more than a smirk.

"There's nae husband alive to read it," he informed her.

"You killed her husband?"

Thayne nodded.

"For abusing her?"

"Nae. I did it for sport."

Her gasp would've been satisfying, except it had all been done before. He'd deal first with her grasping ways; this obsession; the barely concealed lust for him—and only him. That would get answered with his refusal, and then he'd get veiled threats, anger, and then her hatred. He used to pretend ignorance. Now he used bluntness and shock. This was wasting time he needed for something else. He had a full, naked dunking in the loch to take, a change of attire to don, a sup to eat, and a wife to bed.

In that order.

"Wait!"

"Now what?"

Her voice had risen to near scream level, causing him to pivot involuntarily. He winced slightly at the flare through his buttock with the move.

"Have you seen Jamie . . . I mean His Grace?"

"Na' since this morn."

"Is he coming back this eve?"

Thayne sighed heavily, watched her look at how it had increased his chest while he did it and mentally added extra dunking time in the loch. It was the only way to feel clean.

"He dinna' say. I dinna' ask. Now, leave. I've things to see to."

"Like that wench you brought?"

Thayne sucked in one side of his cheek as he considered her. He'd been told her eyesight was failing. How she squinted to see her own needlework, adding to the lines all about her face. How she relied on her closest maid for her dressing, her cosmetics, and the perfection of her costume. He didn't think it a lie, which meant when Sean had carried Amalie, his wife had looked womanly even while using bad eyes. Or Amalie had looked womanly when they'd arrived, held in his arms and swathed in a blanket atop his horse. The duchess had probably already been informed before he reached the stables by one of the spies she paid.

"What wench?" he asked finally.

"The one you brought. And who is, even now, secreted away . . . deep in your chamber. That wench."

She might be attempting to make it sound sordid and brazen and evil. Her words caused the opposite to happen. Thayne swallowed the instant picture of Amalie bathing in her warmed water-filled tub before the fire while the light spread its glow over her woman-curves.

"Tell me I'm wrong."

The duchess had a taunting tone running the words.

"You're na' wrong."

The expression on her face created deeper lines throughout it while hollows formed in both cheeks. He decided failing eyesight would actually be a blessing to her each and every time she looked in a mirror.

"I doona' allow women in a bachelor's abode."

"Some of my servants are women," Thayne reminded her.

"She's a servant? Send her to me."

"Nae."

"You're telling me no?"

"I'm saying she's nae servant."

"Then she is to leave."

"Nae to that, as well," Thayne answered.

"You canna' tell me no. I'm the Duchess of MacGowan!"

"True."

"I demand you send her away."

"Nae."

"Send her away . . . immediately!"

Her voice was at screech level. The room echoed with it. She'd never lost control to this level before. Thayne wasn't the lone one wincing at the noise.

"If I refuse?" Thayne asked.

"I-I-I."

She was a Douglas. Used to getting her own way; if not by force then by threat of worse. Her clan was powerful, directly related to the Stewart line. If the Stewart still sat on the throne, she'd probably have a ready answer and a powerful army backing it up. Thayne watched her assimilate it. There wasn't much she could use anymore. Her lips went tight, forming harsher lines about her mouth. Those matched the ones in her forehead and about her eyes as she squinted. It also lengthened her nose, adding to its size. If she'd had any attractiveness, it was completely ruined.

"Well?" Thayne prompted.

"I'll take it up with . . . my husband."

"You do that."

"I'll not abide a harlot in my castle! If you insist on keeping her, I'll—"

"What makes her a harlot?" Thayne interrupted.

"What else could she be?"

He paused for the full effect; waited . . . and then told her. "She's my lady wife."

He watched her jaw drop. And then her eyes went wide, taking her face out of the wrinkled mess it had been in.

"Your—your—"

Thayne hadn't been so entertained in years. He grinned openly. And then he pursed his lips to say it slowly and distinctly. "Wife. Now, I truly am leaving. I've things to do. Good eve, Wynneth."

He rarely used her given name. It was too informal and he stayed clear of anything giving that impression. Right now, it felt perfect. His departure would have been, too, if he hadn't a slight limp all the way across the floor. Despite how he controlled it, tensed for it, and tightened the muscles to hold it, the wound was still too fresh and raw. He only hoped the pain wouldn't affect his performance later.

When bedding his wife.

Chapter 15

She didn't know what she'd expected, but it wasn't this. Well . . . some of it.

She'd expected a seemingly endless series of steps in the tower Sean entered at a jog. It was impersonal but odd-feeling to be carried by a stranger. He didn't look at her when he stopped as they reached the tower, huffed a few breaths, jounced her as if resettling her, and then started climbing countless wide stone steps that spiraled up into the darkness. She only toyed with asking him to set her down. Speaking to him seemed even more intimate. So she kept silent, chewed on her lip, and looked about her.

The wheel-stair was a spiral, the walls of huge blocked stone, although there were shields and tapestries and weapons displayed intermittently on the walls, interspersed with lit torches in their sconces. The inner walls were also hewn of stone, although it was white instead of the dark gray. She guessed that was for reflection purposes, from any daylight that might filter through the arrow slits, and from the torches.

The stairs felt endless, causing her to surmise Thayne's chamber must be located atop the Great Hall, but she hadn't been counting and had no idea how many Sean kept climbing. It didn't truly matter. She'd know soon enough. There was

an alcove every time the stairs ran along the outer barbican
wall of the castle. At each junction, there were long corridors
fanning out on either side, disappearing into torch-cast
gloom, as well as angled alcoves cut into what looked to be at
least twelve feet of rock. The alcoves were triangular in shape,
fanning from room size to just wide enough for two archers
to stand, each pointing their missiles in a differing direction.
There were furnishings in them as well. Rolled pallets against
walls. Tables. Benches. Some were occupied, too, by kilt-clad
MacGowan men sporting weaponry and nodding before turning back to the view. Amalie avoided meeting any glances
from anyone.

They passed two of those defense alcoves, with gloom-
filled corridors leading from them. She took another guess
that these were halls connecting the castle dwellings, built
alongside, or into the walls. They were dark. Impossible to
penetrate even if she tried and Sean kept climbing without
stopping. At the third one he stopped, huffed for more breaths
and resettled her again, cradling her legs atop his arms without causing the slightest reaction to being carried by a strange
male. Instinctively her body must know it wasn't Thayne.
That was worrisome, but no more than the instant thought of
what he'd promised would take place tonight.

Tonight!

The word sent a shiver through her. If Sean felt it he didn't
remark on it as he turned into a corridor, walked ten steps into
it before turning to his right. They'd reached a large doorway
leading back toward the center of the complex. It looked to be
the same twelve feet in thickness. Amalie guessed this could
be where the Norman Keep had been attached to the outer
wall as Thayne had told her. It could be directly above the
Great Hall, which would be at least three stories. She decided
to check when she had a chance by looking through an arrow
slit. The view was probably spectacular.

Enclosed within the arch was a wooden door of the same

immense size everything seemed to be. It was covered with deeply grooved carvings and hand rubbed with pigments of some kind to give it a color she'd never seen. It was attached to the rock walls with thick leather straps studded with iron bolts. The door had two handles smelted and fashioned of more iron right in the center of it. Sean gripped her with one arm in order to push against one of them.

The door opened not to a chamber, but into another immense hall, defined by torch-lit doorways and more branching halls. If the flooring was wood, it was of a thickness that prevented any pounding sound as Sean stepped along it, his steps sure and quiet. Amalie glanced upward to gauge height but was unable to see anything due to the lack of lighting. The entire place felt gloomy. Dark. Mysterious. Medieval. It was easy to see why the duchess preferred the newer building. Any woman would, with its long tall windows in symmetrical order, carved porticos, and columns and niche containing statuary. No doubt the interiors of that building were light and airy, and open. All of it in direct contrast to this behemoth.

The further they walked, the more movement she sensed happening about them. A glance showed why. The bare rock walls between doors had been covered with tapestries floating from somewhere in the gloom above all the way to the floor. They covered both sides. It was too dark and Sean was moving too quickly to note the colors or materials or artistry, but at some point a MacGowan had tried to make the keep livable. That helped assuage the cold hollow feeling growing in her belly. The one that she was studiously ignoring.

This hall ended at another set of double-doors, identical to the first, both to the wood and pigments, and the depth of the carving. That's where Sean stopped, set her on her feet where she wobbled slightly while he lifted a brass ring and dropped it. The sound thudded into silence.

"Where . . . are we?" She tried for a self-assured tone, but sounded small and insecure to her own ears. It probably didn't matter how one spoke and with what volume. Sound felt like it got swallowed up in the air of the hall. She heard the unmistakable sounds of a bolt being pulled from the other side.

"His Lordship's chambers."

Sean announced it and pushed at the center of the doors at the same time. There were two maid servants, in dark-colored gowns with white caps atop their heads, pulling at the doors as Sean pushed, making it a joint maneuver. Amalie didn't realize she had her breath held until losing it at the sheer majesty facing her.

At first glance the entire wall seemed to be glass. It took several stunned seconds to realize it was due to a sequence of windows, each in a series of three, supported by its own arch, that were designed into a semicircle spanning right out into space. There was a semicircular padded window seat delineating the bottoms of each trio of windows, while at either end she could see what appeared to be the battlements of a balcony. The Romanesque-designed arches framed stained glass that was fitted atop each window, creating a vision of color and design that trailed downward before giving way to clarity midway as it turned to glazed glass.

Amalie's jaw dropped and she didn't do a thing to prevent it. The design was stunning, the execution amazing, and the view beyond even more so.

It appeared Thayne's chamber must be on the top story of the keep, making it taller than the outer walls. That gave it enough height to view the lake they'd traveled around and there was a mountain on the far shore that the setting sun silhouetted into blackness. The last vestige of sunlight burnished the view and turned the lake into liquid, gold-tipped aqua. It looked fairy-like and absolutely unreal.

The impression didn't fade the longer she stood there, taking in the beauty and fantasy bordered by window frame. It was impossible to create something of such wonder and beauty, and yet, here it was . . . right before her eyes. In a Highland castle owned by a barbaric clan.

It was as unbelievable as it was incredible. She was transfixed and awed; rooted in place. And that was just wrong on every level. Amalie blinked her wits back into place and that just got her more immediate concerns . . . such as the bed.

Oh . . . sweet heaven!

There was a walled enclosure of some sort directly to her left, and beyond the wood partition she could see the bed. She tipped forward in order to look it over fully, and then had to suffer the blizzard of shivers that happened.

Thayne had a canopied bed that looked to own the entire left portion of the chamber, jutting out into the room atop its own pedestal. Amalie had never seen anything so impressive or massive. It looked carved by the same craftsmen as the doors, and must be over Thayne's height, but it was difficult to tell from standing in the doorway, three steps above the floor. The bed was flanked by large armoires, spreading out from it. The wall backing was more rock, but a good portion was covered over in thick panels of cloth in red, green, and black. The solid colors were embroidered with gold thread and attached high to the wall by a shield-thing, before draping out to enshroud the bed. The entire thing radiated power and might. She gulped.

Tonight! And in that bed!

She didn't dare think on it. She wouldn't think on it. It was enough that she'd have to somehow stop him and find a good enough reason why.

Amalie stepped forward and tripped on the first plateau of steps. That gained her Sean's hand at her elbow and chuckles from the servants. She was grateful for the assistance before she shook it off. Otherwise, she might have fallen. Three steps dropped into the room, their shape echoing the semicircle of the windows. The steps might be rock hewn but it didn't really matter. All she knew was they were cold. Chill met her feet through her slipper soles and it didn't abate as she reached the floor. She could see it was highly polished wood. The sheen reflected not only both fires in the fireplaces to her right, but also the myriad torches burning from freestanding torch holders throughout the room. They'd placed rugs about, woven with the red, green, and black color scheme the MacGowan clan favored. They all seemed to be pointing into the room; marking pathways toward the windows, the fireplaces . . . the bed.

There was a seating arrangement around the closest fireplace on her right. The glow created welcoming warmth captured within an arrangement of two settees, three large chairs, and a table. Shadowed hulks of more armoires and some bureaus stood mutely, some against walls, others used for separation of space. The same craftsmen creating his doors and bed looked to have designed and constructed everything in the room. Or someone had gone to great care to make certain of the theme. Amalie walked across massive space to the first fireplace and trailed her hand along the top of a settee, then a chair, then atop the carved wood of another settee as she walked toward the end of the room. She'd never seen such space given over to just one chamber. It was fit for a king. Massive. Silent and foreboding. And vaguely threatening. The impression didn't fade as she walked slowly, keeping her attention on the right, which seemed safer. The walls above and about the fireplaces were covered with long heraldic-themed banners, shields, and more than one arrangement of weaponry she didn't recognize, while the space below had heavy carved wardrobes and couches spaced intermittently along it.

They'd progressed far with the bath. Two more maids, dressed identically to the others, were by the farthest fire, one tending to towels whose thickness could be evaluated by a glance, while the other stood before a carved screen placed behind a hip bath. Or what must be a hip bath, although it was built on the same lines as the rest of his household. Amalie guessed she'd probably be neck-deep once in it. She could see it was already half full, as firelight reflected from the water's surface.

She moved toward it, ignoring the entire left side of the room . . . and that bed.

"My lady?"

One of the servants who'd opened the door bustled past her and dropped a curtsey, stopping Amalie's progress as much with her action as the title. It was the first time Amalie actually heard it and registered what it meant. Her pulse rose along with her brows, but nobody knew of that. Nobody must ever know. She felt so out-of-sorts and odd. Small. Insignificant. Vulnerable. Weak.

The woman addressing her only added to the impression. She was robust-looking: large and healthy. She could probably heft the hip bath single-handedly. It wasn't impossible to imagine her wielding a battle-ax thing alongside her Highland man, in a fight against the hated English. It was entirely likely her ancestors had done so. Amalie quickly quashed the imaginings. If she accepted Thayne as her husband, then she had to accept being the lady of his keep. And that included instructing maids. Neither of which was happening if she looked to be cowering in fear of them. Amalie swallowed, heard her ears pop, and then tipped her head in reply.

"Would you be preferring the bath first? Or a bit of sup?"

"What is your . . . name?" Amalie paused before the last word to clear her throat. She had to get more control of her voice. She sounded like a frightened and insecure child.

"Maves."

The woman bobbed another curtsey. The other maid-servant reached her side and did the same.

"How long have you worked at the castle, Maves?"

"All my life, my lady."

My lady. The title came across her tongue so easily! Amalie's father wouldn't believe this. Neither would his household and any of her acquaintances.

"Who is this with you?" Amalie gestured to the other maid.

"Beth."

"Beth," Amalie repeated with another nod.

"And that there is Elinore. And beside her is Yvette."

The woman pointed toward the two like-dressed women near the tub. Thayne kept a French maid in his household? That was odd . . . considering the way he spoke of them. Amalie filled in the blanks. It was entirely likely the duchess had inserted the woman into his household without his knowledge or permission. He detested anything about the French, and it was clear Yvette returned the derision. It was evident even before the slight curtsey she gave. This woman wasn't friendly and she wasn't welcoming. From across the span of room Amalie felt and saw all of it, the pinched lips in a thin face, dark eyes, and blank look. The other three had open smiles, causing the other to look more dour and ill-tempered. All of which was going to see her dismissed the moment Amalie gained insight into the situation.

And authority over her household.

But before she could contemplate anything further, a knock came at the door and Sean opened them both, allowing a large, imposing MacGowan man to enter, leading more manservants in, all burdened with steaming buckets of water. She watched them troop across the chamber and pour water into her bath, putting so much steamed moisture in the air she could smell it. Sense it. Feel it. Her skin itched with days of travel grime covered by clothing of the same. She knew it would be heavenly.

"I'd . . . like to bathe first," Amalie finally replied.

"Excellent. Elinore! Adjust the screen."

The men left the chamber in the same silence they'd entered while the carved wooden screen was curved about the tub, creating a bit of privacy. Amalie had just taken a step in that direction when the tall lanky form of Thayne's man, Pellin, arrived, loaded with a platter of roasted meat, while another man followed at his heels with what looked and smelled like freshly baked bread and thick sliced cheese. Another brought a pot of stew, while the last carried a wine decanter and two thick glass goblets.

Amalie still stood at the first fireplace and its furniture enclosure, and she turned to watch them place the food on the table, arrange a table setting, and pour the wine. An entire day of little more than old, dry oat cakes made her belly rumble with hunger and her mouth water. Pellin bowed to her, touching a finger to his forehead as he did so, before leading his men back out, almost as silently as the others. Or the loud ringing in her ears was drowning all of it out. She watched Sean follow them out, pulling the doors shut behind him.

"I . . . think I'd rather eat first," Amalie remarked. Maves giggled, as did Beth and Elinore.

She was at the table and pulling out a chair before seeing her own unwashed hand reaching for the bread. Amalie grimaced. She wouldn't turn into a barely civilized barbarian like her husband. Not even if he starved her. She'd bathe first. She sighed and turned back to her bath.

"I've changed my mind. I'll bathe. But we'll make it quick."

Three of them bobbed and giggled and after thirty some-odd steps she reached the bath enclosure. The screened-off area captured the moisture and warmth and glow of the fireplace, making it immeasurably smaller and intimate. Almost safe-feeling. And then it got filled with energy and bustling women. The moment she reached it, Elinore reached up and unfastened the plaid cloaking her. Two of them clicked tongues over her appearance, although nobody said anything. It was Maves directing Amalie to a stool, bending her out over the bath water while Beth worked at her tangled braid. The woman was gentle and expert. Amalie could hardly feel fingers at work, until the fastenings of her gown slid open. She was just shrugging out of the sleeves when a knock came to the doors again, and Maves bid them enter.

Amalie peeked through cutwork in the screen while Sean directed three men bearing the governess's trunks to a spot beside the bed. The trunks looked tiny and ill-kempt and pathetic. Everyone had stopped to watch and wait until the men exited again and Sean did the same door closure. It was strangely comforting to know he stood on the other side of the door. Amalie didn't ponder why. She was just grateful.

And then Yvette went over to the trunks to unpack. Amalie almost stopped her, before realizing it didn't matter. She'd started this journey in the guise of governess and she had no choice but to see it through, regardless of personal sacrifice and where it took her. Besides, she already knew Miss Carsten's wardrobe was bound to gain the French woman's censure. Amalie didn't need to watch it. So, she turned away and tried not to let the thought of Yvette's spying bother her.

Then she forgot the woman's attitude and curiosity as the others motioned her to dunk her head into water that had been warmed just for her. She'd been right. It *was* absolute heaven.

Amalie contemplated the fire at length, sipping occasionally at her second goblet of wine, moving it to the lip of the tub before she dropped it. The glass was well-cut and highly polished, possibly of Venetian manufacture. She studied the firelight reflecting through the wine. This goblet was thick. Heavy. Nearly as much as her eyelids. It was just so easy to lean back against the tub rim and watch the fire. Feel the heat. Enjoy the effects of wine on an empty belly. She sighed.

Her mass of wet hair had been washed, towel-dried, combed through, re-plaited, and piled atop her head, held in place by a large ribbon while she soaked, cocooned in such warmth and luxury, she nearly cried at the emotion it evoked.

"My lady?"

Elinore and Maves moved into her field of vision, holding a large towel between them that had been hanging beside the fireplace, getting warmed. That reminded her. And damned her. She'd been so sure a Scot castle would be primitive, coarse, outdated, barbaric, and cold. Thayne probably deserved an apology, which was all well and good. He still wasn't getting one.

"Your sup awaits, my lady."

Amalie rose, once again gaining the same odd silence her nakedness had first wrought. She tried to ignore it but knew she blushed. She'd heard it all before from her maids at Ellincourt what seemed a lifetime ago. She was considered a pure beauty, as perfectly formed as a Grecian statue. At least that's what everyone spoke of. She'd lost weight due to her father's punishment and then the horrid experience of the journey, but she was still womanly, curved in all the right places, with a waist easily spanned by a man's hands. She didn't need corseting to fit the latest fashions.

Amalie stepped out of the water. She supposed if she had to be held prisoner in a Highland castle, she could have done much worse. The towel was thick. Warm. Both maids rubbed briskly until her skin glowed, and then Yvette held out one of Miss Carsten's gray-shaded robes. Amalie shook her head.

"Is there nothing else?" she asked.

"Nothing clean, madame."

Amalie sighed again. It felt sacrilegious to don a garment fit for the charity ward in such richly appointed chambers.

"Now, Yvette, you just step aside. His Lordship has all sorts of robes available. You just wait right there, my lady. And doona' concern yourself. I'll fetch one for you. His Lordship should've given us time to prepare proper. 'Tis clearly his fault. He dinna' give anyone warning afore taking a bride.

We'll find you something and I'll order the castle seamstress to visit on the morrow. She'll bring her materials and trimmings. You'll see. She'll have a wardrobe fashioned afore you can decide which colors and materials you like best. You just watch."

Amalie silently toasted Maves and her authoritative ways as the woman went right around Yvette in the direction of the bed area. Then Amalie tipped the goblet and finished off her glass. The castle stocked excellent wine, the match to any she'd consumed previously. Or better. It was probably French. She made a face at the empty goblet and then looked at the length of red, green, and black plaid Maves carried around the screen to her.

Amalie unwound the towel and within moments, was covered from chin to floor in such soft combed wool, it felt akin to silk. Warm silk. There was nothing else. No chemise, no belt, and nothing for her feet. Good thing the robe was large enough to encircle her twice, but that didn't help the fact she had to traverse a span of cold polished floor to reach her sup.

There was nothing else for it. Amalie gathered handfuls of the material and sprinted. The maids probably thought her a hoyden. No doubt they'd laugh or hold her in disdain to the other servants. She didn't care at the moment. She was too hungry.

The furniture wasn't just massive. They'd crafted it for giants. Amalie climbed up into a chair, and sat perched at the front of it before any of her maids reached her. Her toes didn't reach the floor, but she felt the chill rising from it before Beth helped her loop the robe up beneath her, making a lump of material to sit atop as well as covering and warming her feet. And then she faced a mountain of meat, bread, and cheese placed at her breast level. She'd need a couple of pillows for a boost if she ate here often, she decided, and then set to work on Pellin's feast.

It wasn't long before she finished, wiped her fingers on the delicately embroidered napkin beside her plate, and sighed in defeat. She couldn't hold another bite. She could barely keep her eyes open. Amalie scooted to the back of her chair, well within the encircling carved wood arms, propped her head on an arm and yawned. She heard the activity as the tub got drained bucket by bucket and then removed. She kept forcing eyelids open as unseen hands removed the feast from the table, leaving the wine decanter and the other glass. She had to stay awake. She couldn't talk sensibly to Thayne about their marriage, otherwise.

She should seek an annulment. She should. And before this farce went any further. They couldn't stay married. It wasn't possible. They were complete opposites. He was a Highland barbarian. She was a gently-reared English-woman. He expected obedience without argue, and she needed a mate who didn't resort to force. If only she didn't feel so wonderful . . . much too comfortable and warm. Perfect.

And then Thayne was there.

Chapter 16

"That chair's too big for you."

Amalie lifted her head and blinked. Thayne was wearing another kilt affair, although this one was in a brighter hue. Or something. Beneath it he wore a broadcloth shirt, with a cascade of ruffles down the front. He'd pulled his hair back into a queue that still looked wet, if the shine was an indicator. And he'd shaved. Her heart palpitated unreasonably and fully.

"'Tis almost too large for me."

"Why . . . did you craft it . . . then?"

Her voice had a little girl stammer to it. Amalie grimaced as she scooted to the edge of the chair and then dropped to the floor, her toes flinching at the chill. The fire had been banked behind her, making it colder than before. It was also dark. She hadn't noted that. She did now. What torches had been lit were out, all except the doorway and the far side of the room. Over by his bed. They'd created an oasis of light with candles. Highlighting. Beckoning. Amalie gulped and slid along the table from him.

"I had large forebears. One of the MacGowan chieftains needed chairs that size to prevent them breaking. Where are you going?"

He'd gestured to the rest of the chairs before reacting to her shuffle around the table.

"You . . . shouldn't be here."

He grinned. Her heart flinched, then surged, then retracted with a painful beat. All of it suffusing her frame with flush. If she wasn't using one hand to hold her robe together and the other to lift the front, she'd have moved one to her chest.

"'Tis my chamber," Thayne remarked.

He'd no right to look like he did. No right to kidnap her and then keep her. He'd no right to own a chamber like this! Or be as wealthy and powerful as he was. And he had absolutely no right to withhold all of that information like he had!

"Then . . . *I* shouldn't be here."

The last word was lost in a mad dash to the door, crossing what felt like leagues of floor, leaping onto each step and crossing it, and then she was at the big wooden doors. Amalie dropped the robe to alternately push and then pull at the handles without effect. She might as well try and move trees. She was forced to stop and look at why. He had the double doors blocked with a bolt across them the width of a body but easily three times as long. Or perhaps four. Amalie narrowed her eyes and swiveled, although the robe at her ankles didn't make the move fully, creating a twist of plaid about her legs that defined the limbs. She'd fix it but she needed her other hand to hold the robe about her and all her attention on the man coming toward her. Thayne hadn't chased her. He didn't need to. He'd locked her in. He had a slight limp to every other step as he came toward her. She started speaking before he reached the bottom of the stairs.

"You locked me in!"

"We're both in," he remarked.

"But . . . how can you lift such a bolt?"

He smirked slightly. "It slides."

Amalie looked over her shoulder and grit her teeth. Stupid.

She'd been aroused from a near-sleep existence and hadn't been thinking. And now, she'd lost her chance.

"There's naught outside this room for you, lass. Save my brother. Is that what you want?"

She gave an involuntary shiver. "All I want . . . is . . . freedom." She knew it wasn't true as she said it. But he'd never know.

"Too late."

"No, it's not. We haven't—" She couldn't say the word but he knew what it was.

"You should've kept your mouth closed, then."

"What? When?"

"Must we go over all this again? Now?"

Amalie raised her chin to look at him and suffered through a full blush as her heart reacted. That couldn't be helped. Nor could the rapid pants for breath she made. She told herself it was due to her exertion and then forced the belief in it. They had two torches lit on either side of the door, and candelabra on each step. Lighting everything easily. Making it impossible to avoid eye contact with him. They were at an exact level, because she was three steps above him. But he wasn't close. The width of his three steps separated them.

"I've informed all of your position in my household. You're the chatelaine. You're granted control of the keys to the buttery, armory, and treasury. You're to receive additional allowance for your needs."

"I don't want it."

"You doona' want an allowance?"

His eyes flicked to how the wool was failing at its job of covering her. She watched him do it. Then he licked his lips, making her rock in place and stumble. That was before he took a step onto the lowest plateau, narrowing the distance between them and forcing her to look up to keep contact with his eyes.

"I don't want any of it."

"Too bad. And much too late."

"Now . . . wait! We don't have to do this. You-you-you . . . have a seaport! You said you d-d-did." He'd moved another step closer, gotten taller, and Amalie's stutter showed the effect.

"Aye," he replied.

"I can catch a ship! I can disappear!"

"We truly do have to go over this again, doona' we?"

"Don't . . . come any closer!"

She released the hold on the material at her throat to stave him off. His approach was more dangerous. The hand she put out to stop him would've come into contact with solid male except he stopped a hairsbreadth distance from her and sent sparks instead. She watched her own hand tremble with the sensation, despite willing it to cease. Nothing was working. And when he took a huge gulp of air, moving his chest even closer, the solid flick of lightning tingle got even worse.

"Lass." He breathed the air out, cleared his throat, and looked slightly discomfited. And that just made her heart pulse again. "I've claimed you. Afore God and man. I gave my word."

"I'll never tell," she whispered.

"You canna' stop your word, once given."

"You can put out more word. Tell them I . . . died."

"You want me to lie? Be just like my brother, Jamie?"

"No," Amalie whispered.

"Good. Because I'll na' stoop to that. You should na', either."

"You can . . . let me go. Get an annulment. The babe is safe. You're safe. There's no need to continue this farce."

"You're truly na' going to keep your word?" he asked.

Amalie narrowed her eyes, hoping it showed disdain. It probably failed and didn't mute much of his impact, either. "I was forced to say it. It was life or death. Or worse. You know that. You were there."

"That's na' the word I refer to," he replied.

She went pink. And then all the way to red. She knew exactly what he was referring to, now. "But that was also forced! As the better alternative!"

"Have you finished this argue?" he asked.

"Argue? I haven't shown argue yet."

"Then what? Fear?"

"I don't fear you." The breathless tone gave that lie away. As did the full tremble of her body.

"I can understand maidenly fear. But 'tis rather late. And senseless. Had we na' been interrupted, we'd have been fully man and wife already. Two nights past. At the hut."

Unfair. The man was totally unfair. She hoped it showed in her face.

"That makes this entire thing senseless. Aside of which, if you make me chase you, we'll have a powerful long night. And a painful one. For both of us."

Amalie gasped and watched his glance flick to her revealed cleavage before moving back. The lighting was also unfair, as it reflected off dark lashes as he blinked. And then a large rush of noise tamped her ears, muting his next words.

"I'm failing to speak the right words, I think."

"There are no . . . right words."

He licked his lips and leaned forward, pushing against her outstretched arm and forcing her to accept the weight. And then he just stayed there, balanced against her palm, his face hovering above her. Threatening. Promising. Sending trill after trill of goose flesh shooting down both arms and centering in the most horrid spot. At each breast tip.

"I'm forgetting the best part."

His whisper was light and sent with breath that ruffled the wisps of hair at her forehead. That sent shivers racing down her back to her feet, and then right back up her legs to join those making pinpricks of her nipples.

"You're fain bonny. Womanly. I've na' forgotten the hut . . . if you ken my meaning."

Her cry echoed to the ceiling as she moved, ducking around his side and racing back toward the table, where it was safer. Solid. And dark, so she wouldn't see so much of him while she tried to speak sensibly.

"You truly plan on making me chase you?"

His voice was a growl, and accompanied by a more pronounced limp as he advanced toward where Amalie was keeping the table between them.

"Yes. I mean no," she replied.

"Yea or nae. Which is it?"

He'd reached the table. She didn't know he'd grabbed the candelabra until he plunked it down atop the wooden surface and looked across it at her. There was something sinister about how the light shadowed and defined every portion of him. The firm jaw. Lengthy eyelashes. Set lips. Broad shoulders. Narrow hips. It was totally sinister. And so completely unfair.

"Well?" he prompted.

"I . . . don't plan on making you do anything."

"Then cease running. I've a hip that nears fire-ache when I move it. You break open my wound and I'll na' be as gentle as I planned."

"That's your fault."

"How so?"

"You're chasing me."

Thayne shook his head. "I doona' ken your words."

"If you'd cease chasing me, you wouldn't have to worry over whether your wound opened or not."

"And if you'd honor your word, I'd na' have to chase."

"My word. Your word. It's all just talk. Nobody will know."

He sighed heavily. Due to the amount of light he'd brought,

it was exceptionally visual and stunning and tongue-tying. Amalie gave her own sigh but kept it silent. Where it belonged.

"I'll know. Now, come here."

"No."

"You disavow your word and now disobey your husband?"

"Only in your opinion."

"In any man's opinion!"

"Not a woman's. She'd understand."

He put his hands on his hips, stood taller somehow, and narrowed his cheeks and eyes to glare at her. All of it put perfect definition to the size and strength of his frame. And the handsomeness of his face.

"How can you do this, Thayne? You don't even want me!"

"Trust me, lass. I want you."

"What of . . . love?" Her voice caught. She pulled her lower lip into her mouth but that hadn't stopped it.

"Who said aught of love?"

Amalie was eternally grateful she hadn't said anything of the emotion as anger pumped through his voice. She was terrified that she already loved him, even knowing how foolish that would be. She didn't need a potent reminder he looked ready to give about it. Her heart reacted to it, pounding mightily and sending the rush of water sound through her ears again. She only wished it blocked his next words.

"Love's nothing more than a woman's weapon. Used to enthrall a man. Keep him humbled and subservient. Obliged to pander to her every wish. It's akin to slavery."

"No, it's not," she replied.

Thayne studied her from across the table, tipping his head slightly. He didn't say anything for so long her heart had time to return to a regular rhythm while the water sound in her ears faded, making everything perfectly focused and clear.

"You saying something with these words?"

"No." *Yes.*

"Good. Now, cease this and come around the table."

Amalie shook her head.

"Doona' make me fetch you. You'll na' appreciate it."

"Nobody's making you do anything, Thayne. Nobody."

"Fair enough."

He nodded, and without giving any warning launched fully across the table, enwrapping her before knocking a chair aside with the fall. They landed hard, Thayne taking the brunt of it on his noninjured side. It still must've hurt. Amalie could tell by the groan from between his lips before the ropes of belly against hers tightened with his next move.

"Damn you, wife!"

He shoved to his feet, keeping her plastered to him with an arm resembling iron. He was favoring his entire right side, using that leg for the move and then balance, while dragging his left leg. He snarled at her, before tossing her over his shoulder as if she weighed little, while an arm stayed cocked about her waist. Amalie kicked and gained his other arm about her ankles. She didn't know why she fought. She knew she'd lose. She had at the inn. She lost just as easily now. It didn't seem to hamper him much as he walked toward the haven of light about his bed, using a more pronounced limp than before. And he was speaking through clenched teeth the entire time.

"I ask her to assist me . . . she disobeys. I doona' want an argue . . . but that's all she does! I beg her na' to make me chase her. What does she do? Ignores it! She does na' obey the least thing! Blast you, wife! And your bonny frame!"

She bounced on the mattress once before facing his entire weight as he launched atop her, shoving her into the softness with his body weight and something more. Something indefinable. Potent. Inescapable. Amalie opened her mouth to gain air and got his lips, instead, dragging kisses from her with the sweetness of his tongue.

"Ah, lass. Lass."

He crooned it to her amid motions that sapped her energy

as well as her will. It was her hands dragging through his hair, pulling it loose from the tie. Hers clutching at his back, digging her nails about muscle that rippled and flexed as if for her delectation and enjoyment.

"I wanted this different. Your first time to be . . . soft. Gentle."

He lifted onto his right side, plying his lips across her jawline to her ear, and sending rivulets of shivers from the spot all over her. Making her thrill to it. Every bit of her: nipples, thighs, her nether region. Amalie bucked slightly up and into him as he stayed in place, sucking gently on the skin beneath an ear, toyed along her ribs. Up her side, going infinitely close to a breast. . . .

And then he grabbed at the material of her robe and shoved it down, at the same time lifting his head, moving to her breast, and Amalie gaped in shock as he lowered his mouth to her and suckled, staying latched despite her lunges to unfasten him. Realms of feeling wove about her, brought into being by the sensations at her breast, and then it softened, turning to something resembling idolatry as he lavished attention to her nipple before moving across to the other one.

Her moans accompanied and urged him, as did the handful of hair she gripped, holding him to her and bucking ceaselessly against him as he brought her other breast to the same plethora of satisfaction as the first. But it wasn't enough. Everything on her knew it. Thayne went further above her, lifting onto one arm in order to peel the robe apart, sending his gaze where she ached for touch and his breath where she needed fingers. Everything on her knew it.

"Thayne . . ."

His name was an echo of softness, whispered into the air as his fingers slid along her thighs, between them, sending shivers flying from his fingertips that hadn't a hope of containment. Amalie lunged up at him, sinuously sliding all along the fabric of kilt covering his groin, thighs, hips. Her hands moved lower along his back, defining a buttock . . . feeling him tense.

She roamed her hands to the front, and connected with such strength and rigidity and size, her entire being flinched, going to a shock of stiffness while her wide eyes were caught and held by his.

"Aye, lass. You ken my need now? Feel my want? And soon . . ."

Fingers touched right at her core, minutely tipping her onto a precipice of wonder, and then he cupped a hand fully about her, lifting her at the same time he shoved between her legs. Amalie was held in place, hovering between fantasy and illusion, caught by realms of wonder sparked with intensity. Volition. Sensory primal need. Want. Ache. She rocked beneath his fingers as they endlessly toyed at her, granting her thrill and forcing her to absorb it. Climb toward it. Ache for it. Her breath followed in small gasps of endurance as she worked for it. Strove for it. Hungered for it . . .

Wonder split the air, sending warmth gushing from where his fingers forced the reaction, and then he lifted her, sliding his maleness over and over along her until she pounded at his back with vexation. And then he arched his hips, shoving her down at the same time, the entire time impaling her on complete and total agony with each increasingly deep lunge he made.

Amalie screamed, sending the cry of pain to the top of the canopy and still further as Thayne continued his assault, pushing time and again into quivering rawness nobody had warned her of. The canopy above blurred with unshed tears, and Amalie screamed again.

Thayne caught the second one with his kiss, holding her agonized cry in the caverns of his mouth, while her entire body tried to escape. Deny. Rebut. He was sending fire where he promised and pain exactly as he'd warned. And he wasn't finished. Grunts filled the chamber, put in place with each of his continuing thrusts, pushing continually into her with ever increasing movements. Jarring her. Bouncing her. Punishing her. Owning her.

Making her absorb and take whatever he gave. As if branding her.

Tears slid from her open and unseeing eyes and more took their place, despite how often she blinked. And then he moved his mouth to her ear, nuzzled the spot just below it and whispered.

"Ah . . . love. That's it. Right there. Ah, love. Right . . . there."

Thayne didn't know what he called her, he couldn't. But Amalie heard it. Her heart heard it, too, sending pulse beats of emotion throughout her frame that chased away pain and replaced it with sensation and feeling and visceral amazement. And Thayne was orchestrating it with every continual move; filling her over again and again with massive thickness, heat, and strength. He'd arched his back and lifted her loins to gain perfect collusion. Fitting exactly where he wanted. Holding her and making her take every bit of him. Again. And again. And more. Moving to a rhythm only he heard.

And then something changed.

Amalie felt a vague stirring at the edge of her consciousness. The feeling ran from where he was alternately filling and then releasing her, to flit outward with lightning bursts. It ran her limbs. Sparked off her heart. Hammered into her senses. Tracked along her belly. Filled her throat. Imbued her center. Again. And again. His motions got harsher, blending with the cacophony of sound in her ears, making a clash of noise that had nothing melodic about it. It was solid pleasure and it was toying with her.

Thayne instinctively knew, too.

Both his hands slammed into the mattress beside her ribs, gaining him a fulcrum to lift above her in order to arch more fully into her, gaining better access and motion. Amalie didn't need instruction. Her legs latched onto the material bunched about his hips, the new position allowing her free range to meet each of his thrusts with one of her own. His eyes opened and bored into hers, claiming her with aqua-shaded beauty no man should wield so easily and with such effect. If this was love, she was fully owned by it. Thunderstruck. Completely.

The emotion shifted with Thayne's increased thrusts. A sheen covered him, imbuing his skin with moisture that had his broadcloth shirt plastered to him, making it difficult to gain and keep a handhold anywhere on him. Amalie settled with running her hands all about him . . . his arms, back, shoulders, learning the musculature, defining the sinew and striation of muscle, moving to his chest and holding her palms flat against him for a time. But it wasn't enough. She shoved against him, before moving her hands all over, up and down and crosswise, earning a snap of friction through both palms and her finger pads, while staying enthralled by the feel of cloth-covered strength.

"Lass. That's it. That's . . ."

He lowered his head as his motions got fiercer. Stronger. All-encompassing and brutal. Heavy and large, with alternating inward and then outward lunges, each breath accompanied by a groan. Stronger. Harder. Faster. Leveraging and giving and sending her soaring, until the world whirled all about her, turning into a kaleidoscope of candlelight-glistened view that had Thayne at its core. Amalie felt it. Ground her hips against his and welcomed the flare of fire followed by the spark of liquid pleasure. Again. Over and over until her entire sphere felt suspended in the agony of effort. And then she felt absolute crushing wonder overtaking her. It gushed over her, seeming to obliterate her very bones before it captured her, filling her experience with such perfect, complete bliss she thought she'd died.

Amalie's mouth opened for a long, silent scream as she

came fully off the mattress and into his arms in an arc of supreme ecstasy, experiencing wave after wave of bliss as it tore through her. Filled her. Flooded her. Owned her and forced her to accept it. Forever.

Her antics seemed to unleash something in Thayne. His body turned into a beast of wildness, pummeling at her again and again, gaining her another taste of the sensation, before he altered it, going insanely stiff and immobile. Amalie held to him as he lifted his entire torso into a slant of seemingly agonized, nonrhythmic twinges that emanated from where they were joined. She couldn't move. She didn't want to. She watched as everything about him pulsed and shimmied and trembled over and over, matching the sobbed breaths he sent all over her.

And then he stopped, poised for several heartbeats of time, where he didn't breathe, he didn't do more than tremble, his eyes scrunched shut and looking the perfect image of agony-tainted ecstasy. And then he fell, denting the mattress beside her with his weight, and tossing her slightly before she rolled onto her side right next to him.

"Oh . . . lass. Oh . . . my."

His whisper held something more than amazement. There was an awestruck tone. Amalie turned her head toward him. He cocked open an eye and then the other. She couldn't prevent the tremor that flew her. Nor could she hide it. She didn't even try.

"Lass?"

He licked at lips that looked swollen. Blinked with lashes any woman would envy. Pushed air in and out with heavy breaths from a supremely muscled chest. The man was perfect. If she'd thought him handsome before it was a mistake. Right now, blessed by flickering candlelight, he was pure male beauty. He resonated it.

"Yes?"

Her voice was missing. Amalie swallowed around soreness

brought on by screaming. Or perhaps it had been sucking for breath her body craved and couldn't gain fast enough.

"Just . . . lass."

"Oh."

Where they'd been joined was still jumping and pinging with sensation, although he seemed oblivious to it. He was on his uninjured right side and running his free hand over her hip . . . to the back of her thigh and then back up, following the dip of her waist and to the side of her breast, issuing shockwaves of sensation from the slightly scratchy feel of his palm and fingers the entire way.

"That was—well. It was—"

His voice ended again, but his brows drew into a frown. It matched the narrowing of his eyes as he looked across and down at her. Her body thudded with the exact plunge of her heart. She swore she felt it drop and swallowed hard against it.

"Y-yes?"

"'Twas enough to break open my wound. That's what."

Chapter 17

"If you'd fetch my sporran . . . I'd be obliged."

Amalie didn't know if her body would work at first. Her belly had tremors running it, while everywhere else seemed to be jumping with sensation. Worse was the sticky and raw and moist feeling at her apex. She sat, leaning on both arms and looked out into semi-darkness. Thayne rolled onto his front away from her. He was groaning as he did it.

"Sporran?"

"Whiskey. I need . . . whiskey."

"You do?" Amalie slanted a glance at him before shying away. It was much too soon for intimate words; too embarrassing. Especially after what they'd just done and the warm glow that still suffused her body.

"'Tis a balm."

"For what?"

"Pain." He was still talking to the covers on the opposite side of him.

"You're in pain?" Amalie asked.

He nodded.

"Good."

He rolled his head and looked at her. "Good?"

"That makes us even."

A smile tipped his lips. Her heart pinged in reply. She'd barely begun to silently berate the unfairness of that before he spoke again.

"It could na' be helped. You had a maiden wall . . . and I'm na' a small man. It will na' hurt again. Promise."

"Again?"

"Next time there'll be nae pain. You'll feel satisfaction."

"Next . . . time?"

"You've my word. Satisfaction."

"But—you got what you wanted." She tried to make the words defiant, but failed.

"Did I leave you wanting? Is that it?"

"I. . . . Uh. . . ." *Wanting?*

"I've na' had this complaint afore. I may have gone too fast, although I thought different. Listen, lass. Listen well. If you're unsatisfied you're to speak up. Na' hold it against me. I'm na' selfish and I'm nae brute."

"Un . . . satisfied?" Her voice dropped on the last syllable.

"Did you achieve pleasure? That's what I'm asking."

Amalie gulped, moved her glance away before returning it; sweated with the blush, and then decided to just ignore his question.

"Didn't you . . . ask for whiskey?"

"Aye."

His smile broadened. Her heart skipped. He was so handsome. It was especially noticeable with the candlelit gesture containing warmth she didn't dare test. It was so inequitable and unfair. Everything was.

"Where is it?"

"Dresser."

He pointed with his far arm out into the room, toward the area about the fireplace where she'd had her bath. Amalie looked. There were several dressers and armoires in the vicinity.

"Nae. Wait. Window."

He moved his arm toward the window seat, where a bundle of plaid and glint of weapon rested. Amalie scooted from the dented area of mattress beside him and over to the side of the bed, pulling on the robe as she went.

"I'll need . . . my robe."

She was at the edge, looking at the drop. She only wore the robe sleeve while the drape shadowed the rest of her. She had an arm before her breasts as he regarded her. Then he grimaced. She watched him do a push-up into the mattress, lifting him while she yanked at cloth. It didn't work. His arms trembled and he dropped back onto his face in the mattress.

"I'll na' look," he offered.

"I can't cross this chamber . . . naked." Her voice held shock. Mortification.

"'Tis but a span of floor."

"Then you cross it."

"Don a shirt. In the drawer."

"Which one?"

"Any."

The word was whispered to the mattress, not her. It was more devastating that way. Amalie took a deep breath, jumped down, and lost the robe for covering. She did gain chill all over her body, not just from the exposure, but from how it seeped up from the soles of her feet. This wasn't fair, either. Her legs even trembled. The dresser beside his bed held more than shirts, but the third drawer gave them up. Amalie had one tossed over her head before starting across his floor. She buttoned the placket as she walked. This shirt was fashioned of thinly woven linen and reached past her knees, making it fairly modest. She had it fastened before she reached the windows, grabbed up the sporran thing and turned back. She wasn't bringing his knives or his claymore or whatever else he had. If he wanted weaponry, he could fetch it. She raced back.

He'd lied. He'd looked.

His expression told her of it as he turned his head, following her progress. He forestalled her with a wink.

"Hand me the sporran."

He held one arm out, reached for his flask, pulled the plug, and twisted further to take a healthy gulp, before holding it back out to her.

"I don't drink whiskey," she informed him.

He smiled, but lost it with another grimace as he shoved the plug back in and dropped the flask on the covers between them.

"'Tis na' for drinking."

"What?"

"I've opened my wound. I need you to pour whiskey on it. I may need it burned again, as well."

"No. Oh no. And another no. I . . . can't."

"You any good at sewing?"

She was very good at gagging. And shivering with reaction. She demonstrated both as he watched.

"Have you na' treated a man afore?" He asked it with an impatient tone.

"I've never even seen a man . . . before."

"You still have na'. You had your eyes shut. And I'm full clothed. Still."

"Thayne—I . . ." Her voice stopped.

"Come back up. I need your help."

"Please no."

"Direct me then. I'll do it. You bring any linens?"

"N-no."

"Fetch some."

He put his face into the pillows and reached back to peel the material away, revealing the side view of a thickly muscled rump; much larger than hers. Firmer. And tanned-looking, which was shocking. Amalie nearly sighed in feminine appreciation. That was even more shocking, as well as being ridiculous. She shoved the impulse aside, and then she was rifling drawers again, grabbing up items before he moved again. It was simple to step up onto the plateau but everything got complicated as she eyed a wicked looking wound. The flesh was blackish all about the edges and swollen with purple-red. It was coated with blood, too. He'd *ridden* a horse with that? Amalie's eyes went wide.

"How does it look?"

Amalie licked her bottom lip before sucking it into her mouth. She moved her eyes to his. "Painful."

"I never even felt it, lass."

Amalie darted her eyes to the wall behind him, where several more candles flickered in their holders. She moved her gaze to include the windows to the right, where the bed reflected back at her due to the curve of it. It was better to face the coverlet at her hip.

"Where did my sporran go?"

His voice was as grim as his expression. Amalie pushed his flask to where his hand was searching. "Don't you have . . . men for this?"

"Na' tonight. I gave orders."

He was fumbling with the stopper, revealing his shake. Amalie climbed up onto the mattress before he got it opened.

"What kind of orders?"

"Leave us undisturbed. All night."

"Oh."

He dribbled liquid as he moved the flask. Amalie automatically grabbed up linens to follow. Then he was pouring whiskey onto his wound, going taut with what had to be agony, and filling the enclosure with groans and curses. Amalie touched minutely to his wound before shoving a bundle of material fully onto him and holding it there. He wasn't paying attention. He was drinking again. As soon as a pinprick of blood showed through, she put a fresh one on, and a third one, and then a fourth atop it.

"How . . . bad is it?" His voice was raw and angered sounding.

"Don't look to me. I'm not checking," she replied, trying for a flippant tone but failing.

He snorted and started a coughing fit, and that made a ripple of movement go through the flesh she was perched atop. Amalie pressed harder, going to her knees to keep the linen in place while she watched for blood seepage.

"If it's bad, they'll na' believe our story."

"Story?"

"The bedding is probably bloodied."

"You have a wound," Amalie replied.

"Had this been our wedding night this cover would be pulled and displayed. Proudly. Atop yonder tower." He pointed behind him at the windows again.

"That's . . . vulgar. Uncivilized. Uncouth. And . . . wrong."

"It's still done."

"Exactly as I just said."

"You argue without reason. And little in fact. My grandparents consummated their union with forty sworn witnesses to the event. Right in here."

"Wit . . . nesses?" Her voice sounded as faint as she felt.

"How else can the clan assure legitimate MacGowan offspring?"

"The normal way."

"And how is that?"

Thayne lifted to his elbows and swiveled his head to look back at her, making him undulate beneath her hands. That sent tingling all through her fingers and up her arms. Amalie nearly moved from him before catching it.

"They wait for the birth."

"Bairns are oft-times early . . . leading to questions and issues. Legitimacy. Right to succession."

"Like . . . Mary's baby?" she asked.

She was surprised at her own daring. She truly was. She

watched with baited breath as he stayed silent and still, the only sign it bothered him was the slightness of each breath. Then, he relaxed, easing back onto the mattress.

"Mary's na' a subject we'll be discussing. You ken?"

"What do you want to discuss, then?"

"I want sleep, lass. And a fresh cover. When you're about snuffing candles, you'd best look for another cover for the bed. And a good spot to hide this one."

"Why?"

He sighed heavily, moving his frame and that moved hers. That started tingles through both arms again. Amalie frowned at the sensation before forcing it aside.

"I have to repeat everything to you. Everything. I need a fresh one because this coverlet is bloodied and ill-used. I doona' wish them taking it on the morrow."

Amalie's frown deepened. "I have to repeat my words, too. You've a wound. Wounds bleed." She shuddered but stopped the gagging reflex.

"You've a stubborn streak with no ear open for a listen. They've na' heard of any wound. I doona' go about shouting of wounds because that equates with weakness. Only a choice few of my Honor Guard ken the extent of this. All anyone notes is I've arrived with a new bride. Without warning. Tradition dictates a show of purity, and I doona' believe there's a Scotsman alive who can best a herd of clanswomen intent on tradition."

"But . . . we claim a child."

"Which is exactly why we have to hide the cover."

"Why can't I follow what you're saying?"

"If I want Mary's wee one to stay here and be brought up by me, I have to continue the story of her being mine. And yours. That's why we have to keep the secret. Forever. You ken?"

"We don't have to let them in."

"Sooner or later, we'll be for leaving this chamber. And they'll be a-waiting. Like wolves to a kill. Trust me."

"This . . . is barbaric."

"Doona' tell me it's na' practiced by the Sassenach."

"It's not."

"I doona' believe it. The Stewart king just lost the throne due to it."

"No, and no. You're woefully ill-informed. And it didn't *just* happen. Nearly two years ago he abdicated and fled to France. It had nothing to do with his queen's failure to get witnesses to a consummation, but at a birth."

"Same sort of issue."

"No . . . it's not. The queen is well past childbearing age, and then she compounds it by failing to get witnesses to the birth? A royal birth with no witnesses? Where are your wits? There had to be a reason. If the queen birthed a legitimate heir, why wasn't there a witness?"

"The Sassenach wrong us again. And you argue. This is the issue."

"No. The issue is that Scots are hardheaded and harder-hearted."

He sighed again, moving her up and down with it, while all the same reaction went through her.

"You should waste less time on your argue and more with your duties."

"What duties?"

"You see? I wasted breath earlier. Listen this time. You need to find a replacement coverlet for this one. Look in the wardrobe. Get one that's embroidered in heraldic theme as replacement. 'Tis odd, wife. Look here. We dinna' even get to the sheets. You're fain impatient."

"*I'm* impatient?" Her lips set and then she saw the wink he gave her.

"Then, there's this wound of mine. You've got to check for seepage. Then you've candles to see gutted. All of that afore

I let you back into my bed. And mayhap allow you to sleep."
He stopped and yawned.

"Mayhap?"

"You argue without reason. I'm na' immune."

"To what?"

"You see? Another argue."

"You're avoiding an answer."

"Verra well. You. I'm na' immune to you. Prancing about
while wearing my thinnest shirt. Showing off perfect
woman curves since the light behind you cuts right through
it. That's what."

Amalie lifted her hands from him, crossed her arms to
cover her breasts and looked at him unblinkingly. She
couldn't do anything about the flush that reached her hairline.

"'Tis easy to see why Dunn-Fyne wanted you. And my
brother. As well as any other man we come across. A man
would have to be blind. I'd best seek sleep instead. I'm going
to need it. Why are you still here?"

"I . . ." She didn't know what the reply would have been.

"Sleep. I need sleep. Na' another love bout with her. If I
shut my eyes and ignore her, 'twill be easier to gain. I'll just
lie here. Ignore her. . . ."

"Thayne MacGowan."

"What?"

"You speak as if I'm not here. It's not the first time, either."

"You're na' supposed to be. You're to be snuffing candles.
Finding covers. Staying out of my sight so I can sleep. I've
men to work in the morn out on the list. Unless MacKennah
visits and makes a true fight of it."

"No. You can't fight. Not with that." She pointed to the
wad of linens atop him.

"Oh . . . I'll work. And I'll fight."

"What? Why?"

"I have to."

"That's just stupid. And ill-bred. And barbaric."

"I already ken what you think of me, love. You needn't use such honeyed words."

Love. He said it again and just like that stole her voice. Amalie opened her mouth to answer but nothing came out. She shut it again.

"I have to get to the list and give a show. For a bit. I canna' afford other, lass. Na' with Jamie as our laird. Never could."

"You're not weak. You're healing. And that takes time."

"Hints of weakness mean the same. You ken? Up here, a man is judged on strength. Power. Might. Victories. Against his enemies, and sometimes against his own kin. He needs sleep for all of it. Perhaps you could save further words of pester for the morrow."

"Words . . . of pester?"

He moved onto his side, supporting himself on a crooked arm. "Go. Blow out the candles first. I've changed my mind. I look forward to watching you."

"You can blow them out yourself, then."

"I'm trying to re-knit my wound here."

"So you can rip it open again on the morrow? That's your argument?"

"I doona' argue. I leave that to the wenches of the world. Now, go. Or bear the consequences of disobedience."

"Consequences?"

"Do you wish to ken what they are?"

She didn't need to guess. With the way he moved his eyebrows up and down, it was apparent. "You're uncivilized and uncouth, MacGowan. And crude."

"Next thing you'll be averring is your towels were na' warmed enough."

"Just because you've got servants and luxury at your fingertips, doesn't mean you're civilized."

"You're halfway to consequences already, wife. Just keep arguing. I'm near awake again. All of me."

Amalie gasped. "I've half a mind to leave you to bleed to death."

"I'm in nae danger of that."

"How do you know?"

In answer he pulled at his shirt, taking it from where it was tucked beneath the kilt, over the top of his head before tossing it over the far side of the bed. His antics mussed loose hair with the motion and gave her a perfect view of undulating muscle and brawn. She knew exactly what that described now, too.

"See that?" He pointed to a scar the length and width of her finger on the top of his left shoulder.

"Y-y-yes."

"That's where the arrow exited."

"Someone shot an arrow at you?" Shock colored her voice, closing her throat. It was accompanied by the hand she moved there.

"Na' just at me. Through me. Plenty of blood loss. Nearly died. This became my comparison."

"Of what?"

"Blood loss. What it feels like. How much I can sustain. I was foolish that time. I dinna' burn the wound closed."

Amalie moved her hand to her mouth.

"And see this one here?" He lifted his torso to point at another jagged scar near his waist.

"I don't want to know."

"Why?"

"I'm going to be ill."

"You'd be of little use on a battlefield."

"Please?"

He moved his eyes to hers and smiled. "Doona' fret so. I'm rarely challenged anymore. These scars are signs of why. I doona' lose. You're wed to a MacGowan laird now. You're safe."

"I thought . . . Jamie was the laird."

"I'm his heir."

"Why? Not enough blood on the sheets following his marriage consummation?" She asked it snidely and immediately regretted it.

"Jamie canna' sire a bairn strong enough to live. His offspring all die. Within hours of birth. Even the bastards."

"Oh, sweet Lord. His poor wife."

"Doona' waste pity on that woman."

"But . . . it has to pain her."

"One has to have a heart first, love."

Blast and damn him! Amalie's eyes swelled with moisture at the words and the endearment again. She held her breath and watched him shimmer before her. She didn't dare blink. It would make the emotion real and send tears onto her cheeks.

"You'll learn that soon enough. Once you're gowned proper for presentation. You should go now. Blow out the candles. Fetch another cover."

"Don't watch me."

"She's perched like a naked goddess beside me and tells me na' to watch. Me. Verra funny, lass. Verra."

"I'm not naked."

"You're near full consequences. Near. You want to try for full?"

Amalie put both palms on the bed and pushed toward the side, dropped down to the platform, and stumbled backward without taking her eyes from him. He was at a crawl as she backed across the room, stumbling over a thick rug before turning to run. She'd handle the candles at the table first. There was a long-handled snuffer along the base of his candelabra. She had them out before moving to the plateau of steps and the door. She didn't note how ridiculous it would be trying to tamp the torch flames with the little cupped snuffer in her hand. And she couldn't reach them. Even on tiptoe.

"You would try the patience of a saint, wife. I swear."

She squealed as arms wrapped about her, hoisted her atop his shoulder, where he slapped a hand to her rump to hold her there while limping back toward his bed. The snuffer dropped with a clatter midway across the floor. It didn't matter. She didn't even think of anything resembling a struggle.

Chapter 18

Word from MacKennah came at midday, although pipers had been alluding to it since daybreak, amid the beat of drums and sounds of steel hitting steel. Word came with Jamie's entrance into the inner bailey and to the stables, leading more horses than he'd started with. At least four mounts had women clinging to the manes, while one of them carried a trussed MacKennah clansman, limbs roped beneath the stallion's belly in a picture of defeat. Thayne gave his brother a glance before putting his third opponent down in as many bouts, and then he put his arms wide to the sky, yelling of victory amid clapping and calling and the drum beats that came with each win.

It was better than sobbing the agony.

It was due to Sean that Thayne made a showing at all. The man took one look at Thayne's limp and gave orders; first to escorting him to the alcove of the Chieftain room, next to fetching Angus the castle healer, getting full sporrans of whiskey for drinking and cleaning, and then keeping anyone from witnessing the wound as it got stitched together, every prick on inflamed flesh drawing an unmanly tear he refused to shed. Angus then put some sort of salve atop it before giving Thayne the worst indignity of his life. He'd been strapped with bands of linen to hold the wound together. Like a babe. And all without one word of comment or snicker from Sean Blair. The man's loyalty reminded Thayne of the reason he'd chosen him as his closest Honor Guardsman.

Handling seepage was one part. Nothing could be done for pain except to endure it and turn it to fury and rage and hate. That was easiest out on the list, where the emotion changed Thayne into a beast of lightning reflexes, throat-scraping yells, and brutish blows. The outcome of any challenge was a certainty as soon as it was given. Three clansmen tried it. All three went down. Thayne's wound throbbed ceaselessly throughout the battles, adding to the noise and pulse beats filling his frame until the entire field became not a snow-flecked mud wash, but a haze of red and black.

Then Jamie rode into the grounds, bringing a MacKennah man and several unkempt, weeping wenches. Thayne finished his victory yell and glared across the span of ground at his brother. His brother turned aside as Thayne sheathed his sword and held it in place against his leg. He was at a trot before he cleared the list, dodging chunks of churned-up sod, jumping slick spots, and shoving past Jamie's Honor Guard, before finally stopping, gathering breath. Then he pulled himself to his full height and shouted.

"Jamie MacGowan!" His cry startled more than one of them. The women all turned to him, looking through strands of unkempt hair they didn't push out of the way. A look showed why. Their hands were tied to their saddles.

"Hold there, Bairn Brother . . . while I cancel this thirst."

"You've taken a MacKennah!"

Jamie drank until he needed breath. Pulled the sporran from his mouth and dragged a filthy sleeve across it. "I've taken more than one MacKennah."

"You took MacKennah lasses?"

"Sharp eyes, Thayne. As always."

Jamie tipped his head back and drank again, draining the

flask before gesturing for another. He did the same wiping motion across his mouth when he'd finished.

"MacGowan clan does na' war with women, Jamie. Send them back."

"Nae."

"We doona' take issue with women!" Thayne tried again, in a stricter tone.

"We do now."

"Jamie, see sense. MacKennah will have nae choice but to take in kind! He'll be seizing our women!"

"Mayhap he'll have bonnier bairns to his clan that way. He should be thanking me." Jamie guffawed at his own joke. Nobody else did.

"I'll say this but once more, James MacGowan. Send them back. Now."

"Nae."

His brother was being his most obstinate, and had liquid courage from drink to back him. He licked his lips and looked across at Thayne. And then grinned as if the drink had already affected him.

"You canna' do this. You'll restart the feud."

"You already did that. I'm but playing my part. Ah!"

Thayne watched his brother grab for another sporran and gulp more whiskey down. He waited. Battling on the list had stopped. The pipers and drums were silenced. The very air seemed taut and poised as they all waited.

"You should na' rail at me, Thayne. You should be congrat—congrat—bah! My own tongue fails me."

"Any clansman can rape and reive! You fool!"

"Say that again . . . and we'll be meeting."

"Call it." Thayne pulled his claymore quickly, holding the scabbard with his left hand while yanking out his sword, hearing the satisfactory sound of steel sliding against steel. He lifted the tip of it toward his brother.

His brother ignored him for the most part and patted one

of the lasses' legs before leaning against her. The woman pulled back from him with what looked to be displeasure and disgust. It was probably echoed on Thayne's face. Then his brother belched. Thayne took a step closer to his brother, lifting the sword tip as he went. Jamie's Honor Guard moved back, stepping into the rank of horses and making an enclosure about the brothers.

"Why should I? I'm the . . . laird. By right . . . of birth. You're little save my bairn brother . . . who went and restarted a feud. With our neighbor."

"MacKennah would na' have rejoined a feud. Na' without a meeting! He's sensible. He'd listen."

"You should have wed his accursed daughter."

"That's a-tween MacKennah and me. And the bargaining table."

Jamie swayed backward and took another swig of drink from his sporran, as if there wasn't a sword pointing toward his gullet and everyone watching with held breath. He was smiling when he brought his head back down, and then patting the woman's leg again in a familiar gesture. Of ownership. Thayne hoped it didn't mean what it looked like.

"You . . . should send word to bargain, then."

"I did. We're awaiting word back."

"I'd say you just got it, Thayne lad."

Jamie threw his head back and laughed before moving to drink more whiskey. Thayne stepped in, tucking the blade back behind him, while swinging a closed left fist. His move knocked the sporran from Jamie's hand. Both brothers ignored where it landed in stable mud, adding liquid to the muck.

Jamie stood statue-still, his hand still suspended near his mouth. "You meaning something with that?"

"I'm accepting your challenge, Jamie. You and me. Yonder list. No weapons. Now. Right now."

Thayne lowered his chin, narrowed his eyes, and set his

teeth; ignored the thud of ache hitting the backs of his eyes through his skull. He watched as Jamie shuffled from foot to foot. And then smiled weakly. Ingratiatingly.

"Oh come now, bairn . . . brother. Cease this. 'Tis nae time . . . for battle. We've cele—cele—a fest. We've a fest to put on!"

"You ignore a challenge?"

Jamie grinned with a watery look to his gaze that hinted at his inebriated state. Already. Thayne dropped his shoulders. He couldn't battle a drunkard. It would be a slaughter.

"Just look. See what I've brought."

"I see women. And one clansman. You battle against women now. Is that what you do?"

"MacKennah's the one . . . at fault. Na' me."

His brother was stopping, licking his lips and scrunching his face to make the words. He was also swaying where he stood, one arm still atop the woman's thigh. All marks of drink. Debauchery. Dissipation.

"You disgrace the name of MacGowan," Thayne said softly and stepped back.

"He . . . started it! This swine . . . and his cursed family. They tried . . . to ambush us. And steal my goats."

"What goats?"

"The ones I've brought to . . . roast for sup."

"You stole goats, too?"

"Spare me . . . words. I'll explain all . . . once I've some sleep and another whiskey! Lawrence! More whiskey! And see this carcass . . . to the dungeons!"

Jamie kicked at the man's tied hands, almost falling with lack of balance and earning a groan from his victim. It wasn't the only injury the man suffered. Thayne looked at MacPherson and got a nod. They'd see the man to a chamber and then Angus would be called.

Jamie wove his way across the span to his palace, his Honor Guard about him. Thayne watched him. They all did.

220 *Jackie Ivie*

For differing reasons. Thayne's heart grew as heavy as his sword. He sheathed it without looking.

He'd failed. On his deathbed, his father got a promise from Thayne. He'd been entrusted with hiding Jamie's perfidies. Ensuring the MacGowan name stayed noble. Dignified. Valiant. Feared and revered. Sacrosanct.

He sighed heavily and turned his attention to the problem of the MacKennah women, ordered Sean to see them to his lady wife's side. He needed a drink. But first he needed a good swim out into the loch. He was at a jog before reaching water.

Castle Gowan didn't have a castle seamstress. It had a full sewing klatch of them led by a vocal and particular and exacting one named Millicent. That woman commanded an army of thirty-seven women, all engrossed in sewing, cutting, measuring, fitting, talking and laughing, and sipping tea amidst piles of fabrics, trimmings and patterns of the latest fashions. The last was a complete surprise. Fashions had changed considerably since the "Protectorship" had ended and Charles II, the "Merry Monarch" had assumed the throne. Collars had fallen from their face-framing days, if they appeared at all. Nowadays, a large wide neckline was the vogue, skimming the tops of the shoulders and framing the bosom with a straight-cut bodice. There was rarely more than a strip of lace or ruffle attached. This created a perfect décolletage for jewels or simple enhancement of a woman's assets. Sleeves were now tight and reached only to the elbow. Depending on occasion, laces and ribbons could be attached to drape the lower arms. The front bodice piece was boned and heavily decorated, held tight and flat to the body and ending at a point just below the hips. That's where the skirts were attached, worked up with heavy satins and velvets, tucked and gathered to softly drape about the lower limbs, flaring out on both sides to give any woman a tiny waist and elegant carriage as she walked.

Amalie had possessed gowns near to what they were now designing, although hers were crafted in white and extremely pale colors due to her unwed status. These seamstresses were designing and sewing morning gowns, day gowns, night-gowns, and evening attire in all sorts of hues and shades that made Amalie's breath catch more than once. It didn't seem possible, and yet according to Millicent, fabrics and patterns arrived monthly to Gowen Village, which was the name of their seaport. The particular patterns they were using now arrived not two weeks prior, as well as most of the fabrics and trims. It was spoken aloud how lucky Amalie was the duchess hadn't time to inventory this particular shipment yet. And how they'd been rushed to get all of it to the keep, and waited in an antechamber for the summons before dawn even broke.

Amalie was alone when her new maids had awakened her, shuffling about the room, stoking the fire and pouring water in her ewer. That was followed by a visit from the baby and her wet-nurse. She was then served breakfast of thick browned toast and honey, presented on a silver platter, with a mug of light ale. After that Amalie had been herded behind the screen while manservant after manservant entered, bringing so many sewing items the entire area by the table was given over to it. And on their heels was this battalion of women. Practiced. Ordered. Regimented. And efficient. The entire operation seemed to be.

Throughout the day, food arrived at specified intervals. Late afternoon saw tea being served with hot fresh scones dripping with butter. The activity all about Amalie didn't even pause. Designing and cutting and chatting went on, while the amount of items hanging from the dressing area grew more numerous and more colorful. She studiously ignored the four women earnestly working to get her presentation dress ready for the evening. She and Thayne were required to attend sup at The Palazzo, with the duke and duchess and the rest of the MacGowan family and retainers. In full evening wear.

Amalie closed her eyes on that information and on the instant thought of what her husband would look like dressed for court presentation. In satin knee breeches, stockings, powdered hair, and a long coat, fit exactly to his frame. He was so handsome it didn't seem possible to enhance it. Amalie shivered pleasantly before opening her eyes and returning to idleness and feeling out-of-sorts.

She'd never been around so many women. Every structure save the bed seemed to hold at least two of them industriously plying needles and chatting. It was obvious Castle Gowan wasn't remotely barbaric. It looked well-run and efficient. And orderly. And refined. Civilized.

It was a shame their menfolk had to ruin it.

Amalie looked out over the loch from a perch on the huge curve of window seat. She had her legs tucked up beneath her while leaning against the glass. She was bone weary. And sore. And thrilling occasionally with the memory. Every time she closed her eyes, she got reminded of why. It was better to stay awake and alert but she'd tired of standing. Getting fitted. Checked. Fawned over. Made to pirouette in place while women were asked opinions and gave them even when they weren't asked. She was bored with watching and listening and then trying to ignore them. She had an ache in her head and hollowness radiating with every beat of her heart. She couldn't explain it. She'd been surrounded by humanity all day and yet never felt so alone. Out of place. Odd.

Her interest peaked as bodies came into her field of vision, churning water while they swam far beneath her. Amalie caught her breath at their daring. The water had to be cold. Deep. Wild. She could see the wind-driven water cresting, making white-tipped waves. Swimming in such conditions was foolhardy. And brave.

That was probably her husband out in front. She narrowed

her eyes and tried to see through glazed glass and several stories above the water. Her emotion told her as her heart pumped mightily, suffusing her with blush. She knew it was Thayne. Instinctively and positively. All of that was bad. Troublesome. Annoying. Vexing. And several other worrisome words she didn't dare bring to mind. She didn't know why she bothered listing them. She told herself she didn't care. It didn't mean anything to her what Thayne MacGowan did. Or who he did it with. Or how dangerous it was . . .

Amalie's breath caught again and she gripped her hands together just below her throat as the leader's head went beneath waves. She lost him for a bit before he surfaced farther away than before. Stupid man! Stupid, annoying, frustrating, arrogant man! She told herself she didn't care if he drowned and then worked at believing it.

A huge thump on the door echoed through the chamber, prompting Elinore to open it. That maid had taken up a position atop the highest step, making certain none entered if Amalie was in dishabille, while opening and closing the door for the delivery of a repast, or more ribbon, another sewing knife, or a bolt of material they'd just remembered and hadn't thought to bring from the storehouse, deep in the bowels of the keep.

The new arrival was Thayne's man, Sean. He was attired in a mud-speckled kilt, with mussed hair and a sheen of sweat on him that wouldn't be easy to gain against the chill of late spring in the air. Amalie knew the temperature, since she'd been told of it when first accosted by so many in her chamber. Then, she'd just wanted out into the open air. When she'd argued, Maves had opened the door leading to her balcony and demonstrated exactly how much chill and wet it was outside. Amalie hadn't taken more than a few moments gazing out over the parapet before slinking back inside, defeated.

Directly behind Sean was a grouping of four women who'd seen better times, or something. Sean stood at the top step plateau looking for her. Amalie knew it instinctively and stood to wave. Then Elinore led him through the maze of sewing supplies, toward her, looking like a creature from another planet amid such feminine frippery. The entire time she was conscious of how the thick plaid robe covered every inch of her, yet still managed to leave her feeling undressed and wanton, as if Thayne's lovemaking was emblazoned somewhere on her for everyone to read.

He stopped just before her and bowed. Amalie returned it with a tip of her head. She noted how the room had silenced behind him and then looked at the women. Three looked at the floor. One, with dark red hair trailing in ringlets over her shoulders and a dirt handprint smudging her cheek gave Amalie a look that didn't disguise hatred very well.

"His Lordship requested you to assist him with these ladies."

"He did?"

"They've just arrived at the castle."

"Forcefully?" she asked.

He nodded.

"By . . . His Lordship?"

"The laird. He wished them to visit."

"Just . . . visit?"

"Aye."

"Are they visiting long?"

"Until the MacKennah arrives and arranges release."

"Release?"

He nodded.

"I see." She did, too. Even without the woman's hatred and the others' complete silence. "I believe you should leave now, Sean."

"My lady?"

"You've other duties of greater import and you're disrupting my staff."

His eyebrows rose and what could be a flush started at his lower jaw. "Thayne told me to—"

"I'll handle these ladies. You truly need to return to your duty of protecting my husband . . . from drowning."

"He's swimming."

"Looks more like he's fighting waves."

"His Lordship's the best swimmer in the clan, my lady. He's half fish."

"Not that I've noticed," Amalie answered, to a lot of giggling all around them.

"The lasses might need guarding." He was definitely flushed now.

"I thought they were . . . visiting."

He set his lips.

"Oh leave. We'll not need you again."

He debated arguing further, then bowed. He swiveled without lifting his feet and started across the floor. They all watched him. His exit was given silence until he reached the door. That's when the giggles broke out. It bothered Sean, if the way he dipped his head and the haste he ran the steps was an indicator. Amalie turned her attention to her new charges. The redhead was still glaring. One of the others met her glance before looking hastily back at the floor.

"Maves?"

"My lady?" Her maid bowed.

"Have we enough rooms to see these ladies to separate ones?"

"Please doona' separate us, my lady!" One of the girls, for she looked little older than that spoke up, tears filling her eyes.

"You wish to share a room?" Amalie asked it gently.

"Aye."

"I'll order you baths and fresh clothing. You still wish to share rooms?"

"We're . . . sisters, my lady."

"Sisters?"

Now Amalie set her lips. It was obvious something needed

to be done about Jamie. It was just as obvious her husband
wasn't effective at it. It was an unheard breech of the justice
system and needed to be stopped. She'd heard of magistrates
even up here in the wilds of the Highlands. She had to find a
way to reach one. There had to be some way to stop Jamie
MacGowan from rampaging about the countryside raping and
ravishing and spreading disease. Acting like a hedonistic
despot with his own personal kingdom. Her frown deepened.
From what she'd seen of Scotland, that's exactly what Jamie
thought he was.

She'd been wrong. The castle wasn't civilized at all. It just
carried the veneer of it until one peeked beneath the edges.

"Maves?" Her voice warbled. Amalie had to stop and clear
her throat and hope she sounded more convincing and authoritative. "Would you see these girls to a chamber, order
warmed water sent up, and find clothing that will suit them?"

"Of course, my lady. With your pardon, I'll just go and
speak with the head housekeeper of it. If you'll follow me,
misses?"

She had a head housekeeper? That was another surprise
coating of respectability and civility to life here in this castle.
It was a pure shame it was false. Amalie backed to the
window seat again before another fitting was called for,
tucked her legs back beneath her, and went back to watching
the dark spots of swimmers in the loch.

Chapter 19

Amalie checked again in the huge mirrors brought from the dressing alcove so she could stand and look at herself. She looked perfect. Even the infant seemed to agree as she cooed from her cradle. Absolutely perfect. From the top of her head to the tips of the satin slippers peeking from beneath her hem, those women had created perfection. Once, not so long ago, she'd been gowned much like this, her hair painstakingly curled and pinned into a mass at the crown of her head, with four ringlets left to lie atop her shoulders and skim her back. Just two months ago, at her debutante ball. She'd been excited. Thrilled. Breathless with anticipation. But that had been before finding out the promise of her hand had already been given to an imbecile. Then came their meeting, while he fumbled and drooled and looked at her with watery blue eyes, making her quiver with dislike and something else.

Fear.

Amalie shuddered. She wouldn't think on it.

The image reflecting back at her picked out the reddish highlights in her hair. This style was the rage ever since the French Dauphin's mistress had created a passion for it.

Ladies at court were still required to cinch themselves into a sixteen-inch waist, but they were to leave their coiffure powder-free. Not so the face and shoulders. Those portions were liberally sprinkled if a lady had suffered sun exposure, a disfiguring bout with smallpox, or had a propensity toward sweaty shine. All court ladies were to possess unblemished white skin.

All of which came naturally for Amalie. She didn't even need the small patch at the edge of a dimple to prove it, although she felt it gave her a slight sophistication and allure. She wondered if Thayne would notice. And furthermore where he was.

The household of the duke and duchess dined late, as per the dictates of the French court. Amalie had been given a light repast hours ago, just after the chamber had been vacated by Millicent's army of seamstresses and all of their supplies. Amalie knew they'd repaired to the sewing chambers, somewhere in the bowels of this castle, alongside the storehouses and buttery.

Amalie had no choice but to accept what fate handed her. She was fully Thayne's wife now with little recourse other than take up the role of chatelaine he'd given her. She'd hoped he'd assist her in showing where everything was kept and how the buildings connected through the halls designed into the barbican walls, but she hadn't seen him. Had no contact with him. Nothing.

All she'd had were orders. To rest. Bathe. Get presentable for the fest. Amalie looked over at the baby and smiled, before approaching in a swish of rose-shaded satin to touch a tiny hand that immediately closed about hers. Such a sweet thing. And so fragile. Vulnerable. Beautiful. Amalie already loved her.

"My lady?"

It was Maves, hastening to the door to allow a retinue of Beth, and what might be a steward, attired in MacGowan colors that did little to hide an overly lean frame. Or maybe she was just comparing him to her new husband. Unfavorably. The latter held a velvet-wrapped tray in his arms.

"This is Beathan, my lady."

"Beathan." Amalie inclined her head. The man cleared his throat.

"His Lordship had this sent for you. From the treasury."

She watched him set the tray atop the large table, before bowing and then exiting, with a great show of stiff back and martial-cadenced footsteps. And then the resounding boom of her door closing added to it. She nearly giggled. She'd forgotten Thayne claimed a treasury. He'd given her control of it, as well, and that was just another room she'd have to search out in the depths of this castle. When she went exploring.

Amalie walked toward them, enjoying the swish of material against her lower limbs and ankles. Then she gasped as Maves lifted a tiara fashioned of silver with little pearls dangling from every intricately wrought flower. There was a necklace of the same design that Beth held. It was the perfect touch. And Thayne hadn't even seen her.

Amalie turned back to the mirror and held her breath as the tiara was placed atop her head, offsetting the dark tones of her hair. She was so glad she hadn't insisted on powdering it! The necklace was a bit of trouble, though. It had been crafted for a larger frame and didn't ride the crest of her breasts artfully. Instead, it settled with unerring accuracy right into the curve of cleavage they'd created with her new corset. She spread the chain across her shoulders but watched as the jewels settled right back, as if directing the gaze. Amalie sighed. It couldn't be helped. She was small and everything in this castle wasn't. Even in heels she probably wouldn't reach Thayne's shoulder.

"His Lordship's Honor Guard is waiting for you." It was Elinore with that information from the door.

"His Honor Guard? All of them?"

Elinore giggled. The others joined in. "Just four. They've been sent to escort you to His Lordship. I understand he's awaiting you in the Chieftain Rooms."

"Is . . . that normal?"

Maves smiled. "Women are rarely allowed in the Chieftain Room . . . nae. But as His Lordship's na' been wed afore, I doona' ken if 'tis normal or na'."

"Oh."

Amalie's voice caught in her throat and she knew she blushed. It wasn't said as a rebuke, but it felt like one. She ducked her head ostensibly to work at lifting her skirts artfully before following her maids to the chamber portal, crossing each step plateau, and walking through the width of stone archway that supported his door. And then she was facing four large men she'd never seen before, all attired in Highland wear. With the amount of cloth draped over their broad shoulders and a large feathered bonnet atop their heads, they looked even more immense. And critical. As if she had to first pass muster with them before they'd escort her.

It was a ridiculous notion and she didn't like the feeling but that didn't change it. She raised her chin to look each of them in the eye and waited. And got one grin followed by another before they turned and surrounded her. Amalie hoped they didn't intend to keep this stance the entire way down the wheel-stair, but that was a forlorn wish. The staircase was built wide. Moving with one man in front of her, one at each side, and one behind, presented no obstacle with spacing. They were regimented and took the steps in another cadence resembling a march. Amalie kept pace with one hand holding her skirts, and the other one keeping the necklace from bouncing while sounds of their steps got swallowed up by all the stone about. The only thing that suffered was her nerves.

* * *

What was keeping them?

Thayne reached the end of his raised platform and turned back the other way, ignoring the throb of his wound as the pace kept tempo with his worry. Anxiety. Bother. Apprehension. Potential embarrassment. Concern. He ran his hands along the handles of his skeans, tucking them more securely into his belt as if the last pivot he'd made had jarred them; checked the alignment of his sword against his side; flipped the plaid tartan band back over his shoulder with a rough gesture; readjusted the brooch holding it in place; took a deep breath that chafed against the red ribbon covered in medals and jewels that spliced his chest. The ribbon felt like more bondage atop his black doublet, which was tighter now than when it had been fashioned. That was his fault. Unlike his brother, Thayne fully adhered to the Highland creed that a man could only claim what he could hold. Such a standard required strength and practice and preparation. Continually and ever increasing. All of which broadened his chest, arms, and shoulders. With the exception of his *feileadh-breacan*, clothing rarely fit him properly within weeks of construction. Leaving him feeling constricted. Short of breath. Bound. Imprisoned. And that was before he factored in the starched shirt ruffles at his chin, choking him even though he hadn't bothered fastening the top button.

He'd combed and pulled his hair back to a queue that reached between his shoulder blades. It wasn't a concession to fashion. It made it easier to observe and react. He wasn't powdering it, and he wasn't adhering to any decree of wearing tight curls above both ears. He refused. He also refused to wear the frock coat, knee breeches, and satin stockings laid out earlier, as if the duchess actually thought he'd obey her edicts and wear frippery. Not in this lifetime. And not him. He needed his legs free and mobile, and his sword and skeans handy. If his wife found him uncivilized-looking and barbaric, it wouldn't be the first time. Aside of which, he doubted she'd ever seen correct court fashion and wouldn't be any sort of judge.

Thayne snarled at the shield facing him. That made it easier to start back across the platform toward it, not feeling the seam of his wound flex and stretch, nor seeing the plastered walls two stories in height, the hammer beam ceiling, nor the length of painting all along the roofline done by Valentine Jenkin just after he'd finished Stirling Castle. Beneath that, the MacGowans displayed every manner of banner and shield and weapon and tartan. Most taken in battle; some . . . just taken. It was an impressive room, the perfect backdrop for the MacGowan laird to receive his clan. Sitting in regal splendor in the chair set on this dais. The chair was carved from thick wood. Constructed for his largest forebear's dimensions, it was even large when Thayne sat in it. They'd set it back a bit to allow room to pace in front of it, from one end of the dais to the other.

This delay didn't bode well, and he knew it. He'd given orders to his staff. Sent every bit of feminine nonsense for her use, ordered them to see her dressed correctly . . . but nothing could be done about uncouth manners. Inelegant posture. Lack of training in court etiquette. His Honor Guardsmen had instructions. If she failed to be presentable, she'd be locked back into the chamber and given a late sup, while Thayne would attend the fest alone. Such an act would create more talk and probably more challenges he'd have to meet on the list, but he wasn't presenting her if she wasn't presentable.

All of which was his fault.

It was his mouth speaking the wedding vow, and now that he'd wed a superior servant—and an English one at that—he had no choice but to deal with the consequences. He hoped like hell the glimpses he'd had of charm and elegance in the past few days weren't his imagination.

He gritted his teeth again, spun, tamped down the instant flash of pain, and started back across the platform, listening to the echo of each step. He was alone but that was also his choice. He'd left five of his men in the vestibule beyond the doors. Waiting. Just as he was. Probably wondering at his actions, although no one knew the extent of Thayne's worry or how nervously he paced. It didn't seem possible. All day he'd been trying to banish the image of this woman in the place he'd envisioned always as belonging to Mary. His duchess. His wife. The mother of his children.

Thayne must be walking quicker, since he reached the ends of the platform sooner and sooner and that didn't do anything more than working on the list, swimming until he was exhausted, and then wrestling four of his men into submission had done. It didn't banish it. It didn't change it. It didn't keep the memory of last night at bay, either. He'd put another woman in Mary's place. In his bed. At his side. But he refused to put her in his heart. That was where Mary's memory was firmly ensconced. And just as firmly treasured.

But then there was last night . . . .

Thayne cursed aloud as he spun around for another walk to the end of the dais, his limp more noticeable. He'd bedded the woman and consummated their union. Honor dictated the act, but it should've been quick and abrupt. He shouldn't have enjoyed it as much. Nor done it the second time, making certain of her satisfaction with each thrust. Nor should his loins be bothering him all day for more of the same.

Thayne threw his head back and howled the disgust toward the rafters. The fading sound accompanied the doors at the end of this chamber opening, resounding heavily in waves toward him. Thayne brought his head down, took a deep breath, and turned it to watch his wife from over his shoulder. He hoped she wouldn't embarrass him too fully.

"The Lady MacGowan."

At first he couldn't see her over the heads of his Honor Guard. He caught a glint of silver from the tiara atop her head, brown-shaded curls of a lustrous volume, a span of light rose satin. They all stopped directly before the podium and parted, allowing her to step forward, hold her skirt out with an elegant hand and curtsey. She did it perfectly, with her head tipped slightly to the side, showing a wealth of curls, a glimpse of perfect bosom, and a hint of dimple.

Thayne's jaw dropped. His heart sent a whoosh of blood to the top of his head, and he backed two steps before catching it against the chair's arm. He very nearly fell into the seat and covered over the graceless act with a push back upright the moment his thighs touched wood.

"Good eve, my lord."

She'd lifted out of her curtsey and stood, so slight her head barely reached the bottom of his podium. Thayne walked toward her, the echo of each step showing the limp, and then he jumped down, coming out of his crouched landing with the slightest groan as tartan and ceremony accoutrements settled about him. Then he reached for her free hand in order to bow over the fan she held in it.

"Good . . . eve." His throat was suddenly parched. Thayne frowned slightly as he stood there, huffing the breath from his exertions or the experience of shock, and feeling a complete witless fool.

"Will I pass?" She tilted her head sideways a bit to look up at him.

"What?"

She giggled. His ears cursed him with noise matching his increased heart rate, and he barely caught the tremble of his hand before she felt it.

"This is a magnificent room."

She tipped her head up farther and looked about as if he could move his eyes and follow.

"What?" Thayne replied again.

"It fits you."

"It . . . does?" His voice was still croaked and showed little ability to form words. He was having a hard enough time breathing and sucking for moisture in his mouth and blinking. The woman was incredibly beautiful. Stunningly so. He was almost afraid to touch her. He tightened his fingers on hers without thinking.

"You. Dressed as you are . . . in Highland evening attire."

"Oh." Another one word comment came out of his mouth. His men started hiding grins and shuffling their feet.

"You're magnificent . . . but I suppose you already know that."

She may have thought she was whispering but the room had great acoustics. Her compliment went right to the rafters and started more than grins. He could hear chuckling. Thayne flushed; in front of God and her and nine of his Honor Guard. He swallowed and forced the reaction away. It didn't work but he wasn't surprised. Everything else he'd tried was failing.

"Are you sending me back to my room . . . or taking me with you?"

"What?" Thayne pulled himself to his full height and attempted to glare down at her. It didn't work and he didn't need her dimples as proof as she smiled to herself.

"It's painfully obvious."

"What is?"

"The decision you were making. Aside of which, I'm truly hungry."

"Decision?"

"Whether I'm attending with you. Or staying behind."

"Oh." Thayne cleared his throat and dropped his voice an octave. "You're attending."

She smiled fully. Dimpled. And took his heart. Just like that.

"Is it a long walk?"

Thayne had to do something before she realized the emotion hitting him squarely between the eyes, before it suffused through his entire frame. What he was feeling had no description. He was rocking in place without moving, thrilling with shivers without end, and wondering how he was supposed to hide it. He'd never felt this way. Ever. Not even Mary had engendered this sort of physical and emotional response. He moved his eyes from her and blinked at moisture until the double doors came back into focus. What had she asked? Walk? At the moment the walk across the floor looked enormous.

"W-w-walk?" He should have waited to ask it. Thayne grimaced at his voice and the stammer. Then he endured the tremble at the end. In this room all of it was obvious as the sound ended.

She giggled again. His men shuffled feet and grinned. He reddened proportionately.

"I was told we were attending sup at your brother's Renaissance Palace."

"Oh. Aye. We are." He had to get beyond one and two word sentences but couldn't imagine how.

"Then . . . shouldn't we be starting?"

Thayne made the mistake of moving his eyes back to hers. He lost his voice, and then his hearing with the duration and depth of the pulse beats in his ears. He might as well have a drummer at both sides pounding away at their stretched skins.

"What?"

"The sup. Won't we be late?"

"Sean?"

"The carriages are at the door, my lord. Per your orders."

"Carriages?"

His wife asked it so sweetly, tipping her head to one side and fluttering her lashes up at him, as if she didn't know the distress she caused him! Thayne pulled in a semi-ragged breath, licked his lips, and suffered the noise in his ears rising to a crescendo level.

"'Tis raining."

"Should I fetch a wrap?"

She trailed a hand across her skin just below her throat, touching perfect unblemished skin and shifting the necklace he'd sent to her. Thayne's eyes were hooked on how the off-white shaded pearls caressed and molded before the weight of the center jewel pulled them back into the shadow between her breasts. Thayne watched the flesh warm to a shade akin to the satin that got to touch it. And then the necklace got lifted slightly by a trill of goose flesh beneath the strands.

He tried to physically stop the surge of motion propelling him the one step between them, but didn't fully succeed. All he could do was turn his lurched movement into one that looked like he was ready to escort her by pulling her hand up and into his chest, putting her to one side, and then swiveling them toward the doors with an ungraceful motion. He covered it over by starting off, slowing his steps to accommodate two of hers while his Honor Guard dropped to their sides and rear. His steps got faster, taking her to a skip of movement before they reached the portal, and he didn't even feel any wound.

He couldn't wait to present her. She was lucky he didn't lift her in his arms and carry her.

Chapter 20

The Ducal residence exuded light, and noise, and the crush of humanity.

Amalie could see light streaming out into the castle ground, flicking off raindrops with the sheer volume of it as they approached. It hadn't taken but a few minutes to cross the ground in a coach and six, although the amount of work just getting their ride prepared for the trip seemed wasteful. She appreciated it as Thayne's men held covering over their heads from the top of the coach to the vestibule entry, keeping everything dry and in presentation shape, despite the rainfall.

The moment they entered the hall, it was clear why he'd gone to such pains. The reception room was ablaze in candlelight, coming from a dozen chandeliers hanging partway from the ceiling. The light was reflected off the white plastered ceilings, sending light down on the inhabitants, making it the exact opposite of the gloomy dark halls in Thayne's house. Carved wainscoting trimmed the walls, defining a line from the dark paneling on the bottom to where enormous paintings soared up into the ceiling. Amalie had seen paintings such as these. Ellincourt Manor claimed several of them from Italian masters, but the amount of them displayed here was awe-inspiring. Paintings were displayed adjunct to each other, atop each other, above the doorframes, and on nearly every available bit of wall, unless a sconce or window had already claimed the space. Paintings filled the entire room with color and beauty.

The room seemed filled with people, too, making it difficult to transverse. Amalie kept a hand on Thayne's arm as he progressed through the throng, his Honor Guard about him, carving an opening for them. The noise was hard to hear over, and then the duchess had added an orchestra to the fest, the notes filtering down from the minstrels' gallery where they played.

Manservants were everywhere, delineated by not only the small black hats atop their powdered wigs, but they all wore green jackets and white knee breeches and stockings that comprised their uniform. There wasn't one thing Scot about any of it.

And the duchess was dreadful.

The woman was standing under a wooden trellis that was laced throughout with a myriad of fresh blooms. The entire structure was vainly attempting to frame the Duchess of MacGowan with beauty. The duke wasn't anywhere in sight.

"Her Grace, the Duchess Wynneth MacGowan, kinswoman to Douglas Clan and the house of Stewart! Presenting Lord and Lady Thayne MacGowan!"

They got announced by another French-clothed fellow, using a volume that stopped most of the conversation. Amalie pulled out of her curtsey, keeping a hand on Thayne's forearm as the duchess looked at Thayne with an expression Amalie didn't want to decipher. And then the woman moved her attention to Amalie.

"So. You're the servant."

The duchess held a lorgnette to her thin nose to peer down at Amalie with one hand, while the other flicked at herself with a fan. The woman was overdressed, overpainted, wore enough perfume Amalie's nose twitched, and looked old enough to be Jamie's mother. Easily. Nothing alleviated her thinness, pale complexion, lack of beauty, and myriad lines running her skin. She was worse than dreadful. She was a caricature of the word.

"I'll na' abide insults to my lady wife, Wynneth."

Thayne's low-voiced reply conveyed the threat. His arm tightened into the consistency of an iron bar, as if reinforcing it. Amalie's fingers tingled atop it. That sort of reaction wasn't going to be helpful in a social gathering, of any kind and in any country; even here. Amalie glanced up at him. The duchess was making the stray hairs at his forehead move with the speed of her fanning and the proximity she'd achieved by stepping near him.

"I believe my former occupation is governess, your grace." Amalie relaxed her lips into a slight smile, attempting a shy demeanor. The duchess looked back down to her, but took another step closer to Thayne.

"You don't look old enough to leave a schoolroom, let alone teach in one."

"How right you are. It just seemed so much easier to escape the betrothal arranged for me by pretending to be a governess."

Thayne made a choking noise this time. Amalie studiously ignored it.

"You were . . . betrothed?"

"It was an arranged marriage to the Duke of Rutherford. He was imminently suitable. My father thought it a perfect union. Thank goodness Thayne came back when he did. I was quite running out of time."

"Your . . . father?"

"The Earl of Ellincourt. It's an ancient title, bestowed after the Battle of Agincourt. Surely you've heard of that, even in Scotland?"

"The Earl . . . of Ellincourt?"

The woman had lost some of her bravado and the ability to put sound in her words. She'd also backed up, taking her fanning with her. A look showed Thayne's hair ruffled. The rest of him wasn't in that condition. He'd stiffened into a statue of nonmovement, while his eyes were narrowed to slits. Amalie obviously couldn't expect much help from that quarter, but it didn't matter. This exchange of words was almost exactly what she'd playacted with Edmund, and she'd faced worse than a harridan with bitter words and features. The recent past was an excellent example. Amalie turned back to the duchess's look of total malice. The woman didn't understand prudence and tactical maneuvers.

"You . . . expect us to believe you're . . . a member of the peerage?"

"Your hearing is excellent, your grace. Congratulations."

Thayne might have found that amusing. His frame shifted slightly, and the restraint he'd placed on his arm slackened. He might even be smiling. Amalie didn't move her eyes from the duchess to check.

"You weren't waylaid on your way to employment at the Kennah Castle? You weren't forced to claim a foundling bairn? You didn't trick your way into the MacGowan clan by handfasting with my kinsman, Thayne, against his wishes?" Her voice warmed on the name. Now, it was Amalie's turn to stiffen.

Amalie trilled a little laugh. It sounded brittle and forced even to her ears. That wasn't good.

"You have a very vivid imagination, your grace. Or your spies aren't worth their coin."

"You're denying you're the governess Miss Carsten?" The voice had lost its warmth. As had the duchess's features. She looked carved from deeply grooved marble.

"It is a bit of a puzzle, I admit. I'm actually Lady Amalie Beatrice Evelyn Matilda Ellin. That's a lot of names, but I am the only daughter of the sixth Earl of Ellincourt. Actually, I'm the only surviving child of the earl. I only pretended to be a governess. It was an excellent disguise, wasn't it? I even think Thayne was fooled."

She watched the duchess and Thayne exchange a look above her head.

"I suppose you're claiming the child, too?"

"Baby Mary?"

That was risky. Thayne's immediate intake of air warned her, but he'd already proven he wasn't of any use in a social confrontation. She was on her own.

"You named the child . . . Mary?"

"I just call her that, your grace. She's not baptized, as of yet."

"Send the child to me. I'll foster her."

"I'm afraid that's not possible, your grace."

"I demand it."

"You can't wish to separate a child from her mother? And my husband wouldn't allow it. Thayne?"

Amalie looked up at him and squeezed his arm.

"I believe we've taken up enough of Her Grace's time. There are other guests to greet. Wynneth."

Thayne dipped his head in a semblance of a bow, before moving away, pulling Amalie with him with such speed, her slippers slid along the floor more than once. He didn't check his pace, and didn't stop for anyone in his way. They simply moved before he reached them. Further introductions were impossible, social pleasantries the same. Then he shoved aside a dark maroon drape and led her out onto a beautifully stone-worked balcony, with an overhang of more stone. He dropped her arm then as if she'd become vile. It felt cold and private, and vaguely sinister, especially in the dark and rain. Amalie rubbed at her upper arms for warmth and courage as she looked out at a courtyard too dark to see.

"Enjoy the view?" Thayne asked in a steely tone that matched the elements.

"I've seen better," Amalie replied.

"You ken why we're out here?"

"Creating gossip, I assume."

He stepped right up behind her, but didn't touch. He didn't have to. His size, force of breathing, and the heat emanating from him, all worked in concert to create something vastly different than the amorous man of last night, or the romantic one of just a quarter hour before. This one was solid menace. Amalie's shivering worsened.

"I do na' allow falsehoods into my life."

"You'll need to be more specific, I think." And she had to move away, or her tongue wasn't going to work. Amalie stepped closer to the stone balustrade, and considered gripping it for support, even with how it dripped with rainwater.

"Any falsehoods. Ever."

"You want her to take Baby Mary from us?"

"Her name is na' Mary."

"Then assign her a different one, but in the meanwhile she's Mary. I like it and it quite agrees with her."

He put something that could be words, cursing, or just a growl from between his teeth. Amalie gripped both hands to her arms and hugged herself.

"We are na' discussing the bairn, but your loose tongue."

"Define loose tongue."

"The one spouting falsehoods and innuendoes. That one."

"Very well, Thayne, I admit putting a few innuendoes into my words, but I had to do something. You weren't any help."

"And the falsehoods?"

"The only lie I told was about the baby. You're not going to get me to change that. I'll not give Baby Mary over without a fight. A large one."

"You? Fight?"

"Yes, me. I may not have any strength to shove a sword through the woman, but I've got a mind and a tongue, and I know how to use both. In the event you missed it."

"I'd na' allow her to take the bairn."

His voice warmed. Everything about him seemed to do so. Amalie didn't dare turn about to check. Love for Baby Mary's mother must be the reason, and that just hurt; much more than she wanted to consider or deal with. She had to get the emotion covered over first.

"Good."

The word limped out, but it was the best she could manage. Amalie licked at her lips and shuddered. Stupid man. She'd just gone through a taut experience with an enemy and then got chastised over it. Adding to that was a good dose of how little he cared. It was obvious. The whole of Thayne MacGowan seemed devoted to the memory of another woman. There wasn't much left over for Amalie.

"So. We'll return to discussing your other falsehoods."

"Thayne." Amalie turned, lifted her face to meet his eyes, and the gulp that happened hurt her throat. The man was still breath-stealing, sending messages that her body seemed primed and ready to hear. Amalie felt her heart stutter before resuming a heightened beat that sent heat where everything had been cold. And then he put his hands to his hips and tilted his head, looking amused. Or the weak light was lying. "I didn't tell any falsehoods. I really am the only daughter of the Earl of Ellincourt. We claim ties to the throne. I have a vast dowry."

"And I'm the Sultan of Constantinople."

Amalie's lips tightened. "Is it so hard to believe?"

"You forget, lass. I'm the one taking you from the posting house, the man binding and gagging you, assaulting you. None of which could have happened if you were a lady of the realm. You ken it as well as I."

"All of which shows I created an excellent disguise. Admit it, Thayne. You were fooled."

He sighed heavily, moving the mass of man and sending

warm heated breath all over her. "This is gaining us aught of value, and I've no desire for further argue."

"Well, at least we agree on one thing, although the other should be readily apparent."

"And what would that be?"

"The thickness of your skull."

He chuckled. "You are wicked amusing, wife, even if a tad quick with your tongue. I almost pity my brother this eve."

Every sensation changed to a solid numbness. "Your brother?"

"You're placed beside him for sup. 'Tis a placement of honor."

"Oh no. I refuse."

"You canna' refuse."

"Is that why you had me dressed like this, Thayne? To entice the monster again? Although, faith, I cannot see why you worry over his lusts here. The man probably gets more exercise running from his wife."

"If he touches you, I'll kill him."

Heat from that statement radiated through her; fully, completely, and overwhelmingly, cancelling out cold, rain. Dark. If she blinked just right, she could swear, there was light just about everywhere.

"I've given Gannett instruction. You'll come to nae harm. He'll be at your back."

"Why can't I sit beside you? It's not uncommon."

"I'll be given the place of honor beside the duchess."

Amalie couldn't help it. She giggled, and not just at the way he said it. "Sounds fascinating for you."

"I'd pitch the lot and haul you back to the keep, if it were up to me, wife. I want you to ken this."

"Then, why don't you?"

"Too much clan watching. Evaluating. Wagging tongues over it."

"Gossip? You worry over gossip now?"

"If keeping the laird of MacGowan's true nature hidden is worry over gossip, then aye. I do so."

"Then why did you bring me out here? No doubt they're all whispering over this little excursion to a secluded balcony."

He sighed. "They all ken our status as newlywed. They also note our attraction to each other. Why . . . I've heard it said I'm unable to take my eyes from you. Word is reaching the clan now over my haste to claim you, and the why of it."

"To save your skin?"

He grinned, revealing the shine of teeth. "'Twas mainly due to my besotted state, I hear. My betrothal contract got trumped the moment I met you . . . and fell in love. All ken a love match. Women of any ilk go all dewy-eyed and soft over such a thing. This little bit of time will simply add ballast to it."

"And here you just berated me for the telling of false-hoods. Thayne MacGowan. For shame."

He didn't seem to like that. The instant intake of breath accompanying the straightening of his back to his full height wasn't her only clue. He'd lost his smile, as well. And then he stepped close, put a finger beneath her chin and tilted her face up, and wrenched apart her world.

"Who says it's a lie, love?"

He shouldn't have said it.

The reality hit even before the words left his lips, and a split moment before her stunned look. He was in luck that a servant cleared his throat before parting the drape and inviting them back into the fete. He didn't know what her reaction would be. He still didn't, what felt like hours later, as the meal progressed, course by course; wine and ale flowing freely while conversation got louder and more jovial all about him. It was akin to attending a play. Watching, but not participating.

Jamie was vastly entertained by Amalie's wit, as was

Gannett behind her, if his recurrent grin was any indicator. Thayne wasn't. If he didn't know better, he'd swear he was suffering shock such as blood loss caused, or something closely related to it. Nothing had taste. Nothing had definition. Nothing had sound to it. Except his wife . . . the beauteous, false-tongued Amalie.

Sweet heaven! *He'd told her he loved her!*

And worse. It was true.

The duchess said something at his side. Again. It didn't really matter what the woman said or what she did. She'd been speaking and tapping at his arm, and attempting to garner his interest throughout the meal, with as much success as a stray hair might have. Thayne wasn't capable of paying attention to anything other than his wife. She was like a beacon of light in a morass of dark.

He'd *told* her he loved her?

He hadn't learned his lesson well enough with Mary? His declaration of love was the catalyst behind her marriage to Dunn-Fyne. She accepted his hand that same afternoon! Thayne had reeled with the betrayal, cursed her time and again, hidden his sobs over the heart-pains, and wondered why she hadn't loved him as much as he did her. The pain lasted for months, until it became anger . . . and finally, the acceptance.

And for the first time, he knew how wrong he'd been. On all accounts. Mary had loved him much more than he suspected. More than she could control. That's why she'd chosen an abusive man with a history of ill-treating his spouses. She'd sacrificed herself for clan honor. *His* clan honor. To make certain he wed with the MacKennah lass. To keep from starting a feud. Exactly what he'd been honor-bound to do. He gulped down his wine goblet, twisting his face at the vinegar aftertaste. Mary had done that and what had he done with such a gift?

He'd betrayed it.

Another laugh came from Jamie, and he lifted his tankard in a salute to Amalie, before winking over at Thayne. Thayne stiffened; shoved his chair out prior to standing, flexing his bandage-wrapped wound; moved to stand. Sean's hand on his shoulder stopped him. Brought him back to the present: the woman at his side, the over-rich dishes, the nondulling effects of wine. He'd do better changing to whiskey.

Chapter 21

Something was wrong. Amalie didn't know how, or why, but in the span of that horrid supper, Thayne seemed to have changed. It didn't seem possible, and yet, there it was. *He'd told her he loved her.* She'd been existing in a realm filled with bubbles, floating along on such a euphoric sensation because of his declaration . . . and now he'd turned morose. Silent. Brooding.

And he wouldn't meet her eyes.

The carriage ride that had seemed so short before now stretched interminably, while the thud sound of each heartbeat grew in her ears. Each breath echoed through her chest. She could swear she heard every flick of her eyelashes. He probably should have dimmed the carriage lantern a bit more. That way, she wouldn't have to get glimpses of him every time she got brave enough to look for them. Amalie licked her lips, drew a breath, and broke the stillness with what sounded exactly like it was: a trembling whisper.

"Thayne?"

He didn't reply, although he turned his head away and dipped his chin. She fancied he shuddered, too, but that was just fanciful. Amalie cleared her throat and tried again, and this time got sound.

"Thayne?"

"Aye?"

He answered the shuttered window. That wasn't encouraging, but at least, he had answered.

"Is it always that way?"

"What way?"

Being in love. The flight of spirit. The illusion of heaven. The joy. Didn't you feel it, too? Amalie blinked until the instant unbidden moisture behind her lids evaporated and her throat worked. "At . . . the palace. You know . . . the supper."

"More times than na'."

"Oh."

The carriage reached the front portal of his keep. The door opened. Thayne vaulted out. A hand was put in to assist her, and Amalie groped for it, without being able to see it. Damnable tears. She wasn't the type to cry, she usually had no trouble staunching this sort of weakness, and yet now the stupid emotion wouldn't stay buried. She kept blinking on the carpet that covered first rock-hewn steps, and then more rock-hewn floor. It wasn't working. The path was a blur.

"Sean? See Her Ladyship to our chambers."

She could sense him leaving, lifted her head, and worked at focusing on where he stood without allowing one tear to drop. And then found she couldn't even stop her own tongue. "You're . . . not coming?"

"Of course, I'll be attending you, wife. Doona' lock the door."

His face was unreadable. Impassive. Stone-carved. His entire frame looked to have that affliction as he bowed, swiveled on his heel, and walked from her, his limp noticeable even with the horde of men surrounding him. As if he needed such a guard from her.

Sean stayed behind, fidgeting at her side. Amalie wondered absently if he'd gotten the assignment through some misdeed, and then shook herself. She was an English-bred noblewoman in a castle full of Scots. It was obvious to her. She wasn't wanted, nor was she liked. Fair enough. But Thayne wasn't just a liar. He was the best actor she'd ever imagined. He must have said he loved her to make her more amenable to being Jamie's entertainment for the evening.

Just as he had at the brewer croft.

Amalie straightened and turned to Sean, facing the center of his chest, or thereabouts. She didn't look higher.

"Well, Sean. Come along. We might as well get this over," she informed him.

"My lady?"

"The escort to my chamber. I'm ready for the climb, if you are. Although . . . you probably shouldn't converse with me. You'll get further reprimand."

"Reprimand, my lady?"

She moved rapidly, forcing him to the same pace, in the direction of the stairs, moving around the odd bit of table or bench in the way as she went.

"It's painfully obvious you're a miscreant, Sean. Or you'd be with His Lordship, doing whatever it is men do when they're avoiding their wives."

"My lady?"

"You got the short straw, Sean. Confess."

"My lady?"

"What?" Amalie rounded on him, reaching a view of his upper chest this time. He didn't have any resemblance to her husband's size, at all. It was getting easier to see, too.

"You're heading toward the Chieftain Hall."

"And my husband? Oh dear. That won't do at all, now will it? Very well. You lead. Escort me. Wasn't that your task?"

He put out an arm. Amalie took it, and got turned around again. They'd reached the correct tower hall before he spoke again. Amalie looked toward his head, but it was difficult to decipher features with the gloom, even interspersed as it was with lit torches in their sconces.

"My lady, if I could speak?"

"Is this the wrong stairs, too? I'm going to need smelling salts before I reach the chamber at this rate, Sean. I'm warning you. We Sassenach are weak creatures. Surely you've been taught that."

He chuckled. "I've a confession to make, my lady. If I might be so bold?"

"Oh please. Whenever is a Scotsman *not* bold?"

"I am na' being disciplined. I'm being honored."

"Of course you are. Step lively now or I'm racing you."

"My lady?"

Amalie grabbed up her skirts and started running. He had her at the fifth step, and was waiting at each landing for her to finally arrive, huffing for breath; one handful of skirts, and the other holding the necklace from jouncing, before starting up the next. By the time they reached the last one, Sean was laughing, while Amalie had rarely felt so silly. She didn't need a mirror to see how red-faced and ridiculous she looked. She still longed to thank him for changing any desire to cry. He gave her time at the door to gain her composure before knocking; winking at her while she fussed with each fold of her dress, and then every strand of her hair.

Maves answered the knock, looking stout and efficient, and eternally Scottish. She had Beth at her side. Greeting them was the added touch to a complete restorative, and Sean didn't even wait for a word of thanks. Honor indeed! He was whistling as he jogged from her. Amalie imagined him running to join in the keg of ale they'd decided to split open and then drink.

Men. She'd never understand them.

It was a laborious process to disrobe, unbraid her hair for brushing, decide on an elaborate, feminine-looking night rail, before finally getting settled into that enormous bed, watching the fire glow from across that huge span of floor. She wasn't used to such space, nor was she used to the solitude.

At least, she wasn't since Edmund had passed on. Most nights, she'd snuck into his room and slept curled at the foot of his bed. None had known how close they were, because no one truly cared what a daughter did with all her spare hours. Amalie blinked rapidly on the tears of self-pity, counseling herself over them as she did so. Like always. Tears were for the selfish. The weak. The unrestrained. Not her.

But she missed Edmund. She missed the comforting weight in her arms that was Baby Mary. And she truly missed Thayne.

A knock came at her door, echoing oddly through the measure of space. Thayne knocked now? What sort of behavior was this? Amalie slid to the edge of the bed, slipped a thick robe on, and then padded over to the door, running from rug to rug as she did so. She hadn't known the floor was this cold.

"My lady?"

It was Maves; her hair in some sort of arrangement of tied strips of material, and in her own nightclothes. She had a candlestick in her hand.

"Yes?"

"'Tis the bairn. She—"

There was more but Amalie wasn't listening. She raced past, intent on the rooms given over to a nursery. She ran up one more swirl of the steps, any light from Maves's candle long behind her, not even aware of the cold stone on bare feet. She didn't need directions. She just followed the heartrending cries. She was no longer the stoic Englishwoman in a castle full of the enemy. She wasn't a woman scorned. She wasn't a runaway heiress with a plan. She was a mother with a distressed babe, and she didn't care who saw it.

They had a fire roaring in the fireplace of the nursery, stifling the area with warmth. One of the nannies was in a rocker with the babe in her lap, rubbing along her belly. There were others in the rooms, rubbing their hands together, murmuring amongst themselves, and Baby Mary was kicking and squalling through all of it.

"Mary!"

Amalie had her in one swoop, cuddled against her heart, crooning to the little down-covered head. She didn't even note the tears sliding down her cheeks.

"We dinna' wish to disturb you and the master, my lady, but the bairn! She would na' quiet. She's like to make herself ill with that amount of crying. We were that worried."

"Aye. She would na' even suckle."

"She's so weak. We dinna' wish her to pass without a word to you or—"

"My baby isn't weak!"

Amalie interrupted her with the announcement and then she snarled at all of them. She'd never felt such a warm surge of heat as the one that flared through her. The room was absolutely silent, and then the baby made the slightest coo sound, ending the tension-filled moment. Amalie snuggled her closer, breathing infant smell and sniffing against an onslaught of tears that would shame her if she gave vent to them. That's when the nanny stood, setting the rocker to a floor-thumping sway with her missing bulk.

"Well, will you look at that? I'd heard of it, but disbelieved it until now."

Amalie tightened her arms about Mary.

"Heard what?" one of the other women asked.

"That the bairn has taken to her. Exactly like the master."

"And just why wouldn't they, Mistress MacGorrick?"

The antagonistic tone wasn't lost on those in the room, although Maves was clearly out of breath. Amalie felt her standing beside her, adding a right flank to her defensive position. She didn't bother checking. She couldn't see through the veil of tears in her eyes, nor did she want to move her nose from the top of Mary's head.

"Why . . . her being Sassenach and all."

"She's wed to the master, and that's good enough for me. Should be enough for any of you. Mistress MacGorrick. Elsie. You too, Bett."

"Word is, she forced the wedding."

"Take a good look at Her Ladyship, mistress, and then hold your tongue. She look capable of making a MacGowan do anything he has nae mind to?"

The amusement from that statement rippled through the room. Mistress MacGorrick's tone on her next statement didn't sound like she appreciated it.

"Does na' always take size and brawn to force a man. You ken it as well as I do, Maves . . . for all your Sassenach leanings."

"I serve Her Ladyship. As wife to our future laird. And I suggest you do the same."

"The next thing you'll be averring is it's a love match."

The woman's scorn showed her disbelief of that. Maves's reply was loud.

"Aye. That's exactly what I'm saying. I've a verra good inkling of such, and I'll attest it now."

"Well, I've been told he had the choice given to him. 'Twas death or her hand. That's what I heard."

"You heard wrong."

A chorused gasp answered Thayne's announcement, the full male timbre of his voice surprisingly loud in the room. Everyone turned to face him, Amalie included. He had some of his Honor Guard with him, packing the space. If he meant to frighten them, he succeeded. He took another step forward, holding one hand on his sword hilt. And then he glared at the women behind her, moving his eyes to encompass all of them. Amalie had never seen anything so raw and so dominating. No wonder Jamie feared him.

"I give orders for my wife to be in my chambers. I expect them obeyed."

That was too much. Amalie sucked in air, choking with it

while her entire frame started trembling. She didn't care how grim and terrifying he sounded.

"Later, Amalie."

His tone, as well as the words, shut off her throat. If it wasn't for the baby, she actually considered having a fit of hysteria, much like her father often accused. And if she knew what it entailed.

"Nor do I tolerate open dissent in my household."

"'Twas na' as Your Lordship thinks."

"All things are different than they appear, Mistress MacGorrick. Even this. You'd do well to remember that in the future. The rest of you need think on your words, your intents, and your futures."

"Futures, my lord?" The words were hesitant. Frightened.

"I doona' harbor vipers in my midst. This will be dealt with. For now, I'll be to returning to my chamber. And I'm taking my wife with me. Amalie?"

"I'm not leaving the baby." Amalie forced her voice to work. She was shocked when it did.

"I dinna' suggest that you do," he replied.

"She's . . . coming with me?"

"Us. The bairn is coming with us."

He took a step toward her, somehow enveloping with warmth and security. The men made a passage between them for her and the babe, closing it as they passed, adding even more security. Maves led the way. Amalie didn't know Thayne was at her back until he started giving more orders.

"Grant? Secure a cradle. Len? Send word to the clan for another wet-nurse. One with a bent toward loyalty. Euan? Check the stables for goats."

"Goats?"

The door shut behind them, echoing in the hall, and making a torch flutter.

"We'll need the goat milk. For the bairn. In the event Len fails, or takes over-long in his search."

"Oh. Aye."

The group had halted and now formed a circle with her at the core. Amalie didn't notice how she'd been separated from her maid until Thayne spoke again. He was using his authoritative voice again, the one that created shivers.

"Who are you, and why have you accompanied us?"

"Maves, Your Lordship. I'm Her Ladyship's maid."

"Is she?"

He addressed Amalie. She lifted her nose from breathing in delicate baby smell and nodded. Thayne regarded her wordlessly for a moment before turning back to the maid.

"Then, how is it my wife is at the nurseries getting harangued by women with sharp tongues and na' secure in her bed as ordered?"

"T'would be my fault."

"Yours?"

"I . . . forced her, you see. She was all set in Your Lordship's chamber. Abed and waiting and then—"

"I see nae bonds about her. How did you manage such a feat?"

"The bairn . . . would na' quiet. Nanny MacGorrick fetched me, and I . . . thought if she had her mother . . . she'd calm."

"Her mother?"

Maves straightened. "Exactly as I've been told, Your Lordship."

Thayne looked down at her for long, heart-pounding moments before finally smiling. "Verra good, Maves. Grant? We may continue."

"It appears I had the right of it, too. Do you see how the bairn takes to her? I vow, the moment she felt Her Ladyship's touch, the wee one ceased all her issues. 'Twas the most heartwarming thing. I vow, started tears into my eyes. 'Tis clear the bairn kens her mother. There's nae clanswoman in Scotland would believe different."

"Phib?"

The named came on a breath from Thayne. One of the men moved forward, holding on to Maves's elbow as he took to escorting her down the steps. Amalie couldn't tell what he said but she could guess from the woman's reply.

"You? An issue with the lasses? Come on, man. You're one of Thayne MacGowan's Honor Guard. What issue could you have with the lasses other than working to peel them from you after a bit of showing on the lists? Truly? Well, there's a bit of a potion I'll see fetched for you. That is, if Her Ladyship nae longer has need of my services?"

Maves looked back to Amalie, midsentence. Thayne answered for her.

"I've got the wife fully in hand. She'll have nae need of services until morn. From you or any other party. Except perhaps Len. With the goat milk."

Maves was turned down a hall at the next landing, chatting the entire time with the hulking man beside her. Torchlight was futilely trying to dent the gloom between sconces as they passed through it. Amalie watched them go and then looked up at Thayne.

"You did that on purpose."

"What?"

"Handed Maves another assignment to see her on her way and out of yours."

"I did that?"

"There's probably nothing wrong with the man, either. Is there?"

"Your maid appears to have a bent toward speech . . . of the nonending kind. Phib has a great knack for listening."

"He does?"

"He's tone deaf, my lady."

"Aye. Reads lips, if he must."

The information came from two of Thayne's Honor Guardsmen. They were all grinning.

Amalie couldn't hide the amusement, although hers came with a chuckle. "I see."

"Come along, wife. I've a strong yen toward my chamber. And some time alone with my wife."

"And your babe?" Amalie added.

He flicked a glance to the bundle in her arms and everything on his features seemed to soften for the barest fraction of time. And then it changed to the stern visage he'd presented in the nursery. "Aye. Her, too. Come. The night has na' gotten longer. And I need my bed."

They started off again, Thayne leading this time. The man was so mercurial! He gave heat-inducing statements and glances one moment, and then chased them away with cold looks and acidic rejoinders. He was sending her emotions down a torrential waterfall one moment, and then sealing them in a frozen pond the next. Maddening. Impossible. And it wasn't lasting much longer.

The chamber didn't seem as barren and cold once they arrived, had the fire stoked, and Thayne dismissed everyone. His Guardsman, Grant, was certainly efficient. A cradle rested near the hearth where Amalie had been bathed what seemed days ago, rather than hours. Baby Mary was a comforting weight in her arms. Amalie recognized just how comfortable as she placed her into a nest made of knitted blanket and spun linen. She tugged a chair close, the sound of wood sliding loud in the stillness. Then the bolt rasped into position, making an even louder disruption. Amalie forced herself to watch the baby. She didn't know where Thayne was, although every bit of her seemed aware of him.

"I dinna' fetch you back to watch the bairn sleep."

He used the stern voice from the confrontation in the nursery. And he was between her and the bed; shadowed by the candelabra at the bedstead behind, lit by flickers of light from the fireplace. He stood to his full height as he regarded her. Unsmiling. Unblinking. And then he flicked the catch on his brooch, releasing the shoulder-fastening of his attire. A bit of a shrug had the plaid material drooping into a loop at one hip, held in place by his belt.

"She . . . may wake again."

"That she may. And in the meanwhile, I've need."

He pulled on the ruffled front of his shirt next, revealing buttons, and those he worked loose. When he had the garment gapped open in the front, he moved his fingers to the ties at his shoulders, releasing his sleeves. Those he pulled over each hand. He did it by touch, since his gaze didn't move from hers. Amalie's heart ratcheted into her throat as she watched, making everything feel warm.

"Must you be so . . . blunt?"

A ghost of a smile touched one side of his mouth, lifting it, before it disappeared. "Blunt? Me?"

Amalie nodded.

He removed the shirt and dropped it atop the pile growing at his feet. "If you find me blunt, surely 'tis nae surprise. I am, after all, a Highlander."

"You seek to exercise your . . . husbandly rights? Is that it?" Amalie choked midway through it, but got the words out whole and full-voiced. She didn't drop her gaze, either, although a tremor went through her.

"Ah, love. That is a vast want. Na' a need."

"You want me naked on your bed? Is that it?"

He sucked in his cheeks, putting a pout to his lips as he considered her, or her words, while Amalie grew even hotter with the blush.

"I'm certainly na' averse to such a display, if you so wish."

"Isn't . . . that what you wanted?"

"Later, perhaps."

"Later?"

"I've a need for a bit of nursing first. My bandaging needs seen to. You do recollect I'm wounded?"

Amalie was on her feet. "Why didn't you say something earlier?"

"And miss hearing you speak of your wifely rights? Amid such blushing? Grant me some sense, wife."

"Amalie. My name is Amalie."

"Aye. I ken. Amalie. But, according to the list you gave Wynneth, there's a vast array of other names to you as well. True?"

"Yes."

"I could get fond of Evelyn."

"You want me to see to your injury or not, Highlander?"

"You doona' like Evelyn?"

"How badly did you hurt it this time?" She put a hand to his upper arm and steered him toward the bed, and docilely he allowed it.

"We may need linens again."

"You broke it open? It was your fighting on the list, wasn't it?"

"Nae. And aye."

"Yes and no. What kind of answer is that? How could you do something so . . . ill-advised? And how could your men force it?"

"You ask many questions and in an order a man canna' recollect. I dinna' say I broke it open, love. And nae man forced me. I was challenged."

"And of course, you have to meet every challenge. Here. Get up. On your belly."

Amalie patted the bed and waited until he did as she asked, watching for any sign of pain that might filter through his features. It was the only gauge of pain she trusted. He wasn't forthcoming with much else. And then she had Thayne MacGowan stretched out fully before her. Unclothed to the waist. Changing the temperature in the chamber to overwhelming heat. She slipped the buttons of her robe from their holes and then shed it. She had to swallow to keep her voice from demonstrating how it affected her.

"If I canna' meet a challenge, there might be wondering as to the why of it. And that could lead to—"

"I know. I heard this already. I just don't understand how your men could be so cruel as to challenge you. Aren't they supposed to protect you?"

"'Twas more men than mine on the list today, and the healer is most at fault."

"The healer challenged you, too?"

"Of course na'. His handiwork was behind the severity of my challenges."

"Didn't he care for your wound? What kind of healer do you have in this castle? And . . . just what is this?" Amalie had lifted his kilt up, and found him wrapped in ill-used linen.

"You laugh, and I'll spank you. I vow it."

Amalie dropped the material and leaned until she was beside his face. "Why would I laugh?"

"I'm wearing a loin-wrap."

"Looks more like a swaddling—"

"I'm warning you, Amalie Evelyn."

"I don't understand you men. Who cares if you wear swaddling? It did its job at protecting your wound. I take back everything about your healer. The man shows uncommon sense. Did he burn it again?"

"The man used his needle. And atop that, he's placed moss. Or something of that nature. And then he made me promise to keep it all in place by wrapping me."

"He sewed it?" Amalie made a face and moved to looking over his backside again.

"Aye. I've heard no end to insults and slurs over it. I canna' even fault them. Had it been another, I'd have joined in."

"What is wrong with you men?" Amalie checked about the edges of his wrap for a fastening, getting her fingertips dirtier with each touch. He was also tensing every time, putting a white tint to every scar on him. He had quite a few, and they were in all sorts of places and sizes. She reached to trace one scoring his spine, before stopping her own fingers.

"You'd be best served with a blade. Here."

He stretched, moving enough the scarred flesh contacted her fingertips. The resultant spark flew her wrist, rounded her shoulder, and speared her heart. Her eyes were wide as he unerringly pulled a knife from behind him to hold its handle first to her.

"Thayne . . ." Her voice trembled.

"Go on. Cut. I doona' offer such to many lasses. You ken?"

Amalie started slicing, and then talking. It kept her mind off what she had to do. "You need to give it time to heal. Stay abed. Tomorrow."

"I canna'."

"You're not going on the list again, are you? Because I—I'll just tell them you're abed and . . . can't be disturbed."

"You ken the talk that'll start?"

"They'll think I'm ravishing you within an inch of your life, of course. And if they're too dense to think it, I'll just tell them so." She got the entire thing out before the embarrassment stopped her, sending her heartbeat into rapid, sharp beats. She'd blame the playacting with Edmund later, although it seemed he'd been right. Bravado was always best. Do first, worry later.

He twisted his upper body to face her, and then he winked, drawing a gasp. Amalie tried very hard not to give it, but it was useless. Her entire frame knew it.

"You make a verra tempting case, but I've other plans. Sadly."

"You have other things . . . more tempting than . . . me?"

She almost got the entire thing out before her tongue tripped. She also suffered the full body flush at such immodest words. She didn't have to see it. She felt it. She also had this wrap undone, lifting a mash of leaf-filled unguent with it. His healer looked to be extremely gifted. There wasn't a sign of blood anywhere.

He groaned, turned his face into the cover, and mumbled words into it. "Amalie Evelyn. I'm doing the honorable thing here."

"Honorable?"

"Aye. Just and fair. Exactly as was done for me."

"Then, I didn't hurt you?" She wadded the used linen in a ball and dropped it to the floor.

"I have forced you to accept wedlock with me, and then I forced a consummation. I've done naught to your wishes."

"Thayne MacGowan. You said you loved me."

There was a long silence where she could have sworn he held his breath. And then he sighed heavily, moving the mass of scarred back flesh she watched.

"Aye. That I did."

"Did?" Why couldn't she just let it go? Did she have to gain torment, too? Amalie blinked rapidly on emotion her heart just kept sending to her eyes.

"I did say such."

"Was it a lie?"

He shook his head, moving his nose on the bedding. "Nae. 'Tis true enough. But . . . I dinna' expect love to have so many sides, or so many pitfalls. Nor this much guilt."

"Guilt?" Amalie started working at the buttons at the throat of her night rail. It was feminine and covered in lace, and bedecked with little pearl buttons. It was also modestly fastened to her neck. Stupid design.

"I'd heard Highlanders were the dense sort . . . but I had no idea to what extent."

He rolled toward her, anger probably lighting his gorgeous blue-green eyes. But it changed, their color darkening rapidly as he watched her pull apart the neckline of her gown.

"Amalie." He was using his authoritative voice, the one from the nursery earlier.

"Does this look like you're forcing me . . . husband? Or do I truly have to ask?"

Her answer was a wide grin, then perfect, amazing words, and then hard, sculpted arms lifting her. Arms that trembled.

"Ah . . . Amalie, love. Naught ever looked so . . . I'd have to be a saint. I love you. Did you na' hear me?"

Yes.

Her heart answered, and then her soul.

Chapter 22

Midnight fog clung to every hollow, hiding his approach, exactly as he'd planned since sneaking from the castle yester morn. After placing a kiss atop his wife's sweetly pursed lips, and one to the baby's forehead. With luck, he'd make it back yet for Mary's wake and interment. If he rode all night; and if the MacKennah laird gave him time to talk before reacting.

Thayne held a hand up, halting the line of horses containing the MacKennah women, three of his Honor Guardsmen, and a litter containing the man Jamie had tortured. The MacKennahs Jamie had taken were all wrapped in their own plaid, gagged, and tied in place atop their mounts. There wasn't any other way to approach stealthily. Every one of his unbidden captives had refused any courtesy, and spit in his face when he'd asked for cooperation. Thayne couldn't blame them. He'd have done the same.

Fog coated everything, wetting their cloaks and hampering breathing. It was perfect for his approach to the MacKennah stronghold. Unfortunately, it was also perfect for hiding defenders. They were already too close. Any closer and he'd be risking capture for his men, too.

"We leaving them here? Finally?"

Sean whispered it at his shoulder. Thayne shook his head.

"You *want* to get captured?"

Thayne shook his head again.

"Then what?"

"You stay. I escort them. Alone."

"Nae."

The man was joined by Grant, shaking his head as well as mouthing the refusal. This left Phib at the rear, guarding.

"'Tis nae request, lads. I'm ordering it."

"You crazed?"

"Just hoping to dampen this feud afore it starts up again."

"They'll kill you on sight."

"Na' likely. The man has too much sense. Killing the MacGowan heir means full war. He's na' that stupid."

"You canna' expect us to sit idly by, awaiting the man's act. We're your Honor Guard, Thayne."

"Aye. The best men from it. But you'll stay here as ordered. Readied. I've a pass into his dungeon, at the verra least. You'd na' be so lucky."

"A stay in his dungeon is worse than bad luck, Thayne! We've heard tales."

"Aye, but at least the man will let me live. If I allow your escort, you're all three dead men. Now, go! Before our words bring a MacKennah out to check."

Both men backed slightly at Thayne's tone, or how he reached for the back of his sett, making a cowl about his head, fitting it about the sword hilt peeking above his shoulder.

"You get taken and they'll demand a hefty ransom. They'll probably take a few slices from your skin, as well."

"Hand me the rein. Back a hundred yards up the drum, and wait."

"For what? Your cry of pain?"

Thayne smirked. "You hear a lone wolf howl, you'll ken I've been taken. A hoot owl means all's well. You'll obey?"

"We still say you're crazed, but aye. We'll do as ordered."

"Verra good. Sean? You stay closest. The others move

back, within sighting distance of each other. Send Phib to the end. He's got the fastest horse."

"You wish him to use it how?"

"To get word of my fate to the castle."

"You're insane, Thayne MacGowan. Fully."

"Na' truly. I've a bit of hope the laird will be of a willing mind to settle this. And I've warm pockets to make it a bit easier to swallow."

"A MacKennah settle anything without bloodshed? Unlikely."

"This is ill-conceived, and foolhardy."

"It's still happening. Give me the rein and prepare lads. Bear word back to Gowan Castle, and Jamie's duchess."

"The Douglas?"

"Aye."

"What's she to do with this?"

"She's the lone one with funds to meet large demands, should my forty pounds fail to impress sufficiently. You have instructions. Now move. All of you."

The men nodded. Thayne was given the reins to the lead captive's horse, and then he watched his men meld into the fog cover before kicking at Placer's sides. The stallion scrambled on the incline before regaining his footing. The resultant shale slide made enough noise, he should be well announced and noticed. Good. Stealth wasn't needed now. He fully expected to get challenged and addressed. The sooner the better, as far as he was concerned. If he got too close, the watchmen would need disciplining, and that might anger the MacKennahs worse.

Of course the entire plan was foolhardy. But he had to do the chivalrous thing and try to stop this feud, so he could go back to his wife. He didn't know love felt like this, making a man feel weak and yet strong; quick-witted and yet eternally slow . . . warm with glow, and saturated with awareness. He could've sworn she spoke on her own love, between her cries of pleasure. Maybe it had been wishful listening. Didn't truly matter. He'd just try harder to get her to say the words next time. Thayne couldn't believe his luck, and that he'd gained what every man longed for—a love match.

His men thought he wanted to be out here, a day and a half ride away? Risking a stay in MacKennah's rotten dungeon? Not likely. Stealing from her side, in the predawn chill had been the last thing he wanted. He'd toyed with waking her to his plans, so he could see her luminous eyes once more, but he hadn't wanted them clouded with worry. And she looked fain comfortable in his bed.

They didn't wait for him to say anything.

Thayne heard the hiss sound of an arrow release a moment before it slammed into his right shoulder from the front. The man had a great arm and he was close, otherwise the blow wouldn't have knocked Thayne backward, tumbling off Placer. He pulled the captive's reins as he fell, soundlessly mouthing Amalie's name. He didn't have time to do more than groan before another attacker guaranteed his silence with a head-hit. And before then, he heard the pure sound of a hoot owl.

Damn his rotten luck, anyway.

The waiting was the hardest.

Amalie paced the bedchamber, jiggling Baby Mary in her arms as if the infant was fussy. She wasn't. Of all the inhabitants of Castle MacGowan, Baby Mary was the least disturbed by news of Thayne's absence. Four days now! Four days that right now seemed the longest of Amalie's life. She'd listened to rumor over how the MacKennah laird would receive him, and what might ensue during the negotiations. But no one knew anything, all of them speculated. Jamie got more morose and bitter with every flagon of brew he drank, speaking drunkenly and loudly over Thayne's actions in returning the MacKennahs without one word of permission. That was just a loss of good ransom money and bargaining position. According to Jamie, he was going to challenge Thayne to the list over it when he returned, and this time beat him into his proper place. And all the while the duchess kept up appearances for her group of hangers-on, continuing her evening soirees as if nothing unusual were happening. Although last night she'd requested Amalie attend her own company in her own home if she couldn't keep her presence from putting a damper on the festivities.

That was no punishment. It had been a chore to prepare and attend sup at the Palace, and once there, she'd had to play-act like she hadn't a care in the world. Amalie must have lost her talent for acting. She'd thought her continual concern well hidden and then Thayne's man, Phib, had returned. The jubilation started before the man finished his words. Phib told them Thayne had succeeded in gaining the MacKennah chieftain's ear. Now all they had to do was wait out the negotiations. It wasn't anything too out of the ordinary.

Well . . . maybe it wasn't an extraordinary occurrence for them, but for an English noblewoman newly-wed to one of them, it was more than strange. And uncivilized. And just plain barbaric. There was nothing normal about kidnapping neighbors, requiring ransoms, or enjoining clan feuds. Nothing.

And Thayne was still missing.

No one else seemed concerned about it, and whenever Amalie voiced hers, she got sidelong glances that could mean anything, but looked to signify her ignorance and naivety. Both of which descriptions fit. Exactly. They couldn't know the extent of it, though, and she didn't speak of it. Perhaps if she'd had a decent courtship, with time to know her groom, she'd be less prone to anxiety. Perhaps here, a man disappeared for days on end all the time. Perhaps she was behaving just a bit hysterically over the length of his absence. And maybe she should just drink the posset prepared for her overwrought nerves, say a prayer, and settle into the big lonely bed without Thayne, just as Maves had recommended before bidding her good night.

Amalie sighed, stroked the baby's back absently, and turned for another crossing of the chamber. She'd moved all the rugs into a path resembling skipping stones, keeping her slipper-clad feet from the worst of the cold while she traversed the immensity of this floor. She also wore a thick gown, with a cloak over that. She hadn't worn night attire since Thayne had first gone. She wasn't hysterical. She wasn't overwrought. She wasn't a bundle of nerves, like her countrywomen were reputed to suffer. She wasn't prone to faints that required smelling salts.

She knew the trouble. She was in love.

There! She admitted it. She'd fallen in love with Thayne MacGowan. And to an extent she'd have dreamt, if she'd known it existed. It was such a wonder, the world shone with new promise . . . and yet at times such as these; deep into the night; every moment dragged to such an extent, it was near insufferable. She didn't know love could make her feel vulnerable and weak, but it did. It also made her hypersensitive to everything. She didn't care what was said, Amalie knew something was wrong. She felt it. Her recent experience with this land primed her for it, and then her newly awakened love guaranteed it.

She knew deep in her soul Thayne wasn't a guest of the MacKennah clan. He was being waylaid, and it wasn't with his permission. And she already knew the only thing that could waylay a Highlander was another Highlander with a larger force. Her husband was out there somewhere, maybe injured . . . or worse! His household may think they knew him, but they were completely off the mark. There wasn't any way Thayne MacGowan would miss the interment of Lady Mary into the family crypt, and yet, he had. They'd done the ceremony yesterday. Amalie hadn't attended. Not only was it too hurtful to be reminded of Thayne's prior love for the woman, but the MacGowan clan followed Catholic doctrine! They held Catholic ceremony as if it were completely legal and authorized. Thayne could even be a practicing Catholic. She didn't know. They hadn't had time to discuss it, and if he didn't return, they might not ever get the chance. And as much as that should bother her, it got overshadowed by the waiting. She just wanted Thayne back. In her arms, and in her life. While he still had life.

The nights were the hardest; when she had nothing to occupy her mind except images of Thayne being incarcerated . . . beaten; chained against the wall of a dungeon; tortured. Amalie chewed on her lower lip, breathed in baby scent, and stopped at the fireplace. Warmth and light drew her, catching her attention on the red center coal before she blinked and stepped back. The warmth felt wonderful but dried her eyes, and they already felt filled with sand that scratched and burned. The light was also welcome. She should've had more torches lit, except the maids already gave each other significant looks over her request for them. They didn't know how long Amalie stayed awake pacing. Fretting. Imagining. She turned from the fire and looked over all the pools of gloom, scattered throughout the room, and then the dull thud of a knock hit at her door.

Since Amalie was at the fireplace closest to the door, she was at the bottom step when the door opened slightly, allowing Maves to peek her head in.

"Oh, thank the Lord. You're still awake. And dressed."

"What's happened?"

"It's bad, mistress. May we enter?"

"How bad?"

"Verra bad."

The last was a male voice. Amalie stepped out of the way so Maves could enter, followed closely by six hulky men: Honor Guardsmen. Thayne's men. Two of them looked travel-weary.

"They've got the laird!"

"Something's happened to Jamie?"

"Na' Jamie—although they'll need to send a party out to stay him . . . I meant the true laird. Thayne! Oh, dear Lord!"

Amalie's heart seemed to pause with a hurtful pressure before restarting with such a loud pounding she couldn't hear at first. Then she realized she didn't have to. Her soul heard it.

Thayne's been taken. He was held prisoner in the MacKennah stronghold. The MacKennah clan is demanding a ransom. A huge ransom. The duchess hasn't funds enough to pay it, and so she did nothing. Nothing! Just kept about her party as if it didn't matter. The duke has set out on a rescue mission, with full intentions of starting a war.

Thayne's been taken. That part echoed, matching each beat of her pulse.

A message got delivered before daylight tied to an arrow shaft, aimed at the tree beside Sean's head. Sean rode throughout the day to get here with it. They'd show it to her, but Jamie took it. He was using it to gather clansmen to the cause. Nobody knew what to do. Who to turn to. Where to look. They hadn't enough silver to pay it. Not without next quarter's payment and it wasn't due for another month! The MacKennah chieftain wasn't giving them enough time! They had to deliver funds in full and they had two weeks before the amount got larger and Thayne's stay worse.

"How much?"

Amalie's voice was solid and firm, surprising not only her, but the others as well. The lone exception was Baby Mary, who still slept peacefully in her arms.

"Two thousand!"

"Pounds?" Her voice faltered. They were right. It was a huge ransom.

"Aye."

"Two weeks, my lady! Sweet heaven! What's to happen now?"

"Control yourself, Maves. We've got a lot to do, and not a lot of time to do it in. Fetch me a quill and parchment. Bring them to . . . the table there."

Amalie got more than one open-mouthed look at either the words, or her tone. She'd have joined them in amazement if she wasn't locking every emotion away so it wouldn't interfere. Nothing about her voice or frame gave away the absolute fear permeating every bone as she did the best playacting of her life. And then found, as she continued, that it turned into reality. She'd never felt more calm and in control.

"You're writing . . . a letter?"

"Not just a letter. An appeal. Any of you men capable of riding?"

They all managed to stand taller, as if offended, somehow. Amalie ignored their bruised pride and headed for the table. She didn't step on one rug, and didn't even feel the chill.

"Well?"

Amalie looked up at them from the table. Maves had gathered an inkpot, a quill, enough parchment to pen a short story, and hovered at one side with a wax-tipped stick.

"'Tis na' that far to MacKennah land, my lady."

One of them offered the reason. Amalie huffed.

"Shortsighted. I'm not speaking of the MacKennah clan. I'll never acknowledge them in my world. Not in this lifetime. Not after this. Try to do a good deed, and look what they do? They're absolute heathens. I need a rider for England."

"England?"

"Anyone capable and willing to ride, without rest if necessary, to Ellincourt Castle? It's near Leeds. Anyone know it?"

"Aye. I've seen it. Great stone castle, built of yellowish stone?"

"That's the one. If the earl is home, his standard will be

flying. It's got a Stag Rampant in silver, on a field of blue. Anyone willing and capable of riding that far?"

"Write your missive, my lady. I'll take it."

Amalie smiled at the man. He looked sturdy and capable. "Do we have enough funds to pay for fresh horses for the journey? I know I should have checked with these things, but I always thought there would be time."

"I'll check with the steward, my lady."

One of them bowed and left. She didn't know his name. She didn't know most of their names, although she recognized Sean as the most weary-looking and dirty. He looked mud-spattered, his face lined with more of the same. Amalie smiled at him and watched him frown.

"What now?" she asked.

"Will the earl accept . . . a missive?"

"Didn't any of you believe me? I truly am the daughter of the Earl of Ellincourt. I've got an enormous dowry, and it sounds like we're going to need some of it. Maves? Take the babe so I can write."

Amalie handed over Baby Mary. It warmed the area about her heart to see how the babe immediately woke and started fussing, but then she put her attention to composing words that wouldn't give her father apoplexy.

Chapter 23

"Ah . . . *Jesu'!*"

Thayne choked on liquid fire that ate through his chest wall as he breathed it in. He was then curved into a ball of defense in order to hack the concoction from him, wracked with spikes of ache the entire episode. His body didn't belong to him, or if it did, someone had found a way to send it beneath the wheels of cannon. Either that, or he'd been assigned time on the rack, pulled in so many directions it was impossible to pinpoint the agony with any degree of accuracy. Then full consciousness settled the pain right in his head, where it seemed his mind was at war with his teeth. It felt like he'd lodged in the jaws of some huge beast, getting squeezed between skean-sharp teeth that ground together in excruciating agony. There was nothing for it. He'd rather die.

"Good. I see you've decided to rejoin the living."

"This . . . is . . . na' living."

He couldn't get the entire sentence out. His voice gave first, and then his strength, as he collapsed back onto what might be a pallet if it had any give to it, but instead felt like a chunk of planed wood.

"'Tis more than you had before. Now, open up and take your medicine."

"Before—?"

She didn't let him finish, using the opening of his mouth to send more fire onto his lips, then his tongue, and he spat before it could poison him further. Her laughter over how pathetic he'd made the act infuriated him. Thayne fought the choking reaction even as it consumed him, bringing worse blows to hammer through his skull, while he battled blurred vision to bring her into focus. And failed. He realized it as coughing plagued him, liquid from within him made breathing nearly impossible, and through it all her laughter tormented him. Thayne gripped the left side of his support, concentrating with every fiber in his being, to will air back into his body. He knew then he was definitely atop a bit of planking, and it wasn't very thick since it flexed within his fingers with his grip. He no longer heard her laughter, but knew she was still there. He felt her. Not helping, just watching . . . and waiting.

Tears streamed down his face. He ignored them. Heavy loud thudding filled his ears, and he welcomed it, as he did the continual agony that accompanied it. To feel such pain meant he wasn't dead. MacKennah bastards hadn't killed him. And that meant he still had a chance at this life . . . if he managed to get this spate of coughing under control. And finally, he managed it.

Thayne lay spent, sucking tiny increments of breath that came with an accompanying wheeze. He was damp with sweat, weak with exertion. Every bit of him was exhausted, as if he'd just come from the deepest section of the loch. He pulled each tiny intake of air as the sweetest gift, and then she laughed at him again.

"Something amuses you, Crone?" His voice came out lower than normal. Harsh. Like he chewed on gravel. But it did come out.

"Just watching the great MacGowan chieftain. Crying . . . like a little bairn. And over a little whiskey."

Thayne shoved an arm across his eyes. His left arm. His right wouldn't obey the instruction to move. He flexed the fingers on that hand and felt them respond. Good. He'd taken an injury, but he still had his arm. And he wasn't tied. He turned his head toward her and worked at controlling the thud of pain through his head as he attempted to see.

They were in a small room; rock-walled with tapestries across the opposite wall. It was windowless and dark, without benefit of a fireplace. He couldn't tell her features or her age. She was wrapped in a MacKennah plaid clear to her throat, while another hooded her head. If she hadn't placed a candle on the stool beside her, he'd not be able to see that much.

"I'm na' the chieftain," he told the shadow that contained her face.

"Liar."

"You mistake me for my brother."

"Oh. Nae. I ken exactly who you are."

Thayne pulled moisture into his mouth and licked at his lips. "What's been done to me?"

"You took an arrow in the shoulder. Doona' fash that. We pulled it out and then sealed it. You're in luck 'twas Torquil the Younger coming upon you. His father would na' have missed."

"I meant . . . my head." And curse it for not just flying off and saving him the trouble.

"Oh. That. Torquil has a heavy fist with his ax handle. You've been dead to the world for nigh a day and a half. You can thank your luck again, though. His father would've seen your skull cleaved through."

"Without trial?"

"Oh. Doona' fash yourself over testimony and such. The clan you'd brought with you spoke up for you. They had leagues to say of treatment. We had to release them from their gags in order to hear it. 'Twas enough to get you a spot in a hangman's noose, na' just a nice stay in the sickroom."

"They're the liars, then. I did naught to them, save return them."

"You going to deny you up and wed with a Sassenach, too? Betraying a betrothal contract to the MacKennah clan?"

Thayne took a deep breath, stretching his chest wall as he held it; listened to the solid, reassuring pumping of his heart as it hammered into his ears; endured each thump as they drummed through his skull. If this pain didn't lessen, he'd rather have his head cleaved off and done, he decided. Thayne let the breath out.

"Are you . . . the healer?"

"Me? Nae. I'd as lief see you cold. 'Twould have been an easy matter as you lay there."

"Then, why dinna' you?"

"Seeing you suffer is much better. Immensely so. 'Tis why I offered to watch you this eve. I'm to speak the moment you wake so we can see you put into your proper place."

"And what is that to be?"

"Depends on what you tell me."

"Well." Thayne turned to contemplation of the darkness above him and addressed his words there. "You've watched me. I'm awake. You should probably go tell someone."

"I need the answer first."

"To what?"

"You willing to gain an annulment from your Sassenach bride?"

Never.

Thayne made a shrug, but the instant shot of pain through his shoulder made it a poor gesture, and one he immediately tensed to withstand. And one she probably saw. He released the motion slowly, in infinitesimal increments, until he was flat on the plank again. Then he worked at consciously loosening all the muscles he'd put into play, until all that was

left was the head pain, and it had settled into an angry throb
that vied with his set jaw for viciousness. Strange . . . even if
he concentrated, he couldn't feel the Dunn-Fyne blade wound
on his buttocks that had harried him for nigh a week now.
That was odd.

"Well?"

"My marriage is consummated, mistress."

"So? She may be infertile. And I hear tell she was unwilling. What if she leaves you of her own accord? Would you
obey clan honor then?"

Thayne stiffened that time, and had to stop the instant
reaction as pain accompanied it. Amalie leave him? Never.
And if she tried, he'd hunt her down.

"Well?"

"I'm for the dungeon, mistress. Cease your balking and get
me there."

"Recollect you started it, then. MacGowans always start
this."

"You still here? Can you na' see me to the dungeons any
quicker—"

That was stupid. Thayne couldn't halt the groan as she
smacked at him, hitting somewhere near his new wound,
sending some of the pain from his head to his shoulder. But
before he could turn the agony into sobs, she started her own,
heartbreaking in its volume and intensity. Thayne blinked
until moisture no longer blurred his view in order to face her
again. The woman had both arms wrapped about herself
and was rocking in place, wailing softly, and then she was
stumbling through near-unintelligible words.

"My sweet lass. Sweet . . . Damn you, MacGowan. Damn
you! You doona' ken what you've done to my bairn! My sweet
lass! I'll send you to hell for it. You hear?"

She'd gotten over her initial bout of sobbing, for her voice
toward the end didn't have the slightest tremble.

"You're Lady MacKennah, then?"

She nodded.

"There are worse things than na' having me for a son-by-law, mistress."

His attempt at levity fell flat. She rose from her stool to stand above him, blocking the light. This way, he couldn't see anything about her, but didn't need to see the hatred from her voice.

"You dare laugh?"

He wasn't laughing. He barely had enough moisture in his mouth to swallow. Even then, it was dry and more a gulp.

"I'm na' the lone man in the Highlands. Surely your clan has other suitors."

"After a jilting by the MacGowan laird?"

Thayne worked at sitting up. Everything on him fought his action. It seemed to take forever, but at least the woman backed a step. His body was angry but not as much as his head. If anything, the thudding pain was worsened by his move, to the point his belly retched in disagreement. He fought that, as well as the peppering of dots that hampered his vision, making the room swirl in a kaleidoscope of color that had her candle's flame as its core. He probably looked as ill as he felt.

"I'm . . . prepared to sweeten the girl's dowry."

"My daughter is a pariah among her own. There is na' a man who would offer for her now, regardless of your coin."

"You've na' heard . . . my offer."

"He's awake? And you dinna' tell us?"

There was a door in the wall toward the end of his pallet. Thayne made the mistake of turning to face the man who stood there, moving his head in a direction it didn't wish to go, and couldn't support. And that's when he went down.

She'd been wrong. Waiting was nothing compared to the worry she now added in. It would be much worse come nightfall, though. She didn't have to guess. After watching the men leave with Maves, she'd spent what was left of last night living through worry that had no boundaries. She'd been helpless with it. Stricken by it. The entire night was one of restless energy that had no outlet, hysterical thoughts that had no end, and furious motion that accomplished nothing.

It hovered with her through the day, regardless of how she kept her thoughts and body occupied. She'd started directly after seeing Baby Mary back to the nursery and to her new wet-nurse. She nodded briefly to Nanny MacGorrick and the others. She didn't upbraid them. She didn't even look at them.

She had a household to survey and nothing but time, so Amalie drafted Maves as her guide, and an Honor Guardsman for escort. They sent her a man called Stout Pells, not to be confused with Thin Pells. He was probably as tall as Thayne, but he hadn't a bit of him devoted to anything stout. Amalie looked him over but didn't ask. If this failed to keep her mind occupied enough, she'd have more than enough time to ask for meanings and memorize names.

They started at the chambers beneath the Great Hall. According to Maves, there was an outside entrance. It wasn't in use much except for emergencies, such as fleeing a besieging force. There was a narrow staircase leading down from the kitchens, for accessing foodstuffs and drink. They'd use it later. For this descent, Maves took her down the stone steps that looked to have been carved into the sides of the castle when it was first built. Amalie kept a hand on the wall, while the other held her skirts, and her concentration on not tripping on the badly worn stone, and she should have known the first stop at the end was the dungeons.

She nearly quailed, but that would give the worry and fear she hid form and reality. She'd also have to get past Stout Pells. Amalie pulled her shoulders back and looked into each room shown, with a pent breath before easing it out. The dungeons were old stone rooms. There were six of them, three on each side of the hall, all smelling of damp and age. And they were bare of occupants. The thick oaken door at the end was sealed with a lock larger than her fist. Stout Pells had to put a shoulder and effort to shove it open, giving possible meaning to his moniker. Maves was voluble with her delight that he'd been the man assigned to them, since they hadn't kept a prisoner down here for some time, and the door witnessed it.

The rooms on this side of the ground floor were mostly storerooms: well-organized and well-stocked. Stout Pells held the torch high, shedding light on all the riches accumulated there. Enormous sewn sacks containing barley, oats, and millet were stacked higher than her head. Wooden slats made an aisle through the center so the oldest could be used first. It appeared Thayne had an eye for organization and preparation. She wasn't needed here.

The next series of rooms were devoted to barrels containing ales, brews, and meads. According to Maves, Thayne had his own aleswoman who oversaw his brewery. He also had his cooper making the barrels, and his own method of dating and logging each barrel, so none need drink a vinegar brew unless they wanted that sort of thing. The rooms were a maze, crafted with walls of wood. Stout Pells gave her the explanation without asking: Spirits were kept separated. The walls made access and tallies easier.

Amalie's housekeeping skills obviously weren't needed here, either.

The corner room was given over to the healer when needed, it held several long benches, a small fireplace on the far wall, and a rock rimmed well in one corner. Constructed when the foundations were first laid out, but rarely used now, there was still a bucket drawn each week to make certain of the water.

The other staircase was timber-constructed, and creaked with age. She could see about getting that replaced. And if it helped part the cloud of worry dogging her, she'd even try wielding the ax to chop the wood.

The steps led straight to the kitchens. Amalie would have known without being told. The smell of bread baking, meat roasting, stews and broths cooking, and chattering gave every indication of a hive of industry. Clanswomen were involved in every form of food preparation when they entered, and all of it immediately stopped. Amalie kept her head high and met each look as it was given her, although most kept their heads down and dipped into curtsies as she greeted them. Her presence put a decided damper on the buzz of words she'd heard, as well as the warmth she'd felt, until by the time she left, the place had the same chilling aspects as the rooms below. She was aware of dislike and animosity, but hadn't been slammed with it before.

So, MacGowan clan didn't accept or like her yet. That was something she could work on, as well as the stairs. She'd wonder over how later. It was enough she had another assignment to stir through the mantle of worry.

She was led into a tower stairwell, and from there along a hall carved into the rock, and then, surprisingly, into a small chapel, with a little nave and altar built of stone. Maves explained that this one had been built back in Norman times, for the laird and his immediate family. It was out of use now, and felt it. There were three cloister windows of stained glass lighting the altar, and an air of peace and sanctity that begged one to enjoin.

Amalie did a quick walk-through before moving into another hall, and that ended at a large wooden, iron-studded door that led outside. She started gathering quite a few more participants to her tours of the outbuildings, most of them silent and sullen-looking. She told herself they were just curious about the new mistress, and then she worked at believing it. It was still difficult to ignore the dozen or so women trailing along as she toured the larder where the milk was curdled and cheeses hardened; the paneterie where the baked goods were stored, some of them hardening into stone-consistency for preservation. Stout Pells gave her the reason as he broke one and handed a portion to her. Amalie didn't even wipe her hand before taking it, gaining his grin in reply. The cakes were dry, gritty, and fairly tasteless. She sucked absently on it as they continued their tour. Some of the oatcakes got berries added when they were in season. That made them a bit more tasty. Or a man could swig a good gulp of whiskey to assist with the swallowing. Either way, these cakes were a Highlander's friend when on a long journey.

. . . such as reaching the MacKennah Castle and Thayne . . .

Amalie stumbled as they reached the smoke shed, disguising it as clumsiness so nobody would notice the instant stab of fear she'd displayed. It was much better to stay occupied. She put her attention to the two huntsmen as they explained how game meats and fish were prepared, usually getting sliced into long thin slabs for smoking. Amalie smiled and nodded, and stifled any queasiness, and got more than a smile or two in reply. And then Stout Pells gave her his arm to lead her to the next set of buildings.

None of the women surreptitiously watching them had anything resembling a smile on their faces. Most looked wary. Amalie did her best to ignore them, just as she had the workers in the kitchens. It appeared that MacGowan clansmen were more accepting of Thayne's bride than the women were going to be, but she'd work on it. She had Maves on her side already, and the rest probably needed time.

And that she had a lot of. At least, until Thayne was back. *Thayne!*

Amalie forced the reactive tears down, swallowed convulsively on any sobs, and forced her mind back to her tour. She didn't dare give in to emotion. Not now, in front of clan that wasn't accepting of her in the first place.

Beside the smoke shed was the game shed, where meats

were hung and ripened. Past that was the spiked roof of their two-story dovecote, and beyond that the sheds for drying hides. They didn't reach it. Maves spoke of her concern over wet grasses and the effect on their skirts and slippers, and Amalie hadn't even felt it.

When Thayne had spoken of her assuming the role of chatelaine of his household, and taking up the keys to it, she'd assumed it needed work. Now, she knew the truth. His household was a model of efficiency and organization. Her spirits dropped further as she realized it. She wasn't wanted here and she wasn't even needed.

She followed Stout Pells to another heavy oaken door set in the walls, this one leading to yet another torch-lit hall that echoed with voices and footsteps and activity she wasn't allowed to enjoin. In here, out of reach of any sunlight, the dampness of her lower limbs was obvious. Amalie shivered noticeably, and wondered why even that didn't pierce the depression settling all about her.

They got waylaid at the tower stair by a servant she didn't recognize, although Maves definitely did. She'd make an excellent head housekeeper, if she had aspirations above being Amalie's ladies maid. She stepped in front of Amalie protectively.

"You have chores to see to, Graven."

"I'm bearing a message."

"Out with it then, and return to your dusting duties."

"The Duchess of MacGowan is asking for the Sassenach."

Maves got bigger somehow, or maybe it was the fact Stout Pells had moved forward, sending torchlight onto her which tended to make her shadow bigger. Amalie's mind worked on small bits of information, rather than the entirety of the whole. It was self-preservation and she knew it. She didn't know how else to handle such dislike, distrust, and what bordered on outright rebellion. There wasn't any training her governesses had ever given in it.

"The *mistress* has more to do than listen to the likes of you. Inform them Lady MacGowan will attend within the hour. Once she's presentable. See to a carriage. Stout Pells? See us to the Chieftain Chamber. I've had enough of this woman's tongue, and will see to it once I've settled the mistress. You can rely on that, Graven."

"I mean nae disrespect to the lady. . . ."

Maves pushed forward and the woman in front of her gave way, backing without looking. "Return to your chores, Graven. Now."

"The duchess has requested her presence immediate-like!"

"None can cross the inner bailey courtyard with any speed, Graven. You have your orders. Now hie your arse out of my way."

"The duchess is na' at her palace. She's here. In the solar."

"In that event, the woman can wait just as well here. Give her the message. And now, Stout Pells, could you please see Her Ladyship to her chamber?"

It took more than an hour before Amalie was pronounced ready, her hair braided and wrapped neatly atop her head and then covered with a caplet, a linen under-dress skimming her frame, and over that a skirt and bodice of silver-toned satin while ermine trimmed her sleeves. She looked regal, and aloof, and aware of her consequence: the epitome of aristocracy. Only the chill of her hands in their gloves betrayed any emotion. Amalie had Maves to thank for all of it. More than she could say, although the woman wasn't having any of it. As far as Maves was concerned, Amalie was their new lady. She'd been chosen by Thayne in a love match, and that was good enough for Maves.

The duchess was sitting stiff-backed on a hard chair, situated beside a deep-set window, a manservant standing at either side of her. There was a fire in the Great Room on the other side of the fireplace. Welcome heat radiated from the hearth. That wasn't what had situated the duchess. It was the large peacock-shaded tapestry on the wall behind her, providing a painterly backdrop for her deep ruby gown and like jewelry. She was in full court attire, complete with a powdered wig, white painted complexion, and panniers. She looked ridiculous.

"Your grace."

Amalie approached, curtsied, and then moved to a chair closer to the hearth. She chose one with a high wooden back and a needlepoint cushion that had probably taken months to complete. Better to keep her mind on mundane things. Little things. Inconsequential things.

"You've taken quite a spell to reply to my summons."

"Truly?" Amalie put her attention on smoothing her skirts over her legs, hiding the tremble. And the cold. And what she refused to label fear.

"Now that you've arrived we can talk. Dismiss your servant."

"Whatever you've come to say, I'm certain Maves won't interfere."

"Are you disobeying an order?"

"Say what you've come for, your grace. You're keeping me from household matters."

The duchess pulled back visibly at the insult, and then her face twisted into an even uglier expression. It matched her tone. "Jules? Rene? Wait for me in the hall."

Amalie watched the two men bow before leaving, their footsteps in tandem across the floor. The duchess then turned to her expectantly.

"Maves, you may leave."

"My lady, I really must—"

"Now, Maves."

The woman tightened her lips, gave the duchess a blank look, and then followed the manservants from the room as well.

"Now, we can talk."

"No. Now you can say what you've come to say, and

then follow your servants from my house. That is what will happen."

"Very well. I'll be blunt. When do you plan to abide the ransom note?"

She was right. That was blunt. Amalie considered her for several moments. "I've made arrangements for the funds," she finally replied.

"I don't mean that, you fool. I mean the other part."

"What . . . other part?" Amalie's voice was almost inaudible. She'd never fainted. She wasn't about to do so now. The floor beneath her looked hard. Unforgiving. Cold. She clenched her hands and worked at seeing through the odd arrangement of dots that came out of nowhere to hover in the air between them.

"You mean . . . they didn't tell you?" The woman was prolonging the moment, obviously enjoying it, for her voice carried laughter and something more: nastiness.

Amalie shook her head.

"The MacKennahs will accept dissolution of the marriage."

"My marriage can't be dissolved. It's been consummated."

"Not if Thayne wants out of that hellhole, it hasn't. You ever see a dungeon, Miss Carstens? It's not a place I'd want to see any man."

"My marriage has been consummated. There is no annulling it."

"Minor detail, dear girl. If you're not breeding, no one will ever need to know, will they?"

"I'll know. And Thayne will know."

"You're not wanted here. You're not needed. Why would you stay?"

"Because I'm married."

"Words said before witnesses. Nothing more."

"Binding words, your grace. Or have you forgotten the man I wed? His word is his bond. Always."

"Your stubbornness may kill him!"

The duchess was getting animated. Two spots of dark purplish shade on her cheeks exacerbated her pallor.

"Scottish feuding may do that. Not me."

"He'll still be just as dead. Is that what you want?"

Amalie's heart felt like a giant had gripped it in his hand and squeezed. Her breath caught and the room swelled to immense proportions, making her tiny and insignificant. Then it returned. If this was fainting, she was in severe trouble. No wonder women carried smelling salts.

"This is wasting time, while Thayne is imprisoned! Maybe injured. Don't you care for him at all?"

I love him.

She almost said it. Tears obliterated the woman for a moment. Amalie breathed slowly and studiously until they disappeared. The duchess stood and approached her, pulling a ring from her finger and dropping it onto Amalie's skirts.

"If you love him, you'll do the right thing for him, his honor. And the clan. You'll free him. See this ring sent back to me. Don't take too long. His life hangs in the balance."

"Leave. Now."

It was Amalie's voice and words, but she didn't hear herself making them. The duchess's progress across the room and through the door was soundless as well. As was the door closing. All she heard was the worry closing in. And this time it brought pain.

Chapter 24

The MacKennah dungeon lived up to every expectation. The slab of stone Thayne woke atop was a perfect example. As was the absolute dark and cold. Despite knowing the stupidity, he groaned, alerting any observers. That was followed by a pent breath, awaiting the outcome. Nothing. They'd placed him on his back in here and then left him. Trust a MacKennah to have little in compassion and less in hospitable efforts. Thayne brushed his working hand down his front. Good. He still wore his plaid. They'd put it back over his bandaging. That bit of linen was tied into place, and not budging. Still good. He also wore his thick woolen trews, too. All of that stood him in good stead for this ordeal. At least he wouldn't die of the cold and chill. Not at first, anyway.

He reached his hand out to the side and touched spongy dampness. That proved another point. Their rooms weren't water-tight. Trickles of moisture slid down moss-covered walls, pooling into a depression between the wall and the stone slab he was atop. The ceiling was beyond reach, granting him room to sit, at least. There was fresh air coming from somewhere, muting the antipathy and decay that permeated the air. All in all, he was facing grim odds. Especially if they didn't see him fed.

Thayne sucked in a breath and sat, leaning forward in a slump as he absorbed the instant thumping pain through his temples. He told himself it was better and then worked at believing it. At least his teeth were calm and his jaw felt like it might work at something besides clenching. He rotated, putting his feet to the floor, thanking his luck they hadn't taken his boots, either. Thayne sat, breathing in and out, testing the space for any other occupant. But he knew the truth. He was stalling.

He put his working hand to his knee, pressed, and found his legs wobbled, but supported him for a hunched position until he knew the height of the room. It was getting easier to see, as well. There wasn't enough light to tell if it was day or night, but enough penetrated the gloom to give him a dim outline of a door. A wave of his hand above his head gave him room to stand fully, and he did so, keeping the reaction unspoken as his head throbbed at the move, and then his shoulder and arm joined in. And then, damn it all, everything on his body decided to hate him just for moving.

The door was three steps away, constructed of stout wood that contained slivers to this side, and didn't even have a handle, nor even a window for checking a prisoner. Odd design. And stupid. Any checking on him would have to open the door first. He'd have a chance to attack . . . if he had found any strength and mobility for it. Thayne stood with his forehead against the wood, waiting for his head to cease sending arrows of pain through him. And failing. There was nothing for it. Thayne retreated to his slab and collapsed into a sit to ponder his luck.

He was injured; he was locked in without benefit of food or a bucket for his needs; he was shivering already. At least he wouldn't die of thirst. He could suck it from the walls if he had to. He probably wasn't the first man to do so, and he wouldn't be the last. But food was going to be his real issue. His belly was an empty hole, assigning a measure of time to his incarceration. At least a day. Perhaps more. And then he wondered what his Amalie was doing.

Was she, even now, ensconced in his bed, worrying over his absence? Was she cuddling the bairn for solace? Did she even care that he'd gone missing?

And would she truly consider leaving him?

The groan this time had heart-pain at its core. Thayne bit it off and made a face at the outline of the door. His Amalie would never leave him. She loved him as he did her. She had to. Even if she hadn't voiced it, her frame told him of it more than once. Hadn't it?

Thayne sighed heavily. There was nothing for it. Pondering the workings of his wife's mind was as worthless as trying to dig his way through these walls. He settled onto his back again. It was better to be unconscious. And maybe, if he was lucky, he'd dream of being back in that big bed with her.

"Thayne?"

The feminine cant of the whisper brushed against his ear. Thayne swiped at it. He was dreaming, and it had been so real it was already causing apparitions to plague him? He must have been down here longer than he'd thought.

"MacGowan!"

The whisper came again, louder this time. It was still feminine, and now it came with a shove against his injured side. Thayne growled and rolled to face her, disguising the pain with the move. It was a lass of perhaps a decade and a half: slight, almost faery-like. She held a candle aloft, putting a halo image about her, while shedding light enough to see her glare at him. In his dungeon? Thayne blinked and then swiped at his eyes to look again, regardless of the pain it caused through his skull. Nothing changed. She was still there.

"You awake? Finally?"

"Go away."

"Hush!" She put a hand to his lips as if there were some-one in this benighted hole that could hear him.

"We must hurry!"

"We?" Thayne brushed her hand aside to sit, bending for-ward with the same slouched position as before while he waited for his head to absorb the pain to a manageable level. It was difficult to think around it, and he put his hand to his forehead for support. He'd never had such an injury. Every move sent a wave of sickness through his frame that made him shudder to suppress it. He was surprised she didn't notice.

"I'm going with you."

"You are?"

"Are all MacGowans as dense as you?"

"Dense?"

"You are na' escaping without me."

"I'm escaping?" Thayne must have slept too hard. The MacKennah dungeon didn't have an escape route, and faeries such as this slight thing didn't exist. And maybe, if the throbbing in his head would cease for just one small moment, he could ponder out why all of this didn't just dis-appear.

"If you doona' put some speed into it, you'll na' be going anywhere. Now move!"

She yanked on his hand, as if that would do more than tickle. Thayne thought of laughing, but that would just hurt too much and he was already handling as much pain as he could bear.

"Cease that and move aside. I canna' stand if you're in the space."

"Finally! I truly thank the fates I'm rid of you."

That didn't make any sense, but nothing else in the be-nighted hole seemed to. She'd stepped back, taking her light with her, though, and that meant he had to stand. Thayne nar-rowed his eyes, pulled in a breath, held it, and forced his legs to support him. He'd been right about her stature. The lass was so slight she barely cleared his waist, and stood looking up at him expectantly. Thayne shoved the breath out and stretched warily, working movement where numbness still lingered through his limbs. That was odd. He'd been injured before. He'd slept on stone before. He must be getting old.

"Verra well. I'm up. Awake. What more do you wish of me again?"

"Haste would be nice," she replied and put a hand on her hip as if to augment her dissatisfaction with him.

"Haste? To where?"

"Holy—! You MacGowans are a dense lot. You're escaping . . . and you're taking me with you!"

"I doona' think I . . . can do that."

"You think I'm setting you free without penalty? I'll be cast from my clan. You ken that, doona' you? Now, come. Follow me. And try to be silent and small, rather than a great hulking loud beast. Can you manage that?"

A great hulking loud beast. That was a new descriptor. Thayne would've smiled, but he was afraid it might hurt. "I'll do my best, Faery Maiden."

She had the door cracked open and looked out into a dimness that still hurt his eyes. Thayne blinked and tried to focus.

"My name is Mary. You hear? I'm nae faery and if you call me that again, I'm leaving you to rot."

Thayne groaned. This was a dream. It had to be.

"What is it now?"

"Your name is Mary."

"So? You have a problem with that, too?"

"Surely you have another name I can use?"

"Margaret Beatrice."

"Verra good. Lead on, Margaret Beatrice. I'm at your heels."

Unfortunately, the last was true. She tripped as his boot clamped on a cloak that was way too large for her, and consequently dragging on the floor behind her. He reached for her to keep her upright. And then had to back away from the instant reaction.

"You touch me again, MacGowan, and I'll carve on you!"

A little skean appeared in her free hand, aimed right for his groin. He didn't doubt her familiarity with it, either.

"Verra well. Next time, I'll let you fall."

"If you'd keep your great big feet to yourself, it would na' be of issue. Now come. Follow me."

He'd been wrong. It wasn't a dream. It was a nightmare. Light from their torches speared his eyes, making a colorful circle about them, and that created even more havoc in his head. She turned away from the brightest section, and Thayne nearly thanked her. That was before she led him into a tunnel with dirt sides and a ceiling that didn't clear his head.

The thump of his forehead on a beam sent him to his knees, with both hands about his head, while his belly retched in waves of sickness that each felt like a blow slamming against the back of his skull. Then, it was over. Thayne was on his side, curled into a ball, and weeping dry sobs. He didn't even care who saw. He'd rather be in his cell.

"Get up."

His tormentor knelt at his side, disgust clear on her features. Thayne rolled his face back into the damp earth smell beneath him. "Go away."

"What's wrong with you now?"

"I'm injured, lass."

"Where?"

Was she blind? He couldn't even use his right side. "Arrow shot . . . and then ax hit. I should be dead."

"Who would do that to you?"

"Your clan." Anger tempered the words and motivated more than it hurt. That was odd. He spent a few moments evaluating. His head no longer felt like it wanted to fly off. He felt weak, but the agony of hammering had cleared. He ran his tongue over his teeth, testing for pain and got none. It was a miracle . . . exactly when he needed it. Thayne pushed into a squat, and rolled his head atop his neck, reveling in the lack of pain.

"Impossible. I heard them. You're much too great a prize. They would na' hurt you."

"Verra well. I imagine the wounds."

She'd moved to a stand. Thayne went to a stoop to match her, and ran his hand along the top of the cavern to test height. Not enough and it was getting shorter. And it was slimy with wet.

She made a sound resembling another curse.

"I'm injured, lass, but I'm na' dense. Where does this tunnel go?"

"Outside."

"Along the moat?"

"I doona' ken. I've never taken it."

Thayne swallowed the instant retort. It didn't truly matter if his escape was poorly planned and worse executed. What mattered was that it worked. And hopefully, she had food packed somewhere. And a horse.

She had neither.

She'd resorted to taking his hand the deeper they went. Then, they'd been forced to a crawl, and before they reached the opening, he'd had to shove rocks and mud aside for access. He'd also taken the lead. She also failed to mention the shale ledge they reached when finally he shoved a boulder in front and heard it career into empty space.

Then he was out; on his back and breathing in huge lungs of rain-moist air that tasted of such freedom, he nearly crowed the delight. He'd have stayed there, reveling in it, if she hadn't gone to her feet, pulling sodden cloak about her, looking at him with such an exasperated air, it instantly deflated his joy. That's when they began the climb. It felt like hours later they reached the top of the drum, dealt with the lack of a horse, dry clothing, and food. All the lass claimed was an oatcake that she tore in half and shared with him. If it wasn't for a burn of icy-cold water they happened across that he used to fill his belly, he'd have howled the despair and damn the consequences.

There was nothing for it. They started walking.

Amalie didn't believe in prayer anymore. She hadn't since Edmund. Prayer was for the weak, the frail. The helpless. Prayer never solved much. All prayer netted was sore knees and an aching head. Nobody knew about it, though. Amalie still prayed. She gave it lip service, especially on the Sabbath. Anything else would be sacrilegious and heretical. So, she prayed . . . but her heart wasn't in it. Not since the night Edmund had died and prayer hadn't done a thing to stop it.

She hadn't told Maves what the duchess said, despite the prodding and beseeching, and then bullying. The maid would only argue it. She'd counsel Amalie to await her reply from the earl. Hold tightly to everything she felt. Have faith.

Wait, when any moment could be Thayne's last? Have faith, when she knew exactly what these Highlanders were capable of? Hold tightly . . . to what? Perhaps if it was her life they threatened, it would all be so different. But it wasn't. It was Thayne. And she loved him.

What looked so clear in the daylight hours, got indistinct and ragged when pondered deep in the night, with nothing to defray it. Nightmare visions of suffering warred with her attempts to sleep, and praying did little to mute them. Amalie didn't dare wait for her father's reply, or even if he'd give one. To do so, meant she toyed with more than their stupid pride. To wait meant she played with something more precious to her than her own life: Thayne's.

Amalie watched the glow of fire embers reflecting on the ruby ring she held, trying to decipher meaning from the mesh of red and purple hues. Then she blinked, sending tears down her cheeks. It was probably nearer dawn than eve. She was exhausted and yet still sleepless. She'd walked her limbs into a state of exhaustion that had them twitching, she'd drunk the potion Maves had brought; she'd even tried to find the oblivion of sleep in Thayne's enormous bed. Nothing worked. And nothing muted it. Even the hours she'd spent on her knees hadn't done a thing to dent the emotion seeping into her every limb.

It wasn't worry that dogged her every breath now. It was much worse.

Baby Mary slept peacefully over near the bed. Amalie looked over at the cradle and felt her features soften before another tear blurred the image. She already felt the heart pain that would be empty arms. She suspected it would multiply as the effect of losing Thayne added to it. Her only hope was to pretend it didn't exist. Bury it. Falsify it. And fear it to the point she daren't close her eyes.

She didn't know why she still hesitated. She'd been pondering it all night already, through prayers that didn't change anything, and tears that did less. Maves might grieve her departure, but everyone else would be glad to see the end of her, especially if it meant the return of their laird. She didn't need to question it. Every look betrayed them.

I love him.

Amalie bowed her head to the needlepoint-covered chair seat again, her mind blank and her lips still. Love didn't seem much of a blessing. It had too much agony attached. First when she'd lost Edmund, and now this. Seems she was fated to be heart-sore. Strange thing about fate. Why . . . if the post carriage had been running a half hour late, none of this would have happened. She wouldn't have tripped, or if she did, no

Highlander would have caught her and altered her existence. Her second-class room would have been empty and bare, or if there was anything of Mary Dunn-Fyne left in it, Amalie would probably have taken the innkeeper to task over it and found other accommodations. She'd have gone blithely about her journey to the MacKennah household, been ensconced in the schoolroom, and by now she'd be counting her luck she'd managed to escape.

A half hour of time, perhaps less. Such little time separated the almost giddy sense of self-confidence she'd felt then from what was turning into a depth of heartbreak and loss she didn't know how to absorb. The combination filled her, leaching into her very soul, touching the place prayer didn't penetrate, making her feel old and feeble and weak. She must not have suffered enough after Edmund. She hadn't learned her lesson well enough. Loving someone meant you'd do what you had to for them. You'd sacrifice. You'd do whatever it took. You'd do what you had to, even if it killed every bit of you. That's what loving meant.

And that's why she was still here; attempting prayer. She was girding up for what she was about to do. Thayne MacGowan wasn't going to spend another moment in any dungeon cell, injured; perhaps dying. Not when she could change it. What she wanted didn't matter. What they felt mattered even less. The ruby in the ring winked at her, granting her the tiniest measure of courage. She should probably thank the woman for giving her this lifeline, allowing her back into a sham of life. But she wouldn't. She wasn't ever going to think of this place or this time again. She was going to cut it out of her life and watch it disappear over her shoulder, and do her best to bury it.

I love him.

A sob escaped before she could halt it, and Amalie clenched her hands together on the chair, asking this time—

not for a change from her fate, but for the strength to see it through without one person guessing what it cost her. The words were jumbled and indistinct, and filled with anguish as she begged for a small measure of courage to do what she had to do.

The baby began whimpering, the sound blending in with Amalie, so that, at first, she didn't even hear it. She tried ignoring her, hoping the babe would cease. She'd need all her strength to leave Baby Mary. It was already ripping her heart from her breast just thinking of it. She didn't dare lift her to comfort her. The cries got louder and more strident, and more heartrending in their intensity. Amalie lifted her head and looked across at the cradle, watching the little fists flail above the carved wooden rim. And then she sighed, and got to her feet.

There was nothing for it. She'd have to see the child comforted and asleep again, or she'd never be able to leave. She put the ring on the table, was at the babe's side, lifting her, and then cuddling her, and feeling such a swell within her breast as the babe cuddled into her, that she staggered against the bed. The babe went to hiccoughs, while both hands wound about locks of Amalie's hair, as if the child knew of her decision.

But that was foolish. Impossible. Imaginative. And yet no matter how calm and asleep the baby looked, every time Amalie attempted to put her back in her cradle, she'd awaken and start wailing again. Each time took longer to soothe her too, making it an exercise in patience to jiggle, then rock, and then pace, and then jiggle some more, until finally Amalie climbed into the enormous bed with the babe, and held her close, breathing deeply while the babe snuggled. That's exactly when she knew she couldn't do it. She wouldn't leave. Not when there was hope.

Amalie settled into the mass of pillows at her back, pulled

the linens up to cover them, and yawned with a force that stretched the side of her mouth. She felt replete and aglow, as if something momentous had occurred that was beyond her scope of understanding. If she could get her fogged mind to ponder, perhaps she'd gain meaning. For now, it was enough that her arms felt as full as her heart. And for the first time since the ordeal began, she slept dreamlessly and soundly.

Chapter 25

Dawn brought a sun that tried to penetrate the fog-covered ground, pierce the drizzle, and send some warmth onto any occupants out in such dreary conditions. All it really managed was to illuminate every bit of why Thayne felt so cold, wet, weak, and miserable. Each step slogged with the wet slurp of mud, and then got accompanied with shivers. They were an easy mark, not only for pursuers but for any clan wretch intent on making his name. Taking a MacGowan plaid of this quality would be a coup. Taking it from the MacGowan laird's brother would be even better.

They'd have to seek shelter. He didn't turn to ask Margaret if she agreed. He tried to completely ignore her. He already knew she considered him the weakest, densest lout because she continually told him so. The last had been the one time he'd asked for a rest, and then further why she'd set out to rescue a man without packing one bit of rudimentary equipment, such as a dry change of clothing or a bit of food.

Thayne slicked a hand across his face, sluicing moisture away. The act rubbed his palm along stubble. His Amalie probably wouldn't like being nuzzled from a jaw like this. It usually took a week or more for his skin to feel this grizzled, which was the main reason he kept it scraped off. A man unable to grow a decent beard just provided a lot of amusement at his expense. Better to say he deigned to follow Roman style, leaving little for an enemy to grasp during battle than the real reason. His beard growth now gave him a timeline for his incarceration. He'd been there a week, or close to it.

Thayne jumped a small burn trickle, saturating the ground, and then turned to give his rescuer a hand over it, although it was more a toss. That wasn't intentional. She went airborne due to her diminutive size and lack of weight. She barely kept her feet and thanked him with a scrunched up expression that would dampen her chances for suitors. Once she'd grown enough for such and changed her mind about the state of matrimony.

He now knew she was his betrothed, she considered it a blessing to be free of him, and she truly wondered at her father's anger. No clan should want ties with a clan sporting men as weak and dense as him. She'd helped him escape in order to spare herself the ignominy of a life of shame such as her father had imposed on her. She didn't like Thayne. She expected to be rewarded. He was to get his new English wife to sponsor her into society down in Londontown. Mary Margaret wasn't going to bury herself in the Highlands, amid such harsh rules and clan rigidity. No. She wanted to make something of herself.

In London?

Mary Margaret Beatrice MacKennah would have little chance. Thayne had experience with a society that whispered and cold-shouldered someone for either speech, mode of dress, or lack of sophisticated manners. He'd have disabused Mistress MacKennah of such dreams, but he found it suited him to let her believe them. She could find out for herself. It was payment enough since she appeared to match her mother's temperament. Her lack of compassion shone throughout every spiteful word she uttered and every disgusted look she gave him. He'd rather have her silence.

Without warning, an arrow spliced the ground between his legs, stopping him mid-stride. Thayne immediately put out his good arm and shoved Mary behind him, and she immediately began haranguing him over it.

"Lout! Imbecile! I've had about enough of your man-handling, and oafish—"

"Hush!"

She shoved at him with puny arms that hadn't any effect. And then he yanked her off her feet for good measure.

"Let . . . me go!"

"If you value life, hush!"

He hissed it over his shoulder, and watched realization finally dawn as she saw the shaft still quivering between his feet. Then she became a dead weight, of less than a sack of grain.

"Halt!"

The order seemed to emanate from every direction through the fog layer, stopping him as if they'd known he debated sprinting up the hill and diving to the far side. And then the forms of armed men began taking shape. Lots of men, bearing lots of arms. Thayne stood at his tallest, facing them in a weakened state, shielding the lass at his back, and completely unarmed. His luck was cursed. As always.

There was nothing for it. He sucked in breath and shouted his own order back at them. "You friend or foe?"

"Depends on your clan!"

The answering shout sounded familiar, as did the plaids they wore. Thayne blinked and then stared.

"Grant? Is that you?"

"MacGowan? By the Saints! Lads! Come quick! We've found him! 'Tis the chieftain! Coming right out of the morn at us!"

"I am na' my brother!"

Thayne was intensely tired of being mistaken for Jamie. Especially by one of his own Honor Guard. It made his reply harsher than he intended. He also eased the girl back to her feet, but held to her, in the event she wasn't ready. Grant stopped in front of him, planted his sword, blade down into the ground, and went to a knee. He was joined by more of them, all doing the same.

"My laird."

"What is this?"

Thayne's heart stumbled as he assigned meaning. But that would mean Jamie was dead, and that just wasn't worth considering. As much as he'd detested what Jamie did, and how many he hurt, it still pained to think him gone.

"A vow of fealty. To the new Chieftain of the MacGowan clan. You. Thayne Alexander MacGowan."

"No."

"Aye. The duke . . . he, uh . . . he passed on two nights past."

He'd lost his only sibling, and hadn't even felt it? Thayne's knees wobbled for a moment before he forced them to keep him standing. The lass at his back stirred slightly.

"How?"

The men were getting back to their feet. None would meet his eye. Thayne had to ask it again. "Tell me how. You. Grant."

"He fell from his horse and broke his neck. I'd as lief say it happened during battle, but 'twould be a lie."

"He broke his neck? Jamie?"

"Aye, and died afore any could even reach him. Without pain."

"Where is he? Close?"

"Nae. We sent him back to the castle. Yester-eve. Seemed best at the time."

"Best?"

"'Tis powerful hard to rally men when their leader lies dead in his tent. But now that you've arrived, we can enjoin the bastards in battle and—"

"Nae. There's been enough feuding over a slight. And trust

me, lads. The bride would na' have taken my hand in wedlock, even had I been available."

"Nae?"

"Na' only would she na' have me, but she has nae qualms about speaking on it to me, either."

"She does na' want you? The MacGowan?"

"Oh, for pity's sake! Could you finish this later? I'm hungry. And cold."

The lass interrupted them, stepping out from behind him, with both hands on her hips, to look up at the horde of men about them. She hadn't gained much in stature or presence. Her resemblance to a sprite seemed more acute than before. He amended that. She looked more like a little angry sprite. Thayne watched them all look at her and start grinning.

"Forgive my manners. Lads? Meet Mary Margaret, formerly of MacKennah clan. My rescuer."

"I canna' possibly forgive your manners, Thayne MacGowan, since you've failed to exhibit any. But I suppose . . . if any of you men have food?"

Sean stepped forward and handed her what appeared to be an oatcake sprinkled with berries, and added a strip of dried meat. Thayne's mouth watered just watching her down it, without one word of his needs.

"You hungry, my laird?"

Someone asked it. Thayne looked up from contemplation of Mary as she chewed and swallowed and then demanded more. He shook himself. She wasn't the only one blessed by his marriage to Amalie. His luck must be changing.

"I'm more in need of whiskey, and then a warm fire. And then I'll look to filling my belly. We have any of that? Close by?"

There was a chorus of 'ayes,' and then someone shoved a flask into his hand.

* * *

The MacGowan clan appeared to run on a system of barter, much like a medieval fief. She'd decided to continue her exploration of the keep by checking the storerooms above the kitchens. These branched out of a hall that paralleled the Great Hall upper balcony. They could be reached from either the great wheel-stair that led to her chambers, or she could use another set of steps designated for servants and the like. The balcony had several openings between stone and wood-framed columns, giving a decent view to happenings down below in the Great Hall. There were platforms that jutted out at intervals along the walkway, for accessing the chandeliers. There was also a minstrel's gallery.

Thayne had a room slated as his treasury. She'd been forced to hide her disappointment that all his treasure consisted of fashioned goods. According to the steward-at-arms, Thayne had taken all the coins with him when he'd first gone to the MacKennahs. He'd left behind a locked room containing boxes of jewelry and gem-encrusted articles, while chests containing accoutrements worked in gold and silver lined the walls. It should amount to a good portion of the ransom amount, if the MacKennahs were amenable to barter and payments.

Another room contained the barter he must have accepted for rents from his clan. Amalie counted more than eleven bales of raw sheered wool ready to be carded, alongside uncountable spools of threads, ready for the dye shed, or perhaps the weaving looms. That sort of industry was undoubtedly based in one of the outbuildings she hadn't toured yet, since the dying and drying of wool created a noxious environment.

And then Jamie's body arrived, changing everything.

Amalie had just finished checking the embroidered bed linens, when the sounds of shouting, booted feet, and clanking of weaponry filled the Great Hall beneath them, sending her to a balcony edge. Maves, Stout Pells, the others who'd accompanied her, and even the steward filled space along the balcony.

"Lady MacGowan! We've come in search of Lady MacGowan! Someone fetch the woman."

Amalie clenched her hands at her breasts to hide the trembling. Nothing could be done about the cold. Stout Pells answered for her, in a loud booming voice that seemed to echo. Everyone looked at him in surprise. She hadn't known he possessed such a voice. She wasn't alone. Just about everyone looked surprised.

"Speak your piece, Angus MacGorrick! And then I'll decide whether Her Ladyship can attend you or na'!"

"The duke is dead!"

"Jamie?"

"Escort Her Ladyship to the chieftain room! Now!"

"Aye!"

The noise below her swelled, turning into a mass of men who filed through the door that led to the rooms she'd met Thayne in the night of her presentation. Odd. It felt like it had happened months ago. No. Years.

"My lady?"

Stout Pells held an arm out for her escort. Amalie took it and worked at smoothing any stray hairs that might have escaped her caplet back into order. Jamie was dead? Because of their stupid feud? Perhaps even now, the clan was in battle to free Thayne . . . and these men wished to see her? They didn't blame her, did they? They couldn't. It wouldn't be fair. But . . . if they did blame her, they wouldn't up and punish her without a hearing? Would they? They couldn't. Just because she hailed from the south was no reason to blame her. And then her mind filled with images of what form the punishment might take, before she could stop it.

Her hand shook on Stout Pells's arm. He ignored it. The steps seemed endless, her feet like they belonged to someone else. At one point she tripped and would have fallen, if Pells hadn't yanked up on his arm at that moment. He didn't say anything, and she didn't dare ask. They had a large assemblage following them, and more clan members joined them in the Great Room once they reached it. To her, the observers felt expectant and excited, rather like a wolf pack encircling a kill. Amalie didn't dare look at any of them, and kept her eyes on the floor directly in front of her skirts. She told herself it was just her imagination; then started silently praying she was right.

The sound of steps got swallowed up in the noise generated by such a large crowd. They reached the enormous oaken double doors, and someone pounded for entrance. By now, her hands weren't the only cold portion of her anatomy. Everything on her body shivered with the chilled sensation. If it wasn't for Pells's assistance, she didn't know if her legs would continue holding her. She clung to his arm as he shoved his way through the mass, creating a wake in a sea of bodies. They reached the dais, but a glance showed it to be empty. Pells stopped, and that meant Amalie had to.

"I've brought Her Ladyship. As bid. You may speak now, Angus MacGorrick."

Pells's words rang out, making an audible vacuum in the room. It felt like everyone pulled in a breath and just held it. Waiting. Then there came shuffling sounds and the clanking of weapons. Amalie glanced up and then stilled as man after man went to a knee in front of her, his sword planted blade down into the flooring, with his head bowed against the hilt. They filled the space until it looked like a sea of bowed heads all around her, punctuated with sword hilts.

"What . . . is this?" Amalie cleared her throat after the first word, since it warbled.

"I'm Angus MacGorrick, uncle to the laird. As the elder of Clan MacGowan, I've come to pledge our fealty, your grace. As have we all. Lads?" The old man who'd been leading them lifted his head and addressed her. Amalie felt Stout Pells's movement as he also took a knee.

"Your . . . fealty?"

"Aye. To the new Duchess of MacGowan."

She really was going to faint. Amalie reached out blindly and connected with someone's hand on his sword. It was probably lucky that it was Angus MacGorrick. He took it as a sign to stand, and did so, going directly in front of her, forcing her gaze up.

"We pledge our loyalty to you. Now. As wife of the new chieftain and laird, Thayne Alexander MacGowan. May you both live long and prosper."

The words echoed in the chamber and then died away, leaving a resonating hollow feeling.

"What should I do now?" She leaned forward to whisper it to Angus. It was probably heard by those about them due to the acoustics in the room. Angus winked.

"Advise the men to rise. Too much time on the knee can be harmful to a man's health. And speak loud and clear. We'll make certain you're heard."

"Oh." Speak loud and clear? In front of so many? Amalie had often pondered with Edmund what going on the boards as an actor would feel like, if she'd been born a male and had that opportunity. She found out at this moment that it was more than frightening. It was terrifying.

"Rise. Please."

The words warbled. Angus shouted them for her. Then Stout Pells added an echo of them and some words of his own. "The duchess accepts! Now, move aside and allow her a path!"

A path. Right to the raised dais containing chairs that looked like they'd been constructed for giants. Amalie followed a trio of elders, Stout Pells right behind her, as she was taken to the dais and seated in a chair that made her feel like a dwarf, and probably look like one. She had elders on both sides of her, Angus on her right while Stout Pells stood just to the left of her chair back.

"First item of business, your grace?"

Good heavens. She was at a war counsel, and worst of all, they expected her to lead. Nothing could have prepared her for this. Except those afternoons when she and Edmund had fought the Spanish Armada. Amalie smiled and rubbed her hands, not just for warmth, but because she was excited.

"I would say we must get my husband released, but I'll leave that in the hands of competent men such as yourselves."

She'd said the right thing. As it was announced, and then re-announced, she could see open grins and nods. Not to mention Angus MacGorrick was looking at her like a kindly grandfather. If, of course, it was her imagination of how a kindly grandfather would look, since she'd never had one.

"Fair enough. Next?"

"Was Jamie . . . I mean, the late Duke of MacGowan . . . a Catholic?"

"You insult the MacGowan clan with such a question, your grace!"

Angus went a shade of purple, as it looked like he controlled his words. Amalie said words that just came to her, without any thought or any preparation.

"Then, we must see Jamie's body readied for a proper burial, in the only right and proper church, and that means the Church of England!"

That announcement didn't need to get repeated. Cheers broke out, ringing off the walls. Angus nodded and turned out to the crowd.

"See to it. You? Garrick! Take Leeman, Sean-the-Younger, and Pitt. You have an issue with the dowager, you come tell me!"

Rustling and crowd noise followed the announcement. Amalie assumed it was due to the departure of the specified men. She leaned toward Angus again. "What issue might they have with the duchess?" she asked.

"Hopefully one that'll get her arse thrown off the land. And this time, for good!"

This time? There sounded like a good story in that bit of information but Amalie didn't pursue it. "Good thing I am the lesser evil, eh?"

"I never said such, your grace. I never even inferred such a thing."

"It's all right. I said it for you. So." Amalie rubbed her hands together in a semblance of childish glee. That was probably what brought grins to every bearded face she looked into. "Why should we let them start anything? I say we go and have an issue with the dowager now."

"My lady! I mean, your grace!" It was Maves, moving forward to stand at the base of the podium that just reached her breast line. "You'll need time to prepare! Time to get presentable!"

Amalie stood and shouted her answer. It got repeated anyway.

"Presentable? I'm the wife of the laird of Clan MacGowan. There isn't anything about me that isn't presentable! So, tell me . . . who's with me?"

The answer was blurred from many throats but wasn't mistakable. They might hate her because of her lineage, but they hated the French-court raised duchess even more. Amalie took Stout Pells's arm for an escort again, although this time the crowd parted easily so she could reach the front of the mass. Angus was on her other side, while the other elders strode beside him.

They made quite a retinue crossing the inner bailey grounds, especially as it appeared word was spreading, and the crowd size had grown apace. It had seemed a lengthy distance to the Palazzo when she'd undertaken it at night. And in a carriage. And with Thayne at her side. It had seemed to take a lot longer than the few minutes it took to traverse it now. She might as well have wings on her feet. She didn't even feel the damp of the ground mists or late afternoon chill since any daylight was blocked by the height of the walls. They arrived on the heels of the clansmen Angus had sent, who were attempting to gain entrance.

Stout Pells held her back as Angus took command, sending shouts and orders that saw the front force of the crowd reach the double doors and push them inward. Amalie watched from several yards back as the wood bowed with a loud groaning sound, and then burst wide, tumbling men forward.

Several effeminate-looking servants blocked their path at first, brandishing canes, chairs, a fireplace poker, and one of them had a torch stand.

"Cease that or face a bruising! Andrew!"

One of the largest men Amalie had ever seen stepped through the crowd, and slammed a long spear-thing into the floor. The room resounded with the boom of noise while several cracks appeared in the parquet flooring. But it worked. The servants dropped their impromptu weapons and fled. From the back hall, another man appeared, his wig askew on his head while the buttons on his coat were half fastened. The heels of his shoes clicked with his haste in approaching them. He stopped just shy of the behemoth that was Andrew, looked him up and down before turning to Amalie. And then he spoke in a supercilious tone that was meant to put her firmly in her place and almost succeeded.

"We were not prepared for a visit, Mistress MacGowan. You are to leave."

"Bow your head in deference, Cousin MacGorrick, and that's an order. This here is the new Duchess of MacGowan. I'll thank you to keep a civil tongue in your head, or I'll be for carving it out for you. And ye ken already how much I'd like that."

Angus used his cane for emphasis, tapping it rapidly as he stepped up to stare down the man. His threat must mean something, for the man went even whiter than his face paint. Then Wynneth spoke up, looking down on them from the dim gloom of the stair crest. She had four servants on either side, and looked exactly as overdressed and ridiculous as she'd looked the first time Amalie had seen her.

"What is this? I've just been informed of my bereavement, and this is the behavior of Clan MacGowan . . . to their late chieftain's wife?"

Her voice carried just the right amount of warble. Amalie could feel the reaction in the crowd about her. The woman was good with her acting. Very good. But Amalie was better. Hadn't she spent her entire childhood acting out emotion-charged dramas like this one? She took a deep breath, stepped forward, and curtsied.

"Begging your pardon, my lady, but your men might need help with their hearing. We did knock."

There were chuckles coming from about her, whether at her childlike voice or her words, she didn't know.

"Oh! And your door must have worm-rot. Just look. It didn't withstand my knock!"

She lifted her hand for effect, and got more laughter and some applause, all of it bringing a wonderful feeling of omnipotence. No wonder men went on the boards to act! It was exhilarating.

"What do you want?"

"No pleasantries? No comments on my . . . appearance?"

"You look like a *peasant*. Is that what you want to hear?"

The word was infused with insult and rudeness. It wasn't lost on the crowd. A ripple of something unpleasant went through those about her. Amalie knew why, but the woman facing her was immune. Amalie looked like every other woman in the crowd.

"Very well. We'll speak of other things. Perhaps you'd come down from there so we could speak in a normal tone, and not shout?"

"Say what you've come to say and then leave. You're damaging my floor."

Amalie put her hand up with her index finger outstretched. "Very well, we'll shout, then! And the floor is one of the reasons for my visit, Wynneth."

"My proper title is "your grace." You are to use it when addressing me."

"Not anymore, my lady. Thayne's wife is the new duchess."

Stout Pells announced it in his booming bass voice. Wynneth looked to waver, but had it immediately covered over as she resumed glaring down at them from her superior vantage.

"And as such, I'm here to assess my new lodgings . . . damage and all!"

"Your new lodgings?"

"Surely you didn't think you'd be allowed to stay in the Palazzo, did you?"

"This is my home!"

The woman's voice rang out stridently. Amalie waited for her to fling her arms wide to encompass the entire area. If the woman had any notion of using drama to sway a crowd, she'd have done it. Amalie was rather disappointed when nothing happened. So, she took a deep breath and spoke her next lines, as if someone had scripted them for her.

"That is a real problem, Wynneth, dear. It seems the Palazzo belongs to the reigning duchess, and that is me. Actually, I believe the entire estate is in my control now, and that includes this building. As such, I've decided to move my household here for a bit. With some changes, of course."

"Changes?" The woman's voice choked.

"There's a lot of French-style furniture I'll see to removing . . . as well as religious icons that jar with the true faith. And look here. There's some obvious damage been done to this floor. Remove your spear Andrew, and let me look at it. Yes. I do see a bit of replacement is in order. And let's not forget the front doors. They were obviously defective. Made of weak wood. For shame." Amalie clicked her tongue for effect. The crowd seemed to enjoy that, as chuckling broke out.

"You'd . . . evict me?"

The woman had finally lost some of her bravado. Her voice actually dropped on the words. Amalie smiled up at her and approached the base of the staircase.

"Eviction is such a strong word. I believe I'm doing the right and proper thing by seeing you moved to a dower house. Surely the MacGowan clan has some sort of arrangement of that sort? A small abode for a dowager duchess with only a widow's portion to sustain her. Don't we, Angus?" She turned her head to address him.

"To be sure. We—"

"Silence!"

Amalie had been mistaken. Wynneth still had some arrogance and haughtiness left. She had a hysterical note to her voice, too. The room quieted to an uncomfortable silence. So Amalie did something that instantly broke the tension. Everyone laughed, and they were directing the amusement at the dowager duchess. Stupid woman. If Wynneth thought to best Amalie now, the woman was naïve.

"Yes?" She drew the word out, making three syllables out of it.

"You take a lot upon yourself, *governess*."

She put a snide, condescending tone on the word, as if it actually had meaning. Amalie had to give her one thing. The dowager duchess had courage. Misguided, conceited, and supercilious courage, but she faced them as if a horde of backward serfs had gone rampant. Amalie sighed heavily, put both hands on her hips, and leaned back so her words would get the best projection.

"Whatever I might have been is immaterial, for I am clearly the Duchess of MacGowan now. And you'll begin packing your household for removal. Or I'll assign members of my household to assist. You ken?" Amalie used the Scot word and knew it was the right thing as a swell of approval seemed to encase her.

"You truly think to usurp me? You . . . upstart! You've nothing more than ties to a man who might be dead!"

"Oh. He's not dead. Why . . . I already know he's escaped. He's on his way back to me. You'll see. And all of this is words while you stall. I've given the orders to pack your household for removal to the dower house, and you're to begin immediately."

"If I refuse?"

"Andrew? Do you have kin?" Amalie turned to the giant fellow and looked way up to ask it. He grinned and nodded.

"Good. Request them to my employ. I seem to be in need of strong backs at the moment."

"Thayne escaped? You're daft. We all know he's locked away in a MacKennah dungeon because of you!"

Silence hit the space again. Amalie narrowed her eyes as she turned back to the duchess, who'd come down four steps toward them. She didn't have one servant with her. They actually seemed to be backing, fading into the shadows of the upper halls. The woman had decided to try and sway the crowd now? More stupidity. The dowager duchess was an amateur. Amalie waited several long moments as the silence just kept growing, and then she spoke, clearly and concisely, and with sarcasm gleaned from years of practice. Years.

"How . . . odd. I distinctly recall being told a feud started from Jamie's wedding to you. Ancient history, but there you are."

"Ancient? Why, you—!"

Amalie interrupted her. "This is really tiresome. I've finished speaking my orders. I'll be assigning a contingency of clan here to oversee your removal. Good day."

Amalie turned around, and waited for a path to open for her.

"I can pack my own household!"

Amalie pivoted back. The man, Andrew, had moved into her vacated spot to stand, looking up at the staircase. He had his spear in a vertical position, point upward. He was intimidating, and obviously meant to be. Amalie couldn't have asked for a better finale.

"Oh. I don't send them to assist with packing. I need them for other things, such as an accounting of the treasury. There might be two thousand pounds locked away that could've already been used to get my husband released. Who knows? It might have spared your husband his death. Oh! Another thing . . ." She reached into her bodice and pulled out the ruby ring; held it high for everyone to see, and then moved to place it on the lowest stair. "I don't believe I'll be needing this."

The duchess was finally speechless. She also looked paler than any paint. She might even be weak-kneed, if her grip on the stair railing was an indication. Both hands looked like claws wrapped about it. Amalie waited for her to answer, and when nothing was forthcoming, she nodded. It was the perfect ending for a play. Perfect. Edmund would have been proud.

Chapter 26

Nobody had warned her about the aftereffects of truly acting a part . . . nor that there was a price to pay. Amalie sat in the big bed and watched as Maves poured her another mug of warmed mead. There'd been a feeling of euphoria that lasted clear through the evening, chattering with Angus and his family—which included the sharp-tongued nanny. The woman still didn't appear fond of Amalie, but she did smile once. Then, after bidding everyone a good eve, had come exhaustion. Tiredness had rolled over her like a wet bog slide, making it a near impossible feat to reach her rooms, and another one to prepare for bed. That's when indecision and anxiety set in. She replayed every moment through her head enough times to set her teeth to grinding.

She'd done the wrong thing, said the wrong words, offended those she needed to admire . . . done something wrong. And the worst was claiming to know Thayne had already escaped. What devil had stolen her wits, making her say something so patently false? The night hadn't held any answers, and the morn gave more of the same. Maves called for her early, telling her the elders requested a conference with her. They were waiting in the chieftain room. As if she truly was a Highland chieftain of such a wide-flung clan.

Amalie received Maves's guidance without asking. With that, came another maid to assist with clothing her in suitable attire for such an event. Less than a quarter hour later she was escorted from her room, a tartan shawl atop her white muslin over-dress, an ecru-shaded linen chemise beneath that, thick-soled boots on her feet, while a lace-trimmed caplet sat atop her wound braids. She checked in the chamber mirror before leaving, wondering how ludicrous she appeared. The mirror must have been in on the fantasy. She didn't look remotely English. Or weak. Or anxious. She looked official and in charge of any situation. Her heels had echoed off the stone steps of her wheel-stair, and after she'd been announced—with a long and extremely Scot-sounding name and title—those heels had echoed off the walls, pantomiming a confident, strong stride.

It was a lie. All of it felt like one, especially when Angus had opened the meeting by asking if she could give them Thayne's location, so a scout could be sent out for him. Angus already had the lad picked out: his youngest grandson and namesake. The boy was twelve, but had a wiry strength that belied his age. He'd ride for Thayne and return with word afore nightfall. All they needed was the direction and length of ride. If she'd be forthcoming with the information, they'd be most appreciative.

Amalie had swallowed on the instant fright, clasped her hands in a grip that made her fingers white, and told them she didn't see things as perfect as she wanted, when she saw them. One of the elders had asked if she were fey? Fey? The word must convey something appropriate and it was better to agree than look like the liar she was, so she nodded. And that had satisfied them.

Now, late into the night, she was sleepless and Maves hovered over her, worry in her every word and gesture. Amalie couldn't tell the woman what was wrong. She'd even moved Baby Mary back to the nursery, so she wouldn't be

tainted by Amalie's presence. She hadn't known she'd feel this
way from lying. There was self-hate . . . and there was disgust
at her own actions. There was no way around it. She'd been
lying to everyone for too long. From the moment she'd bar-
gained with her father, the earl, over her trip to London and
then stepped into Miss Carsten's identity, she'd been lying.
One more shouldn't matter. But it did. And something else
added in. It didn't bother her that she'd lied. What bothered
was that this particular one was bound to be discovered, and
then she'd be exposed. And that was enough to keep a saint
restless and haunted.

There was only one thing left to her. Prayer. It seemed to
work before, but she wanted to be in the ancient Norman-
designed chapel to do so. Nothing else seemed clean and
hallowed and sacred enough.

So Amalie pretended sleep until Maves left, softly shutting
the door after tapering all but one torch. It was easy to fool the
maid. After all, lying and acting were what Amalie did best.

She couldn't find a robe. The one she tried had too many
sleeves, and then she found another aperture. Amalie threw it
to the floor in disgust and swung a large tartan blanket thing
around her shoulders instead. It was warm, and if she put it
like a cowl atop her head, concealing. The floor in her chamber was cold. The one outside in the hall was even colder. She
probably should've donned her new boots, or at least a pair of
slippers. She wasn't going back for them, though. The cold of
a stone floor on bare feet could be more punishment.

She'd been wrong earlier. There was something much
worse than waiting and worrying. Dread.

Pellin was handling the cooking. By the third bowl of stew,
Thayne felt like his legs might actually hold him for the journey and his working arm would cooperate. They told him
the stew was nothing more than week-old broth, added to

with turnips, onions, and a good sprinkling of barley for thickening. Every bowl was accompanied by freshly fried oat-cakes almost too hot to touch. He'd shoveled in two with every bowl of stew. Everything he ate tasted like absolute ambrosia. It might have helped that they'd opened two kegs of mead the moment he'd arrived. The entire copse where they'd camped turned jovial, filled with energy and merriment and male boasts of strength and prowess, amid toasts to his continued health. It was impressive to watch. Heartwarming.

Mary Margaret didn't agree. She'd given him a sour look that conveyed her disgust, before getting escorted to the MacGowan chieftain tent erected for Jamie, but was now his to claim. He didn't care. She could have it. He wasn't using it. After the second tankard of mead, he wasn't doing much more than lying on his back looking at the smoke from their campfires as it drifted among the trees. Aside from which, his eyelids wouldn't cooperate. His last conscious thought was how lucky he was with Amalie. She had a quick wit, perfect form and face, and a loving temperament to match. Mary Margaret was the complete opposite. Any man gaining Mary Margaret's hand was in for a lifetime of scolding, nagging, and termagant manners. Yet somehow he'd avoided all of that by being there to make a catch.

He'd call it luck, but he didn't have any except the bad kind.

He could get a cot. The ground was hard, cold, and slightly damp. He wasn't moving. Any lingering pain from his injuries got muted nicely by either exhaustion or mead. It was heaven. Absolute, complete . . .

"Thayne! Quick, man!"

It seemed the next moment someone shoved at him, forcing him to open sand-filled eyes to a late afternoon sky, holding a lot of light for the amount of drizzle coming down from it. Thayne immediately swung, had his fist caught in a giant-sized grip and got hauled to his feet, where the idiot released him and forced him to make his knees cease wobbling, and in the next moment keep his head from flying off his shoulders with the pain that arced through it. Thayne howled with reaction, and slit his eyes to face MacPherson, looking broader and more immovable than ever.

"We'd . . . best be under attack!" Thayne cleared his throat to drop the octave after the first word. Otherwise, he sounded like he was whining, and damn it all, that was starting a worse thump in his head with the increased heartbeat that probably meant anger. Good thing. The emotion also seemed to pump life back into his deadened limbs and awareness into his fogged mind. It also made the pain from his myriad injuries start up, as if he needed the reminder.

"Angus is here. Rode all day. He's got news for you!"

Thayne licked his lips, put his good hand on his hip, and glared over at MacPherson. "There are legions of Angus's in the MacGowan clan! Be specific, man!"

"Angus MacGorrick."

"Na' likely, man. MacGorrick's seventy if he's a day. He should na' even sit a horse, let alone ride it that far. Aside from which, he's my senior clansman. He's got the running of the clan until a MacGowan returns! The man would na' shirk that duty."

"Na' the elder. His namesake and grandson."

"He's but a bairn."

"True." MacPherson grinned, splitting his beard with it. "But I would na' call him that to his face. He's a mite sensitive about such."

"Well . . . if it's of such all-fired import, you had to accost me, cease stalling and take me to him!"

Thayne took a step, wavered, and then took another, and before he crossed to the stabling ropes, he had his stride under control. Or was making a good showing of it. He didn't know what was wrong with him. He'd drunk too much. Or something.

The lad standing beside the horse looked too frail and young to have controlled it long enough to mount, let alone ride any distance. That alone was worth admiration. Thayne approached him, and the lad went to a knee in deference.

"Rise, and tell me this message that is so important, it brings you all the way out here, young Angus!"

"I-I-I . . ."

The lad stood, looked up at Thayne, and then stammered. He was hard-put not to shake the boy.

The lad stopped and swallowed. Everyone about seemed to be grinning.

"Take your time, lad. We're na' going anywhere. Someone should fetch him a bowl of stew and a tankard!"

The boy flushed, and then said two sentences that completely stopped Thayne's heart.

"The castle is secure. And the duchess is leaving."

Amalie is leaving me?

"Nae!"

The word burst from him, sounding more like a sob than he liked, and then Thayne knew exactly how much anger could fuel him, as everything went solid and real and perfectly tuned and energized.

"Get me a horse. A fast one. Now."

"I'm riding with you."

"Nae, MacPherson. You'll slow me down."

"Will na'!"

"Then stay because I need you to guard my rescuer."

A horse materialized from the herd, saddled. Readied.

"You canna' ride alone! We're your Honor Guard!"

Someone was arguing. Thayne turned on him and snarled the answer. He didn't waste time deciphering who it was. "Get Pellin, then. I'll take him!"

"And face fare cooked by Grant?"

"Fetch . . . Thin Pells, then! He's a grand horseman. Move!"

His tone galvanized them. Thayne watched through eyes

that wouldn't cease watering up. He blamed it on lack of sleep, over-imbibing of the mead, and the scratchy feel every time he blinked. Damn her! She was not leaving him. He wouldn't let her. He'd chase her all the way to London if need be!

It seemed to take forever, but wasn't more than a heartbeat of time before the short hefty figure of Thin Pells emerged from the mass at a jog. Good thing. Everything on Thayne was ready for the ride. He didn't feel one bit of pain from anything other than where his heart was supposed to be. And blast it all! That hurt the worst.

He didn't wait to see if Thin Pells was in the saddle before turning and kicking his stallion into a league-eating pace. Dusk fell about them, turning into mist and rain-choked night. It took all his concentration to stay in the saddle with only one workable arm, dodge obstacles, and still maintain speed. Thin Pells was with him every stride, sometimes taking the fore, when the path got too treacherous. Thayne would've argued that, but he was locking every bit of emotion close inside, so not one bit of the heartache could leach out. He'd thought it hurt when Mary MacGowan had jilted him for Dunn-Fyne. He'd been a fool. This hurt was gut-ripping and strength stealing. The only thing he could do was bury it. Send it to the lowest reaches of his core. And that only worked if his mind and body stayed focused on the ride.

Sentries spotted them as soon as they reached MacGowan land, recognizing and then sending the message out, using their bagpipes to telling effect. The swell of sound grew, apace with clan who came from their crofts, holding aloft torches to guide them. Thayne let Thin Pells take the lead, give the signals, make the path clear.

The castle was a huge black block of stone against a lighter blackness, the façade broken up by torchlight coming from the sentry posts. It was enough. They clattered down the wooden bridge, between the first gate towers, and across the drawbridge that got lowered without having to once break stride. The alert was getting sounded through the bailey as they crossed it, Thayne's eyes seeing too much activity in the stables, while at least one cartload of goods looked ready to transport. He was in time. *Thank God.* Relief slammed into him, weakening him for a bare moment, before anger took its place. His Amalie expected payment, too?

His roar of anger had at least one of the clansmen milling about looking, and Thayne swallowed on the end of his shout. Rage was the perfect emotion, and much better than heartache. Thayne embraced it as they reached his keep, using the rage to shove from the saddle, ignore the reaction on barely knitted flesh in his buttock, pat the stallion's sweated rump, and then leap steps into his keep. He didn't even notice his shoulder had broken open, leaching blood down his arm. It didn't matter, and he didn't feel it. Nothing mattered, other than finding his wife and stopping her.

Someone hailed him from the barely lit Great Hall. A guardsman. Thayne waved his way, but didn't look. He was at a run before reaching the wheel-stair, and at a full run down his hall. If need be, he'd ram right through the door. It wasn't barred. It wasn't even closed. It wasn't yet dawn, and his wife didn't bar her bedchamber door?

The chamber held only his wife's maid, standing at the bottom of his bed and wringing her hands. She looked up at his entrance. And then her mouth dropped open.

"Where is my wife?" The words ground out, carrying every bit of the anger he felt.

"My laird! You're here! It's . . . a miracle!"

"Where is she?"

Thayne took a step into the room, then another, and if the woman didn't speak up soon, he was going to reach her, and he didn't know what might happen then.

"I doona' ken. She was feeling poorly, and I just came to check."

He'd reached her and locked every muscle to stop, look down at her, and keep from reacting.

"Your grace?"

Thayne turned his head. There were more than a dozen clansmen filing into his chamber, as if they had purpose and permission to do so. Had his wife been in that bed, Thayne would be challenging, and then he'd be punishing for daring to enter her bed chamber. That would be a pure shame, too, since it was Angus MacGorrick at the forefront, leaning heavily on his cane.

"What?" The word came tersely from between his teeth.

"You . . . escaped?"

"Aye."

"'Tis good. Verra good. The clan will welcome this, my laird."

The man went to a knee, followed by the entire rank of them.

"Later, MacGorrick. Do you ken where my wife is?"

"Nae, but—"

The man was taking his time in replying, just as it took time to regain his feet. And Thayne was getting frustrated.

"I want to find my wife! I need to see her! Does nae one ken where she is?"

"I can help, your grace."

Stout Pells stepped into the chamber, strode through the group, approached Thayne, and went to a knee before him. Thayne looked to the ceiling, pulled in a huge breath to stay the expletive from getting launched from his mouth, and then looked back down.

"Rise, and speak of it. Now."

"'Twas my duty to guard her. . . ."

"She's na' here, Pells! Is this what you call guarding?"

He'd failed. Fury and frustration colored the words, taking out his anger where it wasn't deserved. Stout Pells considered him for a moment and then grinned.

"My apologies, my laird. She's in the small chapel. I dinna' escort or disturb her. She'll come to nae harm."

Thayne didn't hear the entire bit of it. He was already out the door.

Her prayer had been answered before, gaining her serenity, and calm, and making everything right in the world . . . and if God would just be merciful one more time. Just one! She vowed to always tell the truth. Always. Unless the truth was hurtful. In that event, she'd keep her silence. All she needed was just one more miracle. Thayne. She needed Thayne. She needed him in the flesh. Alive, breathing, and whole. In front of her. That's all she needed.

Amalie reached to lift the edge of her plaid again, holding it against her eyes, so it could soak up the tears. Stupid emotion! It wasn't doing anything other than making her nose run, and giving her an ache in her head. The tartan blanket wasn't long enough to reach her head anymore, since she'd layered it onto the floor beneath her knees. The stone floor in this chapel was even colder feeling than the hall. But she'd been right. The entire room exuded serenity. Calm. Sanctity. If there was any place God could hear a prayer, it was here.

"Amalie?"

Amalie lifted her head at the dusky whisper. And then she swiveled her head and saw him. She rubbed her eyes, and looked again. He didn't disappear. Thayne stood in the doorway of the chapel. Thayne. Her Thayne. In the flesh. Then her jaw dropped.

"Thayne?"

It took longer to stand than it should, since she'd wound the blanket about her legs, but once she reached her feet, he was still there. It couldn't be an apparition since he was halfway down the aisle toward her, and he was still Thayne. Still real. Breathing. Wounded. Her eyes narrowed at the blood dripping off his right arm.

"Thayne?"

And just before she expected to be swept into his arms he stopped, narrowed his eyes at her, and then lowered his jaw. It started another trill of shivers throughout her limbs at that look. Dangerous. Lethal.

"They tell me you're leaving."

"What?"

"Me. They tell me you're leaving me."

"No, I—"

"Amalie."

He interrupted her, going to both knees at her feet, and then he grabbed for her hand. "I love you. Please don't leave me. Please."

"Oh, Thayne, I wouldn't—"

"I'm begging you! Please? Does na' my love mean anything?"

Amalie's eyes filled, blurring the view. She nodded and swallowed. She didn't think her voice would work, anyway.

"I have na' been the best of husbands. I ken we hadn't the choice, but given all that—am I that bad? Canna' you see your way to allowing me a little time to make it up? I'll do all you ask. I'll allow the wee one to be christened Mary. I'll take fewer chances. Damn! But I'm mucking this up with every word I speak!"

"Thayne."

She'd been right. Her voice choked off. She had to sniff in order to continue.

"This past week has been hell. I canna' even apologize for

it. 'Twas my fault. But I dinna' think the MacKennahs would truly take me. You're na' speaking. Please doona' tell me that means what I think it does."

"For the love of—"

"I'll try harder. I've nae experience with a love of this depth. I thought it pained when Mary left me. I was wrong. 'Twas as nothing next to how this feels! I doona' ken what else to say? Please say you'll give me another chance? Please?"

"Thayne—"

"Nae! Wait! I was wrong. I canna' stand to hear it!"

He lifted his uninjured arm and swiped it across his face. And then he started shuddering. Amalie went to her knees right in front of him, and forced his face up to hers. She'd always known he was the most handsome man she'd ever seen, but with the depth of emotion in his eyes at the moment, there was nothing more beautiful. Heart-stopping. Totally.

"What fool said I'd leave you?"

"Any of them. All. Jesu'. I canna' bear it."

He tried to put his head down again, but she held on. And then she had to bend down in order to peer up at him.

"I can't believe you're here. Whole. Alive. I'd been praying, and I—words fail me." So did her voice.

"You're leaving me. That's what you're saying?"

He pulled back, and she watched him tighten everything on his frame, until she could see a pulse beat on his chest through the muslin of his shirt. It was unbelievably eye-catching. The man should wear more. A lot more.

"Leaving you? Thayne. Look at me. I love you. I wouldn't leave you for anything. Ever. Did you hear me? I love you."

"You . . . love me?"

"Tell me who spoke this horrid thing and I'll go and behead them for it. Don't look at me like that. I've been leading a large Highland clan. I can think of lots of things equally bloodthirsty as punishment."

He blinked, sending a tear trail down one cheek, and then he stared. "You're truly na' leaving me?"

She shook her head and smiled.

"But they told me the duchess is leaving."

"She is. Good riddance to her, I say."

"They meant . . . Wynneth?"

Amalie nodded and he finally got his good arm about her, pulling her right against his chest. She wrapped her arms as far about him as she could and breathed in his scent with her nose against his throat. He was real. Alive. Cold. Wet.

"You're wet," she pointed out.

"Aye. 'Tis a damp night for riding."

"And you're injured again."

"Doona' fash it. 'Tis naught."

"You're bleeding. Again. What did they do to you?"

"'Twas but an arrow."

"They shot an arrow at you?"

"And tapped my head a bit with a battle ax. I've got a thick skull. Barely felt it."

"Those MacKennahs best guard their backs. I'm going to repay each and every injury. I vow that as well. We'd best get you to the healer."

"I'd rather get ensconced in my bed. With you."

"Thayne!"

"I love you, Amalie. Truly."

"And I you. But, Thayne?"

"Aye?"

"Your . . . men." She almost didn't get the word out since his lips hovered atop hers.

"My men probably think I'm daft."

"Not the ones watching you."

"Watch . . . ing?"

He spun on his buttocks, grimacing slightly as he probably reinjured himself, and finally got a look at their audience. Most were Honor Guardsmen, although Maves was at the front, dabbing at her eyes.

"Have you been here long?"

Thayne asked it and got cleared throats and some half-answers.

"Ah . . ."

"Well . . . you see . . ."

"We dinna' wish to intrude."

That was Maves. Thayne went to his feet, grunting with the effort. Amalie assumed it was due to just using leg strength. He should just put her down, but she knew he wouldn't. And she wouldn't let him.

"You're all to find your posts and return to them. And that's an order."

"We're just so glad to see you back, your grace! And safe."

"It's a miracle!"

"Do any of you ken an order when you hear one, or do I need challenge you?" Thayne asked.

"Your grace!"

Bowed heads and a lot of grinning accompanied their exit from the chapel, until there was just Amalie and Thayne. He lowered to one of the pews, and another slight tic of his lip betrayed how it must pain.

"You're hurt."

"I've got you in my arms, love. There's naught else I can feel."

"Oh, Thayne . . . wait!" She put a finger to his lips, catching the pursed kiss. "I promised God I'd do something if I got you back."

"You were praying for that?"

She nodded. Thayne moved away from her fingers to run

his tongue along her earlobe, starting thrills that had no place in a house of worship. Amalie shushed the thought.

"Ah . . . love. I do believe my luck is changing. And for the better. Finally. Although I've got a bit of confession to make, too."

"You go first."

"That's hardly fair."

Amalie pulled back and regarded him, and then raised her brows. Thayne responded with a heavy sigh that ruffled his hair.

"Verra well. I've brought another Mary home. My rescuer. She fancies a bit of season in London. With your sponsorship."

She blinked rapidly, and then smiled. "Is that all?"

"Wait 'til she speaks. She's got more than a few rough edges to her. She's more an unhewn log."

"Sounds fascinating." Amalie giggled.

"And . . . now yours?"

She looked at the wall behind him, and then back at him. And then just said it.

"I've done a bit of lying."

"Truly now?"

"I . . . told them I knew you'd escaped and were coming home."

"Does na' look like a lie to me. I did escape and I'm home."

"But I didn't know that!"

"Perhaps you're fey, love. Or perhaps the heart knew what the world didn't. Maybe true love works that way. You dinna' lie about loving me, did you?"

Amalie shook her head vigorously.

"I'm a-feared I'll need to hear it in words, lass."

"Is that another Scot law I should know about?"

"Nae. I just wish to hear it."

"Fine. I love you, Thayne MacGowan. And now, let's get to our chamber, so I can see to your latest injuries."

"What if I've got other plans?"

"Thayne!"

His lips took hers, and Amalie could swear their hearts touched.

Chapter 27

A loud thump came at their door, and then Thayne's whisper at her ear finished teasing her awake.

"The castle had better be under attack or I'm hurting someone."

Amalie giggled as he unwrapped from about her, leaving morn chill in his wake. She pulled the coverlet higher, and burrowed beneath it.

"Just see that you don't break open your wound again. We had a devil of a time stitching it back last time."

"The leg's fine. Healing well."

"I don't mean the leg. What of your shoulder?"

"That old arrow injury? Away with you, woman. That's been scarred over a fortnight past. You should worry more about my opponent. Now, they'll be needin' the healer long afore me."

The thump came again. Amalie cracked open an eye and watched her husband of ten weeks toss on a long shirt, hiding nakedness that still caused her to sigh in appreciation. He was right. The arrow mark was just a purplish pucker now, but he'd taken a blow just above the knee from a practice bout with one of his Honor Guard. It was recent enough he limped slightly. He really should take better care of his body. It was a shame to continue to scar such beauty. Then again . . . every bit of him showed strength and purpose, and might. Every scar was proof of it.

And he was all hers. This time, he heard the sigh.

"Keep that up and I'll be coming back to that bed, and to hell with the door."

Thayne had his *feileadh-breacan* tied loosely atop the nightshirt, the end of the plaid trailing along the floor as he approached the door.

"Answer the door, love, before they ram it open."

"Over my dead frame! And you'd best have a good reason for waking my duchess and upsetting my son in the process!" He was at the door and sliding the bolt.

"Your daughter!" She yelled across at him. "And what there is of her can't possibly be upset. She's too small!" Amalie patted the slightest swell of her belly, and felt the same familiar tug at her heart. Her life was full now. So full, it frightened one.

"Details." He waved a hand backward in her direction and cracked one door open.

"MacPherson! Stout Pells! And Grant? What is it? Is the castle under attack?"

She couldn't hear the answer, but Thayne's voice was loud enough.

"You doona' ken? What kind of answer is that? We've got what? A troop of English soldiers? Here? In the outer bailey, awaiting me? What fool let them through the gate? Well? Someone better start jawing and I mean soon!"

There was a bit of masculine rumbling she couldn't make out, and then Thayne stepped out into the hall and shut the door behind him. Amalie sat up and reached for her night rail. Thayne liked to sleep without clothing, and he truly loved cuddling with her in the same state. She couldn't think of one reason to stay him, but it still made her blush.

The garment against her skin was cold, but warmed soon

enough. The robe had the same issue. She added a thickly-woven sett over the whole, cocooning herself in warmth and luxury. Then she girded the floor. The stone was cold. She should have donned slippers. By what light was just touching the loch seen through her window, it didn't even look like dawn had come, yet. She skipped from rug to rug over to the fireplace and stirred the coals before settling a log atop the grate. She then climbed into one of his overly large chairs to watch the flickers of the fire as they took root.

There was a basket atop the table beside her, and she dug into it greedily, munching on a hard oatcake Maves had brought for her last night. According to the maid, Amalie should be suffering every ill effect over the babe, and would need hot tisanes nightly and these cakes in the morn to still illness. But no. Not Amalie. She'd never felt better, and had the health to show for it.

She wondered what was keeping Thayne. Surely even if a troop of English soldiers had arrived, they would be housed and fed, and then sent about their way without any ill will. Scotland wasn't at war with England. In fact, Thayne had remarked just a sennight ago that the Scottish parliament might be absorbed into the one in London, giving them even more voice in politics. Not that she cared, but Mary Margaret MacKennah had still to be pacified, and it would behoove the girl if her Scottish background wasn't an issue. It took the patience of a saint just to sponsor her. Amalie didn't think the governess or dancing tutor they'd hired from Edinburgh were having any luck with the girl, either. She'd almost been ready to accompany Mary Margaret herself, but then fate had intervened with this baby.

Amalie folded her hands about her belly, cupping the small swell, and loving the warmth that seemed to emanate from about her heart. It didn't truly matter what gender the babe was. She was happy. And she knew Thayne was but teasing. He'd better be.

The door opened again, the sound loud in the stillness, and Thayne walked back in. She couldn't tell what look he was giving her as he walked toward her, but something about him seemed different. He reached the other side of the table and just stood there, looking across and down at her, with a guarded expression she couldn't decipher.

"What . . . is it?"

"Apparently, we have a visitor. From the south. An Englishman of some renown and status. I was informed that his title goes all the way back to the Battle of Agincourt, when his forebear was knighted for bravery during the Hundred Years War."

Her heart stuttered. And she knew. He didn't even have to finish.

Father is here.

"Yes, my dearest duchess, I can see by your face that you know. The Earl of Ellincourt has arrived. By ship. He awaits us now. Why does the man spout his lineage to me? Do I go about telling anyone my forebear was awarded a baronetcy by King David the Norman? Well? And do I add that the earldom was awarded by King Robert the Bruce? And the dukedom? That title goes back to our first Stewart king! I doona' add my ancestry to an introduction."

"You have no need, darling. You have a presence that announces it for you."

"Truly?"

"Oh . . . my . . . yes."

He cleared his throat, and rubbed at his chest. "Oh. Well, there's that. Does he na' also have a presence?"

"He's not much taller than me."

"Poor fellow. I do see his issue. He's a runt. He'll na' find the chairs in my chieftain room of much consolation, will he?"

Amalie giggled. She couldn't help it. Her father always had a large ego. He was in for a true surprise. Especially if he sat in one of Thayne's elder's chairs.

"We'd best see to getting you into your finery, then. And I've got to don my Chieftain *feileadh-breacan*. I sent a message that it might be some time afore we meet as my duchess needs time to prepare. I also summoned your maid; the one that talks too much. The earl won't go unattended. I've sent for Angus and the other elders to entertain him. I've also ordered a keg or two opened."

"Thayne! It's not yet dawn!"

"What Scot can resist a good mead? And what Sassenach can resist a challenge from a Scot? If I doona' miss my guess, we'll have verra mellow visitors afore long."

"Visitors?"

"The earl's brought along a troop of English dragoons. He didn't ken if they'd be needed or na', but he believes in preparing for the worst. He came as quickly as he could in answer to a missive from his beloved but naughty daughter. That would be you. Apparently, you disappeared during a trip to London and he's had men scouring the island for you. He's arrived here now to aid in the release of his new son-by-law, that he dinna' ken he had. That would be me. He's ready to take up the matter of my kidnapping and extortion, since last he heard I was being held for ransom by a heathen clan, which would be the MacKennahs. Good thing I managed to escape some weeks past, with as long as it's taken him to mount a rescue."

"Oh."

His eyebrows lifted. "Oh? Is that all you have to say? Is na' a confession due here?"

"I told you I was his daughter."

"You also said you lied. Remember?"

Amalie leaned forward. "Not about this. I lied about being the governess. Do we have to do this all over again?"

"You still love me? You would na' lie about that?" he asked.

Amalie stood and unwound the tartan blanket before stepping from it and approaching him. She put both hands on his lower arms and slid them all the way to his shoulders before moving right against him.

"Oh yes."

His arms went about her, hugging her into him. "And you truly are an heiress?"

She nodded.

"With a large dowry?"

Amalie's eyes narrowed. "You're playing with a hurting, MacGowan," she warned him.

"How large?"

"Thayne MacGowan!"

He grinned and lifted her. "Just teasing, my love. I'm thinking it'll take a bit of time getting used to."

"It won't change things between us, will it?"

Thayne was already heading toward the bed. "It might help with making the Palazzo livable, since Wynneth took everything but the walls back to France with her."

"You'd best be joshing. We'll leave it as is. Empty. This keep is the proper abode for a MacGowan chieftain. And well you know it."

"Aye, love. I was joshing. I also feel a bit stewed over just how much my luck has changed since catching you."

"Yes . . . that was a good catch, wasn't it?" Amalie nuzzled into his neck, making the words indistinct.

"Aye. And I'm willing to tempt fate a mite further. Do you think your father might be amenable to taking a passenger with him when he leaves?"

"A passenger?"

"Mary Margaret. You have a better idea of being rid of her?"

They were at the bed. And Thayne had a good idea of what he was doing to her senses as he set her atop the mattress and started pulling his clothing off.

"Aren't we supposed to be preparing to meet my father?"

She managed to get the sentence out before he kissed her, taking her breath and then her senses.

"Later. Much, much later. He's being well entertained by my Honor Guard and the elders, and the best mead this side of Hadrian's Wall, and I'm being better entertained by my wife. My loving, beautiful, amazing, wealth—"

"Don't say it," she warned, lightly running her hands over his chest, bared now and golden in the dawn glow.

"Verra well. I'll na' tease. Just yet, anyway. Do you always win?"

"Oh . . . yes," she replied.

And it was true. She did.

Books by Bestselling Author
Fern Michaels

___The Jury	0-8217-7878-1	$6.99US/$9.99CAN
___Sweet Revenge	0-8217-7879-X	$6.99US/$9.99CAN
___Lethal Justice	0-8217-7880-3	$6.99US/$9.99CAN
___Free Fall	0-8217-7881-1	$6.99US/$9.99CAN
___Fool Me Once	0-8217-8071-9	$7.99US/$10.99CAN
___Vegas Rich	0-8217-8112-X	$7.99US/$10.99CAN
___Hide and Seek	1-4201-0184-6	$6.99US/$9.99CAN
___Hokus Pokus	1-4201-0185-4	$6.99US/$9.99CAN
___Fast Track	1-4201-0186-2	$6.99US/$9.99CAN
___Collateral Damage	1-4201-0187-0	$6.99US/$9.99CAN
___Final Justice	1-4201-0188-9	$6.99US/$9.99CAN
___Up Close and Personal	0-8217-7956-7	$7.99US/$9.99CAN
___Under the Radar	1-4201-0683-X	$6.99US/$9.99CAN
___Razor Sharp	1-4201-0684-8	$7.99US/$10.99CAN
___Yesterday	1-4201-1494-8	$5.99US/$6.99CAN
___Vanishing Act	1-4201-0685-6	$7.99US/$10.99CAN
___Sara's Song	1-4201-1493-X	$5.99US/$6.99CAN
___Deadly Deals	1-4201-0686-4	$7.99US/$10.99CAN
___Game Over	1-4201-0687-2	$7.99US/$10.99CAN
___Sins of Omission	1-4201-1153-1	$7.99US/$10.99CAN
___Sins of the Flesh	1-4201-1154-X	$7.99US/$10.99CAN
___Cross Roads	1-4201-1192-2	$7.99US/$10.99CAN

Available Wherever Books Are Sold!
Check out our website at **www.kensingtonbooks.com**

Thrilling Suspense from
Beverly Barton

Romantic Suspense from
Lisa Jackson

See How She Dies	0-8217-7605-3	$6.99US/$9.99CAN
Final Scream	0-8217-7712-2	$7.99US/$10.99CAN
Wishes	0-8217-6309-1	$5.99US/$7.99CAN
Whispers	0-8217-7603-7	$6.99US/$9.99CAN
Twice Kissed	0-8217-6038-6	$5.99US/$7.99CAN
Unspoken	0-8217-6402-0	$6.50US/$8.50CAN
If She Only Knew	0-8217-6708-9	$6.50US/$8.50CAN
Hot Blooded	0-8217-6841-7	$6.99US/$9.99CAN
Cold Blooded	0-8217-6934-0	$6.99US/$9.99CAN
The Night Before	0-8217-6936-7	$6.99US/$9.99CAN
The Morning After	0-8217-7295-3	$6.99US/$9.99CAN
Deep Freeze	0-8217-7296-1	$7.99US/$10.99CAN
Fatal Burn	0-8217-7577-4	$7.99US/$10.99CAN
Shiver	0-8217-7578-2	$7.99US/$10.99CAN
Most Likely to Die	0-8217-7576-6	$7.99US/$10.99CAN
Absolute Fear	0-8217-7936-2	$7.99US/$9.49CAN
Almost Dead	0-8217-7579-0	$7.99US/$10.99CAN
Lost Souls	0-8217-7938-9	$7.99US/$10.99CAN
Left to Die	1-4201-0276-1	$7.99US/$10.99CAN
Wicked Game	1-4201-0338-5	$7.99US/$9.99CAN
Malice	0-8217-7940-0	$7.99US/$9.49CAN

Available Wherever Books Are Sold!
Visit our website at **www.kensingtonbooks.com**